THE ROTTEN WITCH

THE COVEN: FAE MAGIC BOOK 3

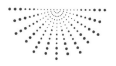

CHANDELLE LAVAUN

PROLOGUE

TENNESSEE

January 24ᵗʰ, 2019

I LOVE MY SOULMATE.

I love my soulmate.

I love my soulmate.

I really did. One hundred and a million percent. But sometimes, especially lately, she made me more nervous than anyone else in my Coven...not because of what she might *do* but because of what she might *know*.

Royce cleared his throat. "Tegan, pumpkin, you're doing that creepy thing again."

Braison shook his head. "You can't stop her, she's not in The Coven."

Tegan arched one eyebrow and pointed to her head. Her crystal Coven Leader crown appeared instantly. "Y'all made me Coven Leader, remember? So, yes, I can. And I will."

Everyone looked to me in perfect unison.

The problem was...she was just so much smarter than all of us. I had no idea what she knew about Savannah Grace or why she wasn't letting Saffie's new friend go home. But I was smart enough to know there *was* a reason. And I was smart enough to just not want to know. Ignorance was bliss and all that jazz.

More than that, I loved that my new Coven Leader companion was bolder than me. Constance hated making decisions. My soulmate loved it and did it naturally. Tegan Bishop gave zero fucks, and I enjoyed that a bit too much.

I grinned and leaned back in my seat. "Be careful what you wish for, folks."

Savannah chewed on her bottom lip. "Okay, so I'm staying here but you'll tell my parents, right?"

Tegan nodded.

Shit, woman, what do you know?

Why is Savannah not allowed to leave?

Maybe I don't want to know. Maybe I just let Tegan handle it. She's Coven Leader now too. I don't have to make ALL the decisions. I can let her.

There was a lot going on. I had enough on my plate. Enough stress. Enough worry. Tegan would let me know once there was something I *needed* to know in regard to Savannah. For now, I could just let myself enjoy a single meal. And if I didn't hurry, I wouldn't get seconds. Most of the table was almost to their third servings.

"Can I stay too?"

I glanced over, then did a double take.

Gigi.

The shifter who can't and won't control her shifting and gets people killed.

GREAAAAAT.

I cursed. "I forgot you were here."

Gigi grimaced.

I can't let her stay. I shook my head. "No, you have to go."

Gigi paled. "But—"

"No." I held my hand up. *Please, Gigi. Don't make this*

harder than it already is. "You already got one of my people killed. I won't have that happen again."

Shit, that might not have come out right. Maybe she can—

Gigi looked to Riah with wide eyes and my resolve firmed. Anger surged inside of me. She got her supposed best friend killed, and instead of pleading with me and promising to learn control, she looked to *Riah.*

I clenched my teeth, and my voice came out in a growl, "Riah is not here to clean up your kills."

Gigi bit her lip and turned to her friend. "Savannah?"

"What do you want me to say?" Savannah closed her eyes and cringed. "I'm sorry but...*I died* Gigi. Because of your inability to control your shifting. I've begged you to work on that for years. You didn't and I died. *My* Coven Leaders have ordered me to stay here."

This was one of those moments where I hated my job. I hated having to be the mean one right now, to be tough on this girl who was a danger to everyone around her. But I couldn't help but wonder who would be next. Which one of the people at this table would fall because Gigi shifted in the wrong moment? The truth was that the only people in this room I had no emotional attachment to were Savannah and Gigi. One of them was my responsibility because she was a witch. As Coven Leader, she was one of *mine.* But Gigi was a shifter...and I was going to let *her* King decide how to handle this.

"Where am I supposed to go?"

I shrugged, trying to keep my fear and anger concealed. "I can't order you where to go, but I *can* order you to leave my land."

Her presence terrifies me. Tegan squeezed my hand under the table as she spoke into my mind. *We have enough to worry about. It's hard enough to keep our whole family alive. We can't afford this risk. I can be the bitch if you want me to be. Just look at me and I'll take over. I'll do it so you don't have to.*

3

My chest tightened. The fear bubbling beneath the surface was now a volcanic eruption.

"So I just go home to Salem and do what?"

"I'd say I don't care what you do, but it's my job to keep this realm safe and you're an endangerment to everyone around you, including yourself. So Koth will be hearing of this, and I'm sure he'll have an opinion."

Gigi's face fell. "*King Kothari?*"

Yes, he IS your King. I bit my cheek and breathed through my nose. I had to do this. I had to be tough. At the very, very least, she needed some tough love if Savannah's death wasn't a major wake up call. Which it clearly wasn't.

Savannah grimaced. "I know you said you didn't want to... but maybe you should go to SOMA and learn?"

She said she didn't want to learn? What in the actual fuck? What is her problem? I didn't know, but there was only one person who was going to find it out. "That's a good idea, but it'll be up to Koth to decide if it's safe enough."

Riah cleared his throat. "I recognize that this is not my place to speak, however, I sense trouble on our horizon, and I do not think we want to risk a repeat of today...just in case I am not here to reverse it. Or it is beyond my reparation."

I squeezed Tegan's hand.

Heard, babe. Tegan sighed and stood. "I'm sorry, Gigi, but it's best if we send you off now."

I got to my feet beside her. "To Issale."

Tegan snapped her fingers and a white portal box opened up behind her. "We're not trying to be mean here..."

We're just terrified you'll make us lose another family member. You get that, right? I stared at her, hoping she'd hear the words in our eyes, the ones we weren't saying. The ones I didn't have the strength to voice out loud.

"I know." Gigi closed her eyes and nodded, then got to her feet. "It's okay. I'll go."

Saffie leapt from her seat and charged for her. I turned to look at Tegan and our eyes met. Not for the first time, I wished I could speak telepathically with her.

But those big pale green eyes locked on mine. *We're doing the right thing, babe. We have to be harsh here.*

Gigi stepped back from Saffie and Savannah and turned toward us. "Okay."

I nodded and stepped right into Tegan's portal.

I love my job.

I love my job.

I love my job.

White light flashed over me and then my boots sank in the snow of the mountain. The crunching of dead leaves and ice echoed between the leafless trees. It was already dark in the mountains of Vermont, but that was fine. I liked the dark. The air was bitter cold, like shards of glass against my skin, but ever since Michael's sword magically connected itself to me, I didn't get cold— at least not like I used to. My grandfather was an angel. *The* archangel. I was still not used to that.

Out of respect for Koth's rule and his land, Tegan portaled us to arrive just beyond the magical border of Issale. From the outside, shifter home country looked like the rest of this mountain—completely undeveloped wilderness. But I knew from past visits here that once we stepped over the border, the Kingdom of Issale would be staring right back at us. I admired the primitive way Issale lived. It spoke to who they were as a species and why they were put on the Earth in the first place.

To any innocent human passerby, nothing would be amiss. Only the most sensitive of the sapiens would catch a faint fiery scent, but they'd assume someone had made a fire—as the magic told them to think. I wondered what a civilian witch might feel standing here. Would they feel the hot tingle of power in the air, the rumble in the ground, or the warning in the wind?

Because I did. It hit me the moment I stepped through the portal.

Koth was near.

Heat flared in my chest and then Tegan jumped through her portal with Gigi beside her. I looked back and found Gigi staring at the magical border in front of us with outright fear in her eyes. Her normal, darker complexion paled.

Let's get this over with, babe, Tegan said into my mind. She met my gaze, then nodded for me to lead the way. *I told Koth it was us.*

Not that he didn't know, I thought to myself as I spun and marched through the snow.

We were quiet as we walked, yet none of us were calm. Gigi's energy was frantic and pulsing. Any moment she'd undoubtedly shift accidentally into a penguin. And I felt like shit for doing this, for having to bring her back *here* and in the way I did it, but she'd left me no choice. I could not coddle her emotions when she could cost me my family. That was a risk I would never take.

Tegan, on the other hand, was as calm and cold as the snow under our feet. She felt no remorse for the girl who refused to even *try.* This was why Tegan was my soulmate and my co-Coven Leader. We were yin and yang. On the outside I seemed calm and calculating, while she was the emotional reaction...but on the inside, we were actually opposites. In the words of Jackson Lancaster, I was a hot bloody mess inside while Tegan was ever sure of everything.

Get your head on right, dude. Koth needs the facts, not your feelings.

The magical border in front of us was invisible to the human eye, but I saw the shimmer in the air and felt the wave of its raw power. I slowed my pace so that all three of us stepped over the border together.

We made it three feet inside Issale when a black wall of

darkness shot out of the forest from right behind us. It rushed right for us in alarming speed. Gigi gasped — and turned into a penguin. She squawked and flapped her fins. The darkness stopped inches from us and then massive purple eyes glared down from twenty feet up.

I smirked. *Koth.*

Tegan chuckled in my mind. *Dirty trick. I approve.*

Koth growled and streams of smoke billowed from his nose down onto Gigi. The ground rumbled under our feet—which was surprisingly dirt, *not* snow. Black wings shot out, blocking the moonlight from beaming down on us. Gigi squawked again.

In less than the blink of an eye, Koth stood before us in human form—shirtless and wearing black jeans and boots. His long brown hair was wild, but his purple eyes were *blazing* with rage. In human form, Koth was six feet and eight inches of muscle, anger, and power. I wasn't afraid of him, nor was Tegan, but I knew we were in the minority on that.

Koth didn't acknowledge us with even a glance. He just glared down at penguin-Gigi who still hadn't shifted back even though her King stood in front of her. He growled and a wave of power left his mouth, slamming into Gigi's penguin face—and she was human again.

Gigi gasped, her eyes widening. Her whole body was trembling. She licked her lips, then did a weak bow. "M-m-my L-l-l-lo-ord."

He snarled and stepped around her—*and turned back into a dragon.* Without missing a step, he ducked his head down and growled in her ear. She screamed and then was a penguin. *Again.* Koth's growl was low and full of rage as he stood to his full height. Gigi turned and did a little waddle, like maybe she was trying to bow.

In his dragon form, Koth was over twenty feet tall. From a distance, his scales looked black as night, but up close they swirled with little streaks of color, like an oil spill or a picture of the milky way. His violet eyes were the same color and intensity in both forms, just differing in size.

A large shadow swooped over our heads. I expected it to be Silas, but when it landed I saw it was the giant eagle form of their shaman, Elan. He squawked and then sat on the ground behind his King. Koth growled and shifted back into human form. The dude was so fast at the change that my eyes never had a chance of watching what it actually looked like. That was definitely a *King* thing, as I'd seen the other dragons shift and it wasn't that fast.

"*Shift,*" Koth growled between clenched teeth, his violet eyes laser focused on Gigi.

Gigi squawked.

Koth narrowed his eyes and ducked his head down so his eyes were closer to hers. "*Try harder.*"

She waddled side to side but remained a penguin.

"Yes, *you can,*" he growled back.

A weird scream-like sound came out of her.

Koth's eyebrows shot up. "What did you say to me?"

Gigi was hysterical now.

Koth crossed his arms over his chest and glared at her.

Elan hung his big eagle head and sighed. A little tornado of leaves coiled around him, rustling his feathers, and then he stood behind Koth in human form. Like this, he was much less physically intimidating. He wasn't quite six feet tall and was very slender, and the way his hair curled into tight ringlets gave him a very youthful appearance—from a distance. Up close the dude was creepy as hell, not unlike my own soulmate. Elan glanced to us with golden eyes, then looked to Gigi and his eyes changed about fifteen colors in rapid succession. Black lines shot out over his face before fading away like they never happened. He cleared his throat.

Koth sighed and held his hand up. That same wave of power I felt a few moments ago shot out of his hand and slammed into

Gigi, turning her back into a human. Again. Gigi had tears running down her face and her fingers were trembling. She kept her eyes on Koth.

And you thought you were harsh? Tegan said with a chuckle into my mind.

Koth put his hands on his hips and cocked his head to the side. "Gigi Cortez."

I frowned.

It's her real last name, shifters who leave Issale must use an alias, by order of the King, Tegan answered my unvoiced question.

I nodded.

Gigi bowed real low this time. "*My Lord.*"

When she stood up straight again, he narrowed his eyes. "Have I *ever* harmed one of my own people on accident or intentionally?"

"No," Gigi answered quickly.

"Have I ever used physical discipline on any of my own people?"

"No, no, my Lord."

Koth ducked his head down and growled, "Have The Coven physically harmed you?"

"NO! No, of course not," Gigi cried in a panic. She looked to us with teary eyes, then back to Koth. "They've been welcoming and nice, I swear. The Coven did nothing to me—"

"I know that," Koth said with a frustrated sigh. At that point, he looked to Tegan and me for the first time and nodded, then turned his glare back to Gigi. He bent over so they were eye-to-eye. "Then why are you so afraid of me right now?"

Gigi opened her mouth and then shut it.

Koth stood up straight and cocked his head to the side. "I felt your fear the moment you stepped out of Tegan's portal and every step thereafter. I am your King, your protector. I am no demon or monster who would ever harm you. Your shifter eyes knew damn well it was me coming through the trees...and yet you were terrified. Why?"

"I...I...*I don't know*."

Koth closed his eyes and sighed, pinched the bridge of his nose. "Where are your parents?"

"My—my parents, my Lord?"

He opened his eyes and arched one eyebrow. "Yes? Are they not here? Did they not bring you here?"

Gigi shook her head. "Why would my parents bring me here, my Lord?"

"Because they've called us several times in the last few weeks worried about you and your inability to control your shifting." Koth looked to us. "Obviously, I am aware Tegan's portal delivered you all here, but I assumed her parents had been the cause of that. They called us frantically yesterday, saying you'd run off with The Coven. They were worried you'd shift and get yourself killed."

Not far off.

Gigi looked to the ground. "I did not know my parents were in contact with you."

"But you did know that you cannot control your shifting, didn't you?"

She nodded.

"And you also knew that despite your parents' efforts to get you back here to train and then to the new school in Manhattan, you refused to do either."

She nodded again.

"And now you've been escorted to my door by the Coven Leaders. I cannot wait to hear this." Koth glanced to us. "Congrats on making Coven Leader, Tegan. Elan is a bit of a spoiler alert walking."

Tegan grinned. "Can't say I know the type."

Elan chuckled and shrugged. "She gets me."

Koth smirked. But then he turned back to Gigi and his smile

vanished. "Well, Gigi? Care to explain yourself or shall I ask the rulers of this entire realm to tattle on you? Because we both know you're in big trouble."

Gigi just stared at him with her jaw hanging open.

He waited for a solid minute before shaking his head and turning to us. "Tenn? Tegan? What happened? Please do not sugarcoat it for me. Did someone get hurt?"

"Everyone is alive and well right now," Tegan said quickly.

"Right *now*?" Koth groaned. "What happened?"

I cleared my throat. "As you know, Gigi and one of our own, Savannah Grace, have been taking care of our friend Saffie while we could not."

"Savannah is the wild one? The one who uses black magic recklessly?" Koth frowned and nodded to Gigi. "Her parents have been worried about that one."

"I assure you that the only wildness in Savannah Grace is in her spirit. She uses black magic, yes, and we'll be addressing that. However, from what I have learned myself, she uses it with the upmost caution and care. I also spoke with her mother who says Savannah does not do any black magic recklessly." Tegan frowned. "Except for once, but that was a moment of fear and desperation as Saffie had been kidnapped by the Seelie fae and taken from our realm, and she was trying to get her back—a measure we all know we'd attempt ourselves."

Koth whistled under his breath and nodded. "Understood. I always thought Savannah was good people, but Gigi's parents were worried."

"Savannah will be remaining with The Coven for the immediate foreseeable future."

Koth arched one eyebrow at Tegan and then glanced to me. "Because of whatever happened today?"

I nodded. "We got Saffie back, partially in thanks to Savannah's black magic that Tegan adapted in her own wicked way. Because of the friendship Saffie had with Gigi and Savannah, I allowed for them to stay with us after we got her back so that they could spend some time together. Saffie had earned that. I even let them accompany us to Crone Island to see Saffie's mother. It was while we were there, while The Coven was tending to Kenneth, Savannah and Gigi went down to the shore to wait for us...and a damn kraken attacked."

Elan shuddered. "Hate those."

Koth smirked and shook his head. "Please, continue."

"Gigi shifted. Savannah, being the good friend she is, picked Gigi up and tried to run *with* her...and the kraken speared Savannah like a shish kebab. Tegan and I were a split second too late. We got there right as the spearing happened. Had Savannah and Gigi both been running on two legs unhindered, they would have made it far enough away—of that I have zero doubts. I'm quite fast and Tegan is...Tegan."

She smirked. "Thank you."

"We had the kraken gone instantly. I mean, Keltie was there and just waved him off...but Savannah died. Fortunately, Saffie's soulmate is a Seelie fae with a very unique healing gift and he was able to bring Savannah back to life."

Koth sighed long and hard. "She's okay?"

Tegan nodded. "She's back to normal as we speak, at least physically. But that's why she's staying with us for now."

"*Partially* why," Elan said with a wink as black lines spread across his face again.

I clenched my teeth. GREAT. TWO *people know something I don't.*

Koth cursed.

"I allowed for Gigi to stay long enough to see Savannah back on her feet, and to enjoy Emersyn's southern cooking, but I'm afraid I cannot allow for her to remain with us a moment longer. I do not have to explain to you what my Coven members mean to me or how I refuse to risk a single one of their lives more than it already is on the daily."

"Of course." He turned to Gigi with a pointed glare. "She is *mine,* after all. Thank you for bringing her to me."

"I wouldn't even attempt to know how you prefer to handle this situation." I frowned and looked to the girl in question. She hadn't spoken in a while. "Gigi?"

She looked up at me with sad eyes. "Yes?"

"I am sorry about this, you understand that, right? I know you would never had intentionally gotten Savannah, or anyone, hurt. Accidents happen to the best of us, but you're a risk to my family I can't take. You get that, right?"

Her face fell but she nodded. "Of course, Emperor."

"He is too nice. You understand that also, right?" Koth growled. "You understand that you got your supposed best friend *killed* because you refuse to learn control...right?"

She nodded and a fresh round of tears slipped down.

Koth shook his head and put his hands on his hips. "Explain it to me, Gigi. Why not learn? You could've come to me at any single moment, and I would have taught you myself. Dragons have the hardest time with control because of the power we wield and yet not a single one is allowed to leave Issale without proving they have control. Why not come home for help? Why not go to SOMA when it opened? Hell, Maddox goes there."

"I didn't want to," Gigi whispered.

"WHY?" Koth growled.

She shook her head.

"WHY, GIGI?"

"*I just want to be normal!*" She cried and shook her head. "I don't want to be *this.* I just want to be human. I want to live a normal life with normal problems. No demons. No shifter hunters. No Lilith."

Koth narrowed his eyes into little slits. "Let me see if I've got this right...you refused to learn how to control your shifting because you want to be human?"

She nodded quickly.

"Do you even understand how idiotic that sounds? How can you live a normal human life if you shift into a penguin every time the toaster pops? Huh? If you learned control, then you could go *anywhere* and live whatever kind of life you wanted, and no one would EVER know your truth? *How is this not obvious to you?*"

"I just...I don't....I just—"

"You want to be human."

"Yes," she cried.

"Fine." Koth lifted his left hand. Black smoke shot out of his palm and slammed right into Gigi's face. It coiled around her so tightly she became completely invisible for a few seconds before fading away. A white cloud popped out of Gigi's chest and flew into Koth's hand and then absorbed entirely into his skin. He dropped his arm and nodded. "Congratulations. You're human now."

Gigi gasped, her face as white as snow.

"*Elan,*" Koth barked.

"Yes, my Lord?" Elan strolled over to stand beside him.

Koth kept his eyes on Gigi. "Gigi here is officially a shifter who cannot shift. Have Silas fly her home to her parents. You will explain to them, and her, exactly what that means now."

"I'm...I'm...*human?*"

Koth glared. "For all intents and purposes, yes. You may always return here if you are in danger. But your family must move—"

"*MOVE?*"

"Yes, *move.*" Koth shook his head. "Salem is a city of magic, danger, and blood. Elan will ensure that you and your parents are relocated to a city where demons and Duenill do not meet for tea on the regular, do I make myself clear?"

She nodded, her lips trembling. "Yes, my Lord."

Koth tipped his head back and shot a stream of fire into the night sky. "Elan, go. Now."

Silas immediately landed in front of us in dragon form and that stony silence of his.

"Silas, escort Elan. He will tell you the plan."

Silas nodded and turned to follow Elan and Gigi out the backside of the clearing.

Koth watched until they were gone, then turned back to us and sighed. He scrubbed his face with his hands. "I am too young for this shit."

I snorted. "I feel that."

"And thank heavens for that. No one else gets it." Koth shook his head. "I am sorry you had to deal with all of this. I am especially sorry for Savannah."

"Ya know, I don't think Savannah is." Tegan giggled. "She's kinda into the dark and creepy and I think this will just play into her personality well. I can see it now. She'll get in someone's face and be like, *I died once, bitch. TRY ME.*"

Koth and I both laughed.

Then I cursed. "Is she going to be okay? Gigi? And is that permanent?"

Koth pursed his lips and shrugged. "It can be."

"A King thing?"

He grinned. "I have the power to give and take a shifter's magic, yes. Never have I done so permanently, but it would take a hell of a lot to convince me to give Gigi's back. In fact, I'm not even going to tell her it's possible. She must feel a punishment of some kind for her actions, or lack thereof."

"And she needs to be an example," Tegan said coldly.

Koth shrugged. "Not all shifters want to be what we are. Not even some dragons, and it's a coveted gift. I have to maintain the safety, and secrecy, of our people. But I don't have to explain that you two."

"Nope," Tegan and I said at the same time.

"She'll be fine. She'll either flourish in her human life or she'll realize her errors and make amends." Koth shoved his hands in his pockets. "Until then, her family will be relocated to a safer city—of their choosing, of course."

"I am sure Savannah will want to know of her new location. Would you mind relaying it to us once you know?"

"Absolutely, Tenn. She is not being hidden. Savannah may visit whenever she wants, though please ask her not to use any black magic on her as it is not safe for our kind."

"OH, that's ominous." Tegan grinned.

Koth's eyebrows rose. He pointed to her but looked to me.

I sighed. "Just ignore that. She's a weirdo."

"Right. So how is Kenneth?"

I smiled. "We had to strip him of his Mark, but it saved his life. He is alive and well in Eden as we speak."

Koth sighed. "Good. That's great. We were all praying for him."

"Thank you." I glanced to Tegan and then back. "All right, well, we hate to take any more of your time, so we'll be heading back now unless you need us for anything else."

"We're all set for now, but thank you." Koth bowed his head. "And thanks for bringing Gigi to me."

Tegan opened up her portal right behind us. She winked and gave a grin. "You know where to find us if you need us."

Koth chuckled. "Likewise. Be well." And then he was gone, vanishing into the darkness.

"Is that how it feels when *I* do that?"

I grinned and took her hand. "No, kitten, it's much, much creepier when you do it."

She beamed and her eyes sparkled. "That's the nicest thing you've ever said to me."

I rolled my eyes. "Shut up, butthead. Let's get back before all the food is gone."

She giggled and took my hand. Together, we stepped inside Tegan's portal—

"*MOM,*" Cooper screeched.

We strolled back into Headquarters and found all of them cracking up and Cooper in obvious visible distress. He was all red and sweating.

Tegan smiled and sat back in her chair. "What did we miss?"

"I'm afraid to ask," I grumbled. Mocking Cooper usually happened at my expense. "I just want to eat."

CHAPTER ONE

TEGAN

January 31ˢᵀ 2019

It was a bright, beautiful sunny day with bold blue skies and not a single cloud in sight.

And it made me want to pluck someone's eyeballs out.

The cool ocean breeze did *nothing* to ease my anger. This was all my fault. I was better than that. I was faster than that. I should have gotten to them in time. I should have—my phone vibrated in my hand, cutting my self-hating thoughts off. I looked down and found a text message from Constance to our group chat. I held my phone up a bit higher so Tenn could read it over my shoulder. He was sitting on the sand beside me.

'Henley has not moved in hours, still sitting in Hidden Kingdom,' Constance wrote. *'Should we be concerned the camera was removed? Tegan?'*

Tenn groaned under his breath.

I focused my mind on the sounds coming from the spell placed behind my ear. Around me, the ocean's waves were calm and soft, but in my ear I heard children screaming and giggling, carnival music off in the distance, and a couple arguing in Spanish. I recognized these sounds instantly, and not because I'd been listening to it for days...because Hidden Kingdom was a special kind of place for us.

And for the shadow demon.

I typed a quick response to Constance, '*No. She's still there. I can hear the park around her. And I know she hasn't discovered my listening spell.*'

"What's he doing?" Tenn whispered. "He knows we haven't moved. He knows we're here and preoccupied...why not strike while we're down?"

I took a deep breath and tried to ignore the onslaught of memories from my time as Queen of Darkness. I leaned into him. "Because he wasn't expecting us to be down. It takes time for him to...settle into the body he possesses. It has to adapt to the physical limitations of the human body."

"You mean he has to sleep? He didn't last time."

"Yes, he did. He took her earlier than anyone realized, and then he used Emersyn's power to give him strength enough that night in Hidden Kingdom." I grimaced. "And then it was ME who gave him the strength to enact all his dirty plans."

Tenn shuddered. "I still hate that you did that, even though it's over."

That almost made me smile. I kissed his shoulder. "This will be over for Henley soon enough. Our plan is working so far."

Our plan...was potentially my craziest plan to date. I sent one of my best friends to be possessed. We caught a coincidentally lucky break by the shadow demon needing to adjust to a human form, otherwise sitting here on this beach waiting for Bentley could have been catastrophic. As it was, the shadow demon only made mediocre trouble. Some demon attacks here and there, but we had enough help from the Knights of Florida that it was handled.

We just needed Bentley back. Once we got him, we could

figure out how to get Saffie into Seelie to save the others. And judging by the intensity of her magic slamming into me from where she sat a few feet back...she was ready to blow. Not that I blamed her. If it had been Tenn, I would've been gone already. There would have been no reasoning with me. I just needed a safe way to get Saffie into Seelie. I owed her that much.

A giant gust of wind ripped off the water and slammed into me, blowing my hair off my shoulders. Tenn sat up straight. I jumped to my feet, my magic coiling around my hands instantly. *I felt that. What are you?* Tennessee stood up beside me, his power radiating against my skin. My Spidey senses were downright pulsing. Something was coming. The air was sharper, the ground warmer. I wiggled my fingers to feel my magic. *Come on, Bentley.*

I felt each Bishop get to their feet behind me. The energy moved like a wave over the sand. Each time it hit someone, they flinched and hopped up.

"What is that?" Savannah whispered. I couldn't see her, but I felt her magic stir in a panic. "What is it? I feel something but—"

A ripple sliced through the perfectly flat turquoise ocean water. The sound of my Coven-mates drawing their weapons almost made me smile. If this was another attack, we'd be ready. But I didn't think it was, or maybe I was praying it wasn't. My stomach tightened into knots.

A wave shot up twenty feet off the shore. It rushed toward us, moving faster than a natural wave could. The water turned jet back. Bright orange and red flames blazed from within the wave. The water turned thick and gray with red and orange molten lava. Each time the lava hit the ocean water, it hissed and white smoke billowed into the air. The lava cracked and hissed as it hit the sandy shore. Thick gray and white smoke poured out into the blue sky.

Fire burned a vertical line in the sky going upward from the wave. It flashed and flickered, then the fire split apart like flames eating parchment until it left a black hole. Except it wasn't a black hole. This was uneven and misshapen. A black night sky twinkled with stars. It was like someone had cut a hole out of the blue sky.

A figure stepped into the hole, filling the space but cast in shadow. The smoke surrounding them was filled with flames. Behind them, a ball of fire shot across the night sky. I tried to look, but all I saw was smoke and flames. The figure walked forward, moving out of the hole, and I saw broad, muscular shoulders and a long body. It was definitely a man, except every inch of his body was black and gray like he'd been burned. He stalked toward us like he was walking on solid ground, like there wasn't fire and brimstone in his wake.

I sucked in a deep breath and held it as the rest of the world blurred away.

Streaks of burning orange fire covered the man's blackened torso as he walked.

The second his feet hit the white powdery sand, slivers of black and gray chipped off of his body until he looked completely normal. *Human.* His skin was tanned, or maybe he was just grimy and ashy. He was shirtless, wearing only low-slung black pants and black boots. His upper body was chiseled tight like a sculpture. Lean, sharp cut muscles covered his arms and shoulders. The ash on his skin made the ripple of deep-cut abs more pronounced.

Fire scorched like bolts of lightning across his skin, moving over his body in random places but not staying there.

The lava, smoke, and fire receded back into the hole faster than it appeared.

"What are we bloody lookin' at here, lads?"

"Anyone know who this is?" Easton whisper shouted.

The guy looked up and all I saw were crescent moons made of fire around his pupils.

He was still walking toward us, but everything seemed to be in slow motion. With every step he looked more and more human. Dark hair fell in wild, dark waves over his shoulders. My heart stopped. I knew that face. I knew the shape of those eyes and the—

"*Oh my God,*" I breathed. "*Bentley?*"

Someone gasped.

He stopped in place and held up a left arm that was chiseled with muscles.

The black *V* Hierophant's Mark was a stark contrast to his skin. He looked up with eyes that shined that bright, brilliant, *familiar* gold. "Yeah, it's me."

Bentley.

BENTLEY.

OH MY GODDESS.

IT WORKED.

Relief and shock that our ritual worked swirled inside of me, but my mind was blank. Because standing in front of me was not a nine-year-old boy but a man. My gaze scanned over his face again and again. He looked like he was maybe my age, or older. He looked like Bentley but different. He looked like our father but with Mom's hair. He had to be the same height as Cooper now.

There wasn't a sound around us. Even the ocean had gone silent as we all just stared. I didn't think any of us were even breathing. My brain was just screaming, *Bentley, Bentley, Bentley.*

It felt like an hour, but I knew it was only a matter of seconds before our mother was charging for him at full speed. Bentley's gold eyes widened and locked on her. He seemed to brace himself like he wasn't sure what was about to happen... and then she tackled him so hard they stumbled back a few steps.

A heartbreaking sob left her lips and carried through the

wind as she coiled her arms around his now big shoulders and held him tight. Bentley closed his eyes but not before I saw his expression shatter. His face scrunched up and his arms squeezed around her, lifting her off her feet. A few moments later, Mom pulled back and Bentley lowered her to the sand. He looked down at her with guarded gold eyes.

I couldn't see Mom's face, but I did see the way her hands trembled as she reached up and cupped his face. She sniffled and ran her hands through his knotted long hair. "Welcome home, love."

Dad was suddenly there next to her, though I didn't even see him move. His face was red and his eyes bloodshot. Without breaking stride, he reached out and grabbed Bentley, dragging him into his chest. Dad was still two inches taller and much bigger, but the closeness made my heart skip. My breaths hitched. My pulse pounded so hard in my veins they drowned out whatever my father was saying to Bentley.

"Breathe," Tenn whispered right in my ear. His warm hand took mine and squeezed tight. "Breathe in, kitten."

I sucked in a shaky breath.

"Exhale."

I let it out and leaned into his arm. My grip on his hand was probably too tight but he didn't mention it.

We did it. He's back. He's OLD. I failed him. He aged too much. It's my fault. Oh, GOD, how long did he suffer in there? Why didn't I send Saffie sooner?

"Keep breathing, kitten," Tenn whispered into my ear again.

A loud, broken whimper came from right behind me—and then a blaze of fire brushed over my right arm. I looked up and all I saw was long blonde hair and bright orange flames—

"*EM, WAIT. FIRE!*" Deacon shouted.

But Emersyn did not wait. She moved like a flame on gasoline.

Dad stepped back from Bentley and glanced over his shoulder, then dove back out of the way just as Emersyn tackled our *little* brother. Bentley's eyes widened, but as Emersyn's arms wrapped around his neck, those flaming orange crescents flashed in his eyes. Glowing fire-like lines shot down his arms. Black smoke coiled around their bodies. Emersyn was shaking she was crying so hard.

Deacon cursed and hurried over. He pressed his hand to Em's back. "Butterberry, love, let's not set him on fire. Come on."

Bentley looked right into Deacon's eyes, not *up* like he used to. They were the same height now. *No, wait.* Bentley was taller, though, by maybe an inch. I didn't know what Bentley was feeling, but whatever it was Deacon and Dad were picking up on it because they both had to physically pull Emersyn off of him... and then she collapsed into Deacon's arms.

Cooper strolled forward, his hands on his hips. He walked up to Bentley and stopped so they were almost nose to nose.

Bentley stiffened. His gold eyes locked on Coop's.

But then Cooper scoffed. "I'm still bigger."

Bentley's gaze dropped down to Coop's chest and arms and then back up. He opened his mouth to say something but never got the chance because Cooper wrapped him in a big bear hug. And not the kind of hug dudes gave to their friends while trying to still look cool. This was a *real* hug. When Bentley leaned *into* him, my eyes watered. But when his hands fisted the back of Coop's shirt, I just bloody lost it. Tears poured down my face.

Tenn's thumb rubbed circles on the back of my hand.

Cold fingers gripped my other hand, making me jump even though I knew it was Bettina.

She bumped her hip into mine but didn't say anything.

Cooper jumped back and wiped at his face, and an awful sound slipped out of my throat.

Uncle Kessler chuckled and swooped in, still towering over Bentley. I wanted to watch their interaction, but my gaze betrayed me and landed on my dad wiping tears off of his face. I groaned and buried my face in Tenn's shoulder. I needed to go to Bentley. I knew I did. I wanted to. But I was stuck. Frozen. I was falling apart. My little baby brother, my mini-me, was now as tall as Cooper. He was grown. He had *abs*. And it'd only been four days.

Bettina squeezed my right hand—and then she was gone.

The suddenness made me look up just as Bettina tackled him in a hug. She was there from the very beginning of his life. He was always like a brother to her, too. *He IS your brother, Tegan. Get over there.*

As Bettina backed away, I nodded to myself and took a deep breath.

And then Bentley looked up and our eyes met.

There was no one between us, just sand and a whole shit ton of emotions. The beach was so quiet I could hear each of my teardrops hitting the ground. Bentley seemed just as locked up as I was. I didn't know what my problem was. This was still Bentley. He was back. He was *alive*.

He took a step forward, then stopped. His face fell and the expression in his eyes broke me.

And then it hit me...he hadn't smiled. Not once. No smirks. No winks. No playfulness. No devious grins and scheming. The face looking back at me felt foreign even while it was utterly familiar at the same time. His Mark looked exactly the same. The Hierophant's locket hanging on his chest was pulsing with power I knew. His magic was entirely familiar.

It was Bentley...but was it *Bentley*?

My heart could handle him being older, but I was terrified I'd lost *him*.

Those big golden eyes were watching me. Waiting.

I took a step forward, then stopped.

His energy skipped and pulsed. It felt suddenly wild...and nervous. He was nervous about my reaction.

So I licked my lips and said, "What creature sat in the corner the first time Harry Potter visited my office in Hogwarts?"

He just stared at me in silence with an odd expression as I held my breath. Waiting.

"Are you mad?" Jackson said under his breath in both concern and confusion.

And then it happened.

Bentley smiled.

Not the fake kind. Not the pose for a picture kind. Not even a happy kind. It was the silly, devious kind of sideways grin that was one hundred percent my little brother. "A grindylow."

I wasn't sure who ran to who, but the next thing I knew we were hugging.

He chuckled in my ear and even though it was a deeper sound now, it was still entirely *him*. "Goddess, I missed you, weirdo."

I sniffled and pulled back so I could see his face. "For a second I thought you were gonna let me down."

He arched that one right eyebrow like he always did. His grin turned crooked. "I'm almost as reliable as Jackson's British-ness saying the exact next line of the movie naturally."

Jackson's eyes widened. "What?"

Bettina threw her head back and laughed, then wrapped her arms around him. "I'll show you later, Lancelot."

And then the wolves descended on him, or that was what it felt like. Everyone else rushed to him, surrounding him in the largest group hug I'd ever seen. And it was everyone else. Koth and Silas towered over my Coven-mates as they ruffled Bentley's hair. Even Maddox and Savannah, who barely knew him, had joined in. Hell, even Tenn was in there—actually, he'd somehow made it to the middle of the pile. I heard Olli howling and then he was sitting on Koth's shoulder, punching and licking the air. Albert barked and then half the pile was tackled to the sand in his attempt to get to Bentley.

I hung back just to watch this moment. We'd done it. We'd gotten Bentley back. None of us cared that he was older. It just mattered that he was *here*. We still had a lot of problems to address, but for this brief moment my heart was happy.

And then I heard a sniffle from behind me.

My heart stopped. I didn't even need to look but I did anyway.

Saffie.

Her eyes were puffy and as red as her hair. She watched the happy pile of hugs with a half-smile and a heavy stream of tears.

I cursed and hurried over to her, then wrapped my arm around her shoulders. "*Hey, hey, just breathe, okay?*"

She nodded and leaned into me.

"This is a victory for us, Saffie. We needed him back and we got him. It worked." I squeezed her tight. "I know he'll have read the note and he'll know the answer. We will not stop until we get Riah and the others back. You know that, right?"

She looked up at me and nodded.

"Cassandra?"

I looked up at the sound of Bentley's voice and found him staring at the former Hierophant with a wild grin on his face.

"Hello, my little successor." Cassandra giggled and gave him a quick hug. She stepped back and squeezed his shoulders. "I left *very* detailed instructions for you before I died."

"Yes, and I made *very* detailed questions for your return."

She winked. "I can't wait."

"Wait, hold up." Easton waved his hands between Bentley and Cassandra. "You can't know her. She died before you got here."

"Wait, did you say *for your return?*" Chutney shrieked. "You knew she was coming back?"

Bentley tapped on the Hierophant's locked hanging on his chest. "It's a long story."

"One we'll get to later," Cassandra said with a coy smile.

I couldn't wait to hear *her* story because I knew there was something else there.

"Yes. Later." Mom cleared her throat and shooed everyone away from Bentley. "I want to get him looked at by Katherine now that he's home. Just in case."

"Bentley?"

Everyone froze at the sound of Saffie's soft voice. She hadn't yelled or even spoke up. It was barely more than a whisper, yet we all heard it.

Bentley turned toward her with a shattered expression in his eyes. "Saffie."

"Where's Riah?"

CHAPTER TWO

SAFFIE

"BENTLEY?"

Everyone else froze.

I felt awful for interrupting their rejoicing. They deserved it. I didn't resent them for the happiness that Bentley had made it home alive and well. *I* was thrilled about it too. But I couldn't handle it a single moment longer. My heart was breaking. I couldn't wait any more.

Bentley turned toward me and the look in his eyes was like a dagger to the heart. "Saffie."

"Where's Riah?"

His shoulders dropped and his face fell. He shook his head. "I can't say for certain."

My lips trembled. The whole world seemed to be shaking.

Bentley hurried over to me, then took my right hand in his. He held it up in front of my face and tapped on the crystal glyph on the back of my hand. "Do you see this? What color is it?"

I sniffled. "Green."

"That means he is still alive." Bentley ducked down to look

me in the eyes. "It's not even red, which means we still have time to save him. Okay?"

"O-okay." I nodded and licked my lips as he dropped my hand softly. "When was the last time you saw him?"

Bentley frowned. "What day is it here?"

"January 31st, 2019," Tennessee said quickly.

"*What?*" Bentley shouted. He spun around with wide eyes, then exhaled and bent over with his hands on his knees and hung his head. "*Are you fucking kidding me?*"

"*Bentley,*" Devon hissed. She was smirking.

"Four days? It's been four days?"

"Yes," we all said in perfect unison.

Bentley stood back up right and scrubbed his face with hands that were covered in scars. Then he shook his head.

"How long has it been for you, Benny?" Tegan asked with narrowed eyes.

Bentley laughed, but there was no humor in the sound. "Seven years."

Silence.

Braison cringed. Deacon cursed. Maddox shoved his hands in his hair while Koth closed his eyes.

Seven years. It's been seven years. That's fine. He's six hundred years old...seven is a blink of an eye, right? RIGHT?

Tegan pursed her lips. "So, you'll be sixteen this month?"

Bentley scratched the back of his neck. "Yeah."

Tegan grinned. "You're still the baby of the family. Cool."

Emersyn snorted and then buried her face into Deacon's chest. Cooper giggled. Devon and Hunter shook their heads. Everyone else just stared at her weird.

"What? These are important things to note." Tegan shrugged and winked to Bentley. A white portal box opened up behind her. "Get inside, y'all. Bentley's got some shit to tell us, and if I want to listen, then I need to at least be able to watch Henley."

Bentley's face paled. "Shit. I was hoping you'd gotten her out by now, but I guess it's only been four days."

"I'll fill you in on that as well." Tegan pointed to her portal. "Go on, y'all. Get."

We all rushed through the portal, which placed us right back in Kessler's living room in his house in Tampa. Constance, Daniel, and Kenneth were watching the big screen television that was hooked to the hidden camera in Henley's dermal piercing on her face. I knew exactly where she was the second I saw the screen. The shadow demon liked his hiding spot in the carnival section of Hidden Kingdom.

Bentley was pounced on by the three adults who hadn't been on the beach with us. The rest of us took seats and got settled in. Well, *they* did. I paced the glass wall while chewing on my thumbnail.

"So, before we get to me..." Bentley pointed to the screen and then turned his back to it to face the room. "What's been happening with her?"

"We got a coincidentally lucky break—"

"*WHAT?*"

"Royce," Tennessee growled in warning.

"Let me explain?" Tegan smiled to Royce, then turned back. "The shadow demon has to adjust to being in a human body— no, I don't know why or how that works. I was planning on asking Riah. But that's how it worked last time. Except, last time it possessed her before any of us knew it and remained hidden. It then tapped into Emersyn's energy to try and open the Gap... and then I gave it the strength it needed."

Several people started to talk but Tenn growled so they stopped.

"I'm not sure why it's worse this time, but I suspect it's because Henley is in rougher shape than she was before. Alas, it has to rest a lot. It did not expect us to be down or I'm sure it would have pounced. In fact, I think it's so weak because it's tried to attack us these last four days." Tegan looked to Bentley and shrugged. "The Knights of Florida have handled those situations while we worked to get you back."

Bentley nodded. "But we should be ready for it to make a real move any time now."

"Exactly." Tegan glanced around the room. "That basically catches you up for us. Now it's your turn—"

The front door flew open and slammed into the wall. Sunlight poured in, casting the person in shadow. But as they sprinted down the hallway toward us, I spotted a familiar head of auburn hair.

Katherine slid to a stop and gasped. "BENTLEY?!"

His cheeks flushed. "Hi, Katherine."

"Oh my *Goddess,*" she mumbled and hurried over. "How old are you now?"

"Sixteen."

"Did you age naturally or through magic?"

"Is that a trick question?"

"*Bentley,*" Devon hissed.

Tegan chuckled.

Bentley sighed. "Naturally."

Katherine dropped a huge black bag on the coffee table and then pointed to it. "Sit. Now."

"Katherine, I feel—"

"Like you were in another realm for seven years even though it's been four days here? Yes, I'm aware. Sit." She snapped her fingers and pointed back at the table. "We have to make sure you're clean and healthy just in case."

Bentley sighed and plopped down on the wooden coffee table as she asked.

"Good." Katherine glanced around the room. "Go ahead. Talk. I can work while you interrogate."

Tegan smirked. "All right, Benny—"

"What happened?" I blurted out. When no one answered

me right away, I turned and marched over to sit on the couch directly in front of him. "What. Happened."

Bentley was staring at the ground, but when I sat he looked up. "You have to understand that time in Seelie does not work the same—"

"I know that—"

"No. I mean *within* Seelie." Bentley leaned forward with his elbows on his knees as Katherine ran her hands over his bare back. "On Earth, time works the same everywhere. There are time zones, but it's otherwise consistent. In Seelie, it depends on where you're at. So, the others might not have experienced as much time as I did."

I nodded. "Where were you? What happened when Sage took you?"

Katherine pulled one of Bentley's arms up and made him sit up straight.

Bentley took a deep breath and slowly let it out. "Sage delivered us all to the King and Queen, and whoever was in their court watching. Riah...Riah tried to smooth talk him but the King didn't buy it or let him talk long."

A whimper left my lips. Someone grabbed my hands and squeezed, but I couldn't tell who it was through the fear rushing through me.

"So Sage betrayed us. Betrayed Riah." Easton cracked his knuckles. "Riah was lied to this whole time?"

Bentley frowned. "I'm not entirely sure about that—"

"*How can you say that?*" Braison shouted, his face flushed.

I nodded. I wanted to know why he thought so too, but my mouth would not open.

"I'm not saying she and Thorne are bad or good, I'm just saying I'm not sure." Bentley held up his hands. "I mean, Sage didn't need to take all five of us. She is plenty capable of just grabbing Riah and leaving. Yet she took us all. And as soon as Thorne came out, he asked his father if they needed to keep all of us...as if we were coincidental. It doesn't make sense. But also...if she hadn't taken me, you'd never make it into Seelie to get to the others."

"Which makes me think this was all part of their twisted plan," Tegan said.

"The one Riah claims Thorne and Sage are running." Jackson cursed. "He wasn't lying, so if they did betray us, then Riah was just as surprised."

Obviously.

"*What. Happened?*" I heard myself growl.

"I was wearing a long-sleeved shirt, and I was obviously a child, so I don't think the King realized that I was in The Coven..." Bentley narrowed his eyes and stared into space, like he was reliving the moment that was so long ago for him. "Sage was quick to get me out of there, too. I will spare you of the details of their conversations. You do not need to hear it. But Sage suggested bringing me to the Wild Night—"

I gasped. "Oh no."

"What?" Tegan looked back and forth. "What is that?"

Bentley's eyes darkened and those orange crescents flashed in his eyes. Orange, lightning shaped marks shot across his bare skin. "I do not wish to speak of it right now, but your imagination won't be far off—I assure you."

Hunter groaned.

"The Wild Night is the outer banks of Seelie where time runs the fastest, this is why seven years passed for me...but the others..."

"What did they do with them?"

Bentley cursed. "I was dragged out of the room before I could hear—"

"*You don't know?*" I cried.

"I made a friend while there. Her name is Ziva. She's a half-breed like Saffie who was stolen from Earth and thrown into the Wild Night. She has her own set of skills that allow her to move around unnoticed. She went looking for answers for me, and yes, she did get them." He jumped and cursed as Katherine dumped some liquid on him. Then he shook himself. "From what she was able to learn..."

"Just tell it to us straight, Bentley," Deacon grumbled. "Rip the band-aid."

"The Queen took Landy, though Ziva insists that she saw her in the meadow *with* the Queen unharmed. Amelia... Amelia..." Bentley cringed. "Amelia was sent to the King's private chamber."

Deacon sank to the floor and buried his face in his hands. Red lightning flashed around his fingers. Emersyn dropped down and wrapped herself around him.

The room was silent a moment and then Maddox of all people cleared his throat. "Are you...are you saying what I think you're saying? That he...took her?"

Bentley grimaced. "I'm saying that is certainly the intention he made clear to the entire court...and no one has seen her since."

Maddox cursed and spun away with a growl.

"According to the rumor around Seelie, a former Coven member was being tortured for information—"

The entire Coven groaned and cursed.

Bentley frowned up at Katherine as she jabbed him with random crystals. "Obviously Paulina is the only one who fits that description. But the rumors also suggest that she's giving them one hell of a fight, so there is hope. And she'd never betray us. That goes without saying."

"And Riah?" I leaned forward and gripped Bentley's hands. "Please, tell me."

"He's alive. Your soulmate mark proves that." He waited for me to nod, then grimaced. "But...Commander Zachariah has been sentenced to death for treason."

A violent sob ripped up my throat and my whole body shook.

Everyone reached for me. I felt at least a dozen hands holding me tight. It helped a little.

"Listen to me, Saffie. The King *loved* Riah. He is furious over the betrayal and he wants to make Riah suffer for it—"

"Seven years though?" Savannah shrieked.

"Well, that's just the thing...time doesn't run the same, but from what Ziva says the Wild Night is the fastest. If Riah isn't dead yet, which we know he isn't, then it stands to reason that it probably hasn't been very long for him at all. Especially if the King wanted to torture Paulina first, or have his fun with Amelia—"

Deacon gagged.

"I'm not saying to take our time getting in there. I'm simply saying that soulmate mark will turn red once the countdown really starts."

"But then it'll be too late!" I hissed.

"No, I don't think so," Tegan said softly. She started to pace the small area while tugging on her bottom lip. "Tenn and I have both experienced red for each other. Each time it was when something significant happened, but it wasn't game over."

"What are you saying?" Cooper frowned.

Bentley shrugged. "That if the King wanted to make Riah suffer and torture him before killing him...that glyph would be red when that *started*. And he wouldn't hurry through it."

Tegan nodded. "So the suffering hasn't yet begun. Most likely."

I let out a strangled kind of half scream, half whimper. "I have to get in there. I have to get to him. I can't wait any longer."

"Bentley..." Tegan stopped and turned to her brother. "What's in the locket? What does Althea's note say?"

CHAPTER THREE

SAFFIE

Bentley looked to Cassandra who was leaning in the corner. "Did you not tell them?"

"She did," Tegan answered. "But I was hoping for more."

Bentley put his hand out to Katherine. "Please, can we pause the health inspection for a minute? We all need to focus on this, and I can't think when you do that."

Katherine patted his shoulder. "Of course, but I will finish later."

He grinned. "Of course."

She winked and then walked into the kitchen.

Bentley cleared his throat. "Okay, so I don't know what Cassandra already told you...but Althea's note is not complete. She isn't wrong, she just didn't know she was missing part of the information. And this is complicated shit, so bear with me here, okay?"

Everyone nodded and leaned in closer. Bettina pulled out a notepad. Tegan's Book of Shadows was sitting open in her lap. No one made a sound. Or maybe I just couldn't hear them over the thundering of my pulse.

"Althea's note says there's an archway north in the forest of

Canada—and yes, she describes it because she was there herself. She even sketched it to be thorough. This archway is the entrance portal into Seelie." He took a deep breath. "But the first thing she didn't know is that it is also the entrance into Unseelie."

"WHAT?" everyone shouted.

"Quiet," Tenn growled.

When everyone fell silent again, Bentley nodded. "This is potentially the most important part of the entire process. Because Althea did not know this. So everyone hear my words clearly, if you fuck this up, you go to Unseelie and there's no getting you back. Got it?"

Tegan cursed.

Royce grumbled. "I don't like this."

Everyone nodded.

"Now, once you get to the archway, there's a special incantation you must say in order for it to open. Like the chamber of secrets, right? But if you say it wrong, that's how you enter Unseelie instead. Althea *did* know this incantation, and yes, she wrote it. And yes, I know it. I have it memorized just in case something happened to the locket." He held his hand up. "However, I'm not going to give out that information just yet. We'll burn that bridge when we get there. Because that's not the only problem."

"What else?" Tenn asked from the back of the room.

"As with everything with Seelies, there's a price to pay for entering." Bentley took a deep breath. "But the trick is, you won't know what the price is until you've walked through...and have already paid it."

Tegan cursed again. "So, you say the spell, walk through, and the price is taken instantly."

"Yes. And you'll have to guess what it is they took from you, for it might not be obvious." Bentley tapped on the locket. "Althea recommends using that memory spell she put in the

Book of Shadows, but my gut tells me it won't be memories they take."

"What's the next problem?" I heard myself ask, though my own voice sounded far away. When everyone looked to me, I shrugged. "I know there's more, so what is it?"

"Well...first we have to find it. That's the other part Althea didn't know." Bentley rubbed his hands together and shook his head. "The archway is inside the Land of the Lore."

A cold chill slid down my spine.

No one spoke.

Bentley nodded, like he understood what everyone was feeling. This was not something any of us had ever heard of before.

"The Land of the Lore is...well, it's basically a foggy magical essence that flows like a river through the forests in Canada. Inside of it are what you might call forest sirens, like shadowy nymphs. They sing a siren's song and lure people into the fog..." Bentley shuddered.

"Then they get stuck like the Bermuda triangle."

"I don't understand." Kenneth scratched his jaw and stared into space. "How does this entrance into both Seelie and Unseelie exist without The Coven having any knowledge of it? Or this Land of the Lore?"

"Because the magic repels ours. Think of it like two of the same charged magnets and how they push each other away. The people who are lured inside are typically humans or civilians."

I whimpered. "How are we supposed to find it, then?"

"Can't Tegan just portal us there?" Easton asked. "Or no?"

Bentley shook his head. "Tegan cannot portal us there, nor can she use her magic while there. I'm not saying don't send her as an escort. I'm just saying she's emergency backup and that's it. Because the Aether Witch's magic *is* earth magic. It's our elements and power *here*. But the Land of the Lore isn't really *here*. It's complicated. We're going to have to use a cloaking spell of some kind to try and conceal our magic because it will literally hide from us."

Tegan cursed. "I get it. But where is it? How do we get there?"

"I don't know. I know what it is, what it looks like, and how to get through it once we're in it...but I don't know how to find it because it's always moving."

"Bentley," Tegan leaned forward and narrowed her eyes. "What aren't you telling us? What are you really not wanting to tell us?"

Bentley groaned and pushed his now long hair back off his face. He glanced to Royce and my heart stopped. I had a really bad feeling about this. My stomach turned and flipped inside out. Tears pooled in my eyes. *Please don't say what I think you're going to.*

"There is literally only one way someone can intentionally find the Land of the Lore...but Althea did not know this information. And in my seven years *in* Seelie, the only thing I've been able to learn on it—"

I whimpered and shook my head. *No, no, no.*

"—has something to do with the moon." Bentley's face fell and his gold eyes turned sad. "We need Henley."

CHAPTER FOUR

BENTLEY

I STOOD in the warm water, letting the gentle waves of the Gulf of Mexico roll over my feet. The water used to seem warm to me, like sitting in a bathtub compared to the water in Charleston. But seven years in the Wild Night changed that, among many other things. At least the sand was still powdery soft between my toes. It was surreal to be standing here barefoot with my jeans rolled up to my knees. I couldn't remember the last time I just...relaxed.

It was at least seven years ago.

The rest of The Coven were still inside playing their spy game on the shadow demon, but Dad must've said something to Tegan because she ordered me to go outside and take a deep breath. She'd left her portal open, though, so I could still hear everyone despite being miles away. I knew my entire family was watching from just inside Uncle Kessler's house. They weren't going to let me out of their sight for a while. Tegan must've ordered them to leave me be. That was the only explanation for this solitude. I'd have to thank her for it later.

I just needed a moment to...I didn't even know. Catch my breath. For the last seven years, all I focused on was gathering all the information I could and trying to get home. I hadn't stopped to prepare myself for what would happen once I got home. I'd known time worked differently there, Ziva had reminded me of it often, but I clearly had not expected *this*. Of course, it all made sense now—all the visions I'd seen of myself those last few weeks before I was taken and of me being an adult standing next to my family. Ziva had tried to prepare me for the possibility. She was right in the end.

Ziva. My heart hurt thinking of my friend. She was my best friend. We'd been through a lot together in seven years. I hated that I had to leave her, even though I had no choice. The wormhole could only take *me*. I'd promised her over and over we'd get her out of there, and I was going to make sure we kept that promise. I just prayed we weren't too late.

Raw, hot power slammed into my back. The low tide rushed forward, raising a few inches higher. Energy pulsed through the air and rippled the water. My own magic surged into my hands, igniting the marks of the Wild Night in my arms. My pulse quickened and my nerves tightened, ready for an attack—

"Just me," a deep voice rumbled from behind me, and it instantly set my body at ease.

Tenn. I glanced over my shoulder and watched him saunter toward me. Tennessee Wildes never truly strolled. He never looked that calm. All of my tension just evaporated. Most people were nervous around him or straight out scared, but for me Tenn was a calming presence. I knew no matter what happened, he'd have my back without question.

As he crossed the beach toward me, the sun shining down made the two gold bands on his left forearm sparkle like metal. His soulmate crystals on his chest and back of his right hand were bright pink and glistening. He wore his standard uniform, and the V-neck black shirt let the top half of the glyph stick out. I couldn't even count how many times in the last seven years I'd thought to myself *if only Tenn were here.* And now he was.

43

My emotions choked up inside of me, so when he did finally stop beside me...I had nothing to say. There simply was too much. My heart and mind were a bit too heavy. I didn't know how to process my thoughts for my *own* sake. How was I supposed to voice them to someone else?

He met my eyes and nodded once, then turned his mismatched gaze out to the horizon. His long black hair was only an inch or two longer than mine at this point but significantly more disheveled and wilder. I wondered what he'd think if he knew I let mine grow out because of him, because in my panicked mind it made me feel stronger. Just thinking it now made me feel...unhinged. Almost seemed silly now. But it was the little things, little thoughts that kept me going.

I wanted to tell him that, but my throat was tight and my mouth was dry. Instead, I turned and eyed the horizon. He didn't say anything and I couldn't bring myself to either, so for a few moments we just stood there in the water in silence. It was calming, comforting. Tenn wasn't my family, not by blood, but there was just something about him. Ziva had asked me once if I *liked* him liked him—I guess I'd talked about him too much. But I didn't. It wasn't like that. It was just...the dude had been through so much in his life already. A normal person would've snapped or broken down, yet he grew stronger and stronger.

As the only child in a Coven of powerful teenagers and adults, I'd looked up to that.

Suddenly, Tenn cleared his throat. "I know that instinctively you want to be alone right now, to flee from the closeness of this big group we call a family...but don't push them away."

"I..." *I don't know what to say to that.* Tenn wasn't a man of many words, so when he did speak, I made it a point to listen.

"They're pretty good at respecting privacy and emotional limits, even if it seems like that can't possibly be true." I must've made a face because Tenn shrugged. "When Easton jokes about you suddenly having more chiseled abs than him and Cooper combined, that's just his way of breaking the ice. And to make you smile. In his mind, if you're laughing at how ridiculous he is, then you're not thinking about what's bothering you."

I opened my mouth and then shut it. I'd never thought about it like that.

"Also, try to remember that Deacon can feel your desires, so if he's saying something ridiculous he's trying to help you." Tenn smirked. "And Coop, well, he's the most overprotective one in the whole damn group. I can't decide if he should never procreate or if he should have like a dozen kids. Could go either way."

"How did you do it?" I heard myself suddenly blurt out without any warning.

Tenn looked down at me with a curious gaze. "Do what?"

"Go on after realizing you'd lost twelve years of your life with your family?"

He stared out at the horizon again and was silent for a long moment before he sighed. "I won't lie and say it's easy. I won't say I don't catch myself feeling overwhelmingly sad at what was robbed from me, or that I don't feel rage and the need to break shit because *someone* has to pay for what was done... because it sucks. It sucks more than I have the words to express. And I know exactly how you're feeling right now. Because even though you were alive this whole time and experienced every single passing day, suddenly everything is different."

My breath left me in a rush. He got it. He understood what I was feeling and trying to say. I couldn't get my mouth to work, so I just nodded.

"There are so many things I wish would have happened— things I wish I would have known..." he closed his eyes and shook his head. When he opened his eyes again, he stared down at the water by our feet. "Except I can't change any of that. I can't get my parents back. But I *did* get my sister and uncle back. Yes, I missed out on twelve years' worth of memories we could have had together, but at least I have them now."

My heart was pounding. I wasn't sure anyone was going to understand how I was feeling yet he did.

"It's horribly cheesy, but it's true. I thought Timothy died, so when my memory came back, I grieved all over again but worse. Hope was in Eden for *months*. I knew she was. I was the one who told Dean to keep an eye on her. And she was Hope the whole time." Tenn exhaled roughly. He reached up and tied his long hair into a messy bun on top of his head. The pain in his eyes echoed the roaring agony inside of me. "Every time my emotions get the best of me, I remind myself that I have them here and now."

A strangled kind of half-sigh, half-groan left my lips.

"How did I do it, you asked?" His eyes snapped to mine and held my stare. There was no judgement in his stare.

I nodded.

"I do it by reminding myself of the pain I felt every single day my memory was gone. For twelve years it tortured me because I knew, *I knew* I was missing people. I was haunted by the ghost of memory. I thought I'd never figure it out, and I definitely never thought I'd actually get my memories back. And getting my sister and uncle back? I never even dreamed of it." He glanced over his shoulder toward Tegan's portal into Tenn's childhood home. "Any time I'm losing it, I just look at them. I didn't have them in my past but I'm not going to let anything prevent me from having them in my future, and that includes my own fragile emotions."

Silence.

Well, shit.

My chest was tight. It felt like the world was closing in around me.

He turned to me. "You were in Seelie for seven years, and unlike us you experienced every single day of it. I don't even

46

have to ask to know that the hope of seeing your family again kept you going. I can see the scars on your body. I can feel it in your magic. Your time in the Wild Night hurt you severely and it will leave its mark, but you're home now. You're with us. Sure, you're not the little nine-year-old we expected to get back but you *are* back. You're alive. You don't know what the last few days were like for them, I mean for all of us, but especially for them. When you were taken—"

"What? What happened?"

"Each and every Bishop charged for the tunnel, including Hope and Deacon. Savannah had to use black magic to stop Emersyn. Tegan was so shattered that she actually forgot she could teleport herself—and that's the only reason we were able to stop her. I had to use every ounce of magic inside of me to stop her from getting inside the tunnel. And in case this wasn't obvious, none of us left this beach until we got you back. We all sat right where you were taken, waiting for our spell to work."

"And it did work," I whispered. It was a stupid response, but I was struggling here.

"Exactly, Bentley." He smiled softly. "It did work. We got you back. Sure, we're all going to have to adjust to this new reality, but I promise you, from experience, that if they had to choose between this and you dying, they'd choose this without hesitation. Death is a real possibility for all of us in The Coven. We kept waiting for Saffie to deliver the news, except you returned to us."

I wanted so badly to say something, anything, but I couldn't get my body and mind to work. So I just nodded.

"Darkness will come, but when it does, cling to the memories—"

"Of the good times?" I asked with a smirk.

He chuckled and shook his head. "No. Of the *pain*."

"*What?*" My jaw dropped.

He shrugged one shoulder and smirked. "You have to fight

fire with fire. Remember how it felt to be in the Wild Night, and it'll make all of this a dream come true."

Despite the pain trying to drown me...that made me smile.

Tenn winked and then turned. He stopped and arched one eyebrow. "And if that doesn't work, just think of how much more fun you and Tegan will be able to get into now that you're not a little kid who can't fight."

I snort laughed, but it felt good. Foreign but good.

Tenn squeezed my shoulder, then walked away back towards the portal.

"Hey, Tenn?" I half-turned.

Tenn stopped a few feet away and turned back to face me.

"Thank you."

He smiled and nodded. "I promise it gets easier."

Get inside! Tegan shouted into my mind. And the way Tenn stiffened I knew he heard it too. *Henley. NOW*.

CHAPTER FIVE

SAFFIE

I FELT Tenn and Bentley fly into the room behind us. Both of their souls burned like fire but from very different flames. Tenn's soul burned with the fire of Heaven. It was strong and steady—almost so hot it was cold. I couldn't use my Death Cards gifts on him, couldn't even try to tap into his spirit. It would consume me. Bentley's on the other hand was volcanic, like flames bursting through the ground to scorch everything in its path. I'd never seen lava, but I imagined that was what his spirit felt like.

Sometimes it was annoyingly distracting to be the Death Card.

I'd lived for three centuries. I'd gotten pretty used to feeling other witch's magic. Even with the power upgrade into The Coven, I'd adapted to the magic around me quickly...but their spirits were a ball game I wasn't quite sure why I'd been called to play. I'd always been partial to the life in the people around me, I'd always felt it, but *this* was too disorienting. It was too much. I needed to pay attention to the screen on the wall for Henley. Tegan heard something suspicious so we'd all gathered around to watch, but I couldn't focus.

I was feeling everyone around me too much.

Even with them just sitting there in silence, I heard too much. Some worse than others.

Royce's spirit was screaming so loud it made me flinch.

Braison's was dark. I felt him slipping into the shadows and it terrified me.

Tegan's was unnervingly ice cold.

The dragons could have been literal balls of flame beside me.

Bettina and Deacon's spirits were sharply vicious, ready to destroy anything.

And despite Bentley's return, the rest of the Bishops' spirits sang for revenge.

I wasn't sure how I was supposed to focus on *my* job with all of this. Because this wasn't like the Devil tapping into everyone's desires—no, that was surface level stuff. Deep down in the darkest pits of them, *this* was soul wrenching,.

Then again, feeling *theirs* was the only distraction strong enough to keep my own at bay. My mind screamed, *Riah, Riah, Riah,* over and over in the back of my mind. Like a constant buzzing in my ear, a sad song playing on repeat.

I'm coming, Riah. I promise. I just have to find out HOW first.

And my answer lied with Henley.

"Where is she?" Bentley growled in that deep voice none of us were used to yet.

"*I don't know,*" Royce whimpered and buried his head in his hands. "I hate this, I hate this, I hate this."

Hunter placed his hand on Royce's shoulder, but his golden eyes were locked on the screen. "It's obviously a big city, but I can't place—"

"That's downtown Miami." Tenn marched forward. "Southeast 3rd Avenue."

"I don't like this," Deacon grumbled. "There are too many people in Miami."

"*Exactly,*" Tegan said calmly. "Everyone be ready."

I stared at the screen, wanting nothing more than to scream and cry and break things. My legs bounced with the need to *move.* I tugged on my hair and chewed on my lip. Henley was walking down a city street...*whistling.*

Everything looked completely normal. The sun was setting in a beautiful array of reds and pinks, and the glass windows of the skyscrapers reflected the sky from every angle. The streets were crammed with lines of cars and humans in suits walking on the sidewalks. Henley stopped at a corner and waited for the walk sign to cross the street. I didn't know what Tegan heard to make her worried because everything looked—

Fire exploded out the side of a building in front of Henley. Thick black smoke filled the screen.

We all gasped.

A white portal opened up in front of us and everyone charged, not waiting for orders from our Leaders. I was up and flying along with them in an instant. We came out in the middle of chaos and destruction. In every direction, bright orange flames burst from windows in the tall buildings. Shattered glass rained down on the streets—but a rainbow cloud turned it to dust.

The ground rumbled under our feet. Heat slammed into my back. Screams ripped through the madness and echoed off the steel and cement.

I gripped my citrine crystal and felt the cool slide of my golden armor covering my upper body and then the comfort of my sword hilt suddenly in my palm. But I froze, and not because I wanted to. I knew how to fight. I *wanted* to fight. But something was pushing down on me, pinning me in place. I gasped and pushed against it, but it wouldn't budge. It was heavy and dark...cold like...

Death.

I feel death.

There was too much of it. It was suffocating me. And it wasn't all *new* death. Some of it was very, very, *very* old. The world closed in around me in dark vibrant blues until I couldn't see a single thing. I felt their pain, their sadness, but most of all their fear.

The dead were calling for me.

I closed my eyes and focused on their silent cries for help. *Just hold on for me, okay? I need to help them, then I'll set you free. I promise. Just let me SEE.*

The pressure eased, not completely but just enough so I could breathe and move my arms. My feet were still glued in place, like they didn't trust me to let me move even an inch. They were too afraid I'd leave them, and that broke my heart.

I took a deep breath, then opened my eyes and gasped.

There were demons *everywhere.*

The sky was littered with flying black monsters straight out of nightmares. But the dragons were shooting like rockets, burning them to ashes. Emersyn rode on Koth's back, sending rivers of fire through the sky. Everywhere I looked, The Coven was in action. They hadn't hesitated. They knew *just* what to do and did it.

"Saffie!"

I jumped and looked to my left just as Bentley slid to a stop beside me. "Yes?"

Big gold eyes bored into me as he took my hand. "Where's Henley?"

"I don't know, I—" I gasped as an idea formed. I pushed out with my magic. "Friends, help me. Find my friend with the demon inside of her—"

"The shadow one," a deep voice whispered behind me.

I glanced back only to find a hazy blue form.

Bright blue light shot out of the ground like water rising

until it took the shape of people. In perfect unison, the spirits sprinted across the street and into a wall of flames.

Bentley rolled to the balls of his feet and dropped my hand. "Tell me when you feel her. They won't hold him long."

I nodded and kept my eyes on the line of blue spirits. All around us was fire and destruction, but I pushed it out of my thoughts. I didn't have words to describe what Henley's soul felt like right now, while she was possessed, but it stood out from everyone else's.

"*Now.*" I gasped and pointed. "There."

Bentley darted forward without hesitation. He was halfway across the street when a horde of glowing blue spirits hauled Henley out from within the flames and smoke. They had her by the arms, dragging her toward me. But the shadow demon was stronger than them. They'd just caught him by surprise. Big red eyes snapped up to me, and Henley's pretty face grimaced—

Bentley emerged from *behind* Henley, tackling her to the ground.

I gasped as her face slammed into the charred asphalt. The Henley-demon hissed and snarled. Bentley pushed up off her and then flipped her over so her back was on the ground. He pinned her down with his legs and a hand to her chest, like he was choking her, but then growled and slammed his free hand over her face.

Henley screamed so loud windows shattered next to us. The moon dropped lower in the sky, glowing a neon yellow. White magic spilled from her palms.

"*HENLEY!*" Royce wailed from behind me.

But it wasn't Henley. Those disgusting red eyes blazed from her face.

"HEN! BENTLEY, NO!" Royce cried.

"*Friends, stop him!*" I ordered to the spirits.

A wall of glowing blue spirits shot up and blocked Royce's

path. He screamed and cursed and fought against them, yet they held him in place. Pinned to the ground on his knees.

"BENTLEY, NO!"

What are you doing, Bentley? He looked like he was suffocating her.

Black smoke billowed out from under them as the shadow demon fought back.

Bentley let out an evil little chuckle and then those bright, glowing orange crescents flashed in his eyes. Orange lightning streaks sliced down his arms and across his chest, like fire was bursting from his skin. His long brown hair was braided back out of his face, though I'd never seen him do it.

The shadow demon screamed, using Henley's voice to bait the others to interfere.

But the spirits weren't allowing anyone near.

Bentley growled and a cloud of orange magic and black smoke spilled from his palms. It coiled around Henley's head, then shot back up into Bentley's arms. Those orange lightning bolts pulsed and flashed like they were absorbing something—

Henley rocked side to side and then vanished into a cloud of smoke.

Bentley sat back on his heels as white light flashed from inside the Hierophant's locket dangling against his chest. He closed his eyes and frowned.

"*Henley,*" Royce whimpered. He tugged against the spirits' hold.

"Release them," I told the spirits and the blue haze in the street instantly faded.

The Coven descended upon us all at once, like they'd been there the whole time. I glanced over my shoulders and found shocked faces. Deacon sprinted to Royce and then sank to his knees beside him.

"Bentley..." Hunter strolled toward him. "Son?"

Bentley opened his eyes, but they were back to gold now. "Yes?"

"*Yes? YES?*" Royce shrieked. "WHAT DO YOU THINK?"

"I didn't hurt her, Royce," Bentley said with a sigh. "He just wanted you to think so."

Tenn cleared his throat and stepped forward. "You know that's not a sufficient—"

"*Saffie?*" An unfamiliar woman's voice said from suddenly right behind me.

I tried to turn but spirits were still holding my feet in place.

"*No, I think it's Saraphina?*" Another woman said softly. "*Saraphina Proctor?*"

I glanced over my shoulder—and frowned. Two spirits stood there side by side, just looking at me with sad yet hopeful eyes.

"*Are you Saraphina Proctor?*" the second woman said with a smile.

It was strange to be able to tell how recently a person died. The fresher their death, the paler their color. Their blue was almost unnoticeable. And their forms were much more solid. The ones who'd been stuck here for longer became hazier.

The first woman arched her eyebrows. "*The Death Card?*"

I shook myself, then nodded. "Yes, yes, I'm Saffie. The Death Card."

In my peripheral vision, I saw the entire Coven flinch and turn toward me. But I had to ignore them for a moment.

"Can you two come in front of me?" I pointed to my feet. "There are some lost souls here who have me pinned in fear I will leave them."

Deacon shuddered.

Cooper cursed.

The two spirits hurried to move in front of me. Then they gave me sad smiles.

"Hi?" I was still trying to grasp the concept of talking with the dead.

"Hi. I'm Lisa," the first woman said, then she pointed beside her. *"This is Marie."*

"We are the Majors of Miami." The second woman frowned. *"Well, we were. We fell."*

I sighed. My heart hurt. I hated this part of my gift. Helping the long since deceased find peace was rewarding because life had passed them on so long before. But the ones who had just fallen, who knew they'd just died, they hurt my heart too much. It made me question why I was chosen for this Card in the first place.

"The Majors of Miami."

Tennessee cursed. "Lisa and Marie?"

The two spirits turned toward him and opened their mouths to speak and then stopped, like they suddenly remembered they were no longer living. They turned back to me and nodded.

"Yes, Tenn." I pointed in front of me. "They are here, though they are gone."

Tenn put his hands on his hips and shook his head. "I am sorry to hear that. Are there any others? Others lost here?"

As if the spirits were listening to him, they rose from the ground, filling in the free space in every direction. They stood like statues, motionless and just staring at me. Waiting. Silently begging. Tears stung the backs of my eyes.

"Saffie?"

I nodded. "You don't want to know how many lost are here with us right now."

His face paled. "From today?"

"No," Lisa answered. Then she frowned. *"There are only a handful that fell with us inside headquarters."*

"The rest...have been waiting." Marie gestured around. She glanced to Tenn, then back to me. *"That shadow demon is up to something. It thinks it is tricking you."*

"Thank you." I nodded and then looked to Tenn. "They say

only a few died tonight. The rest...I could not tell you when they fell."

Tegan walked up beside me and put her hand on my back. My golden armor vanished instantly. She smiled down at me, then nodded. "Thank you. Let them rest now."

I glanced around at all the waiting spirits and gave them a small smile. "Time to go home now."

I held my hands up and called on my magic. It swam through my veins and into my palms. Gold glitter sparkled between my fingers. I took a deep breath and then pushed. *Be at peace.*

My magic moved like a wave, gently rushing over every spirit until their blue lights sparkled glittery gold. Each spirit closed their eyes and smiled...then faded away. Warmth seeped around my ankles as those that held me were now gone.

I lowered my arms and sighed as a strange hollowness filled my chest.

My thoughts went right to Riah.

Are they gone? Tegan whispered into my mind.

I nodded.

"Good." She exhaled. "Now damage control."

Royce threw his arms down and rose petals crumbled to the ground. "What the fuck, Bentley?"

CHAPTER SIX

SAFFIE

EVERYONE TURNED BACK to our Hierophant in shock.

"*WELL, Bentley?*" Royce shouted. He gestured wildly. "START TALKING."

"Easy, Royce," Cooper said softly. "Maybe Bentley was getting what we needed."

Braison's face snapped up and his eyes brightened. "Did you?"

Bentley grimaced. "No, and yes—"

"Bloody hell, lad. Not this Tegan style rubbish right now." Jackson pointed to Bentley's feet, where Henley had just been. "I don't care if you're telling the truth. Out with it. Don't be a wanker."

Tegan smirked. "Feels a bit like mutiny, but okay."

"Son..." Hunter shrugged and gestured around. "Please?"

Deacon ran his hand through his hair. "He wasn't trying to hurt her—"

"*What do you call all that, then?*" Royce shrieked.

Tenn held his hand up. With the other, he pinched the bridge of his nose. "Out with it, Bentley."

"Did you get what we needed from her? For Seelie?" Braison asked with hopeful eyes.

My pulse skipped. Hope flared inside of me at dangerous levels.

Bentley shook his head. "I was trying, but he's got too tight of a hold on her for me to get through."

"Get through *how?*" Emersyn pursed her lips and pointed to her own arms. "Because that was not normal Bentley behavior. Is there a gift for Hierophants I don't know about?"

"No."

We all turned toward Cassandra's voice. She moved to the front of the group. "That is not a gift for normal Hierophants. But it is an adaptation of it."

"In English?" Easton sighed.

"He doesn't know, y'all," Tegan said in that scary calm voice of hers. "Right, B? You don't quite know why you can do this and that's why you don't want to talk about it?"

Bentley chuckled and threw his hands up. "Feels a bit like mutiny, but okay."

Tegan shrugged. "Sometimes we just have to admit when we don't know. Surprisingly, for them, that is better than knowing nothing at all. Don't ask me. It's not my language they're speaking."

Bentley smirked at her but then his face fell. "I have this new... gift. What Cassandra meant is that it's an extension of what I could do before but *more*. All Hierophants get visions of the future, though we cannot control what, where, when, or how. We see what we're supposed to see. Yet somehow, and I don't know the answer as to how, I've developed the ability to force visions. On contact."

They gasped.

My eyes widened. "You can see someone's future by touching them?"

"Try me." Tegan thrust her arm out.

Bentley's eyebrows rose. "I won't promise to tell you what I see, got it?"

She rolled her eyes. "I probably already know."

"It's not through the hand." He closed the distance between them, then pressed his hand to her chest, up by the base of her throat. Orange magic coiled around his fingers, and he closed his eyes. Suddenly, he chuckled and yanked his hand away. "Well, okay."

Tenn's face fell. "Nope. Nope, don't like that."

"Will *I* like that?" Cooper growled with a deep scowl on his face.

"Please don't answer that," Hunter said softly. "I don't wanna know."

Easton raised his hand. "So...you just touch someone and you can see their future?"

"Not their entire future, just pieces." Bentley shrugged. "It doesn't hurt—"

Royce scoffed.

"Here, do me." Deacon pointed to his chest. "Show him."

Bentley did the same to him as he did Tegan. He placed his hand on Deacon's chest and let his orange magic coil out. He closed his eyes as he watched whatever vision was shown to him, then he nodded and dropped his arm.

"See, cousin? I didn't feel a thing." Deacon frowned. "Well, maybe a little bit of fear but that's not on him. Is mine better or worse than Tenn's?"

Bentley pursed his lips. "More expensive?"

Deacon sighed. "I can handle that."

"Show me." Royce's face was all scrunched up like he was in pain. He pounded on his chest and nodded.

Bentley repeated the process, ending with a soft smile.

Royce sighed so hard he actually swayed. He scrubbed his face. "I'm sorry. Sorry. I just...it looked so awful."

"That's because of the Wild Night." Bentley tapped on his

arms and those orange lightning bolts appeared. "I will not elaborate more than that, just know this is the result. The smoke is part of it, but it was also the shadow demon trying to get loose."

Tenn scrubbed his face, his silver rings glistening in the lights around us. "Okay, so what *did* you see?"

"At first I was just trying to get the answer we need to get Saffie to Seelie." Bentley shook his head. "I keep trying to force the answer I want with this new gift, but it hasn't happened yet—"

"Let us hope it never does." Cassandra's voice sounded like a song. "For you will regret it."

"I know. I know." Bentley looked to her and the two seemed to have a silent conversation before Bentley shook himself. "Then I was trying to see *Henley*. The real her. I wanted to see if I could...well, anyway, it didn't work. I couldn't get through him."

"But you saw him." Tegan grinned. "What's he planning?"

"I saw three visions. You won't like a single one."

Tegan's grin turned wicked. She rubbed her palms together. "I like that you saw them. Tell me."

"Remember that I see fragments of moments, not the whole picture." His gaze flicked to mine, then back to Tegan. "And I don't know when they'll happen."

Why did he look at me?

What does he know? What did he see?

It's Riah. It has to be. He must have seen something before he went into Seelie and now he wants to look again.

My stomach rolled and nausea bubbled up my throat.

"...Hidden Kingdom—"

Everyone gasped. I cursed. I'd missed whatever he said.

"Then I saw the Riverwalk in San Antonio, Texas, running with demons."

Someone cursed.

"And the last vision was Paris under attack. The Eiffel Tower, to be exact."

"Three attacks on major tourist attractions." Timothy twirled his sword around. "Means we need to be ready to move."

Willow spun around on him. "You think it'll be soon?"

"Yes," Tenn and Tegan said at the same time.

Tenn gestured around the street. "We stopped him hard here."

"I don't know what his plan was here, but we definitely interrupted." Tegan tapped on her ear. "He's been grumbling about it. He's definitely pissed and feeling vindictive. I think we can expect that attack on Hidden Kingdom to be soon and swift."

Lily pursed her lips. "You think he'll strike us where it'll hurt us emotionally first."

"Absolutely," Deacon answered. "But he can't get to Eden so it's feeding off Henley."

"And last time Hidden Kingdom played a big role in their plans." Emersyn pulled her hair up into a high ponytail.

"We need to get Miami settled before that happens." Tenn rubbed his hands together and glanced around. "We still have to do our jobs."

"I'm surprised no one else from Headquarters came out to help," Easton said with a scowl. "What's that about?"

Cooper scoffed. "Tegan."

"Tegan," Kessler said at the same time as his nephew.

She just shrugged. "What's the saying, too many chefs in the kitchen?"

Bettina snorted and covered her mouth with her hand.

Tenn just shook his head. "Babe?"

"We had dragons and a fire-breathing Emersyn. We were fine." She winked. "I didn't want any more civilians out here. I told them to lock it down until we came knocking."

Devon cursed. "They lost both Majors. That's a big hit when this city just went down like this."

"I can stay and serve as temporary Major." Cassandra smiled. "We don't need you worrying about finding a proper replacement in a moment like this. I'm familiar with Miami and the entire staff here. I can get this place back up and running in no time."

Everyone turned to Tennessee, then to Tegan.

Tenn shook his head. "I don't want Constance out and about—"

"What? Can pregnant people not do things?" Tegan frowned like she was genuinely confused by this.

Devon chuckled. "She can do anything she is used to doing."

"So stress is right up her alley—"

"*Easton.*" Lily smacked him in the back of the head.

"Constance, Daniel, and Kenneth are all in Tampa. That's not far, and they can be reached by phone. I'm just saying Cassandra can handle this by herself—" Tegan held her hand up to stop people from interrupting. "Because Miami is well stocked, people. Minors, Pages, Aces, Knights, and Healers. All right here."

"And if I need any more help than that, I can call the others in Tampa."

"Yeah, Chutney could just grab a ride on a dolphin and come down."

I frowned at Willow. "Has she done that before?"

Willow giggled and nodded.

Tenn shrugged. "I guess that settles it. Cassandra, you'll let us know if you need any assistance."

Cassandra grinned. "Look at you being all in charge and good at it. Too bad no one told you—"

"*Shut up,*" he said while trying not to smile.

The group broke into jokes about Tenn and Timothy. That

was the way The Coven worked. Between peril and fear there was a ton of laughter. But I wasn't in that mood. I couldn't hear the humor when my heart was hurting. And the look Bentley had given me a few minutes ago had only made it worse.

While they were distracted, I slid over to Bentley and cleared my throat.

He looked down at me with a sad smile. "I can't see everything, Saffie. I won't know—"

"Please, Bentley." I picked up his hand and pressed it to my chest. "I just need to know if you see him. I need to know if he's in my future at all, or if I'm already too late."

He closed his eyes...and orange mist flickered in my peripheral vision. I wished I could see what he was seeing while he was seeing it. Instead, I just had to stare at him. Waiting. Praying he saw something that gave me hope Riah could be saved still—that he was in my future still.

After a few seconds, he dropped his hand and sighed.

"Do you see Riah?"

He frowned and nodded. "Yeah. Yeah, I see him."

Why doesn't that sound like a good thing?

"GUYS—" Tegan shouted, then covered her ears. Her pale green eyes widened. "NOW."

CHAPTER SEVEN

SAFFIE

A PORTAL OPENED up right in the middle of the street. Before I could even walk toward it, my feet were sliding across the ground as an invisible force dragged me. In the flash of a second, the entire Coven flew through the portal and out the other side —and right into a nightmare.

People were screaming and running by us. We'd been dropped right in the middle of a stampede. Each person's face wore a mask of pure terror. Parents were carrying and dragging their children. The shrieking pierced my ears. The ground shook with the heavy thumping of their feet.

Night had fallen, but the moon sat so low in the sky it lit everything up like mid-day. Not that I needed the light. You didn't live in the same place for three centuries and not recognize it in every condition.

Hidden Kingdom.

There were so many people racing down the pathway that it was hard to see which section of the park we were in. But I knew the curve of this road and the cracks in these bricks. I knew the way the fog seeped up off the water to the left and curled over like a dome. I always hated this section.

The metal sculptures of clowns were moving and walking like they'd suddenly come to life—chasing and grabbing at humans as they fled. Shadows danced through the crowd, leaving hysterical shrieks in their wake. Clowns with neon-colored hair towered over the people with big, glowing red eyes.

I gasped. *NO.*

A soft yellow mist spread out in every direction, even swimming upstream through the crowd charging toward us. Each person who hit it instantly calmed, their screams dying on their tongues. Blue light flashed over our heads. I glanced up and found fireworks flashing and popping. The humans gasped and pointed—their terror now giddy excitement.

"Calmly and slowly exit the park," Deacon's voice purred over the crowd. Red mist slithered through the people like a snake. "Go home."

The combination of their three gifts had the crowd thinning out rapidly. But my eyes had latched on to the fog. It shot up into the sky, blocking out the stars. My body turned ice cold and chills ran down my spine. The fog crawled over the ground. It rolled over my feet and curled around my ankles. Memories crashed in all around me until all I saw was the past. I shuddered and pushed against this attack. I had to be stronger than this.

I stomped my foot and golden glitter flashed from below.

"Where is she?" Royce cried. "She's here."

STOP. I need to SEE. Make it stop—I pushed with my magic and gold glitter exploded out of me. The fog hissed and faded. The clowns froze in place, red blazing eyes locked on me. But their bodies weren't solid. The clothes flapped and swayed in the breeze like there wasn't a form inside of them...they were just floating. They weren't spirits, yet something was making them move.

"There!" Tegan whisper shouted and thrust her arm out.

Chutney screamed and charged forward. She ran in the

direction of Tegan's point, then dove headfirst into a thick bush. Henley and Chutney flew out and rolled across the pavement. They landed in a tangled array of arms and legs.

"LET THEM GO!" Chutney screamed and shot a ball of yellow magic into Henley's face.

Them. Chutney. I gasped. *NO, no, no.* I focused on my new power and searched for their souls, then a little whimper escaped my lips. My stomach turned. I knew their spirits. A gust of wind rushed over my face, so I sucked in a deep breath through my nose. Rage filled my veins. I knew those scents. *THE ANIMALS. He possessed the animals.*

"CHUTNEY!" Royce shrieked and darted toward them.

Chutney wasn't listening and I knew why. She was hearing the animals' crying for help. Sweet, innocent Chutney turned into a menace with a glistening dagger raised high over her head. Everything was happening so fast. Rainbow magic coiled around Chutney's wrist. Everyone dove for them.

I screamed and pushed my magic out. Gold glitter filled the air as far as I could see. The clowns dropped into piles of wigs, masks, and neon clothes, like the clowns had melted into puddles on the pavement. Out of the corner of my eye, I saw my Coven-mates hurrying to Chutney, but time seemed to stand still. It was moving too fast and too slow at the same time. It was like trying to run in a dream.

The clown clothes wiggled and then squirrels, rabbits, and birds hopped out from inside of them. They shook their heads and hurried toward me.

I crouched down and opened my arms. "Come, my friends."

Royce tackled Chutney, pulling her off of Henley.

Henley jumped up and smoke billowed from her palms. The animals stopped halfway to me and turned. Like the flip of a switch, they headed back to Henley. I growled and balled my fists, calling every ounce of my magic into my hands. *How dare you take them.* These animals had been my only companions over the centuries. I would not let them be tormented like this.

"They're *mine*." I threw my magic as hard as I could right into Henley's chest.

The animals spun back to me.

A warm breeze swept through my hair, buzzing like —*FAIRYFLIES!* Out of nowhere, a swarm of fairyflies coiled around Henley's face like a tornado. She cursed and swatted at them. It wasn't going to keep her down, but it was long enough to break the possession over the animals.

"Come on." I waved them toward me. "It's okay."

I recognized each of my little animal friends and they knew me too. The birds flew up to sit on my shoulders with trembling little feet. The rabbits hid under me, clinging to my ankles. The squirrels climbed my arms and tried to get inside of my clothes to hide.

The rest of The Coven swarmed Henley. Magic flashed in every color. Smoke shot like a pillar into the sky and the ground rumbled—

"NO!"

I looked up just as the black smoke vanished.

My heart sank. "*No. Where is she?*"

Royce dropped Chutney and she scrambled over to me. Without hesitation, she picked each furry friend up and hugged them to her chest. She sank to the ground so they all could climb onto her lap. She was crying and talking softly to them as they tried to get closer and closer to her.

"What the hell just happened?" Braison whined and threw his hands up.

Easton spun around with a scowl. "We had her. We just *had* her. What—"

"Tricksy hobbitses," Bettina hissed under her breath. Ice covered her forearms.

Cooper cursed. "We're gonna have to be slicker than that if we want to get information out of Henley."

My breath left me in a rush, and I sank down to my knees. We had her. She was surrounded by The Coven, yet she slipped through our fingers like sand. My eyes burned with angry tears I refused to cry. We had to do better. *I* had to do better. Riah's life was hanging by a thread and all we needed was one piece of information.

Tenn turned and arched one black eyebrow. "What do you have up your sleeves, kitten?"

"*I'm thinking,*" Tegan whispered. But then her phone rang from her pocket. She pulled it out with a curse, then quickly hit a few buttons. "Constance?"

Everyone froze.

Constance sighed through the phone. "She's in San Antonio."

"I'm staying with the animals." Chutney raised her chin and her eyebrows. "You can fight me if you try and make me leave."

Tenn cursed. "Savannah, Lennox, and Warner, stay here. Help her. Make sure the humans get out and the park is secure."

Warner and Lennox saluted him. Savannah gave a thumbs-up but then glanced at their salutes and fumbled to follow suit.

Tenn nodded. "Tegan. Texas. Now."

WE CAME out of Tegan's portal on a dark brick pathway with a flat river on our right and a CVS store on our left. On both sides of the river there was a row of buildings with gold shimmering lights illuminating the shops and paths. Tall trees with long, leafy branches hung low over our heads and draped over the river almost like a tunnel. The dark night sky was peeking through the leaves, but the moon was low and full, shining a sinister gold.

The river was crowded both on the water and land. Humans clogged the brick pathways, laughing and talking without a care in the world. Boats with several rows of humans cruised down the river with neon-colored lights illuminating the water. The smell of food filled the air, making my mouth water and my stomach growl. All of the shops must have been playing different music because several different melodies tickled my ears at once.

It was colorful.

It was beautiful.

It was joyful.

It was too much. Way, way too much. I'd never seen a place

like this, with so much happening all around me at once. I couldn't focus. My gaze bounced round and round. Every flash of light and new sound had me turning. My pulse raced. My magic rushed to the surface. I felt goosebumps cover my arms. My wings fluttered behind me.

I have to get out of here. I can't be here. I have to—

Big, warm hands gripped my shoulders and my pulse instantly slowed to a steady beat. My magic simmered and my wings stopped flapping. I took a deep, shaky breath, then exhaled.

"*Focus on one thing,*" Hunter whispered in my ear. "*Then it won't be too much.*"

Tears stung my eyes. I didn't know what I'd do adapting to the modern world without my Coven-mates. I nodded and focused my gaze on the black and purple head of hair in front of me. *Tegan.* I reached my hand out and pressed my palm to her back.

Don't move, Tegan said into my mind.

Cold, pulsing energy tingled against my hand and little rainbow-colored lightning bolts flickered between my fingers.

I'm cloaking us, Tegan said in my mind. *Nobody move. She's here.*

Now that my eyes had adjusted, I realized that under the cover of these trees it was rather dark, which was perfect for concealing a couple dozen witches and a few massive dragons. I glanced over my shoulder to where Koth stood, but he and his two companions were in their human forms. Which was probably for the best. Dragons weren't easily concealed. But I liked knowing they were back there ready to torch the world at a moment's notice—

The air pulsed around me. It was hot and sharp and stung my skin. My wings fluttered like hummingbird wings. Hunter's grip on me tightened like he was trying to calm me down, but that feeling wasn't *me*. That was magic being unleashed —I gasped.

"GAP!" I screamed.

"BRIDGE!" Tegan shouted at the same time.

White light flashed and then we were at the base of a bridge that arched over the river.

Henley was under it, clinging to the brick like a spider with swirls of purple and blue magic swirling. She'd opened a Gap —*it* did. Not Henley, the shadow demon. Red light flashed under the bridge and then a cloud of black smoke burst from the small Gap.

The scent of maple syrup stung my nose.

Demons.

It happened in an instant, faster than a blink of an eye. Dozens of demons flew out of the Gap and down the river. In the dimly lit area, they were just black blobs with red glowing eyes. Humans screamed and tumbled to the ground. My Coven-mates jumped into action immediately. They charged after the demons down the river with swords and magic drawn.

Emersyn and Tenn dove for the Gap. Black, green, and blue magic flashed.

Jackson and Cooper lunged for Henley. They grabbed her by the arms and held her in place. Bettina covered her feet in ice, gluing her in place. Tegan threw both hands up and fired her magic. Rainbow mist shot straight into Henley's chest.

Those big red eyes glowed brighter and brighter—rainbow magic exploded. It slammed into me, flipping me upside-down and backwards. Long fingers wrapped around my ankles and yanked me down. I felt Kessler more than I saw him, because my gaze narrowed in on the tidal wave bursting from the bridge. It towered almost as tall as the trees and rolled down the river away from us, flooding the pathways and drenching the humans. Demons shrieked and fought against the water, but the tide dragged them over the edge and beneath the surface.

Flecks of rainbow-colored magic dropped down like rain all around us.

As the demons drowned at the bottom of the river, our Coven-mates stopped and spun around with wide eyes all locked on Tegan.

She threw her hands up and shook her head. "Wasn't me."

They looked to Tenn.

He stepped out from under the bridge and shrugged. "It worked."

I frowned and glanced around. My heart sank. "No. She's gone again. Where did she go?"

Everyone else hurried back over, but the humans were panicking.

Tegan held one hand up to the sky and lightning shot out of her fingers, snaking across the sky. Thunder rolled over our heads and rumbled the brick path under our feet. Thick rain-drops fell in sheets up and down the river.

My eyes widened. "Are *you* doing this?"

I expected her to smirk or make a joke, but her eyes were blazing with anger. Her hair whipped around her body as more lightning bolts streaked from her hands.

Tenn looked to the sky and then back to her. He frowned and walked over to stand in front of her, then took her chin in his hand. He ducked down to meet her eyes. "We're still in this, babe."

She sighed, but it was more of a growl. Then she spun around to face the rest of us with glowing pale green eyes. "Yes, Saffie, I'm doing this. It's the fastest way for me to get the humans to do what I want."

"Which is?"

"Forget what they just saw and go home." She tied her hair up in a messy bun on top of her head. "Dammit."

"We've thwarted its plans twice now," Devon said calmly. "They could have been bloodbaths."

Kessler folded his arms over his chest. "We're lucky Bentley saw what he did. We're still a step ahead of him."

Bentley pushed through the others and marched up to Tegan and then stopped. He stared at her for a moment, then lifted his left hand and pressed it to her chest. Those orange lightning bolts flashed up his arms. Tegan's green eyes glowed brighter. The crystal on her and Tenn's chest changed colors rapidly. Tenn scowled and moved to stand between them, his mismatched eyes jumping back and forth.

And then Bentley pulled his hand away and sighed.

"Benny?"

He shook his head. "Not what I wanted to see."

Tegan arched one eyebrow. "We'll revisit that comment later."

Bentley nodded once.

Bettina must've sensed her brother's panic and Tegan's struggle because she walked over and shook both of them. "We're gonna need you two to stay with us here. Where'd Henley go this time?"

Easton raised his hand. "More importantly, how'd he get away again?"

"You zapped Henley." I narrowed my eyes on Tegan. "Why? What were you trying to do? What happened?"

"In October, he-*Henley*- startled me one day and I zapped him with magic on impulse and it knocked the shadow demon out," Tegan said in a rush. Her eyes were locked on nothing in the distance, like she was seeing something else. "It wasn't long. Remember, y'all? But it was long enough for me to get the information I needed—"

"To go Queen of Darkness. Yes, we remember," Cooper said with a smirk.

"Right, to get the information we needed to *win*." Tegan rubbed her hands together and magic flashed. "I was trying to do that again, but it didn't work. *He* resisted so he must have learned."

Tenn cursed. "Which means your old tricks really aren't going to work. You'll need new ones—"

"You need to hit him with more power," I heard myself say.

Tegan smirked. "I like the way you think—"

"No, no." Royce waved his hands around. "No, do not encourage her."

"We're gonna have to, Royce," Deacon said softly.

Emersyn nodded but her eyes were still watching the river. "She—*he*—can vanish too easily. And he's not going to let Henley out—"

"We have to force her back out," Cooper finished.

"I thought we needed her in there still?" Lily asked.

"We do." Bettina turned to Tegan and Bentley. "Because he's still up to something and we need to know what."

"We need to kill him."

"We don't know how."

Bentley sighed. "One thing at a time. We just need an answer so we can send Saffie. Once she's on her way, *then* the rest of us figure out how to kill the shadow demon."

I nodded. Butterflies danced in my stomach as my nerves rushed back to the surface. "Yes. *That.* Let's do that. I need to get to Seelie. Now. I just need—"

"Henley back. For a moment." Tegan nodded and tapped on her crystal necklace. "I can do it, I did it before but—"

"Don't say you're gonna take our magic again," Timothy grumbled.

"*No, definitely not*—" Tegan's mouth slammed shut and her eyes widened.

"*WHAT?*" Royce hissed.

Tegan scowled and held her hands over her ears. "She's groaning and cursing in a demonic language. Things are crashing—I need to *see.*"

CHAPTER NINE

SAFFIE

I WAS NOT USED to Tegan's rapid portal system yet, so when Kessler's living room suddenly appeared around us, it was spinning flipping upside-down. But several hands grabbed my arms and legs—and then I was upright. *Ohhh.* I cursed. It wasn't the room but *me.*

Lily wrapped her arm around my shoulders, holding me in place. "You'll get used to crazy's portals soon. The rest of us don't have wings, so it was a bit less complicated."

I nodded and focused on breathing. My vision was still a bit wonky and my wings were still fluttering.

"Nicely done, guys," Constance said from somewhere nearby. "You handled that quickly."

"I always liked to watch you drown demons." Kenneth chuckled.

"He's somewhere in the mountains," Daniel said in his soft voice. He pointed in front of him while pushing his glasses up. "I don't recognize the forest, but obviously he's not here in Florida."

"And there aren't any humans that we've seen since she—*he* —appeared." Constance pushed her hair back. "But I think you must have done something to him because he's been struggling."

I blinked until my vision cleared and the room stopped spinning. Once I got control of myself, I was able to pull my wings back in. They were popping out on their own much more naturally now, which was both a relief and problematic. Olli punched my leg, so I sank down to the floor and let him crawl into my lap. We were back in Kessler's living room with everyone huddled around the screen to watch Henley. The screen was dark, with only moonlight illuminating the trail Henley was on, so she definitely wasn't near a town.

Tenn sighed and crossed his arms over his chest. "Have you heard from Chutney and the others?"

"Yes. The humans have been evacuated safely." She smiled. "Chutney is singing the animals to sleep as we speak, according to what Savannah just told me."

I grinned. "I used to sing to them."

Everyone turned to me with sad smiles, so I glanced away. I didn't like to remind them of my time of being cursed. It filled them with guilt and pain. I didn't regret what I'd done, so I didn't want them to either...especially now that it was over and I was free.

Henley cursed and her voice echoed through the room. The screen wobbled and then zoomed in on the stone trail. There was more cursing and then the screen filled with a crystal-clear night sky. Stars glittered against the velvety blackness like diamonds.

Cooper gasped. He turned his head to the side, then pointed to the screen. "He's in the Black Hills Mountains."

Royce scowled. "How do you know that?"

"The stars told him."

Cooper glanced to me and winked.

"Babe, do you hear anything?"

"All y'all talking," she snapped back.

Silence.

She snorted. "That was a joke. Relax, y'all."

I sighed. But then the light in the ceiling reflected off the gold jewelry on Tegan's ear, the one Keltie gave her. "Um, Tegan? Can't you use Keltie's jewelry to track her?"

"Yes, but I want to see what he's doing first."

"His last three stops were all heavily populated areas." Bettina gestured to the screen. "There ain't a soul in sight here. So, what's he doing?"

"*There!*" Braison jumped up and ran to the screen, then tapped on a dark blob. "That's a cabin. I can see it through the darkness, can you?"

Everyone shook their heads.

Braison sat back down beside Albert. "Give it a second. You'll see it."

We waited in tense silence as Henley stumbled through a forest. My heart was lodged in my throat and my body twitched. I knew we couldn't be hasty with this demon, I knew we needed a sneaky plan, but my brain kept saying, *I need to go, I need to go, I need to go.*

Henley crashed to her knees and a vicious growl echoed around the room. Black smoke billowed from under her feet—and then she was inside of a house. Or what had to be the cabin Braison saw. The cabin was simple and rather empty, but Henley stumbled and crashed into a table, knocking it and a chair over. She cursed and struggled back to her feet only to lose her balance and slam into a wall. Several picture frames smashed onto the wooden floor in pieces.

Black smoke wrapped around her and then she was in a bathroom, clinging to the shower curtain for balance. It took her a second to get her legs to stop wobbling before she staggered across the tile floored room to a sink. Henley's pale hands gripped the edge of the sink bowl that was stained with red and black residue. I prayed it wasn't blood, but knew it had to be.

A sinister growl rumbled from the speakers.

Henley lifted her head and looked at herself in the mirror. Bright red eyes flashed. "She thinks she tricks us again, but no. We have her right where we want her."

"I didn't like Gollum in the movies, and I sure as hell don't like him in real life," Bettina grumbled.

I gasped. "I understood that reference!"

Bettina snorted. "She really *is* Captain America."

"He's not talking to himself," Bentley said with a growl.

"He's not?" Willow cocked her head to the side.

Tegan shook her head. "No, he's not."

Just then a few smaller demons the size of a cat or dog strolled into the mirror reflection, all of them with big red eyes. They hissed words I didn't know the meaning of—

"It's a demonic language," Timothy grumbled. "I know you're all thinking it."

Tenn nodded. "Do you know what they're saying?"

He grimaced. "Some of it...and they're asking the plan."

My gaze snapped back to the screen.

A dog-like demon growled.

Henley hissed in that same language and then shouted, "Stupid Earthling, human bodies need rest or they'll die. *I said, we wait.*"

Royce groaned and buried his face in his hands.

Henley pushed off the mirror and stumbled all the way across the room until she crashed onto a narrow bed. The screen rolled and flipped, then the wooden ceiling filled the view. One of the cat-sized demons with a weird shaped head jumped up onto the bed next to her and hissed.

"*Tomorrow* we win," Henley snapped. "Wake me if they come."

And then everything fell silent.

"The bastard has guard dogs," Royce said under his breath. "How are we supposed to sneak up on him?"

"*We* don't. *I* do."

Silence.

My heart dropped.

"*Kitten*," Tenn growled. He spun to face her, and the rest of us, and put his hands on his hips. "We are fragile right now. You can't stop speaking there."

"Yep."

"What he said."

"Start talking."

Everyone was nodding and agreeing with Tenn. All I could do was sit there holding my breath, waiting for some sign of hope.

"*Out loud, woman*," Jackson grumbled. "Bloody hell, don't think we don't know you're talking to mini-me over there."

"I'm bigger than her now," Bentley said with a smirk.

"We kinda look more like twins than me and Em do."

"Deflection with humor." Emersyn rolled her eyes. "You're not helping yourselves."

"So..." Kessler cleared his throat. "We need to hit her with more power than Tegan has before."

"Without taking all of our magic again," Cooper growled.

"That wouldn't help anyways. She's already done that." Timothy scratched his jaw. "So that's an old trick."

Bettina cocked her head to the side. "You really took all their magic?"

"*Tegan*."

She jumped at the sound of Tenn's voice. "I'm thinking."

Tenn arched one eyebrow.

Tegan sighed and looked to Bentley.

"Maybe? We'd need—" he frowned and then shrugged one shoulder. "Right. That's true."

Bettina raised her hand. The ground turned pink under her foot.

Bentley nodded. "Combine those—"

"OUT LOUD," Cooper yelled.

Everyone started grumbling and harassing them to speak out loud, but my brain was going to explode. I couldn't take it anymore.

"*Stop!*" I groaned.

Everyone looked to me with shocked faces.

I balled my hands into fists and clenched my teeth. "Everyone in this Coven has a role to play and skills to use. Secrets, scheming, and knowledge are *theirs.* They have thousands of years of knowledge at their disposal and you distracting them by demanding they think out loud is only going to slow them down. And *by the way,* you never, ever, would have won back in October if Tegan had told you the plan."

No one said a word, but I felt their eyes on me. I felt their tense energy.

"There are four people who may not have a lot of time and are waiting on *us* to save them. From what Bentley says, we need one single piece of information so that I can go in there and get them. My *soulmate* has been sentenced to death because he helped The Coven." I pressed my fingers into my temples. "So, let me make one thing clear...I do not care what Tegan's plan *is.* I just need her to *have* one, okay? Because they've all worked so far. I know you all care and want to help... this is how you help. Just let her do what she does. *Please.*"

Tegan crouched down in front of me and took my hands in hers. Those pale green eyes were soft and warm. "I'm going to get you in there, Saffie."

"I know. I trust you."

She squeezed my hands, then stood up straight. "Keeping secrets isn't easy. It's hard for me, too, for a variety of reasons. I don't have a firm plan yet. I need to look at the Book of Shadows. I need access to the Hierophant's locket."

"This knowledge we have is a burden more often than a blessing," Bentley added softly.

Tegan gripped her crystal necklace and the Book of Shadows appeared in her hands. "The shadow demon *has* to sleep because Henley's body requires it. Bentley saw it attacking Paris, so I think it's fairly safe to assume that's where he's going next. My mind is spinning with words and images right now. It wouldn't make sense to any of you. Just let us think. I promise I'll have a plan by the time he moves again."

"If he's sleeping, then we need to be as well." Tenn twirled a silver ring around his finger. "I don't want anyone going home, despite them being so close, just in case we need to move at a moment's notice, so it's a Coven slumber party. Tegan, can you get our friends back from Hidden Kingdom before you go digging in your brain?"

She nodded. "I'll get them. I'm going to stay up to watch Henley but also to plan—yes, I took Katherine's potion again. Yes, I'll be fine. Everyone go to sleep now. I'll wake y'all in a few hours to eat and discuss the plan."

Hunter frowned. "Wake me up to do the cooking. *Please.*"

CHAPTER TEN

SAFFIE

T<small>EGAN CLEARED HER THROAT.</small> "Right, so is everyone finished eating?"

"Nope, don't like this," Royce grumbled and shook his head.

Timothy chuckled and rolled his eyes. "You have a crazy plan none of us are going to like so you waited until we finished eating because it would've ruined our appetites?"

Tegan grinned. "Exactly."

I froze with my fork halfway to my face and my stomach turned.

"*Ma'am,* how was I supposed to eat in the first place?" Savannah gestured around the table wildly. "Everything here is covered in maple syrup. How do y'all even *do* that?"

Easton picked up the bottle of syrup and chugged it, then sat it back down and licked his lips. "We kill demons and we kill breakfast."

Lily sighed and looked away from her boyfriend. "You get used to it."

Savannah arched one eyebrow. "Eating the smell of demon blood, or Easton?"

"Both," everyone else said in unison.

"All right, weirdo." Bettina pushed her plate away from her and rubbed her hands together. "What do you have for us?"

"I have a plan that none of you are going to like," she said with a grin.

Bentley, who was seated beside her, leaned back in his seat and crossed his arms over his chest. "Let 'em have it, T."

"Brace yourself, babe." Tegan ran her hands through Tenn's hair. "Anyhoo, nobody freak out, okay? But I'm going to use black magic."

Tenn cursed violently. He leaned forward and buried his face in his arms that were crossed on the table. The muscles in his arms and shoulders tensed. His long black hair fell over his forearms.

"WHAT?"

"NO."

"Are you *that* crazy?"

Savannah snorted. "*It's about to go down.*"

"Whoomp, there it is," Braison sighed and pinched the bridge of his nose.

Tegan rolled her eyes. "I said nobody freak out."

I raised my hand and caught her eye. "Why black magic?"

"Because *he* uses black magic and in all my experience with him in October, I never used it. So, he won't be expecting it from me." She pointed to her left and right. "Now, I'd like to remind everyone that Lennox and Savannah here are experienced in black magic, so their job will be to watch my ass."

"Got you." Savannah nodded. She actually looked excited.

Lennox shook her head and grinned. "Oh, I can't *wait* to see this."

"Henley would approve," Emersyn said in a rough voice. "So I approve."

I leaned forward. "Do you think that will be enough?"

She shook her head. "No, but that's why Bentley is going to...well, do whatever it is that Bentley does now. That smoke and lava thing. But if y'all are done flipping out, I have more to the plan."

I leaned forward and held my breath.

Chutney pursed her lips. "Are the dragons outside? Or did you send them home?"

"Wait, where's Deacon?" Royce frowned and looked around.

"Yeah, we should wait for Cooper and Willow." Warner scowled. "And Devon."

"They left," Hunter and Emersyn said at the same time.

Jackson ran his hand through his hair. "Bloody hell, this is gonna be like that trap with Joseph in the courtyard, isn't it?"

Tenn's head snapped up. His mismatched eyes darted around the room. "Cooper isn't here?"

Tegan cleared her throat pointedly. "May I have the attention of the class, please? I brought Mom, Cooper, Willow, Deacon, and the dragons to Paris right before I woke y'all because Henley wasn't there yet and it was imperative I had them in location, ready to strike, and fully cloaked in place."

Tenn tied his hair up in a messy bun just like Tegan's. "What do *we* do?"

"I'm going to cloak everyone. When I say to, you'll attack the demons." Tegan stood and rubbed her hands on a napkin. "That's all I want y'all to worry about. Wait and then kill demons. Bentley, Saffie, and I will handle Henley."

I gasped and sat up straight. "Saffie?"

Tegan smirked. "*When I say to*, raise the dead like you've never done before and command them to grab ahold of Henley. That's all you have to do, okay?"

My pulse quickened and anxiety rolled through my body. I nodded rapidly.

"Good. Let's ride." Tegan snapped her fingers and a portal opened. "When you come out the other side, you'll be cloaked.

Do *not* attack demons until I drop the cloaking, or you'll kill each other."

Despite the lack of information and details, the rest of the group rushed through the portal until only Tenn, Constance, Daniel, and Kenneth, and I were left. Constance was propped up on the couch with Albert and Olli sleeping beside her. Kenneth and Daniel moved to sit in front of the screen.

Tenn and Tegan stood on opposites sides of the portal just staring at each other like they were having a silent conversation. So I took a deep breath and hurried through the portal...then slid to a stop.

Fresh white snow covered the ground. The morning sunlight shining down made it almost too bright to look at it. I squinted and wrapped my arms around myself. The air was cold —a fraction of the Florida temperature I was dressed for. But with a flick of my hand, I was back in my oversized sweater and jeans I wore back in Salem.

I looked around but saw no one else. I stood in front of a park bench all by myself—*no, wait.* I felt them. I felt their magic beside me like little balls of heat, like a warm current in the ocean sweeping over me. It amazed me what Tegan could do. We were invisible in the broad daylight. Sure, there was some kind of park on our left because there were a bunch of trees and bushes all covered in snow, but I didn't see the Eiffel Tower that direction.

I'd never seen it in real life, but I'd seen it in movies and from my understanding, it was massive. I turned to my right slowly, carefully looking at everything so I wasn't caught off guard. There was a big open field covered in snow with a row of trees that had died for the winter. Despite the chilly temperature, there were dozens of humans hanging around the field taking pictures. I followed the direction of their cameras and my jaw dropped.

The Eiffel Tower was *huge.* I didn't think I'd ever seen

something made by humans that tall. It was a dark bronze color and made of metal.

The air pulsed with raw, hot energy behind me. I gripped my crystal bracelet, ready to summon my sword, when a wave of fresh rain scent hit me. *Tennessee.*

She's coming, Tegan said suddenly into our minds. *Everyone stay here. When you can see each other, that's when you move. Tenn, stay back and stay low. Your aura is not subtle.*

I could have sworn I heard him growl.

Showtime, Tegan purred. It was a lethal sound that sent chills down my spine. *Do not attack until you can SEE. Trust me.*

White lightning flashed between the massive metal legs of the tower.

Steady... Tegan growled.

More lightning shot out from beneath the tower and traveled up the metal structure. Humans screamed and scurried away from it, all of them looking to the cloudless blue sky in confusion. And then I heard shrieks of terror.

The ground rumbled.

My magic rushed to my hands. My pulse quickened.

I wasn't sure what summoning the dead was going to do for us, but I trusted Tegan. *Raise the dead like you've never done before,* Tegan's words echoed in my mind. I just prayed I didn't mess this up—that I wasn't the one who caused us to fail.

Hold on, Riah. I'm almost there.

Demons surged from under the tower, rushing out into the field in a stampede of horror.

I felt my Coven-mate's panic. It was killing them to wait.

Benny, NOW! Tegan shouted into our minds.

I gasped and watched in front of me, but I couldn't see them. They were still invisible and their auras were lost to the sudden madness and mayhem around us. The demons weren't attacking the humans but running alongside with them—like they'd been instructed to get *out*. And that made my blood boil.

A cloud of black smoke billowed from the middle of the Eiffel Tower, then slithered down to the ground. Henley emerged from within it with glowing red eyes. She threw her head back and let out a maniacal laugh—black and orange mist slammed into her chest in perfect unison.

I held my hands out to my sides and wiggled my fingers. *Spirits, are you here with me?*

The ground turned bitter cold under my feet. Fingers like ice gripped my legs. I crouched down and more hands grabbed my arms and shoulders.

Black magic coiled around Henley's body. Orange lightning and smoke covered her face.

Ok, spirits. We need your help. I flexed my fingers out and let a little gold glitter fall to the snow.

I felt the spirits' energy brighten and grow bold. They wanted to help, and they were ready.

SAFFIE!

I pushed with everything I had in me and lunged to my feet while throwing my hands in the air. *RISE!* The ground rattled. Snow fell from tree branches. Humans and demons stumbled and dropped. Bright blue, green, and yellow mist broke through the snow and ice on the field and shot up into the sky.

Gold glitter exploded like fireworks in every direction.

Beneath my feet, green grass and wildflowers popped up in rows, shooting out in lines.

SPIRITS, RISE. RISE. RISE.

Spirits formed from within the colors, but there were so many I couldn't see one from another.

GRAB HENLEY. HOLD HER. NOW.

The spirits swarmed Henley in an instant, circling her from every direction. Hands of blue, yellow, and green gripped her body.

Rainbow magic rippled through the air and then my Coven-mates were standing beside me. In my peripheral vision, explosions of fire and smoke burst above the buildings. Blue mist flashed and the air turned a soft yellow. The humans stopped moving and closed their eyes *and then they lay down like they were sleeping*. Red lightning streaked through the field. Each time it hit a demon, it jumped *up*.

Tenn growled and shot into the sky, flying with his gold wings and slicing Michael's six-foot long, glowing sword through demons. Emersyn sent rivers of fire across the field to the demons. The rest of my Coven-mates charged into battle, easily leaping over the sleeping humans. Bettina, Royce, Savannah, and Lennox raced toward Henley.

I wanted to go too, but I was afraid to break my hold.

White light flashed—and then I was standing between Tegan and Bentley, who were firing steady streams of magic straight ahead.

Henley was on her knees in front of me. She trembled and thrashed, trying to break free, but the black mist and smoke still covered her body.

"Hold her," I shouted and raised my hands in front of me. *"Reach through and hold her."*

The spirits reached up and stuck their ghostly transparent hands through the smoke— Henley screamed. Royce sank to his knees, covering his mouth with his hands while mumbling words to the Goddess.

The smoke crackled and popped with little sparks.

And then it was gone.

Henley lifted her head, and her eyes were a brilliant sapphire blue.

Royce whimpered and dove for her—

"Don't touch me!" Henley shouted. Her eyes went to me. "Don't let go, Saffie."

I nodded and kept my hands raised.

"Tegan, what? Why are you risking this—"

"We need you. We have to get to the Land of the Lore."

Henley frowned. "I don't know what that is."

"Henley, listen when—"

Henley gasped. Her eyes widened. "*BENTLEY? OH NO.*"

His eyes were sad but still sharp. "Yeah, I'm big now. Listen, in Seelie, in the Wild Night, I discovered the Land of the Lore. It's a foggy magical essence that flows like a river through the forests and hides within it a gateway to both Seelie and Unseelie. And its magic is made to repel The Coven so we'd never find it. I'm told the only way to find it intentionally has something to do with the moon."

Her gaze snapped to Tegan. "That does not bode well for you, Tegan. Don't you *dare* go anywhere near that gateway, and try not to use your magic for any reason. You might not make it back out if you do. You understand?"

Tegan's face was pale, but she nodded. "Understood. Agreed. But we need you, Henley. We have to send Saffie in to save—"

"Riah, Paulina, Amelia, and Landy. I know." She shuddered. "*He* had nothing to do with it, but he's enjoying your pain. I have all kinds of spells for summoning the moon, obviously, but if it repels Coven magic, then none of *mine* will work. Bettina are you here?"

"I'm here," she said in a rush and jumped forward.

"Your angel magic will be required here. Tap into your mother's talents and make a spell. Don't fight it, okay? Whatever words come to you—remember, they've all worked so far." She hissed and bared her teeth. "*T, hit me again.*"

Without hesitation, Tegan zapped her with black mist.

Royce whimpered.

"*Hold her steady,*" I told my spirit friends.

Henley exhaled. Her eyes were still blue. "Use these words in your spell—"

"Hold." Bettina held her arm out and pressed her finger to her skin and whispered words in the angelic tongue. "Go."

Henley rattled out a list of words in our ancient language too fast for me to comprehend but each one was being etched into Bettina's skin like she had a pen in her hand. Then she coughed. "Listen, if what Bentley says is true, you'll need a civilian to do this spell. Bettina can make it, but a civilian must perform it, okay?"

"Okay," we all said in unison.

Henley snarled and I felt the fight inside of her as *it* tried to come back. "Hematite. Obsidian. Moonstone. Diamond. Selenite. Labradorite. Those going must bathe in the moonlight and moon water with these stones, then wear them in. But those going *into* Seelie MUST take them off before going in. Okay? Got all that?"

"I've got it. Promise." Tegan smiled. "Anything else?"

"Bettina—*triple mother, single stone, lend your power to be shown.*" She clenched her teeth and snarled. "Start with that."

Bettina nodded.

"And Tegan?" Her sapphire blue eyes sharpened, but the words that came out of her mouth were not a language I knew. It was the ancient dialect of our language, the one used by the originals. I hadn't known Henley knew it.

Bentley gripped the Hierophant's locket and light flashed between his fingers.

"Read the deck, T. Don't decide. Don't fight. Read it." She arched both eyebrows. "Get out fast, you hear?"

"Henley, wait. We got you out," Royce cried. "You're here. It's time to come out. This is over. It's time to be done with this game."

Henley shook her head, but her eyes turned sad. "No, I have to stay. This job is not done yet. He hasn't even begun his plans yet, you need me in here still. You need to be ready. He thinks he's leading you astray, that you'll think this is it, but it's *not*. The worst is coming."

"We can find another way, Henley!"

"Royce, *no*," she begged. "Listen, this isn't the same game as last time. We HAVE to kill him this time, there's no other option—"

"I haven't figured out how to kill it yet," Tegan grumbled.

"I don't know either. He...he *feels* invincible. He acts like it too. He knows something we don't. You need to find out what that is."

My arms began to tremble from holding the spirits in place. "Where do we even start?"

"Riah." Henley's gaze snapped to me. "He's terrified of Riah. I don't know why but he is. Get Riah back, and I bet he has the answer."

Tears stung my eyes. My magic was fading. "Henley, he's coming..."

Henley looked to Tegan. "I trust you."

Then her eyes turned red and she vanished.

CHAPTER ELEVEN

SAFFIE

I wasn't sure of the time difference between Paris and Florida, but as Tegan sent us through a portal back to Kessler's house in Tampa, I noticed the sky was still pitch black. It'd been daylight in Paris, which meant this had been the longest day and I'd used far too much of my magic while not getting enough rest. Savannah was half carrying me, so when we stepped out into the living room Constance shrieked and jumped up in a panic.

"She's fine, she's fine," Savannah assured her in a rush as we waddled toward the couch. "Just exerted herself."

Constance sighed and patted the spot on the couch she'd just been lying on. "Here, lay her down. *Katherine!*"

"I don't like being separated, Tegan," Bettina shouted through the open portal. "Hurry up!"

"Constance? Are you okay?" Katherine yelled as she barreled around the corner and then slid to a stop. Her eyes landed on me. "Lay her down. I'll be right back."

She was out of sight before my head hit the pillow. But *not* before Olli pounced on my chest and licked my face. His white-tipped tail thumped against the leather from wagging so hard. Behind me, Albert acted like a warm full-body pillow.

"Hi, baby." I chuckled and ruffled Olli's long ears. "Hi, Albert."

Daniel cursed, which seemed unusual for him. "He hasn't stopped yet."

"Is it just you all back?" Kenneth frowned and swept the room. "Bentley, Bettina, and Lennox...Savannah and Saffie. Where's everyone else?"

"Excuse me one second," Bentley mumbled as he dashed out of the room.

Bettina sighed. "Killing demons. Tegan went to get them."

Katherine flew back into the room and over to where I was. She held an open vial out to me. "Drink."

I took it and drank. The potion was refreshingly cool and sweet. I sighed and licked my lips. "That was tasty."

"Let's see how that does. You might need another."

"Bentley might need one. He used a lot too." Bettina pointed in the direction he'd gone. "Not that he'd admit it."

Katherine rolled her eyes, then marched that way.

Bettina and Savannah both sighed and sat on the couch beside Olli.

Constance scowled. "That does not sound good."

Lennox snorted. "Typical day for us, eh? Speaking of, kinda, not really—anyway—do we still have that pool out back?"

"*That* does not sound good." Constance walked to the window, then turned back and nodded. "Yes, why?"

"Some of us are bathing in moonlight and moon water tonight, and I suspect we'll be needing that pool." Lennox eyed Constance. "How are you feeling?"

Constance smiled. "I'm perfectly capable of crystal work. What do we need? Please, give me something to do."

"We need hematite, obsidian, moonstone, diamonds, selenite, and labradorite." Lennox counted on her fingers. "Yeah, that was it. They also need to be bathed with the people. Once they get out, they'll have to wear said crystals."

Constance rubbed her hands together. "Perfect, I'll get the pool ready with crystals. Those will be good for all of us to have on hand. Let Tegan know I'm out there when she gets back? I'm sure she'll want to be ready to get moving."

Get moving.

To the Land of the Lore.

And into Seelie.

Because we got the answer from Henley.

A wild rush of emotions raged inside of me. I was relieved to have finally gotten the answer we needed, but something about this Land of the Lore unsettled me deep down. And if I was being honest with myself, I was terrified to enter Seelie. But not more terrified than I was to lose Riah. I'd been watching my soulmate glyph nonstop. The gold lines covering my fingers and entire right arm were hard to ignore. Every time I looked, I held my breath, afraid the crystal would be red this time.

I lifted my hand and found it still emerald green.

Riah wasn't okay but he was alive. That was all I could allow myself to think of.

I closed my eyes and pictured his face and the way he smiled.

"Is she okay?"

"Oh, *shit*, Saf?"

"Saffie?"

I gasped and jumped. My eyes flew open only to find the rest of The Coven huddled around me. "Hi?"

"Don't scare us like that." Cooper cursed and shook his head. He picked Olli up and cradled him in his lap, then sat on the couch between me and Savannah. His pale green eyes watched me. "Katherine get to you already?"

I nodded. "Everyone else okay?"

"We all here?" Tenn growled, his voice echoing around the room. "Sit so I can see all of you, please."

Everyone quickly found a seat, either on furniture or on the floor. A few seconds later, only Tegan and Tenn were standing.

Tennessee scanned each face like he was counting. Then he frowned. "Constance and Bentley?"

"Bentley is off being Bentley, but Katherine followed him with potions." Bettina pointed toward a side hallway.

"And I told Constance what Henley said we needed," Lennox said with a serious expression. "She was getting started and said to tell you she's outside."

Tegan looked to the window and narrowed her eyes. "Mom, you can check on Bentley now."

Devon bounced out of the room.

I pushed myself up into a seated position. "We can go now, right? I mean, once we do the things Henley said to do?"

"Henley?" Deacon looked back and forth between me and Tegan. "It worked? You spoke to Henley? Real Henley? What happened?"

Royce groaned and buried his face in his hands. "She was back and then demanded to go back in."

Tegan gave the rest of the group the summary of what happened and what Henley said...and the room fell into a tense silence. I knew we were all thinking the same things.

Bentley sauntered back into the room. "Is Constance getting the pool and stones ready?"

"Yes." Tegan nodded and then turned to face the screen. "He did this last time, just moved around. It means he's planning but not acting just yet."

I narrowed my eyes on the screen to see what she saw—and frowned. All I saw was a blur of gray and black, like perhaps he was in shadow form.

"Henley's okay," Tegan whispered. Then she turned back to face us and sat down on the floor with her legs crisscrossed. "We saw her. She's very much with it and she knew about Riah,

Paulina, Amelia, and Landy. Which means she's *listening*. We need to focus on this rescue mission right now."

Tenn cursed and crossed his arms over his chest, which I was starting to suspect was a comfortable position for him. "We need to decide who is going into the Land of the Lore and who is going into Seelie."

"Aren't those the same people?"

"Aren't those *everyone*?"

"I'm staying to watch my sister."

"It's not like everyone can go into Seelie."

"Exactly. Tegan can't. Tenn and Bettina shouldn't."

"Is it only The Coven that's up for selection?"

The conversation exploded around us. Everyone was arguing and talking over each other. Everyone had a different opinion. Everyone was terrified—that much was obvious.

Deacon whistled so loud we all hissed and covered our ears.

"Thanks, D." Tenn's voice was a deep, low growl. "We cannot and will not abandon Henley. Nor can we let this shadow demon have unchecked freedom to destroy. There are enough of us to split up and still have decent sized groups, especially with a few extra hands. We also are not sending a ton of people into Seelie. We will not risk losing more of us. End of discussion."

"Okay, Son," Kessler said softly. He gestured around the room. "Who do you want where? You know we'll follow your lead."

Tegan gripped her necklace and light flashed. The crystal changed into a deck of black cards that had metallic gold etchings on the back. "Why don't we let the cards decide who is doing what?"

Tenn sighed. "Yes. Thank you. That's perfect."

She winked up at him, then looked to everyone else. "Take a deep breath. The Goddess has not led us astray yet. Let's let her tell us. I'm going to first pull from the deck to see who is going into Seelie."

My stomach tightened and turned. I knew my name was going to be on there—it had to be. But what if it wasn't? What if I was going by myself? What if I had to take others? All of these options sounded equally possible.

Tegan sat the deck face down on the hardwood floor in front of her. She held her hand over the top of the deck and closed her eyes. Rainbow magic swirled around the deck and snaked between her fingers. She took a deep breath...and flipped the first card.

My face stared up at me and my heart stopped.

DEATH. SARAPHINA PROCTOR.

I knew it was coming. I wanted it to come. It *had* to be me. Yet still.

No one batted an eyelash or flinched. Everyone knew I was going.

"Who else is going to Seelie?" Tegan flipped the next card and a girl with strawberry blonde hair and dark brown eyes looked innocently up from the card. *"Willow."*

"Why's it always me?"

Bettina grinned and winked at her. "Because you're a badass, little Neville Longbottom, slayer of horcruxes."

Willow's face flushed, but her eyes were wide and full of fear.

"Okay, next is..." Tegan flipped and chuckled. "I knew it. Lily."

Lily? I leaned forward and frowned. "You knew that one? Why?"

"I second that request," Lily grumbled in a flat tone.

"The fae hate the sun." Tenn shrugged. "So I'm not surprised you were chosen."

Easton looked like he was going to be sick. "Who else is going?"

Tegan eyed the deck, then flipped another card. This one had a girl with black and turquoise hair. She held a mean looking silver sword. On the bottom it said, *Queen of Swords.*

"*Ma'am, tell me I'm not seeing what I'm seeing right now?*" Savannah crawled over on her hands and knees and looked at the card up close. "That's me. On a card. Well, I'll be damned."

Tegan chuckled and flipped another card, but this one was all black. That was it. Only the four of us girls were going into Seelie. I was both relieved that only few were going and terrified that only a few were going. I would've rather gone by myself, but I was so thankful I wasn't.

"Four people."

"And one is a civilian."

Bettina raised her hand. "Oh, Henley said y'all can't wear the crystals into Seelie."

Tenn walked over to stand directly behind Tegan. "Babe, can you read now and tell us who is escorting those four through the Land of the Lore?"

She picked the deck up and held it between two hands, then sat it back on the floor just like it'd been. She tapped her finger on the top card. "Okay. Now, who is going to escort them through the Land of the Lore?"

We all leaned forward with our hearts in our throats.

Tegan slipped the first card, but a bright orange flame burst from it. It swirled around in a circle, then took the shape of a dragon. The dragon roared and flew as a flame but then turned into a gray color and sat down.

Koth chuckled. "Congrats, Silas."

Silas just nodded once.

I kept forgetting our dragon friends were there. They were so damn good at blending into the background, which said a lot considering they were *dragons.* And Koth was six-foot-eight. But when surrounded by The Coven and all their intense magic, the dragon King and his right-hand man just blended. Like shadows in the night.

Tegan smirked and flipped the next card—

"It's gonna be me," Chutney whined at the exact moment her face appeared from the card. "SEE."

"All right, let's see who else..." Tegan flipped three cards real fast.

Timothy.

Hunter.

Devon.

The two soulmates nodded to each other, whereas Tenn and Bettina both stared at their uncle with fear.

Tegan cleared her throat and flipped the next three.

Easton.

"Oh, thank the Goddess," Easton said with a sigh. "I'll at least escort you."

Next card...*Bentley.*

Everyone just nodded. We all knew Bentley was going.

The next two cards flipped together. When Tegan pulled them apart, I saw Emersyn and Deacon's face smiling up at us. I glanced over at them, but they sat in stone cold silence.

"Next is..." Tegan flipped and smiled. "The *Queen of Wands*. Miss Lennox Ward."

Lennox gasped. "Really? I'm on a card? That *is* cool," she whispered.

Cooper frowned. "That's got to be all, right?"

Tegan frowned and flipped—and her eyes widened. Tennessee's face glared from the card under the glittery *EMPEROR* title. There were grumbles and curses around the room, but everyone's eyes were latched on that next card.

"*Pull again, babe.*"

Tegan tapped on the top card, then slowly flipped it over— her face fell. It was *her.*

Bettina cursed.

Tegan flipped another and it was solid black. That was everyone.

"Why are you upset by that?" Hunter frowned. "I thought you'd be relieved you're going with your soulmate."

Tegan took a deep breath. "I have concerns about me going in there, but it doesn't matter. The cards have chosen. Everyone who wasn't named, you'll be staying here and watching Henley."

Everyone else. That meant Royce, Kessler, Constance, Warner, Bettina, Jackson, Braison, Cooper, Kenneth, and Daniel. It seemed too few. I feared for the fate of my escorts.

"Koth, I think you and Maddox should go back and check on Issale. We'll call you the moment we get back. That okay?"

"Thanks, Tennessee. I think that's a good idea." Koth glanced outside. "Mind if I speak with Silas before I go?"

Tenn nodded. "Of course. Now—wait. We need a spell, don't we? The one for the Moon? Hope?"

Bettina looked up from where the words were written on her arm. Her mismatched eyes flashed. "Just give me a few minutes alone, and I'll have this for you."

"Go head, B." Tegan turned her deck of tarot cards back into a crystal necklace. "Lennox, I'll be having her give the spell to you to perform since you're a civilian and chosen for this quest."

Lennox pushed her shoulders back. "I'm ready."

Bettina jumped up and hurried down the hallway. Koth and Maddox exchanged private words with Silas out back, then morphed into dragons and flew off.

Constance walked inside and stopped. "The moon water and crystals are ready. Time to bathe."

Tegan jumped to her feet. "You heard her, y'all. Everyone going on this quest, go get in the pool."

CHAPTER TWELVE

SAVANNAH

I wasn't typically a fan of the heat, so Florida was never on my list of places to live, but I had to admit the salty ocean breeze was refreshingly cool. Especially while floating in a pool in the middle of the night. Anything in the middle of the night was my jam though.

Tenn had said those of us going into the Land of the Lore were to get in the pool...but everyone had. Even Albert and Olli, although they were both out by now and lounging beside us. Katherine had suggested Constance get in because it couldn't hurt and might help ease stress for the baby—and then Royce made a joke about being a baby and needing it. Next thing I knew, we were all in. No one spoke or made jokes. There was no giggling and teasing. This was a serious, tense moment. The Land of the Lore was a dangerous place that The Coven had never been.

I was more worried about Seelie.

Saffie clung to the edge of the pool where Olli had lain. Their faces were pressed together as she ran her fingers over his fur. A few people had gotten out already but everyone else was just floating silently. Tegan and Tennessee were sitting at the bottom of the pool. They seemed to be having a quiet conversation down there and nothing about their expressions made me want to hear it.

I took a deep breath and exhaled, but it came out all shaky. My fingers trembled ever so slightly, and my stomach was in knots. Any minute now Tenn would demand our departure, which I understood since Riah could be killed at any moment. I was glad to be on the rescue team. The dude had literally brought me back to life. I owed this to him. To Saffie. But it didn't make me any less nervous.

Because there was a real chance I wouldn't come back from this trip.

We were the fellowship of the ring marching right into Mordor and the fires of Mount Doom. I'd seen enough movies and read enough books. Someone always fell. Usually more than one someones. I hoped it wasn't gonna be me. Hell, I'd already died and returned like Gandalf, but something in the pit of my stomach warned me not to be too confident.

My life had taken an unexpected turn since Saffie showed up in Salem.

Oh feck. My parents. I hadn't spoken to them since I left Salem...however long ago that was. I wasn't even sure Tegan had called them yet to explain why she'd insisted I stay with them. I needed to call them before I left. Just in case. *Just in case I die.*

I cleared my throat and turned to Timothy. "May I get out? I need to call my parents before I go. If that's okay?"

Timothy glanced under the water to his nephew and Tegan then looked to me and smiled. "I'm not Leader anymore but I see no reason why you can't do both of those things."

"Better now before he decides he wants to leave," Kessler said with a sigh. "Go ahead, Savannah. You can use any of the bedrooms for privacy."

I smiled and started toward the stairs. "Thanks."

"Savannah, wait." Constance gently touched my arm. "Do

not tell them where you're going. It's imperative no one outside The Coven—and our immediate allies—know about this quest."

My stomach dropped. I blinked at her and nodded. "I understand...but...what do I tell them? Nothing? Just act like it's a normal day? *Hey, how's work?*"

Hunter smirked. "It's not about where you're going, Savannah. It's about expressing your feelings to them before you go."

"Your parents have the right to know you're going on a quest with The Coven and that the Goddess chose you for it." Devon pursed her lips and shrugged. "You can tell them that. Tell them you cannot tell them the destination, but it will be dangerous and you wanted to speak with them before going. It's the best you can do."

I stared at them for a long moment before nodding and walking up the steps. Tegan, or maybe it was Tenn, had set up one of those magic rings to dry us off as soon as we got out, so the second I stepped onto the cement I was completely dry. The adults were all watching me. I felt their eyes on my back, but I couldn't handle the emotion in their faces. Or the knowledge.

Instead, I marched into the house, passed the couch where Kenneth and Daniel were propped up watching Henley, and went straight to the kitchen counter where my stuff was. *My stuff.* I snorted. I hadn't brought *my stuff* with me. All I had was my cellphone and a wallet. Sure, there was probably random makeup at the bottom of this satchel, but it was just that—random. We'd left Eden just for a surprise birthday party here in Tampa and we hadn't gone back thanks to the shadow demon. I didn't even have my journal with my spells. I hadn't wanted to forget it here. But I kept telling myself it was better this way. I couldn't lose it in Seelie if I didn't have it.

I grabbed my satchel and slipped down the hallway into the first bedroom I found. But when I went to dial my parents, I couldn't make myself do it. I was a little too raw. So I dialed a different number instead.

It rang a few times and then a voicemail clicked on. *"Hey, it's Gigi. Leave me a message."*

"Hey, G, it's me. Savannah. Listen, I um...well, I hope you're doing okay. I'm going with The Coven on a little mission and uh..." I cleared my throat. "I just wanted to say I forgive you for what happened. I know you didn't intend for that. I'm also sorry about that fight we got into. I think we both knew we were growing apart and trying to ignore that. When I get back, I'll come home to Salem and maybe we can get some pizza and tots or something? Anyway, I've got to go but I wanted to just say...I hope you're good now. Okay. Bye."

I hung up and groaned. *Don't overanalyze that. It's done. You said it. Make the next call.*

It was ringing before I even realized I'd hit the button.

"Savannah?" My father answered in a rush. "Savannah, are you there?"

My pulse quickened and my throat went dry. "Yeah. Yes, I'm here. Sorry—"

"Savannah?" My mom's voice suddenly shrieked into my ear.

"You're on speaker, honey," Dad's voice was tight. "It's really early. Why are you calling at this hour?"

Mom hissed. "She's calling! That's all that matters."

"It's nearly five in the morning. If she was just wanting to say hello, she would've waited at least until dawn."

"Well, I guess that's as good a segue as any." I sighed. "Actually, has Tegan or Tennessee called y'all yet?"

"Yes," they both said at the same time.

"Tegan called a few days ago and told us that you were going to be staying with The Coven for a little while." Her voice was rough, like she hadn't slept. "She said you'd gotten injured and they were keeping an eye on you."

Gotten injured my ass. I fucking died. I shook my head. No point in telling them now. "Um, yea. I'm fine now. It's been a couple crazy days of things...well, going horribly wrong to be honest."

"What's going on, Savannah? What aren't you telling us?"

I cringed and tugged on my hair. "I have to go on a quest with The Coven. A perilous, potentially one-way quest that the Goddess literally said, *Savannah Grace, you're going.*"

Silence.

"Pretty much, yup. So, uh, that's...that's basically all I'm at liberty to tell you. We're all caught up to speed now."

Silence.

Dad cleared his throat. "Will your phone work where you're going?"

"Definitely not."

He cursed.

"Are you going alone?" Mom whispered.

"No, no. Um, half The Coven is going on the first part...and then a few of us finish it."

Silence.

My face was on fire and sweat dripped down my spine. All the feelings were overheating me and stressing me out, but I had to say them. And avoiding them any longer was just going to make it worse. So I took a deep breath and then let it out. "*I just wanted to say I love you and I'll call you as soon as I get home.*"

I exhaled.

There. I said it. It's done. Can't take it back.

They both said it back. I couldn't handle all the feels. It made me antsy and sweaty. I heard their words, but my brain had already half shut off.

"All right, honey, just be as careful as possible," Mom said softly.

"And let us know as soon as you're back safe. Even if it's a text."

I nodded. "Take care of Luna and Freya until I get back, okay?"

"They're in good care. We promise."

"Thanks. Okay, I've got to go now. Bye."

I pulled my phone away from my ear but still heard their voices saying goodbye before I hit the 'end call' button. My phone instantly rang in my hands. I frowned and looked down but didn't recognize the number, and it wasn't stored in my phone.

"Hello?"

"Hi, Savannah," a soft, warm female voice hummed through the phone. "It's Cassandra."

"Oh." I blinked in surprise. "Hello. Is something wrong? Did you try contacting them and they didn't answer?"

She chuckled. "No, I'm calling for you."

"Oh. Okay, what's up?"

"Well, I know you're about to go into Seelie...so I added some things into your journal that you might find useful."

"My journal?" I scowled. "You did? When? Wait, I don't even have it with me—"

"Yes, you do. Check your satchel."

A weird chill slid down my spine as I reached into my satchel. When my fingers found the soft leather of my journal, I gasped. Goosebumps spread across my body and the hairs on my arms stood tall. It was there. In my bag.

"Ma'am, what did you DO?"

Cassandra laughed.

"No. Hold up. I just picked this up and it wasn't in here." I let out a weird little groan and shook my head. *"Ma'am. What are you?"*

"That is a complicated question with a long answer that we'll get to one day." She chuckled more. "For now, well, it's *magic.*"

I pulled out my journal just to confirm that it was mine...it was. I shook my head. "This some sneaky Tegan-style shit, ma'am."

"You'll get used to it. Anyways, I'm sure y'all will be going soon and I don't want to keep you. But if you like what I added, I'll teach you more when you get back. Okay?"

"Yes, ma'am. Sign me up for that. Whatever it is. I'm down."

"All right. Now, just remember things in Seelie might get weird, but trust your gut over your mind and your eyes. Okay?"

"MA'AM, THAT IS NOT REASSURING? WHAT DOES THAT EVEN MEAN? MY EYES? WHAT'S HAPPENING TO MY EYES?" I shook my head. "I beg your goddam pardon, what did you just say?"

Her laughter was musical in my ears, like something straight out of a Disney princess. "Good luck, Savannah."

And then she was gone.

Well shit.

That had me all kinds of jacked up. I couldn't sit in the quiet room alone any longer, so I spun around to leave—and gasped. My feet glued to the ground. Cooper was stepping out of a closet and pulling a gray t-shirt on over his head. My eyes widened and my jaw dropped. My heart did an Olympic floor routine to rival Simone Biles.

Because in front of me was all kinds of bare skin.

It was like he was trying to put that damn shirt on as slow as possible.

I tried not to let my gaze linger in one spot but there was just muscle after muscle—

The gray shirt slid over his stomach, and it was like throwing snow on a fire. My insides were squirming.

I looked up and met his pale green eyes. "Cooper. What are you doing here?"

He smirked. "This is my room."

I blushed. He shrugged. I nodded. He grinned. I screamed inside my mind. His eyes were locked on me, and it was wreaking havoc. Tension reached up from the depths of Tartarus and dragged me down with sharp talons and sandpaper grip. *Never date a Bishop, Savannah. Don't go there, brain.*

"I should go."

"Wait." He held his finger up, then stepped back into his closet and picked something up off a shelf. Then he turned around with long, rolled up black silk in his hands. "I have something for you."

"For me? You have a present for me?" *Oh no, why are you doing this to me?*

"I do believe your birthday is coming soon." He smirked as he walked over to me, stopping with our feet inches apart. "But really, when the cards said you were going into Seelie, I wanted you to have this."

My hands were definitely *not* shaking as I shoved my journal back into my satchel and then reached up to unfold the black material. When I pulled the silk back, my jaw dropped. A pretty, shiny silver dagger the length of my forearm glistened in the dim lighting of his room. It was simple yet elegant. The hilt had gorgeous etchings and an antiqued finished. The blade looked untouched.

"Cooper...this..." I blinked and shook my head. "For *me?*"

"Yes, for *you,*" he whispered, and his breath brushed over my forehead. "This was mine when I was a kid. I don't use it anymore, so I want you to have it—to take with you into Seelie."

My heart fluttered. I peeked up at him and our eyes met. "This dagger looks special. It looks *pretty.* Does this have special meaning to you?"

He chuckled and it did *not* help the fire raging inside of me. "I picked this one because I wanted a weapon as visibly impressive as Tenn's. He had that dagger with the crystal in it *and* his black sword. Both very, very fancy and as a kid I wanted to...not compete but match? Anyway, it's not my style and too small for me. I want you to have it."

He was filling me with all kinds of warm and fuzzies that

my heart could not handle. "That's really sweet, Cooper. Are you sure?"

"Absolutely," he said without hesitation. "Most civilians don't carry weapons and definitely not ones charged with Coven magic. If you're going to ride with us, then you should be properly equipped. And it would make me happy to know this special dagger was yours. Go ahead. Take it."

I bit my lip to stop myself from grinning. I carefully picked it up with both hands and held it in front of my face. As I tilted it, a silvery white magic sparkled along the blade. And then his words clicked. "Charged with Coven magic?"

"Yeah. Cassandra helped me back in the day. It glows in the dark if you press your thumb to the blade." He took my hand in his and pushed my thumb onto the blade, just beneath the hilt, and the blade began to glow like the North Star. "Bentley says it's dark there. I thought this could guide you if you were afraid, or in danger."

My eyes burned but I was *not* about to cry. Too many people were testing my emotions. Yet somehow Cooper was the hardest to handle. I focused on the blade. It reminded me of stars twinkling against the night sky. "*I have loved the stars too fondly to be fearful of the night.*"

"What's that?"

I shook myself. "Sorry, I was...never mind."

"But what was it?"

I kept my eyes on the blade. "Oh, just my favorite poem. By Sarah Williams. Or part of it. Part of my favorite part of it—just ignore me."

"I haven't been able to thus far." His voice was low and rough. "Tell me your whole favorite part of your favorite poem?"

My gaze snapped up to his. The words spilled from my lips. "*Though my soul may set in darkness, it will rise in perfect light. I have loved the stars too fondly to be fearful of the night.*"

He smiled and his eyes sparkled. "That's lovely. And perfect for you."

"Thank you." I cleared my throat and forced myself to look away. "Thank you, Cooper. This means a lot to me."

He nodded and ran his hand through his hair. "You're welcome. I'm sure Tegan could quickly muster up some convenient holster or something. Mine wouldn't fit you—"

"I'll ask her. Thanks." I smiled and tucked the dagger into my satchel. "I'll treat it with care."

He nodded.

I stared.

There was so much to say yet absolutely no point in saying it. It didn't matter how I felt, or how he felt. Not in the long run. *Never date a Bishop,* Saffie had said. It was the saying. Because they always got soulmates. I'd heard Bentley confirm that myself. And I'd heard Bettina and Jackson's pain over what they went through. I didn't want that for me or Cooper. I had to nip this in the bud now before we fell down the rabbit hole any farther.

Yet even as I thought this, my body made other decisions. I watched myself reach out, fist his shirt, and drag his mouth down to mine. Our lips crashed together, and I knew in the deepest pit of my soul this was going to leave a mark. His arms snaked around my waist, crushing my body to his. I slid my arms up and wrapped them around his neck. His warm hands gripped my jaw and tilted my head back to deepen our kiss, but I was already lost.

T-minus two minutes till departure, folks, Tegan shouted into our minds.

We didn't gasp and jump apart, like we both knew we'd made a mistake of epic proportions by allowing this kiss to happen. A small part of me was almost glad I was going into Seelie where I'd be forced to be away from him.

Our lips brushed a few more times before we both stepped back from each other.

Silence and electricity hung in the space between us.

He stared at me with flushed cheeks.

I'd kissed him, so I needed to say *something*. I licked my lips and shrugged. "Just in case I die. Again."

He cringed and shook his head. His face looked pale. "Try to wait until you're with Riah to do that again, please."

I charged for the door like I was fleeing a crime.

"Savannah?"

My feet froze at the sound of his voice.

"Say something so I know you heard me."

"*Yes,*" I whispered.

He cursed and the emotion in the sound made me turn to look at him. He had his hands on his hips as he shook his head and stared at the ground. "Why do I want you to say it? Why? *What have you even done to me?*"

My heart stopped. *It.* We both knew what he was referring to. Neither of us knew why it affected us, or why we liked it. I used to hate it. Loathe it. The very idea of saying it would gross me out. I knew part of me had said it that first time as a joke because I used humor to deflect. But none of that mattered. It was too late for that. We were in too deep.

"Yes, *daddy.*"

He looked up and grinned, then let out a sexy as sin chuckle that would haunt me forever.

"You better be here when I get back, or I will summon your dead ass every damn day." I winked and then spun and sprinted out the door.

Kiwi. Kiwi. KIWI.

CHAPTER THIRTEEN

SAFFIE

T-minus two minutes till departure, folks.

I sighed and leaned my forehead into Olli's. "Time for me to go, O."

He groaned and licked my cheek.

"I know, I'll miss you too. But I have to save Riah." I pulled back and ruffled his long brown ears. "Just stay with Albert, okay? Chutney will be back in no time, and she'll keep you safe until I come home."

I sighed. Again.

"I'm sorry I have to leave you so soon. But I'll be back. *With Riah.*"

I will. I have to be. There's no other option I'll settle for.

Which means it's time to go now.

Now that the time had come, my fears were trying to consume me. Fear for Riah's safety. Fear for my Coven and friends. Fear for what the Seelie King would do once he found me in Seelie. I was a twisted, knotted ball of nerves, but it wasn't going to go away until it was over.

I floated to the edge of the pool where the stairs were and climbed out. The moment my feet hit the cement, my clothes and hair instantly dried. The crystals Henley instructed us to wear were hanging from my neck and my citrine bracelet from Riah was still on my wrist. My wand was tucked into my boot for safe keeping. I was as ready as I'd ever be. I just prayed it would be enough.

Olli hopped over to me, so I bent down and scooped him up and then headed toward the house. I was about fifteen feet from the backdoor when I spotted Tegan and Tennessee standing in the shadows of the house. I froze. I didn't want to eavesdrop, but if I tried to walk by it would interrupt them.

And they looked tense.

Tegan had Tenn's leather jacket fisted in both of her hands. He had her face in his. This wasn't a romantic moment, this was intense, terrified passion. Tenn was whispering something to her, but his voice didn't carry. The soulmate crystals on their chests and hands flashed a deep emerald green. They were scared too. Henley's warning to Tegan worried me but there was something else that lingered in her spirit, something deep down in her aura that unsettled me. Not in fear of her but *for* her. There was trouble on the horizon and by the way they stared into each other's eyes, they knew it.

Sharp pain laced through my chest. I squeezed my eyes shut and then sucked in a strangled, deep breath and sank to my knees. I knew their fear. I knew what they were feeling in this moment because I felt it tenfold. I wished so badly I could just see him, speak to him. To tell him I'm coming, to just hang on.

When I opened my eyes, I found the power couple locked in a passionate embrace and it made my heart hurt. I jumped back up and hurried past them into the house. We were three steps inside when Albert barked from the couch. I walked over and sat Olli down beside him.

"I promise I'll take good care of Olli while you're gone," Braison said softly from beside me.

"I know. Thank you, my friend." I turned and gave him a hug, then whispered in his ear, "I will find Paulina."

He nodded but didn't say anything else. He just plopped down beside our dogs and stared into space.

"Okay. Everyone ready?"

Everyone jumped at the sound of Tegan's voice.

I glanced around the room to my friends—my *family*—and wanted to cry. They were all scared. I saw it in the shifting of their weight and the darting of their gazes. Some of them chewed on fingernails, others fiddled with weapons, and some stared into space. Even the ones staying behind. Because if one of us went down we all felt it.

Despite all the red flags and warnings, they were doing this for me. For Riah. For Paulina, Amelia, and Landy. It was oddly fortunate that I had the rage and determination fueling the fire inside of me to go in there and burn it all until I found Riah...I wasn't sure what fueled them in a moment like this.

"Yo B, you have that spell for me?"

Bettina stood and walked over to her best friend, then handed her a folded piece of paper. "You know I do."

Tegan opened it and her green eyes traveled down its length. Her face wore an expressionless mask, which was telling in itself. She held the paper out to the side. "Lenny, you are now Frodo."

Lennox hurried over and took the paper. She opened it up and read the words, then whistled under her breath. "Intense. I'm on it."

"It's also on Bentley's arm, just in case." Bettina pointed to our Hierophant lurking in the corner.

Tegan cleared her throat. "All right, time to go."

I closed my eyes as they turned to each other. They saying goodbye, just in case they didn't come home. I couldn't watch or listen. Things were too tense, too sad. I couldn't bear the idea of losing someone else in exchange for Riah. But I knew by the edge in their auras they were prepared to do so, and it did something to me. In the words of Savannah, I was feeling some type of way about this, and it was too much.

"Come back to me," Bettina whispered, drawing my eyes open. She hugged her brother and uncle and then stepped back. "Don't be heroes, okay?"

I quickly looked away, only for my gaze to land on Kessler and Hunter hugging. Movement in my peripheral made me turn just in time to see Katherine tackle Timothy. Over his shoulder I saw her teary eyes.

Braison cursed. His eyes were red and puffy. "I hate that I'm not going in there after her. You'll tell her I had no choice, right? You'll find her for me?"

As everyone reassured him, I concentrated on breathing normally.

Cooper walked over to Tenn and hugged him.

Tegan smiled at them and pulled on a leather jacket covered in gold and silver studs. "Oh shit, B, let me activate the listening spell for Henley."

Bettina cursed and skipped over to her.

Royce groaned and bent over at the waist like he was going to be sick. "I swear to God in a cashmere sweater, if all y'all don't come back..." he closed his eyes and shook his head.

Bettina blinked and shook her head. "Whoa, that is distracting. Right. I'm on it. Promise."

*If all y'all don't come back...*suddenly a thought I hadn't considered came to mind. *What if I don't come back?* I'd been so focused on getting to Riah and saving him I hadn't entertained the idea that I might not survive. I should have. I cursed and turned to Kenneth. "Can you do me a favor?"

He nodded. "Of course. Name it."

"Can you call my mother? Tell her where I'm going. Tell her...tell her..."

"I know. I will." He squeezed my hand and gave me a sad smile. "Absolutely."

Bentley cleared his throat. "All right, we need to get moving."

There was a lot of groaning and cleared throats, but they all huddled together in the middle of the living room. I moved to stand beside Savannah. She wrapped her arm around mine and nodded. It almost made me smile.

"Tegan is going to portal us as close as possible. Once there, Lennox will perform the spell that will lead us to the Land of the Lore." Bentley tapped on his necklace. "Everyone have their crystals on?"

I looked down to where the crystals were strung on a leather cord.

"Tuck those necklaces under your shirts so they're less likely to be snatched or broken."

"I do not like the sound of that."

"Savannah, Lily, Willow, and Saffie," Bentley paused with his eyes on me. "Do NOT wear those into Seelie. Henley was adamant that they be removed prior to going through the archway."

We nodded.

Tennessee cleared his throat. "For those of you staying, be careful. He'll know we're gone, and he will capitalize on that."

They nodded.

"Dad, Constance, you're in charge until we get back." Tenn grimaced. "Just stay on Henley. Call Knights to handle demons. You stay on Henley. Let's pray the Goddess watches all of us and all this fear and emotion is for nothing."

CHAPTER FOURTEEN

SAFFIE

When the light of the portal faded, we found ourselves surrounded by darkness.

The air was sharp and cold but fresh and untainted by human pollution. I hadn't felt air this clean in centuries, not since before I was cursed. The nostalgia was a bitter slap in the face. It made me think of Riah and the time we had together when we first met, however fleeting it was. If only we had known who we were to each other. If only I had taken charge back then, like I did in the hot tub, then maybe we would have known. Maybe fate would have dealt us a different hand.

That is NOT helpful, Saraphina.

I groaned. My own name was now a weapon against me. I heard his voice even thinking it in my head. My chest grew tight and my breaths short. *Breathe, Saffie. You're going. You're going to save him now. You're almost there, just hang on.*

A large, warm arm wrapped around my shoulders and a soft golden light glistened in my peripheral vision. I looked up and found Hunter Bishop's eyes of sunshine watching me.

He gave me a soft smile. "There's still time. Just focus on one step at a time."

I nodded, then closed my eyes and took a deep breath.

Lose it now and you'll never save him. Set all other emotions aside.

When I opened them again, I felt my resolve sharpen. A coldness filled my veins and burned like lava through my body. The only emotion I needed was rage, and I planned on letting all of Seelie feel it.

The energy around me was tense and dark and I understood why.

We all did.

I walked forward until I stood at the front of our group between Tennessee and Tegan. We stood at the base of a mountain range that towered into the black night sky. The moon hung low over the trees and glowed a deep orange, yet a soft blue haze clung to the air.

Everything *looked* normal.

But I felt it.

That...off-ness.

It felt like ice sharpened into pin-pricks were dragging down my spine. It made my magic flutter and roll through me in waves. Little purple flowers sprouted from the dark soil beneath my feet. They reminded me of Riah's amethyst ring. My stomach tightened into knots. I balled my fists and clenched my teeth.

"So...um..." Easton cleared his throat in the silence, which made everyone jump. "Where is this place? Because I'd rather not linger here. It's giving me the creeps."

"*Exactly.*" Tegan shuddered, then shook herself. She pointed straight ahead into the mountains. "It's *there*. I can feel it."

"*I ca, too,*" I said at the exact same time as Tennessee and Emersyn.

"I have a bad feeling about this," Deacon whispered.

Savannah squirmed. "I am not in charge here, but y'all, I am losing steam the longer we stand here."

"Oh, thank Goddess. Me too," Willow said with a deep exhale. "Team Freak Out, party of two?"

"Party of three," Lily grumbled.

Tegan sighed so hard she actually swayed into me.

"Nope. Nope, nope. You're not allowed to do that." Deacon cracked his knuckles. "You fake it 'til we make it. Got it, Queen of Darkness?"

"Don't share my secrets, Devil boy." Tegan glanced over her shoulder with a sideways grin and a wild wink. Then she sobered and nodded her head. "Bentley?"

Bentley strolled forward until he was standing in front of all of us. He turned his back to the mountains, and I saw orange crescents flash in his eyes. "The Land of the Lore is alive. You need to listen to what I'm about to say and do *exactly* as I tell you. Got it?"

We all nodded.

"The very nature of this place is built for Seelie and Unseelie. It will try to trick you. It will play with your minds, your vision, the very things you feel deep inside." He pointed behind him without looking. "It will sing you a lullaby more beautiful than you've ever heard and beckon you into its dark-ness...and then it will consume you."

I swallowed through a rush of nerves.

"You're entering the realm of the forest sirens, and if you step off the trail, you will not know what hit you until it is too late." Bentley's voice was rough, like he'd swallowed gravel. "You cannot block your ears or your sight. Its magic is in the air and will reach inside of you. It will prey on the very essence of who you are and break you. Do you understand?"

"How do we protect ourselves?" Tenn asked softly. "What do we do?"

Bentley shook his head. "I know this will be difficult, for some of you more than others, but I will guide you. I have lived the last seven years in Seelie. I understand its magic and its essence. You will need to trust me and do everything I say exactly when I say it without question. The stones Henley told us to use will help protect us. Now, the four of you going into Seelie, I want you in the middle. Let the rest of us handle anything that comes our way as that is literally the reason we're here."

"Except for Tegan," Timothy grumbled from the back.

Bentley gripped the Hierophant's locket and orange magic flashed under his fingers. He shoved it under his shirt to hide it.

Tegan cursed.

"Tegan...you need to be as not present as possible. You're emergency backup only." He stared at her for a long second and I knew she was speaking to him telepathically. He nodded. "You know what it is we fear inside for you. Just try not to do *anything*. I mean it. You're our fast track out of here. The emergency brake. You bust out your magic and we'll either be ambushed or kicked out, or both. Got it?"

"More than you realize," Tegan grumbled. "Everyone, *please* try not to die, okay? Pretend I'm not here."

"One last thing..." Bentley rubbed his hands together. "Silas, stay a dragon. I'm not sure if you'll be able to shift once you're inside, so I wouldn't try."

Silas snorted.

"Okay, Lennox, you're up." Bentley stepped aside and gestured for Lennox to take his place. "You know what to do?"

"You tell me, Dr. Strange." Lennox winked playfully as she hurried forward. She pulled her wand out of her jacket and pressed the tip to her palm. Light flashed as she moved it over her skin. When she was done, there was a glowing rune shining against her dark skin. "Okay, everyone stay behind me. I'm going to do the spell and our destination should reveal itself."

My stomach tightened into knots.

Lennox took a deep breath and then held her hand up

toward that orange ball in the sky. *"Triple mother, single stone, lend your power to be shown. By the light are all things fed, in thy presence I feel no dread."*

The Moon grew bigger and brighter, then lifted higher in the sky. The orange hue lightened until the color was a soft, pale blue that chased away the edges of darkness on the mountains. Tall, towering pine trees stood in stark contrast to the moonlight. It was breathtakingly beautiful, and for a moment I forgot just how lethal this destination of ours was supposed to be. A strange, foreign peace settled into my bones. My mind told me it didn't make sense, but my thoughts were foggy.

"Goddess, guidance, grieving, gone, magic, strife, and silver dawn," Lennox called up to the Moon like they were old friends and the air sparkled like it was raining glitter. *"Phase of fire, fury, and fear, within the madness, mine I hear. Straight of the spirit, peace of mine, I call on you please show your sign."*

Fog lifted from the ground like dawn rising from the horizon. For a moment it hovered, clinging to the pine branches in every direction, but then it began to move. Right before our eyes the fog condensed together so it looked like a river—I gasped. *THAT'S IT! The Land of the Lore!* Bentley had said it was like a river. The fog was thick and white, like a snowy cloud that sparkled under sunshine even in the middle of the night.

"Paint me now in thy light, to walk along the trail of fright. Waning, waxing, crescent, full, within my soul they'll never pull."

Magic rushed out of Lennox's hand and into the river of fog. Normally, Lennox's magic was the same yellow-green shade of her eyes, but this was a paler shade of her indigo hair. This was *not* Lennox's power she was wielding and that fact sent a chill down my spine.

This was the Land of the Lore, a place The Coven had never been.

And we were looking for the entrance.

A single neon-blue flame burst to life at the edge of the forest between two pine trees. It flickered and danced in place with matching blue mist swirling around it as it hovered a few inches off the ground. Lennox took a step forward and another blue flame lit up behind the first. And then another...and another. Suddenly there was a whole row of them moving farther into the forest like a—*TRAIL*.

"*Is that it?*" I heard myself whisper. "*Is that the path?*"

Bentley sighed and stepped up beside Lennox. "Those flames will lead us to the archway. Everyone, follow me and *stay on the trail*."

Tennessee cursed under his breath. "Lead the way, Bentley."

Bentley nodded and waved for us to follow him. We moved as a unit, each of our steps hitting the ground in perfect unison like we'd rehearsed for it. Willow, Savannah, Lily, and I were huddled close together in the middle. Tegan was right behind us, trying her best to blend in.

"Once we're in, you *do not* slow down," Bentley said as we approached the first flame. He stepped through the tree line first, then spun to walk backwards. "Dad, let me know when we're all in."

I straightened my spine and pushed my shoulders back. Fear be damned. I would do this for Riah. I would face anything to save him. The air shimmered blue around the flame, casting us all in a silvery blue haze. My magic *burned* to come out and fight, like it knew the danger we were in.

"Okay, we're all in—" Hunter cursed. "It closed. The opening is...gone."

"It closed us in or—" Lennox gasped and crashed face-first to the ground.

"LENNOX!" We all dove for her at the same time.

Dirt as black as shadows flew up all around her body. The air pulsed like a shockwave, moving away from us and into the forest. My pulse skipped.

I felt her soul beaming with life and warmth. "*She's alive!*"

Tennessee got to Lennox first. He slid to one knee and gently but quickly scooped her into his arms. Her indigo hair fell off her face and swayed under her head. Her arms dangled. He pressed his fingers to her throat and then sighed. "She's breathing."

"She served her purpose here," Deacon whispered. His violet eyes bounced around the forest. "I can *feel* it. The forest wants us, one by one it will come—"

"We need to move," Bentley said with a growl. He rolled his wrists and his skin turned black from the elbows down. Those orange lightning bolts streaked through the charred black parts and into his palms. Flames flickered between his fingers and then two fire-covered swords appeared in his hands. "*We cannot stop—*"

I gasped. My body instantly felt like all the warmth had

been stolen from it. Ice-cold air brushed over my feet and coiled around my ankles. Fingers clawed at my legs and tugged at my jeans.

Saraphina.

JOIN US.

SARAPHINA.

Come with us!

With each silent plea, their hands pulled at my body. I looked down and that white foggy river we saw from outside slithered over the ground and our feet. In my peripheral vision, I saw Tenn place unconscious Lennox into the cradle of Hunter's arms, but my gaze was locked on the hands of fog reaching up for him. I looked up only to find the white fog sliding all the way up Tegan's legs. Her green eyes rolled back, and her body swayed.

"Move. *Go. GO, GO, GO!*" I leapt forward and shoved Tegan forward. "*Go, go, go. MOVE!*"

Tegan gasped and lunged forward instantly. I grabbed Lily and Savannah's arms and dragged them forward. Savannah threw her arm back and snatched Willow's hand to pull her with us. The others looked left and right in a panic, their eyes wide, yet they moved after us.

"*What is it? What do you see?*" Chutney hissed from the back of the group. "I don't see anything!"

"We're not alone," I yelled back as I kept dragging the others forward.

Bentley leapt around and got back in front of me with his flaming swords raised. "*WE HAVE TO KEEP MOVING! NO STOPPING!*"

"OR WHAT?" Easton shouted.

"*They claim us,*" I heard myself whisper.

"What is it?" Easton had Lily's other hand clenched in his grip. He sliced his sword left and right. "I don't *see* anything."

"Spirits."

Saffie? Tegan said into my mind.

I looked up, expecting to meet her gaze, but she'd moved to stand behind me next to Tennessee. Her eyes were locked on the ground.

These souls are on their way out, aren't they? She asked and then her gaze shot up to mine. *They're moving on, right?*

I nodded.

She closed her eyes and reached for Tenn's hand. *I can feel it.*

I shuddered. Weird things happened to Tegan when she got too close to spirits and Heavenly power. The magic here was not of Heaven's making, but it wanted her all the same. I waited until Tegan opened her eyes and looked to me again, then I nodded and mouthed, *I'll warn you.*

She shivered. *Don't you dare risk getting into Seelie for me. Tenn will catch—*

"Whoa, whoa, whoa." Easton hopped around and swung his blade. "What's this stuff?"

I followed his gaze and found that white fog had grown thicker and was rising from the ground all around our group. "The spirits. Just keep moving."

"Spirits—"

Arms made of white fog reached up, swaying unnaturally as their ghostly hands tried to grab anyone in their path. Each of my Coven-mates glared at the hands as they walked. Silas puffed his own smoke at them, and they vanished. Chutney's eyes widened and then she began blowing on them.

"Can these hurt us?" Emersyn asked softly, swatting at the ghostly hands tugging on her long blonde hair.

The hands pulled on us, gripping our clothes and weapons and tugging.

"Just keep moving," Bentley barked. "We don't want to find out."

The others kept glancing up at me with nervous eyes. I

turned to face forward and held my chin high. *Fake it 'til you make it, that's what people say nowadays.* In front of me, Bentley marched confidently into the night. Ahead of him, floating blue flames glistened in the distance, marking the trail to the archway.

Around us pine trees towered into the night sky. Each of their trunks and branches were solid black shadows against the light of the Moon shining through. The air was a foggy, faint blue—almost silvery. It glittered in the distance just beyond our reach. I looked straight up, but there was no end in sight for the trees. We were but ants in *this* world...*and we were being hunted.*

Every few steps something moved from within the trees, but I knew not to look.

I *was* half Seelie. I knew how my other kind worked. I knew their tricks.

If you look, they've got you.

But I'd never felt it this bad before.

"*What was that?*" Chutney hissed. "Over there—on the right!"

My body acted on its own and turned to the right. Figures made of white fog danced between the trees. They twirled in big puffy skirts of smoke, spinning and skipping alongside us.

"*Keep moving,*" Bentley growled. "Join them and you die."

Something cracked under my boots. I ignored it and kept walking, pretending the crunching of every step was twigs and branches. But then I heard it echo behind me. I knew which steps were the boys because the crunch was louder and heavier.

"Don't look down, my dudes," Deacon said softly. "I can feel you want to but don't."

I hadn't meant to look, but in that exact moment the fog swirled away from me and the air cleared around my feet.

Skulls and bones covered the ground.

They smashed under our feet, shattering like eggshells.

Emersyn groaned.

"*Are those bones?*" Willow said under her breath. "Tell me they're not bones."

Bentley glanced over his shoulder. "I must not tell lies."

The forest went eerily silent.

Light flashed through the trees and the air glowed turquoise like the ocean by Crone's Island. Little glowing turquoise orbs floated up from the ground and into the air, rising up to the sky. They reminded me of fairyflies. I smiled and watched them flutter through the trees, flying in swirly patterns like they were dancing. I wondered what they would look like with my fairyfly friends—gold and turquoise together. The thought made the tension in my body ease.

A loud, cheerful whistle rang through the forest. It sounded like music—

"*DON'T LOOK,*" Bentley barked.

I gasped and my steps faltered. Savannah's sharp gaze shot to me and her eyebrows scrunched down low. She tugged on my hand to keep me moving with everyone. I cursed and shook myself.

"You guys hear that, right?" Lily asked in a monotone voice. "Tell me you hear that."

"The whistling." Devon's voice was soft, weaker than I'd ever heard it. "I hear it."

"Don't look," Bentley yelled again. "*Do not look.*"

The whistling grew louder, like it was moving closer to us.

Close your eyes, Tegan said into our minds. *Close them!*

I squeezed my eyes shut without hesitation. I'd thought my Seelie blood would make this journey easier, make me more immune to their tricks...but I was starting to fear the opposite. This was Seelie magic, and they knew mine. This Land of the Lore knew exactly what would make me smile, make me relax... make me forget for a moment where we were.

"HELP!" A women's shrill voice ripped through the whistling. "HELP ME!"

Willow and Chutney gasped.

"*DON'T LOOK!*" Bentley screamed.

A woman's broken sob echoed between the trees. "Please, PLEASE! Is someone out there?"

My stomach tightened into knots. Every single part of me wanted to run to this woman's voice.

"HELP ME! I BEG YOU! HELP!"

"Walk faster," Tennessee growled. "*Move.*"

I pushed my legs to move faster, praying I wasn't walking off the path because I wasn't looking.

"HELP! PLEASE!" The woman screamed. "YOU! I see you! THERE by the blue flame!"

Devon cursed. "That's s-s-strong."

"*Do not look!*"

"COME HERE, PLEASE! HELP ME! I'M RIGHT HERE!"

"*DO NOT FOLLOW!*" Bentley's voice was laced with power.

A cool gust of wind brushed over my back and swept through my hair like someone was running their fingers through it. I rolled my shoulders and opened my eyes—I didn't look but I saw in my peripheral vision that no one was touching my hair. Savannah held my one hand while Lily held the other. The four of us were hanging on to each other because we *had* to get in together. There was a reason the Goddess chose us.

"*Saraphina, stop,*" Tennessee whispered in my ear.

I froze and started to turn to look at him when I realized he'd said Saraphina. Not Saffie. Tennessee did *not* call me Saraphina. Only Riah did. A cold chill slid down my spine. Savannah tugged on my hand, so I skipped to keep up our pace.

"*Saraphina? I said stop,*" Tennessee whispered in my ear

again, his breath was hot on my neck. "*Saraphina, will you wait?*"

"TENN," I said through clenched teeth.

"Yes?" He responded instantly.

"*I asked you to stop and wait,*" that whispering voice of his tickled at my neck again.

"Tenn?"

He cursed. "That's not me, Saffie."

I knew it wasn't. It sounded like him but didn't at the same time. It was smoother, softer.

"*Ma'am,* excuse me, what?" Savannah's face paled. "What's not you?"

"Something with Tenn's voice is whispering to me right now."

"*Oh, hell no,*" Deacon cursed.

I frowned. "Do you hear it too?"

"No..." He was silent while we walked.

Easton cleared his throat. "How did you know she could hear your voice?"

Tenn, the real Tenn, sighed and it sounded like it hurt. "Because my mother's voice has been calling to me for several minutes now."

Savannah groaned. "I beg your goddamn pardon, *what?*"

"I hear her too," Timothy said softly, though his voice trembled.

Bentley twirled his swords. "The deeper we get, the weaker we get at fighting th—"

Chutney screamed.

I spun around just as deep red blood gushed from Chutney's forehead. She flew up, her back arching as her feet left the ground. Her whole body went limp and plummeted back down. We all dove for her, but Silas got there first. His dragon arms snatched her free-fall and pulled her tight to his chest.

Hunter and Timothy were right there, pressing their hands to her throat and forehead.

"She's ice-cold," Timothy grumbled.

Hunter shook his head. His brow furrowed. "But she's breathing."

"What the hell hit her?" Emersyn curled her hands, and I knew she wanted to call on her flames.

Willow gasped. *"There are people! Floating in the trees!"*

"DON'T LOOK!" Bentley cursed violently and flew through the middle of the group. He pulled and tugged on our arms. *"MOVE, PEOPLE. MOVE."*

We all cursed and grumbled and leapt back into motion. Timothy and Hunter were still fussing over Chutney as we walked. Silas marched forward—the lone stone colored dragon among us.

"Easton, take Lennox? I need my hands," Hunter said in a rush.

"Of course." Easton spun and jumped over to him and took Lennox into the cradle of his arms. *"Just keep swimming, swimming, swimming..."*

"Her pulse is racing." Hunter cursed. "She's unconscious but she's panicking and afraid still. If I could use my magic—"

"*Dad*—"

"I know, Son. I won't, but—*wait, Devon?* Devon, where are you?"

"Mom? MOM!" Emersyn cried, her feet planting in the dirt.

Bentley cursed and spun in a circle. "MOM!"

Hunter's soulmate glyph changed to green on his hand. "DEVON?"

"I'm right next to you. What's wrong?" Devon's voice was loud but she wasn't anywhere in sight. "What?"

We'd all stopped now, even though we shouldn't have. Even though we knew the rules.

"Devon, you're not here," Hunter yelled. He stumbled forward and spun around. "You're not next to me!"

"What are you talking about? I'm right here—"

Dozens of Devon clones appeared instantly, standing shoulder-to-shoulder and filling in all the space between the trees.

"*DEVON!*" Hunter's voice was high and sharp. His golden eyes were wide in panic. "*Which one is the real her?*"

We all dove for the Devons around us, swinging our arms through their bodies but finding only smoke. This was the exact opposite as we were supposed to do. We were giving it exactly what it wanted. The sea of Devon's projections vanished the second we touched them but more just popped out.

"Devon..." Hunter stumbled away from the group. He spun in a circle. "DEVON."

"Hunter, I'm right—"

Silence.

"DEVON!" Hunter shrieked.

Tegan cursed and pushed through the group. She sprinted back in the direction we'd just come in. Tennessee was hot on her heels with Hunter behind him. Bentley glanced around in a panic and then raced after them. The rest of us exchanged glances, then sprinted off.

"THERE!" Tegan shouted and threw her hand out to point just off the trail. "I can't leave the trail—"

"*I've got it,*" Bentley said in a rush. He waved his flame covered swords and his orange magical bolts flashed. The air glistened like glass and then the haze vanished. "*MOM.*"

We gasped and froze.

Devon was on her knees between two trees. Her entire body trembled. Her head jerked left and right, up and down, making her dark hair swish around. She mumbled a stream of words, but they weren't coherent. Her eyes rolled in different directions. She gasped and her back arched.

"*Devon?*" Hunter hissed and dove for her, jumping right off the trail. He sank to his knees, then reached out to grab a hold of her.

She gasped and threw her head back. Her whole body convulsed and twitched. She collapsed and flopped on her back like a fish out of water. Her arms and legs thrashed. She swung her head back and forth. Even from here I heard her teeth rattling against each other.

"*Get her over here!*" Tegan screamed from the edge of the trail.

Her body was thrashing so wildly he had to grab her under the armpits to drag her across the dirt and back onto the trail. The second her body crossed onto the trail we all dove for her. Each of us grabbed ahold of her limbs and tried to hold her in place because her body was turning astral, flashing in and out of physical form. Her eyes bounced around faster than hummingbird wings.

Bright red light shined out from her chest like a spotlight.

Hunter cried out.

Her soulmate glyph was *red*.

She was in danger. Imminent, life threatening danger.

My body went numb.

Emersyn dove down and supported her mother's head. Bentley pressed his hand to her chest to use that new magic of his—and his face paled. He shook his head rapidly. Hunter was calling out for her. Everyone was panicking. I heard them shouting and trying to figure out what to do.

Then pale blue light washed across Devon.

Tegan held shaking hands over her mother's convulsing body.

Easton swatted at Tegan's hands. "*No, you can't use your magic—*"

"*I just need to see if I'm wrong—*"

I choked on a gasp. "*TEGAN!*"

She froze. Wide green eyes met mine.

That blue light grew bolder. The air turned cold. The panic in Devon's soul was fading.

"She's dying," I said.

Just then Devon's soulmate glyph began pulsing with red light.

"Fuck that," Tegan yelled and blasted rainbow magic right into Devon's entire body.

Rainbow-colored mist coiled around each of Devon's limbs and through the strands of her dark hair. Her body lifted a few inches off the ground while Tegan's magic went to work. Tegan's arms lit up like a full Moon as power poured out of her like a broken dam. The ground rumbled under our knees.

Light flashed out of Tegan's hands.

Devon's body went still.

CHAPTER SIXTEEN

SAFFIE

Bright white light shot up out of the ground all around us. It poked through the dirt in streaks—*and wrapped around Tegan's wrists*. She gasped and Devon crashed to the ground.

The light rose up and formed into the shape of—*oh shit! SPIRITS!*

Everything happened so fast. I wasn't expecting it *like this*. I opened my mouth to warn her, but they were faster. In the blink of an eye, spirits formed right out from under us. They grabbed Tegan by the arms and dragged her away, leaving a trail of rainbow magic in her wake.

"TEGAN!" We all screamed.

We sprinted after her, pushing ourselves as fast as possible. But it was something straight out of one of Savannah's horror films. The spirits rose and claimed her faster than even *Tennessee* could move. He was at least ten feet ahead of the rest of us, yet she was getting farther and farther from him by the second. She threw her arms out and reached for him. Her wide eyes met mine for a split second and then she was lost to a river of spirits.

I couldn't see her, but I felt her terror like it was my own.

"*DROP HER!*" I screamed to the spirits and pushed my magic, but nothing happened.

These spirits were out of my wheelhouse.

They were on their way home...and they were taking Tegan with them.

I pushed my wings out and flew past the line of spirits following Tegan. Tennessee was a few yards ahead of me, his gold angel wings carrying him *almost* fast enough. They both had their arms stretched and reaching for each other but there had to be ten feet between them. My wings couldn't fly any faster. Those blue flames that signaled our path blew by us one after another.

STOP.

STOP.

STOP!

But my magic did nothing.

The spirits moved faster than a riptide.

The trail took a sharp left turn, then down a steep hill. At the base of the hill, the blue flames curved the trail to the right to go around a glowing blue lake, but the spirits rushed straight ahead *and into the lake.*

The water glowed as bright and unnatural blue as the flames on our trail. A layer of neon-white fog clung to the surface and billowed like steam. The line of spirits didn't slow their speed even a fraction. They charged straight into the lake, sinking beneath the surface. And none of them came out the other side. My pulse thundered in my veins. I knew what this was. I knew what was happening. If they got Tegan deep enough in this lake, there'd be no saving her.

The spirits holding her ran over the surface of the water and then they sank feet-first. Tegan's black and purple hair flew up and over her face. Her fingers flexed and rainbow magic shot out of them—and then she was under.

TENN! She screamed telepathically.

"TEGAN!" We all shrieked.

The rest of us were too far away except for Tenn. He was *fast* on land. but water was his element. He dove headfirst into the lake and vanished beneath the glowing foggy surface.

TEEEEEENNNNNNNN—Tegan's telepathic scream cut off short.

I flew over the lake to try and see under them, but I saw nothing but water—not even my reflection.

My Coven-mates were just making it over the hill and sliding down the steep edge.

Water splashed under me. I gasped and looked down just as Tennessee emerged from of the water—*with Tegan draped in his arms.* Her body was limp, her arms dangling down and dripping water. Tennessee's face was scrunched up like he was in pain. The soulmate glyph on his chest was white, which made no sense. They were only white when they first appeared and never again. Not even in death.

The weight of the water must have been slowing him down because he stumbled through it toward the surface instead of just walking on top like he normally would have. Deacon and Easton charged into the lake, the glowing water splashing all around. As Tenn got closer, Deacon and Easton reached down and grabbed Tegan, but smoke sizzled and hissed like acid.

Deacon cursed and yanked his hand off Tegan's leg.

Easton shouted in pain and I felt it rock through his body. There was a nasty loud *crack* and he crashed to his knees. He started to sink in the water. Red blood pooled on the surface of the lake all around him already. I charged for him. Deacon dove out of the way, cursing and shaking his hand. The smell of burnt flesh carried through the air.

Bentley and Timothy were at the edge of the lake, gunning for Tenn—

"*Don't touch her!*" Tenn yelled and turned away to get out of their touch.

When I got to Easton, I reached down and grabbed his shoulders and then dragged him toward the shore.

"EASTON!" Lily squealed and dove for him.

I sat him just on the shore next to Bentley and Timothy. Easton was groaning and hissing. We crouched down to get a good look just as he rocked back and blood cascaded in a perfect arc. Once the blood cleared, I leaned down and my stomach rolled. Easton's arm was mangled. The bone had snapped and sliced through the skin so it was protruding from his body.

"*What the hell!*" Deacon hissed. He hurried over but was still shaking his now bright red hand. "That was worse than touching Michael's sword."

Lily and Willow rushed to Easton. Silas sat on the shore with Chutney in his arms. Beside him, Easton had laid Lennox on the dirt and Savannah was tending to her.

Hunter came stumbling over the hill, carrying Devon in his arms.

My heart stopped. She looked dead in the way she lay in his arms, but I felt her. It was faint and weak as hell, but it was there. She had a chance. And under the pain and trauma of that, her soul was already fighting to survive.

"Saffie—"

"She's alive." I looked up and met Hunter's tear-filled eyes. "I can feel her fighting it. Get her to Katherine. She still has a chance. Just like Lennox and Chutney."

He nodded. His face was flushed with emotion.

"Oh my God...*noooo*..." Emersyn leapt away from Deacon toward the river.

I spun around just as Tenn stepped onto the shore and sank to his knees. He rested Tegan's body on the dirt, then reached up and tipped her head up...her hair was whiter than snow.

"*Tegan!*" Tenn cupped her face and gave her a little, gentle shake. "*TEGAN!*"

She gasped and flailed in his arms. Her eyes opened and the

color combination sent chills down my spine. The irises were white like her hair, but her pupils and rims were a glittery bright gold.

She looked up at Tenn with her eyes half closed. *"Haven,"* she whispered.

"Yeah, I'm here. I'm here, love." He ran his thumb over her cheek. "I've got you."

She opened her mouth and spewed out a bunch of words I'd never heard before. They sounded angelic. The soulmate glyph on her chest was still white, but it shimmered a faint green color if you looked close. A sloppy smile spread across her face...and then she passed out.

Everyone began to panic. We now had six injured people, only two of whom were capable of walking on their own, and Easton was losing a lot of blood quickly.

Tennessee screamed. *"WHYYYY?"*

"It's the Strait of the Dead," I whispered and pointed to the blue flames.

Tenn's face paled. "No...can't be. That's in the ocean down in the—"

"I know." I nodded sadly. "But this lake connects to it. That's why my magic couldn't control them, not at this stage in their eternity. But this path we're on is literally the path the dead take to the afterlife. That's why we can follow—"

Hot, sharp electric energy pierced my hand and my chest. The pain burned and throbbed like I'd been impaled. I gasped and gripped my chest with my other hand as my breaths grew short. My pulse pounded in my palm, so I held my hand up to see it...

And my heart stopped.

My soulmate glyph was *red*.

RIAH.

CHAPTER SEVENTEEN

SAFFIE

"Noooo!" I screamed and threw my right hand up, waiting for it to change. "NO!"

RIAH! I'm coming, I'm coming! Just hang on for me!

The others crowded around me. I heard their panicked voices and felt the fear inside of their souls. But their words were lost to my ears. My pulse thundered in my veins.

"I'm too late. I'll never make it—"

My glyph flashed and then turned a vibrant emerald green.

Relief rocked me so hard my legs gave out and I fell back. Tattooed arms snaked out and caught me. I saw a flash of turquoise hair and then I was back on my feet again. Bright colored flowers popped out of the ground under me as my emotions raged up and down out of control.

"He's still there. We've still got time," Savannah said in a rush. *"So let's get moving."*

I looked up to the rest of our little group and my heart sank. Tenn cradled unconscious Tegan in his arms while Hunter held Devon. Silas still had Chutney who was still bleeding. Timothy carefully lifted Lennox off the ground while Lily was wrapping material around Easton's bleeding wound.

Emersyn stepped forward and twirled her wrist. That double-sword of hers appeared in her palm with bright orange flames coiling around the blades. She narrowed her golden eyes and snarled. "They can't have what's *ours*. Let's move."

"We've been here too long," Bentley whispered and pulled his swords out while his gaze scanned the forest around us. He glanced over his shoulder to us and those orange crescents flashed in his eyes. "This has not gone unnoticed."

Everyone jumped to their feet and moved back into our little formation.

A soft, faint humming sound whispered through the trees.

It sounded like a softer version of a church's organ. I felt the rumble of the tone in my bones. My gaze locked on the blue flame in front of us. It flickered and swayed in the opposite direction, like it was urging us on. Like it knew something we didn't.

"What is that noise?" Willow asked, her head whipping back and forth.

"*They're coming,*" Bentley growled. "MOVE!"

We leapt into motion, hurrying straight for that blue flame just as voices filled the air.

"*Faster,*" Bentley hissed. "Stay on the trail!"

The voices were soft at first but with every step we took they grew stronger and louder. They were feminine and high. The voices sang but not in words, just this range of notes that seemed to move around us and tickle one ear at a time.

Bentley waved us forward. "Keep walking..."

The voices sang out in words from our right side and a cold slid down my spine. The song moved through the trees, following us along the trail. More voices sang from over on the left and goosebumps spread down my arms. I pushed my legs to keep walking, but my ears were locked on the sound.

It was haunting.

It wasn't human.

But it was one hundred percent familiar...I just couldn't place it.

The voices sang in unison like a church choir, harmonizing in surround sound. My skin tingled. Their song reminded me of old sea shanties from my childhood. They were enchantingly beautiful. Their words sharpened as the tempo of the song picked up and—*wait*. My eyes widened. *I know those words.*

I know this song.

"*GO, GO, GO!*" I pulled on Savannah's and Lily's hands and quickened our steps. "*Move, move, move. NOW!*"

Bentley was already half-jogging. "We must be close, just keep on the trail!"

Willow gasped and froze. She spun toward the forest and started to take a step, but Savannah yanked her back by the hand.

"*MA'AM,*" Savannah snapped. "NO. What you doin'?"

Timothy cursed and then he was suddenly in my peripheral vision, heading for the forest to my right. At the last second, he grumbled and threw himself back onto the trail with us. Silas roared from the back of the group. I glanced over my shoulder and gasped. Silas had stopped and was shaking his head back and forth, his tail whipping through the air. Chutney jostled in his arms. Deacon threw his hand out and hit Silas with red mist. Silas froze, then sighed and shook himself.

They were calling us.

Beckoning for us.

Reaching down into our souls and pulling out our worst fears.

Or *theirs*. These words would not affect one of their own.

There was a reason they were called forest sirens, and it was only going to get worse.

"*Keep moving. Don't —*"

"COOPER!" Emersyn shrieked and stumbled. Her golden

eyes were locked on nothing out in the forest. *"What are you doing h—NO!"*

She charged straight off the trail and into the forest. But there was nothing there. There was no one. Cooper was not there. The forest sirens had sank their hooks into her and reeled her in. Deacon screamed her name and sprinted after her. His blonde hair glistened in the silvery moonlight. The rest of us slid to a stop with our hearts in our throats.

I felt eyes on my back, but when I looked I saw nothing.

"HURRY, D!" Bentley shouted, then glanced behind him in the same direction I'd looked.

He feels that too.

Deacon and Emersyn disappeared, vanishing between the trees.

"We have to move. Now. Now, now, now," I whispered over and over. I threw my hand out and pushed glittery gold magic onto the ground just off the trail. "DEACON!"

Red lightning flashed and struck a few trees.

A river of bright orange flames streaked across the forest.

And then Deacon emerged from the flames and darkness, dragging Emersyn with him. She was screaming and fighting his hold. Fire flicked at the edges of his clothes and hair. She hissed and swung her arms—and her entire body lit on fire.

Silas growled and swung his tail. It slammed into Deacon's back and pushed them toward the trail. They flipped in the air and rolled. Bentley tackled Emersyn, then pinned her to the ground while her flames lashed at him. But everywhere they touched him, his body turned that charred black with orange lightning bolts.

Tenn's body flashed bright white for a split second and then a gust of wind hit Deacon and wrapped around him, blowing out all of Em's flames on his body. He gasped and landed on all fours. Then he instantly scrambled to where Emersyn was pinned down, screaming about saving Cooper.

Savannah's face paled. She looked back and forth between Emersyn and the nothingness of the forest. "He's not here. He's not. It's nothing. Right, *right?!*"

Deacon threw his hands out and a wall of red magic rushed out of his palms. It covered Emersyn's face like a blanket. Her body went still. He growled, then flicked his wrist and his magic cleared.

Her gold eyes stared at the sky above her unseeingly.

The flames vanished.

Cold air brushed over my back. I gasped and stood up tall. My wings fluttered. "Get her up. We gotta go. *Now. Now, now, now.*"

Deacon cursed and then held his hand over her face. Red magic flashed. "Get up and walk on the trail with us."

Emersyn jumped up without hesitation, but instead of that fiery personality she was more like a statue. Bentley grabbed one of her elbows and pulled her along with him. Hunter groaned and it sounded broken.

"I had to put her in a hypnotic state," Deacon said in a rush. "It's reversible. Later."

"Good. *Time to go.*" Bentley swung his other arm. "GO!"

But no one else moved. Everyone, even Tennessee, was looking left and right when they should have been walking. Savannah stared at the spot Emersyn had seen Cooper with a blank face of white.

It was too late.

They'd reeled them in. Deacon couldn't override all of it for all of us. He had to use too much of his power to overpower hers. *Think, Saffie, think.* But the singing was so loud it drowned out all of my thoughts. Most of the group was now back-to-back.

"What language is that?" Easton whispered.

"Ancient Seelie—" I gasped.

I knew this song. I knew these words. I had no idea what they meant, but I vividly recalled a conversation with Keltie

144

about this song and the power it wielded. My pulse skipped. *Worth a try.* I licked my lips and focused on the singing...and then I let their same words roll off my tongue and pour from my lips. Their power burned through my body, instantly filling me with their energy. Goosebumps covered every inch of me. My red hair flicked around my shoulders. Golden glitter spilled from my palms.

Bentley nodded rapidly. He skipped to the front of the group and signaled for us to follow him. Everyone jumped into line and marched on.

The forest hissed and rumbled with every note I sang. It didn't like that I was playing with their own tricks. But *I* liked it, and in the back of my mind that terrified me. I felt fire in my veins. My Coven-mates had stopped buckling to its magic. Their eyes were locked on our path ahead and their feet stayed true and straight.

And then the drums started.

Butterflies danced in my stomach.

The hairs on my arms stood tall.

Bentley gasped and skipped a step. He glanced over his shoulder and yelled, "RUN!"

It was hard to sing and keep my voice calm while running but I had to keep trying. I was Seelie. Even with half their blood, I still could fight fire with fire. They weren't used to fighting their own magic. It wouldn't keep them at bay forever. I just needed long enough to get us to the archway. Once we were in, they could use their magic at full force and get the hell out.

The drums sounded like a stampede headed right for us.

Each beat sent vibrations up my legs and into my bones. The ground rumbled. Every muscle in my body tensed. I sang louder, pushing my voice to move deep between the trees. The trail swerved in a curved path, hooking around one tree and then darting across to another. The blue flames were closer together, illuminating every few feet.

The drums pounded feverishly and my pulse mimicked.

My fingers tingled and I felt myself grow weaker.

I looked down at my right hand. My soulmate glyph was still green. Riah was still alive. He wasn't in imminent danger or fatally wounded. I still had a chance. I just had to get there.

"LOOK!" Bentley raised one of his fiery swords out in front of him.

My eyes widened. The only blue flame left was five times the size of the others. And it glowed brighter and bluer. *Riah, Riah, Riah*—that was all my mind could think of. We had to be close. This had to be it.

We raced towards this flame. No one spoke. We were too focused.

When we got to the flame, we slid to a stop. Bright golden light shined down from the sky like late morning sun. The air had that soft, pale green tint to it. The light flickered blue like an ocean wave rolling by.

And then I saw it.

The archway.

It wasn't at all what I was expecting.

My steps faltered. It wasn't just an archway. It was half of a wall made of old gray stones. It looked like maybe there was once a full structure there. Or part of a wall, the stones were broken off on one side of the archway, but on the other it stretched out to even include a little window. *Who's looking through that and why?* Because it was not an accident.

The forest was full of towering pine trees rowed up one after another, yet in this ring around the stone archway, all of the trees were *oaks*. Massive oaks with branches thicker than my body. The trees' branches stretched out at angles, some of them hanging low over the trail that led to the archway—like they were protecting it. Moss and flowered vines clung to the stones and hung down through the opening of the archway. The air was lighter in this ring of trees. It was a pale blue-green color and seemed to carry a bit of a haze in it.

"We did it," I breathed as my legs burned and begged to stop running. I pointed at it like they could've somehow missed it. "There it is!"

Savannah cursed. "Oh no, ma'am, that is creepy as hell. Of course that's it."

I flew ahead of everyone, then stopped short when I saw the circle of stones on the ground that went around the archway. Every instinct inside of me told me to turn around. To go home. To leave immediately. And I knew why, through that archway was a place just as dangerous as everyone feared it was. But I had to go. Riah's face flashed in my mind. I felt his pulse skip through the glyph, or maybe that was mine. I wasn't sure anymore.

"Yeah, this looks about right," Savannah grumbled as she walked up on my left. "Do we have to do something to cross the circle?"

"Wait —" Willow, who was still clinging to Savannah's left hand, pointed at the ground. "Is Seelie on the other side of the circle or through the archway?"

"The archway." I licked my lips and nodded through the tightness in my chest and lump in my throat. "I suspect the circle is a sort of warning contraption to let the others know visitors are near...so they can stay one step ahead of us."

Lily stepped up on my right and stopped. She reclaimed my hand and squeezed. "Let's go get our family."

Savannah cleared her throat. "Just so we're on the same page before we go in...what's the general game plan for saving them?"

"Destroy everything in our way." A cold menacing rage rushed through my veins. "And give nothing back."

"*SAFFIE!*" Bentley screamed—his voice raw.

We all jumped and spun at the sound of my name—and gasped.

The rest of our group was back a little way and running toward us. Behind them, a bright white light lit up the forest, casting everything in shades of gray. The ground hummed with energy and trembled as something moved near.

How did we get ahead of them by so much?

Everything slipped into slow motion.

The branches hanging low over our heads dropped to the ground *and landed on four legs*. They didn't have hands or feet. Their arms and legs were made of solid white and tapered down to points. Their backs were curved like a humpback but had sharp spikes along the spine. These creatures had tiny round heads with big gaping black holes where eyes should have been.

They turned and lunged forward, tackling Deacon and Emersyn to the ground.

Red lightning flashed left and right.

"EM, FIRE!"

Emersyn raised her hands and flames burst from her palms.

The four of us took a step forward to help—

"NO!" Bentley screamed from thirty feet back. "STOP!"

We froze just as shadows moved from the glowing white forest all around us.

And then the oak trees *moved*.

What I thought were thick trunks were tall humanoid figures that were the same texture as trees. My eyes widened. I glanced left and right and my stomach dropped. We were surrounded. It was an ambush and we fell for it. These weren't the same creatures that Deacon and Em were fighting. These were taller, more human-like. They stood on two legs and had long arms with three branch-like fingers.

And they were charging right for us.

Deacon and Emerysn were still pinned to the ground. Their fire and lightning weren't working.

Bentley leapt over the creatures, slicing his fiery swords through their necks and then flipping mid-air and rolling across the ground. He came out of his roll in a smooth jog and sprinted for us.

Tenn jumped with Tegan in his arms and cleared the distance between us, landing a few feet in front of me. He lifted his leg and kicked one of the monsters in the face, then glanced over his shoulder. "*GO!* We can't use our magic until you do!"

The monsters lunged onto the trail from within the trees. One grabbed Timothy by the throat and lifted him up, then shook him until Lennox dropped ten feet to the ground. He reached for his ice-sword hooked to his hip and grabbed it—

"LILY!" Easton screamed from the back. The monsters were closing in on him. He looked to his right and yelled, "SILAS!"

Silas whipped his tail right at Easton and growled. Easton jumped up and caught the tip of his tail as it swung over his head—*and then Silas threw him.* Lily cried out and moved like she was somehow going to catch him. But Easton landed on his feet and slid through the dirt, then raced for Lily who stood at my side.

Tennessee gasped. "*HUNTE—*"

A humanoid-tree-monster swung its long arm and collided with Hunter's back. Hunter still had Devon unconscious in his arms, so he couldn't brace himself. In a blurry flash, he flew across the trail and slammed into a thick tree trunk. He screamed out and the sound was pure agony. Him and Devon fell straight down to the ground and in the shadows.

That's IT! I jumped forward, ready to fight, when Bentley suddenly slid up in front of me. He caught me against his chest, and we stumbled backwards.

"Let me go! Let me help—"

"NO!" Bentley dropped me and reached into his jeans

pocket. He pulled out a piece of parchment and shoved it into my hand. "You four have to go. Now."

"BUT—"

"*No!*" Those orange crescents flashed in his eyes. "This is the spell. Recite it and go in together, holding hands. GO. NOW. Or we don't have a chance here and neither do our friends *there*."

"Without us you don't—"

"Saffie!" Tenn shouted, his eyes flashed with emotion. "GO and we can use our magic. GO. *GO SAVE THEM! GO!*"

Save them.

Paulina. Amelia. Landy.

RIAH.

Red mist washed over my face and then Deacon shouted. "*We got us, you GO! NOW!*"

I cursed and spun back toward the archway. "Come on, girls!"

Together we leapt over the stone circle and sprinted for the archway. We slid to a stop just before it. I opened up the folded parchment and read the words I never thought I'd mutter. We had to hold hands, so I had to memorize it.

Willow cursed. "Lily? Where's Lily?"

I gasped and spun just as Easton grabbed Lily's face with his good hand and kissed her hard. His blue eyes were shining bright with unshed tears. "I love you. *Come home to me.*"

They were inside the circle, just a few feet back. Lily sniffled and placed her hand to his chest. Her long black hair was braided down her back. "I love you. *Be alive when I get home.*"

"EASTON!" Deacon shrieked and then flew through the air.

The monsters were *everywhere*. The white light was so bright it washed everything out, making it hard to tell what was tree and what was *monster*.

"NECKLACES!" Savannah shouted and yanked the cord off of her neck.

Willow, Lily, and I tugged ours off.

"*Give them to me!*" Easton threw his good hand out and caught all of our necklaces, then hooked them over his neck. He nodded and then jumped out of the stone circle without taking his eyes off of Lily. "GO!"

Bentley sliced his fiery swords through two monsters and turned to me. "*Say it slow!*"

SHIT. SHIT. SHIT. I spun and shoved the parchment into my pocket, then grabbed Lily and Savannah's hands. Savannah gripped Willow's like their lives depended on it. We were just outside the archway, just one good jump away.

"Let's do this, Safferella." Savannah nodded, her blue eyes locked on the archway. "We trust you."

"Let's save our friends," Willow said with a growl.

Lily looked down at me. "Let's get that soulmate of yours."

"Together. I'll recite the spell. Do not let go until I say so." I took a deep breath and focused my gaze on the shimmery blue-green haze in front of us. There were two parts to this spell. The first part I knew far too well. "*For what I seek is deep and dire, I see my words burned in fire. Smoke and ember, cinder and ash, My spell in flames from magic's cache.*"

Behind us chaos roared. I heard our friends—our family—shouting in panicked voices to each other. I heard the rumble of the monsters. I smelled the metallic tinge of witch blood and the sweet sappy scent of Seelie monster.

But I didn't look. Neither did the girls.

Because that wasn't our mission.

We couldn't help them anymore.

There were four other people counting on us.

I took a deep breath and chanted the final lines of the spell to enter Seelie. I wasn't sure what they meant, I didn't speak ancient Seelie, but I felt their power tremble in my bones as I said them. My body turned so cold it burned.

Words appeared inside the archway, written in flickering orange flames.

Under the archway, purple mist shimmered like a curtain.

"NOW!"

Together, we jumped.

CHAPTER EIGHTEEN

SAFFIE

THAT PURPLE MIST flashed around us, robbing me of my sight. But I felt Lily and Savannah's hands still gripping mine. The moment seemed to last an eternity and I knew what was happening.

The price was being paid.

I pictured Riah in my mind and threatened my brain not to forget him again.

The air turned hot and sticky, like late summer in Tampa. The purple mist swirled then turned to a bright sunny yellow – and my feet hit the ground. I glanced left and right to make sure the girls were still with me, and they were. We seemed to be in a yellow cloud. There was nothing in every direction. For a second, none of us spoke.

Silence crashed down around us.

"Are we dead?" Savannah whispered.

Lily sighed and squeezed my hand and shook her head.

I leaned over. "You alive, Willow?"

She blinked and nodded. "I certainly hope so." Her voice was tight. "Um, do you see anything?"

"Just a piss-colored cloud," Savannah grumbled. "Safferella?"

I took a deep breath and pushed my magic out—it answered stronger than it ever had. It flowed through my veins like a river rapid bursting through a dam. Under my feet, green grass sprouted from the black dirt and flowery vines stretched out in an X shape. My eyes widened. I let go of Lily and Savannah's hands and held my own up. Gold glitter poured out of my palms like smoke, filling the air around us. My skin seemed to shimmer. The gold lines of my soulmate mark still covered my entire right arm and chest but now it was glowing like a neon sign.

I looked to Lily. "Are there still lines on my face?"

She nodded.

"Are they glowing?"

She nodded.

I held my hand up and checked my glyph—still green. I exhaled in a rush. And that was when I felt it. *Magic.* I frowned and cocked my head to the side. It wasn't Earthly magic, this was full blown Seelie. My pulse quickened. Except...it felt *good*. I felt stronger than ever.

I felt ready to destroy everything in my path.

"Safferella?"

My lips curved into a little grin. I took a step forward. I knew what this cloud was. This was to immobilize visitors so the Knights could claim them for the King. But they weren't expecting *me*. I held my hands up and pushed with my magic. Golden glitter exploded like a firework. As each little glitter speck moved through the yellow cloud, it vanished inch by inch until the world of Seelie was standing before us.

"That's better."

"That grin you're sporting is making me hella nervous right now." Savannah shuddered. She glanced around. "So, *this* is Seelie?"

This was a marshy riverbed with water that was as aquamarine as my soulmate glyph should have been. A forest towered over us, surrounding us on all sides. Trees grew wild here. Roots and branches were sticking out in every direction and connecting with each other. I couldn't see a sky through all the leaves and branches, but the rays of light poking through were the same turquoise color as the river. Everything else was cast in shadow.

I sighed. "This is at least part of it. Keep your eyes open. This realm is likely to be nothing you've ever expected."

Willow cleared her throat, but then her voice came out high-pitched and a little panicked. "Yeah, um, that's going to be a problem."

We spun to her.

"Willow?"

"*Ma'am?*"

She grimaced. Her dark brown eyes were wide and staring at nothing. It was a blank stare that made my stomach turn. She swallowed roughly. "I can't see."

"*Anything?*" Savannah hissed. "You saw something before? In the cloud?"

Willow shook her head fast, sending her strawberry blonde curls bouncing. "No, that's what I was asking before when I asked if you saw anything. Because my vision went black the second we jumped."

"The price," I breathed, then cursed. "The damn price."

Savannah's eyes widened as realization hit her. She spun on me. "We had to pay a price to enter. One we wouldn't know until we got here. Hers is her vision..."

I nodded, then remembered she couldn't see. "Yes. It appears her vision was *her* price. We would've all paid a different one. Willow, do you feel okay otherwise? Is your magic there?"

She raised her hands and they were trembling, but her blue magic rushed to the surface. "Did it work? I feel it—"

"Yes." Savannah gripped both of her hands. "It worked. You still have your magic, and we're right here with you."

Tears filled her eyes. "Saffie…is this…permanent?"

My stomach tightened into knots. "I can't know for sure. I've never been here. But I would think it will only last while we're here. Or at the very least, I feel like someone back home can heal you."

Savannah glared at the archway behind me. "*Like Riah.* Okay, what about y'all? What ya missing?"

Oh, shit. What did I pay? My magic had already been used. In fact, it was *stronger*. So that wasn't it. I knew Riah. I knew everyone. I didn't seem to be missing memories. I reached up and touched my ears. They were pointed, which was to be expected here in Seelie. I glanced over my shoulder and found my wings twinkling behind my back like clusters of stars. *What did I pay?* I ran my hands over my body—

Lily gasped and grabbed my left hand, then yanked it out in front of me.

There, on the back of my left hand, was a symbol I had definitely seen before but only once…and drawn inside of an old journal. I'd seen it as a young teenager, back before my life got flipped upside down. In the book, back in Salem, the symbol had been drawn in black charcoal. But this…this was a soft pink that glowed just as bright as my soulmate mark. It was a simple mark drawn in clean lines. It looked like an abstract drawing of a butterfly but with one of its wings missing.

"*What does it mean?*" Savannah whispered.

"What is it? What do you see?" Willow shrieked.

"There's a symbol on my hand that wasn't there before, Willow." I rubbed my skin to see if it would come off, but it didn't. I heard Savannah describe it to her in vivid detail, yet my mind was spinning and trying to recall what it meant. "I can't remember what it is. In my youth, when I was your age, I'd made it my mission to learn everything about my other half—

about Seelie and all things fae. This symbol was in that research...though I have misplaced the memory it seems."

"Or they robbed you of that memory," Savannah snarled. "Because they wouldn't want you to remember what you owe them."

"*You owe them something?*" Willow whispered.

"Yes," Savannah and I said at the same time.

My stomach rolled. "I'll have to burn that bridge when I get there—"

"*Ma'am,* that is not the saying." Savannah pursed her lips.

"It is now," I growled. But then I shook myself. I had to stay calm to think straight. "Riah will know what this means. He's a Commander. He'll know. I just have to save him. So let's focus."

And that was when I realized Lily had not spoken a single word.

But she was paying attention.

A cold chill slid down my spine.

I turned to my right to face her, and our eyes met. "Lily...say something."

Her lavender eyes watered. She shook her head and mouthed *I can't.*

"*What'd she say? I can't hear her!*"

"She didn't say anything, Willow..." Savannah said sadly. "Lily, stomp your foot twice if you are incapable of speaking."

Stomp.

Stomp.

Willow cried.

Lily wiped her eyes with shaking hands. But then she sniffled and pushed her shoulders back. *We are wasting time.*

My heart hurt, but she was right. "You're right. We are wasting time. Savannah, you're up. What are you missing? What did you pay?"

Her face paled and she looked more nervous than I'd ever seen her. "I have no idea. I feel fine, or as fine as can be expected. I remember everything. I can see. I can speak...I don't know?"

I frowned. *I'm Seelie and they're making me owe them something. Willow is an illusionist who has been blinded. Lily is a gifted witch who now can't speak. What is Savannah*—I gasped. "Your magic."

She scowled. "My magic?"

"You and your black magic would be dangerous to them. That has to be your price."

"But I can *feel* her magic. It's strong," Willow cried and squeezed Savannah's hand. "Lily, can you feel it? Stomp twice for yes."

Stomp. Stomp.

I loved how quickly they'd found a way for Lily to communicate for the blind girl. It wasn't much but I was low on hope and happy things, so that did it.

Savannah shook her head. "Okay, but I don't understand. I'm not in The Coven, so they wouldn't have a power to take from me. I can still do spells—"

"Name one."

Her face fell.

Silence.

"Savannah? Name a spell. Any spell."

Lily exhaled and scrubbed her face.

Savannah's mouth opened and then closed. Her eyes began to panic. *"I can't. I can't remember ONE. Oh my GOD."*

It was brilliantly sneaky. I almost admired it. *Almost.*

"They took your memory of your magic because you're a spell caster. It makes sense. Everything they took from us makes sense from their point of view." I nodded and took a breath to steady myself. "We just have to push through. We finish our mission and save our friends and get home. Riah will heal you."

"How can I help at all if I can't see? My whole magic revolves around *seeing* things—"

"OH! That's it." Savannah snapped her fingers excitedly. "Willow, did you see that old Ben Affleck movie where he played Daredevil?"

Willow frowned. "Is that the one where he's blind but uses sound to—" she gasped. *"To make himself see!"*

"EXACTLY!" Savannah shook her hand. "Use your magic to give you some kind of vision."

My jaw dropped. I'd seen that film. Back when I had no memory, Savannah and Gigi had hosted an action hero themed movie marathon. "That's brilliant. Willow, your illusions work because it adapts to your surroundings. It blends with it. Use that. Send it out around you and *will* it to match the real thing. Try it."

Willow nodded and licked her lips. She held her hands out in front of her and rubbed her palms together. She took a deep breath and I felt her magic coiling inside of her, ready to burst. She thrust her hands out and that blue mist of hers sprayed like a hose. It flashed and sparkled as it latched on to everything around us...and then it vanished like it'd never been there at all.

"Oh my Goddess," Willow breathed. A tear slid down her cheek. *"This looks terrifying, but I can SEE."*

We dove for her, wrapping our arms around her in an unplanned group hug.

After a moment, we all stepped back.

Willow sniffled and looked right to Lily. "Hi."

Lily smiled and waved. *Ready?* She mouthed.

"Ready." Willow frowned. "But I should not—*WHAT'S THAT?!*"

We spun around to follow her point, but there was nothing there. Just darkness.

"There's nothing there, Willow."

Yes, there is, I thought to myself. Because I felt it.

"Ma'am?"

"THERE—"

Shadows lunged out from between the trees and charged for us. I jumped in front of my friends and held my hands up as creatures as black as night sprinted through the glowing river. They had glowing blue eyes and fangs, but the rest of their bodies were solid black. They looked like bipedal wolves with giant heads. I glanced out of the corner of my eyes and found the forest was denser beside us, so these creatures were only coming from the front.

"Run to our left in five..." I growled and held my hands up high.

The wolf creatures were almost to the edge of the riverbed. I just had to time it right.

"Four..."

I pushed my magic and a cloud of golden glitter exploded in the air. The wolves hissed and shook their heads.

"Three...two..."

I lowered my arms and imagined myself picking up the ground with my fingers, then I thrust my arms forward. Thick tree roots shot up from the dirt and straight up into the tree branches above, forming a solid wall between us and them. The wolf creatures slammed into it at full speed. They howled and hissed as the trees shook.

"ONE! RUN!"

Savannah grabbed Willow's hand and dragged her into a run. Lily and I were hot on their heels, sprinting to our left down a narrow pathway cut into the forest. Up ahead in the distance, a neon-blue light shined through the trees in what seemed to be a clearing of some kind. I felt energy radiating from up above.

"Where...are we...going?" Savannah shouted between breaths.

"I have no idea! I've never been here!" I pushed off the ground and let my wings fly me in front of them. "Follow me. I'll scope it out. We need to find a village of civilians."

They nodded as they ran, all three of them holding hands and jumping over giant roots or fallen trees. I flew ahead. Not far, but I needed to find a direction to go in and my wings voted me the scout. A cold chill slid down my spine and then electricity tingled along the right side of my body—something slammed into my side.

I screamed as my body was thrown into the tree beside me. Pain laced through my back. My wings were pinned to the trunk, so my feet dangled twenty feet in the air. I tried to get loose, but the wooden staff was lodged in *just* the right spot. With a curse, I gripped my citrine bracelet and felt the familiar slide of golden body armor covering my upper body.

A male voice shouted, echoing through the trees—and then several more answered.

KNIGHTS. Had to be. The King would suspect we'd come.

Once my sword hilt hit my palm, I swung my blade up and right through the wooden staff. My wings popped free and I dropped straight down to the ground just as Knights in shining gold armor that perfectly matched mine swarmed in around me.

In the flash of a second, they had me surrounded.

Half of them carried long, vicious looking swords. The others had bow and arrows.

I was crouched down on one knee. My sword was in my hand, which just so happened to be hidden between long strands of neon-green grass. They raised their weapons higher. I raised the grass between us until it stood tall, halfway to their knees. They glanced down at the sudden greenery and scowled but didn't lower their weapons.

My fingers were pressed to the dirt, and I felt the ground respond to my touch. It was the craziest thing. Back home, I knew I could affect the earth, but not *like this.* Royce's face flashed in my mind, and I heard his voice screaming *Poison Roycy!* I suddenly knew how he felt, what this power felt like. I was Seelie, and this land wanted to do my bidding.

I glanced around the circle of Knights surrounding me and recognized every single one of their faces. These were the Knights who'd captured me in New York. These were *Riah's* Knights, and they wanted my blood. I felt it in their souls, in the deepest pits of their existences. Their souls sang the song of vengeance, and for once, we had something in common.

"Hello, boys. I believe we've met."

The Knight directly in front of me, about fifteen feet away, snarled. "I can't wait to tell Zachariah you made it this far only to die at our hands. It will comfort him as the final blow delivers his death."

I smiled. "I *am* Death."

I threw my hands straight up while pushing my magic. Vines covered in sharp golden thorns shot out of the ground at their feet and coiled around their weapons, snatching them right out of their hands. Metal crumbled and wood bows snapped.

I lunged forward with my sword in my hand. Three centuries of fighting made this easy for me. I swung my arm up and released my sword just as I'd been taught. My blade sank into the chest of the Knight in front of me. He gasped and flew back. Flowered vines covered his body in an instant, leaving only his face sticking out of the ground—*and my sword.*

Tree roots lifted off the ground and then slammed down on top of the other Knights, crushing them like bugs under their feet. Half of the Knights were still standing, but their eyes were watching the trees and not me.

"What's wrong, boys? Don't like the trees?"

My magic *sang* in my veins. It wanted more. And for the first time in my life, I was going to let it have more. I held my hands out and wiggled my fingers, searching for the souls once lost here. Life sprang under my touch. Just like back home, spirits rose from the ground in a foggy haze. They were blue on Earth, but here they were gold—just like my magic. *That has to be a sign, right?*

The handful of spirits that had risen all turned to me. I felt their fury and pain like it was my own.

The living Knights tried to move, but my vines had pinned them in place.

I grinned. "*My friends,* finish them."

Without hesitation, the glowing golden spirits pounced on the Knights. They screamed and grunted while I stood there feeling my desire for vengeance grow tenfold.

Silence fell around me.

The spirits rose, then turned back to me with expectant eyes.

"Thank you." I smiled. "Be at peace now."

There was a flash of light and then they were gone.

The only life still holding on came from beneath a patch of neon-colored wildflowers. I walked over and stopped beside it. That mouthy Knight who threatened to hurt my soulmate was dying. He had but a few moments left. I wasn't going to waste them.

I gripped my sword hilt and yanked my weapon free. He groaned in pain and blood filled his mouth. I leaned over and met his stare, then lowered the tip of my sword just above his throat. "His name is *Riah.*"

Red blood splashed in an arc as my sword sank into his flesh.

The old me would never have done this. The old me wasn't cold and ruthless. The old me didn't want to hurt *anyone.* I used to be a gentle soul. I used to care for the wellbeing of everyone. I used to use words over weapons, a smile over vitriol.

But the Seelie King had ruined me, and I planned on returning the favor.

With a satisfied smile and steel in my heart, I turned toward the path my friends had been on. "Girls? You can come out now. They're dead."

But there was only silence.

CHAPTER NINETEEN

AMELIA

It was impossible to tell time here.

The Seelie King had ordered his Knights to deliver me to his chambers what felt like days ago, though it could have only been hours – or even minutes. I hadn't gotten hungry or thirsty, I hadn't needed to use the restroom. I was trapped in a horrible vacuum where everything was lethally beautiful.

The Knights had basically thrown me in here and bolted, leaving me alone. My fingers and hands were sore from trying to smash the windows. There was no other way out. There was no other way *anywhere*. The room was a giant cylinder, I felt like I was inside of a tornado. The walls were made entirely of stained glass that were varying sized squares and shades of blue. It was entirely blue, from one end of the spectrum to the other.

164

Just like his hair.

My stomach turned and my pulse kicked back up.

He was coming back in here at some point and I still had no idea for an escape. There was a part of me that knew escaping the palace was a terrible idea because Goddess only knew what dangers lie out there...but I knew exactly what danger was coming for me if I stayed here.

The King may not have been human but his gaze was *all* male.

There was only one thing he wanted me for.

I gotta get out of here. Think, Amelia. There's an answer here somewhere.

I felt magic around me but it wasn't arcana magic, it was *fae* magic. I knew there had to be a door that was probably hidden in the blue glass walls. The only other door was at the very top of the room, which was at least three stories high but there was absolutely no way for me to get up there. It was just a ledge, like looking up at a cliffside from the base of a mountain. The Knights had flown but I didn't have wings. I'd spent the last *I didn't know how long* trying to create stairs with my magic but either my wand wasn't capable of doing that or I just didn't know the right spell.

My stomach turned again. Any second I was actually going to get sick. I rolled my wand between my fingers and scanned the room *again*. There was still only a single king-sized bed in the middle of the room with a fancy post at each corner that looked like was a living, breathing birch tree trunk. The bed and posts were white but the light coming in through the stained glass made everything look blue.

I refused to sit on the damn bed.

But if I didn't think of a way out I was going to be doing a lot worse than sitting on it.

Bile rose up my throat and I gagged. I bounced on the balls of my feet and spun in circles. *There HAS to be a door, right? A window at least?* I'd already fired every spell I could think of at the glass to break it yet it remained solid and strong.

Up above, the door opened with a click. I pulled my arms behind my back and hid my wand under my long blonde hair. There were heavy footsteps and then two Knights in golden armor and long swords peeked over the edge. Their eyes were cold and sharp. I raised my chin and met their stares.

They smirked and their gazes traveled up and down my body.

My stomach rolled.

Bright golden light spilled over the ledge at the top of the room.

The Knight on the left side turned toward the door and nodded. "She's ready for you, King Atzaran."

HE'S HERE.

I gasped and scurried back until I crashed into the frame of the bed. I heard the soft slide of a door followed by the click of it shutting...and then the flip of the lock that echoed around the room. My time was up. He was going to come down here and... and...I shuddered. And then I realized my wand was still in my hand. I couldn't let him find it. Even with my limited magic I knew having my wand would be my only chance at escaping.

Hide it. I dropped to my knees and turned toward the bed, the only piece of furniture in the room. Up above, the other Knight was saying something in their language to the King. I couldn't see him yet but I heard them use his name.

And his magic radiated all the way down to me, it made the hairs on my arms stand tall.

I had to stash my wand somewhere. There was only one option. I lifted the mattress just enough to slide my wand under it. Then I turned and sank down to the floor, pulling my knees into my chest. My heart sank.

OH GODDESS. PLEASE HELP ME.

I sucked in a deep breath and held it.

And then *he* appeared at the edge of the ledge and my breath left me in a rush. His long royal blue hair hung over the shoulders of his white robe-cloak-thingy. Even from a few floors up his eyes burned like fire flames, the orange color standing out in the sea of blue. He waved a ring-clad hand in front of him and then a staircase shot out from under the ledge and unfolded foot by foot in a circular pattern until it reached the bottom with a clang.

His eyes never left mine.

The only thing between him and me was this spiral staircase.

He rested his hand on the railing then strolled down the stairs. He was taunting me. We both knew he had wings but he *chose* to walk just to torture me, to draw out the moment. This was fun for him. A sick twisted little game. My legs twitched to move, to run, but I knew there was no use. This was the Seelie King *in Seelie*. I was prey. I was breakfast, lunch, dinner, *and* desert.

His eyes were locked on my face as he descended, his own face wore an emotionless mask but I felt the heat rolling off of him. His bare feet landed on the cold white stone floors of his room. I didn't move. I couldn't. I was stuck. My body felt numb and hazy. I should have been more scared, more angry, but as he sauntered toward me I had the sudden sinking suspicion that my calmness was *not* my choice. *He* was doing it.

He stopped about ten feet away and just stared at me in silence. He held his hand up and that spiral staircase curled in on itself and crawled back into its hiding spot under the ledge.

NO! The stairs may have been my only way out.

He arched one blue eyebrow. "Well, well, well..."

Stay calm. Maybe that's not what he wants. Maybe I misunderstood?

"Stand, child," he barked.

I jumped and crawled to my feet as quickly as possible but

my legs were shaking. *He said child. Maybe he wants to torture me for information and not —* I shuddered and his eyes *danced*. Like he was enjoying my fear.

His orange gaze slid down my body *very, very, VERY slowly*. On their way back up they lingered on the small stretch of skin showing between my black thigh high boots and mini plaid skirt. He pursed his lips and cocked his head to the side. "How old are you, child? In your silly little earthling mortality..."

Don't look weak but don't look too tough. "I'm twelve," I growled.

He pursed his lips and eyed my body *again*. But then a slow smile spread across his lips and my stomach flipped. "Not quite the prime age."

Before I could even *think*, royal blue magic the same color as his hair coiled around my entire body. My feet lifted off the ground. Warmth spread through my limbs but the cold air in the room felt like electricity against my skin. For a few moments I was lost in a blue tornado. Lights flashed and magic covered my entire body, tingling and humming in my ears.

The blue magic vanished faster than it came on and my bare feet touched the stone floor. *Wait, BARE FEET?* I'd had boots on. I looked down and choked on a scream. I stumbled backward until I crashed into the bed post.

The body I saw was not mine.

This was a *woman's* body. Not a twelve-year-old. I hadn't even hit puberty yet and he'd just made me skip it entirely. I froze. My whole body locked in place and my breath left me in a rush. I couldn't think. My mind was lost to the differences in my own body. *I have boobs!* And they were huge. I squealed but the sound didn't leave my mouth.

The only thing I recognized were my feet yet they were bigger than before. Gold chains wrapped around my ankles and covered the tops of my feet to connect around my middle toe. Diamonds hung from the chains like charms.

My legs were long like Emersyn's now and perfectly toned. I had hips that curved into a tiny little waist that didn't look any bigger than it was with my twelve-year-old body. This wasn't natural. I didn't look like this. No one in my family looked like this. My mother had died years ago but I remembered her and I had pictures. She was average height and square-shaped, no curves whatsoever. Yet here I was with a perfect hourglass frame.

My breath left me in a rush. I swayed and something brushed over my arms. I jumped, thinking it was *him*, but it was just my hair. My sandy blonde hair was now platinum and hanging all the way to my thighs in a sexy little wave girls spent hours trying to create with tools.

King Atzaran hummed with satisfaction.

"WHAT DID YOU DO TO ME?"

The King chuckled and the sound made my skin crawl. "I believe what *will* I do to you is the more pressing question..."

My jaw dropped. Everything inside of me went blank.

"You were a beautiful little earthling..." He gripped the lapel of his white robe with one hand then slowly pulled it open to reveal a muscular chest. He licked his lips. "I merely gave you the body I wanted to play with."

My stomach rolled. "Where...where are my clothes?" It wasn't important I just wanted to stall him to give my brain time to kick back into gear.

"You don't like what I've given you?" He arched one eyebrow then let his gaze linger on my body.

What he gave me. I clenched my teeth. What he gave me was a slutty Halloween costume or Coachella outfit. I now had on a little white crop top that barely covered the important parts of my new busty chest and let the bottom of them hang out. My new dragon *tattoo* that marked me as Maddox's soulmate was on full display and a giant slap in the face. Like salt to the wound. Right now Maddox looked like an angel in comparison.

A high-waisted skirt that was mostly see-through hung down to just below my knees with a slit cut literally all the way up to the waistband on one side. I had no undergarments on of any kind. It was just this luxuriously soft white material that was definitely the pretty cousin of cotton and body jewelry. Beneath my skirt, wrapped around my hips was a thin gold chain. A string of diamonds hung from that one and hugged my right thigh, wrapping the circumference of it tightly. Apparently the high slit required something sparkly.

Another gold chain dripping with diamonds coiled around my waist and hung over the top of the skirt. But the worst part was on my chest. It was like wearing a bikini top someone cut the material off of and left only the underwire. A string of diamonds hooked over my neck like a halter top then swooped down and around my back. Two strings of diamonds criss-crossed over my breasts and between my cleavage.

I wanted to cry and scream. A hot lump formed in my throat and tears stung my eyes.

But I couldn't let him win. I couldn't let him see just how much he was hurting me.

He cocked a sideways grin that made me scream in my mind. "Those hideous garments were not properly suited for my taste so I gave you something more...*delicious*. Not that you'll be needing them."

I took a step back and my head smacked into the bed post.

He chuckled and yanked on his robe. It dropped to the floor, leaving the King standing there naked wearing nothing but gold chains that crisscrossed over his body like a fence. I kept my eyes on his face. I didn't want to see that. I'd never seen a man naked before, I didn't want him to be my first.

My first...my words rocked through me like I'd been sucker punched. *OH NO.* I knew what he'd intended the moment he sent me to his room but apparently I'd somehow been in some

170

sort of denial until this very second. Or maybe my bravado was wearing off.

He prowled over to me like a tiger on the hunt then stopped directly in front of me until there was but an inch or two between our bodies. Heat radiated out of him like a furnace. He reached up with his right hand and ran his fingertips over my cheekbone...across my jaw to my chin. It took everything inside of me not to shudder and gag. He pushed my chin up, forcing my eyes up to his. He still towered over me with my face at his chest level. He eyed my mouth and licked his lips then slid his fingertips down my throat to the spot between my collarbones.

He made a little grunt that made my stomach turn and then his fingers traced a line down the center of my chest to where the strings of diamonds started. Every inch of my skin he touched turned cold, like my body wanted to freeze him out. He slipped his finger under the chain then ran the back of his finger between my new cleavage all the way down to the center of my stomach until he reached the waistband of the thin silky white skirt at my waist.

"I like you in chains," he purred.

I bit my cheek and shuddered. I didn't like the double implication there.

He leaned forward and chuckled right in my ear. "Enjoying this already? I haven't even started."

My lips trembled. This wasn't fair. I'd just wanted to go to Chutney and Willow's birthday party and now I was the five course meal for a predator. *Don't give up yet. You can think of something!*

His warm fingers traced that chain around my stomach as he moved to stand behind me. Tears pooled in my eyes. *Get to the bed, Amelia. Your wand is there. Try SOMETHING. Just get to the bed.*

His lips pressed to my skin behind my ear...and then he slid them down the side of my neck. His large hands landed on my arms, covering my biceps from shoulder to elbow. Even with this older body I was still a fraction of his size. He pressed his lips on the base of my throat. His teeth nibbled on my skin and a strangled cry slipped out from my clenched teeth.

Just bid your time. He's not going to do it right here standing up. There's a bed in here for a reason. Stay calm, keep your cool. Let him take you to the bed and then grab your wand.

His hands skimmed up over my shoulders. "I think you will only wear chains and diamonds from now on."

WHAT—

His fingers hooked under the silky straps of the top he'd put me in and yanked. There was a rip and then two pieces of soft white cotton flew out to either side of me. Cold air rushed over my now bare chest. I gasped and threw my arms up to cover myself but he caught my wrists and hugged them to my own chest. The breasts pressing against my own arms were foreign to me but it felt just as violating.

He chuckled in my ear again and it sent chills down my spine. "Don't worry, you'll be glad it's cold in here soon." He pulled my wrists and wrapped my arms around his neck, then forced my fingers to grab ahold of each other.

His large hands slid down my arms slowly. Bile rose up my throat but I swallowed it down. My bottom lip trembled. *Just get to the bed. Get to your wand.* I wasn't foolish enough to think I could overpower him physically. He was a full-grown male, and an *ancient* one...and I was twelve – or whatever I was now. I just had to play nice, pretend to submit to him...pretend to not fight back. That bed was only a few feet away. My wand was so close. I had absolutely no idea what I was going to do when I got it but I'd try *something*.

So I gripped my hands tight together. But this new position brought my body flush against his so I arched my back — and my ass pushed directly into *him*. I gasped.

He moaned then it turned into a deep satisfied laugh under

his breath. "I thought you'd like this. Fifteen is a much better age for you I see..." he whispered in my ear and rolled his hips, grinding himself against my ass.

NO, NO, NO! Every nerve ending in my body was screaming in panic.

His fingertips grazed down my arms and then took my chest in his hands. He squeezed and I whimpered. I tried to keep myself together. But I couldn't stop myself from squirming in his grip. At that he *laughed* and grabbed my waist, holding me in place. His hands were so big and his fingers were so long that his hands fully wrapped around my body. His fingers dipped under the waistband of my skirt and my heart stopped.

Oh no. NO, no. Tears rained down my cheeks. There was a small tug and then cold air rushed over the length of my body. A strangled cry left my lips before I could slam my mouth closed. My teeth rattled. My hands and arms were shaking against him.

He *purred* in my ear. "Don't you just love a little...anticipation?"

I can't do this.

I can't take this.

Please, Goddess, save me.

Somebody save me. PLEASE.

My legs were shaking so hard the diamonds hanging from the gold chains on my legs and feet were jingling. His hands returned to my waist except this time there wasn't a single ounce of fabric between his body and mine. It was just his skin pressed against mine and the cool brush of metal chains. I trembled from head-to-foot uncontrollably.

My stomach tightened into knots.

He moaned and slid his hands down to my hips then began to slide his fingers forward—

I gasped and yanked my arms down, swinging both elbows into his ribs like I'd been trained. *NOPE, NOPE, NOPE!* He grunted and hissed. I lunged away from him, diving for the side of the bed, but his large hands caught me by my arms and squeezed tight. His hands dug into my biceps as he lifted my feet off the ground.

"DON'T TOUCH ME!"

"*TOO LATE*," He growled and spun me around. "*And I've not even started.*"

The whole world spun in a sea of blue light. Pain shot up and down my arms. I screamed as loud as I could.

"*Go ahead, scream,*" he growled in my ear. "*I am King, this is MY world. No one is coming to save you.*"

A broken, shattered sob burst out of me. I couldn't hold it in any longer.

He snickered under his breath and *threw me.* I flew through the air and landed face down on the bed. I pushed up and scrambled for the edge to where I'd stashed my wand — he grabbed my ankle and yanked me back, flipping me over in one fluid pull. My back hit the bed and then he was there, kneeling between my legs. He was ready to take his sick game to the next level.

I panicked.

I thrust my leg up as fast and hard as I could and slammed my knee into his groin.

He bellowed in pain and released my leg to grab himself as he buckled over.

I threw myself to the side and dove for my wand. He was growling and cursing. The fury in his voice sent goosebumps over my whole body and made my hair stand tall. If he got ahold of me now – I shuddered just as my fingers gripped the thin piece of wood tucked under the mattress.

His hand slammed into my hip like a brick and I screamed out. His skin was painfully hot now. His long fingers dug into my bare skin. He snarled words in a language I didn't know but I heard the promise of pain in the sound. Everything was happening both in slow motion and hyper speed. I didn't have time to think. He yanked my hips back—I screamed and flicked my wrist back, firing magic from my wand. *DON'T TOUCH ME!*

He gasped and then his hands were gone.

I scrambled off the bed on all fours and crashed onto the stone floor. Pain shot up my arms and legs but I couldn't stop. He was already moving toward me. I rolled over and my eyes widened. He was wearing a straight jacket.

His fiery eyes were wide. He gracefully leapt off the bed in one fell swoop and charged for me. "*YOU!*"

I cursed and fired magic at his legs – *pencil skirt!*

A shimmery white mist coiled around his legs and yanked them together just as a black leather pencil skirt covered his lower half. But that wasn't good enough. He was too agile. I pictured what I wanted in my head and shot magic at his feet. Neon pink roller-skates covered his feet instantly.

I didn't celebrate. I was still *in here* with him. I scrambled to my feet and grabbed my skirt off the floor. *Think, Amelia, THINK!*

Behind me the King roared like a dinosaur. The walls shook and the glass windows rattled. My eyes widened. They *were* breakable. Hope flared in my chest. I gripped my wand and held it out in front of me as I sprinted for the wall of glass.

The King cursed and a wave of wild, hot energy hit my back. I gasped and glanced over my shoulder just as a ball of blue glowing magic flew right at my head. I threw myself on the ground — and his magic slammed into the wall. The blue stained-glass shattered into a million pieces in a massive circle that was twice the size of my body.

This is it.

This is my chance.

I had no idea what lay outside this room but I knew what was in store for me *here* if I didn't jump. He'd underestimated me once but after this he wouldn't do it again. I had to take this chance. I lunged to my feet faster than I expected I ever could and dove head-first out of the hole in the wall. Cold air rushed through my hair and over my bare body. I didn't scream, I didn't want anything to know I was coming...but down below was utter darkness.

Several stories down.

I was free-falling straight to my death.

There was nothing to break my fall. No trees to grab onto and I didn't have wings — *WINGS!* A crazy idea popped into my mind and I went for it. I flicked my wand at my own back and pictured wings. But not just *any* wings. Big golden wings like Tennessee's. I'd seen someone at Comic Con in Manhattan wearing them back in October. They'd looked so real.

I felt leather straps wrap around my shoulders and my waist — my body lurched back like something had grabbed ahold of me. I screamed. *THE KING!* He had wings, he must have gotten loose. I swung my arms back to fight back and my eyes widened.

They were MY wings.

They weren't gold like I'd pictured but snowy white that glistened in the moonlight. Feathers ruffled in the wind. They looked soft enough to touch. But more importantly, the caught the wind and gently carried me down into the darkness.

For a few moments everything was black. Hot air rushed over my body. And then my bare feet slammed into thick, wet mud. I stumbled forward a few feet but managed to catch myself before falling face-first into the mud.

"*Whoa, whoa, whoa...*" I froze with my arms out to the side and my legs steady while my balance caught on.

Way, *way* above my head I heard the King screaming out of the hole in his wall.

I cringed and braced myself but then the night fell silent. I looked up and found myself at the bottom of a very dark, deep, dense forest of some kind. There were so many thick tree branches stretching over my head that I could just barely make out the shape of a castle.

There was a chance he couldn't see me right where I stood but he knew exactly where I landed...and as he said this was *his* world. If he wanted to come down here and claim me he would. Which meant I needed to hide. The Coven was coming. I knew they would. I didn't think so highly of myself to assume they'd risk everything to enter Seelie for me or Landy.

But Bentley Bishop was here. His whole family were Cards. *He* was a Card. He was the Hierophant for Goddess's sake.

And then there was Riah.

That last second before we were pulled from the beach I'd seen Saffie's face. I saw the look in her eyes. They'd taken her soulmate. Coven aside, I knew with every fiber of my being that Saffie was coming. I just had to wait. I had to hide and stay alive until Saffie found me. Once I had her, together we could rescue the others.

I just have to hide.

In another realm.

I sighed and looked around me for the first time really. As I was falling I'd noticed it was dark out and the moon had been shining, but down here the air had that pale blue glow like just before sunrise. All of the trees were black and cast in shadows. The air was hot and stuffy, like that one time I'd gone in the sauna with Aunt Heather. My long thigh-length blonde hair clung to my body as sweat beaded across my skin.

A cold gust of wind slammed into my back. I gasped and stood up straighter. That was a whole lot of air on my skin. And then I remembered. The King had ripped my clothing off of me. My stomach turned and bile shot up my throat. This time, I couldn't stop it. I bent over and vomited. My whole body trembled. My skin felt clammy. And now my throat burned. I needed water. And shelter.

I looked down at my hand and realized I'd grabbed my skirt.

It took me a second to figure out which was the top but once I had it buttoned into place and covering my naked lower body I felt a little bit of relief. Not much, as the material was mostly transparent and the slit gave quite a show but it was better than naked.

My top on the other hand was definitely in pieces on the King's bedroom floor. And these strings of diamonds did not count as a top, they didn't even cover my breasts. *My breasts. I have boobs now. I'm TALL. Did he say I'm fifteen now?* Panic rushed through me.

"Calm down, Amelia. Calm. Down. Survival mode time. Panic and cry once we're home." I reached for my wand and gasped. It was gone. It'd been in my hand but now it was *gone*. "*No, no, no, no. This can't be happening!*"

I crouched down and scanned the ground but it was no use. It was too dark to see anything and my wand was the same color as the mud under my feet. After a few minutes I gave up. I'd have to wait until daylight and come back. I couldn't stay in the place the King saw me land, I wasn't that stupid.

That cold wind slid over my body again. I sighed with relief. I pulled my hair over my chest to cover myself then glanced around. There seemed to be a narrow, almost not visible trail cutting through the forest which meant I was at a fork in the road. There were two options – left or right. I peeked up through the branches to the castle. Left seemed to go closer to it and I didn't want to do that so I turned and hurried down to my right.

I walked for a little while in the dark when I heard the soft trickle of water. Without thinking, I sprinted toward it in a blind panic. The light shimmered a little brighter between two trees so I leapt through it — and slid to a stop.

A dark, marshy river sat before me. The water was flat and still, which didn't make sense for what I'd heard. But then the water rippled from between floating red leaves. I took a step back just as a woman rose from the water and glowing yellow eyes met mine. I froze.

Her skin was gray, with strange dark veins. Pointed ears stuck out through long black hair. Her yellow eyes had no pupil or iris. She grinned and I saw pointed teeth. "Another one."

CHAPTER TWENTY

DEACON

I WATCHED with dread as Saffie, Willow, Lily, and Savannah leapt through that purple shimmery mist and vanished. I closed my eyes. *Goddess, watch over them.*

Easton groaned, but it was a broken sob kind of sound. He spun way from the archway with bloodshot eyes and blood raining down his body. He raised his sword in his good hand and lunged for the closest alien freak monster.

Bentley bounced back and forth across the trail like a pinball on a warpath. Those fiery swords of ice sliced through the monsters like butter. Silas was in the back with half a dozen of them climbing him. He roared and shook his body, but with Chutney in his arms he was restricted.

Tenn was a few feet over from me but the fury and power radiating off of him was literally pushing me back so hard my feet were sliding through the dirt. *"There's too many!"*

He was right. There were too many. This forsaken forest was producing these things faster than a hydra regrowing heads. There were only a few of us uninjured and far too many unconscious for us to carry *and* fight.

I threw my hands out and shot my red lightning at everything that wasn't human. Each time I hit one, they'd freeze for a moment but never long enough. Emersyn stood beside me like a statue. The hypnosis I put her under was overpowering her magic, so I couldn't even make her use it without risking witch's shock for both of us. My stomach turned. I'd used too much on her. I put it on too strong. I'd panicked.

We gotta get out of here.

Tenn scoffed and stomped his foot. A wall of dirt shot up and tackled three monsters to the ground and then buried them. He turned to me with wide, panicked eyes. *Panicked eyes. Tenn.* That made my pulse skyrocket. Tegan was unconscious in his arms and full on white witch. Tenn lost his mind every time this happened. If we wanted his help, we needed to move fast.

"*Got any ideas, D?*" Tenn growled and buried more monsters under dirt.

Timothy cursed violently and dove into the shadow at the base of a tree. "HUNTER! OH GODDESS!"

Bentley flinched like he'd been slapped. He spun and raced toward the shadow his father had fallen into—and his face paled. "*Dad. Wait, wait—don't move!* TENN!"

Tennessee groaned and sprinted over. I followed after him before I realized I'd moved. For some reason I didn't really want to know about, Tenn wasn't moving faster than the rest of us. And I felt his anguish and panic over that too.

We slid to Bentley's side and I gasped.

Devon was just as unconscious as before. Their soulmate glyphs were both still red.

But Hunter's leg was royally fucked. It was one hundred percent broken, though it thankfully hadn't torn through the skin like Easton's arm. My stomach tightened into knots. I turned back and saw Easton's strength was fading.

SHIT! I took a deep breath, then pushed my magic out of me. The red mist slammed into the monsters and they all froze in place.

"Bentley, we gotta get out of here. NOW," Tennessee growled. "How?"

Bentley used his sword to point in the direction we'd come in. "The same way we came in. But as fast as possible. It won't want to let us out."

"Can we use our full magic now?"

Bentley's gaze snapped to me, and the orange crescents gave me chills. "As much as possible."

"Easton! Silas! COME HERE!" I called out, using my magic to get them to our side faster. When they were there, I looked around the group. "I'm not in charge here, but simple math and observation tell me we can't *all* be tied down with injured."

Timothy tugged on his hair. "We can't put them on Silas's back. He needs to be able to move without worry and with them not holding on—"

Tennessee cursed. "Silas, give me Chutney. Someone put her on my back."

"*Deacon...*" Bentley growled, his eyes on the forest.

I pushed more magic out. *STOP.*

Timothy took Chutney from his dragon arms and hoisted her onto Tenn's back. Tim carefully hooked her arms around his neck and her legs around his hips under Tegan's limp body. Magic flashed, then he nodded. "Let's see if that sticks."

An idea formed in my mind. I turned to Em and used my magic in my voice, *"Emersyn, climb on my back and hold on."*

Like a robot, she turned with emotionless gold eyes and immediately climbed onto my back and mimicked Chutney's positioning on Tenn.

Tenn nodded down to Tegan in his arms. "D, can you hold Devon?"

Not easily. "Absolutely. Hand her to me, Tim?"

It felt like this was taking forever but it was only a matter of seconds before I turned with Devon in my arms and found Lennox draped over Easton's good shoulder.

"This is gonna hurt..." Tim said softly and bent down.

Hunter screamed and his pained voice echoed through the trees. The monsters shook and my magic dropped. Those big black holes where eyes should have been stared at us. *And then they shrieked.* Mouths they hadn't just had suddenly opened wide to reveal five rows of sharply pointed gray teeth.

Bentley swung his swords at the ready. Silas reared back like he was ready to pounce.

That was it. Two fighters for all of us and all of *them.*

We were never going to make it.

"Fuck this." I summoned every ounce of magic inside of me, then pushed it out. Bright, neon-red mist exploded out of me and rolled into the monsters like a tsunami. *"Razzle dazzle time. RUN!"*

CHAPTER TWENTY-ONE

SAFFIE

I KNEW BETTER than to yell again, even though I wanted to scream their names until my voice went hoarse. I hurried over to the last place I'd seen them, yet they were nowhere in sight. It didn't make sense. I'd only been a little bit ahead. They'd been *right here.*

Where did they go?

Butterflies bounced around my stomach as fear gripped me. And guilt. If I had just stayed right with them...if I'd kept a closer eye...I groaned and pushed my hair back as I spun in circles looking for them. I'd felt a presence in the forest—that was the reason I'd gone ahead. If they'd been with me when the Knights arrived, they would not have gotten hurt, or kidnapped, or worse. That was why I hadn't looked to them once while the Knights were here.

I'd been protecting them.

Now I was alone.

I gently pushed my magic into the forest around me, but I knew they weren't there. I would recognize their souls in an instant. They would stand out in this world. The living creatures here felt different—foreign. There was a wildness in their spirit. I knew *that* and I'd only just gotten here.

The problem was...I didn't know here.

There was only so much research to be done on a different realm. *Dead men tell no tales, and all that.* But if my experiences in the Seelie tunnels taught me anything, it was that the rules we knew on Earth did not apply here. The people were different. The animals were different. Nature was different. *Life* was different. One wrong step and my friends trapped here would have no help coming.

I had to find Lily, Savannah, and Willow, but I had to find help first.

There was no knowing how many Knights had come out here with the squadron I'd killed. Nor did I know how long their disappearance would go unnoticed. When the King realized they hadn't returned, he would send twice the amount.

Because there was no way King Atzaran didn't expect someone from The Coven.

My stomach tightened into knots. Riah swore Thorne and Sage were on our side. Jackson had even confirmed he was telling the truth. But there was a chance they'd been playing Riah all along. Otherwise, why would they send him to be slaughtered? Why kidnap four other Earthlings?

Unless they—focus, Saffie.

I could loop all night about the *whys* and *what ifs* but that wouldn't help me find anyone. No, I needed help from someone *here.* Bentley had told us to find his friend Ziva. He'd given me a description of her, but I suspected this was hunting for a needle in a haystack. He said she had the ability to sneak out of the Wild Night, so I prayed I wouldn't have to go there to find her... but I didn't know where I *would* find her.

I cursed and pinched the bridge of my nose. Help was what I needed. The palace was out of the question, even if Thorne and Sage could be trusted. I had to seek the civilians—the people who hated their King more than I did. *Just gotta find them. No big deal.*

In every direction I looked, I saw only forest. My eyes would not serve me best here. I needed my magic to do the guiding. So I closed my eyes and just focused on what my magic felt. At first, I only caught the pulse of life in nature, but then I felt a buzz in the air...heard a little hum.

Fairyflies?! I opened my eyes yet still only darkness. I pursed my lips and thought back to when I'd first found *my* fairyfly friends in Salem. They'd been shy at the beginning. I'd had to sit out in the autumn leaves with them. I forced my gold armor to retreat back into my bracelet, even taking my sword. Then I sank to my knees in the cold dirt. The air was hot and thick, but luckily I'd lived through it for three centuries so I barely noticed.

I calmed my pulse by breathing slow, then I held my hands out and ran my fingers through the grass. *"I won't hurt you,"* I whispered.

The blades of grass swayed despite there being no breeze... and then little glowing blue orbs floated up off the ground. They fluttered and buzzed. They looked exactly like the fairyflies back home only *blue.*

I smiled. *"Hello friends,"* I whispered.

They all swarmed me. They flew around my arms and legs, circling my head. Some of them landed in my hair and on my hands. I giggled. A strange sense of comfort fell over me. I'd always been particularly attached to fairyflies.

"I need help," I whispered to them. *"Do you know where I can find someone I can trust? Someone nice?"*

The fairyflies flew in tight circles around my head so I jumped up. Once I was upright, they fluttered ahead of me, swirling in the air. I skipped to catch up to them and then we moved through the forest in comfortable silence. My own wings were weak from the wooden staff so I couldn't fly with them, but they didn't seem to mind.

For quite a few minutes, they led me through a forest with dark gray and black trees, where everything felt dingy and dark. Finally, they rounded a corner and my breath left me in a rush. The forest had parted just enough for a narrow pathway that led to a vibrant turquoise opening at the end. The trees that lined this path were a deep red while the leaves were a glittery gold and orange. These gorgeous leaves wrapped like vines around the tree trunks and clung to the branches. But they also covered the path's floor. It reminded me of an autumn day in Salem.

The fairyflies hovered near while they escorted me to help—and then they froze mid-air.

I stopped short. *"What is it?"*

The fairyflies shot over to me and coiled around my arms *and tugged.*

"Okay, show me."

They darted into the forest with me hot on their figurative heels. I was thrilled to see that this part of the forest matched the pretty colors of the trail, but as the fairyflies led me to the edge of a clearing, all that happiness vanished.

A Knight stood between two trees a few trees over with a bow and arrow in his hands and his aim focused across the little glassy pond. My body went cold. My friends' faces flashed in my mind. I turned to follow his stare—and gasped. It wasn't a person but an *animal.*

Except this was no creature I'd ever seen on Earth. It was majestic and beautiful. It was tall like a moose but with the body of a wolf that was covered in white fur. Tall, pale brown antlers perched on its head with red rose-like flowers covering them. This gorgeous creature had its mouth down to the pond while it drank. I wanted to run up to it and hug it.

And then I remembered the Knight.

Oh no.

He was hunting it. A bonfire of rage burned inside of me. Before I could stop myself or even think about it, I raised my hands to fire my magic into his back when a woman with long rainbow-colored hair lunged from between the trees and tackled the Knight.

I froze. *What in the hell?*

The Knight may have been surprised, but he recovered instantly. He was on his feet and lifting the woman off the ground *by the throat.* My eyes widened. His bow and arrow were on the ground, so he plucked a dagger off his belt and pressed the tip to the woman's throat. Blood trickled down her skin. She stared at him with wide green eyes but didn't cry. The Knight leaned in and growled in her face, taunting her.

I snarled and thrust my hand out toward him.

A sharpened piece of tree trunk soared through the air and slammed into his side, piercing through his rib cage. He screamed out and staggered. The woman fell to the ground. She held her own throat and coughed. The Knight spun and stumbled backwards until he crashed into a red tree trunk. His eyes met mine. I smirked, arched one eyebrow, then fired another piece of tree trunk right into his chest.

The woman jumped back up and turned to see who had saved her—and gasped.

My new blue fairyfly friends fluttered around my left side. I glanced over just as that majestic creature hopped out from behind a tree. It charged for me. I jumped and held my hands up, *and it licked my face.* I giggled and reached up to run my hands through its white fur and sighed at the softness of it.

"Oh, you're just a big fluffy puppy, aren't you?"

It looked at me with glowing pink eyes and I felt the relief and happiness in its soul—*her* soul. She licked my face again, then laid down at my feet with her fluffy tail wagging. The fairyflies flew over and landed on the red flowers growing from her antlers.

"You're a pretty girl, aren't yo—"

The leaves around me rustled and then a dozen of these same animals leapt out. Several of them rushed over to lick my face while others laid down at my feet beside the first one. I glanced across the pond to make sure there wasn't one there but there wasn't. She'd already found me. Their emotions swarmed me. The relief was overwhelming, *theirs* not mine. They were giddy and happy, yet there was a tinge of pain.

I frowned and took a closer look. That was when I noticed that the flowers on their antlers were beginning to wilt. My chest tightened. I didn't know why or what caused it, or if I could even fix it, but my hands flew up to the antlers closest to me to try anyway. My golden glittery magic gently slid from my hands and hugged the red wilting flowers. The animal, this one male, sighed like I'd given him cold water in the middle of a desert. I felt his soul smile as he lay down on the ground, the others watching him carefully.

My magic glistened bright for a few moments and then faded away, leaving perfectly red and thriving flowers. The others stared, then hurried over to me, lowering their heads so I could get to theirs.

I giggled and got to work. "Okay, okay, easy now. I'll get to everyone."

It was only as I was lowering my hands from the last pair of antlers that I heard a woman's voice say something in ancient Seelie. It was the woman who'd tackled the Knight to save the animal. She was speaking, but my entire attention was caught on her hair. It was remarkable. It fell in tight narrow ringlets down to her waist. The roots of her hair were red, blending to orange, yellow, blue, purple, and pink at the tips. It was a perfect rainbow. It made me think of Tegan's magic.

And then I remembered she was speaking to me, so I smiled. "I'm sorry. I do not speak your language."

Her light green eyes widened and stared at me, then she shook herself and cleared her throat. "They are sacred."

My eyes widened. My hands froze. "Oh no, did I do something wrong? Did I hurt them?"

She chuckled. "I think it is very clear they liked what you did quite a bit. They like you."

"They are beautiful," I said with a happy sigh. "Animals tend to like me, and I must say it is mutual."

She walked over and leaned against the tree beside me. There was a strange, reverent expression in her eyes that wasn't aimed at the animals. "They're called vakinyas."

"Well, I can see why they are sacred." Then I remembered that damn Knight. "Not surprised the King's men do not care for that."

"The King cares for the King," she scoffed. "I am Lukat."

I smiled at her. "I'm Saffie."

"That is a pretty name...you are not from here, are you?" She cocked her head to the side. "Yet you cannot be an Earthling...not with the way life is drawn to you."

"I am a half-breed. My father is Seelie. My mother is arcana—" I narrowed my eyes on her. "Do people here know about Earth?"

"Yes," she said with a sad sigh. "Our King teaches us of Earth and the realm he will control once Lilith wins the war."

My stomach tightened into knots. "*If* She wins."

Lukat grinned. "Why did you kill that Knight?"

My hands froze on the soft white fur. "He was going to kill all of us, so I beat him to it."

"Well, thank you for saving me and them," she said, gesturing to my new friends. "Since you are from Earth, and access here is most perilous, I assume you are in need of assistance...and I am going to give it to you. On behalf of myself *and them.*"

A small part of me worried this was a trap, that Lukat could not be trusted...but the bigger part of me knew I was never going to save anyone without help from the natives. And Riah didn't have that much time. I felt it through my soulmate mark, which meant Riah knew it too. *Can you feel me? Do you know that I'm here yet?*

"Saffie?"

I jumped and looked to her. "Sorry, I was thinking. Thank you. I could use help indeed."

Lukat removed her long teal, silky cloak and then wrapped it around my shoulders. The material was refreshingly cool in this heat. "It will be easier if you don't stick out too much. Come with me."

I nodded, then turned to my other new friends and pet their heads. "Okay, I'm going with her now. Be careful, pretties."

Then I spun and followed her in the opposite direction. Her long teal skirt flew up as she moved, like a cape in the wind. The leather corset and daggers strapped to her thighs made me realize this was no delicate flower. She was a combination of danger and beauty. Like everything here.

Lukat slowed so we could walk side-by-side, and I noticed the pretty red freckles covering her face. She whispered, *"It is best not to speak in these parts. I will lead you to the village."*

I nodded. Not talking was fine. It allowed me to focus on my other senses more.

With every step, Seelie was taking my breath away with its beauty. We walked around a tree that had to be twenty feet wide, and my jaw dropped. The trees had changed from a deep red to a bright vibrant purple the same shade as Tegan's hair. The leaves were neon-pink like Bettina's magic. They hung from branches and littered the ground. Some of the orange and golden leaves blew onto the pathway and the combination of them with the neon-pink was happiness for my eyeballs.

Up ahead the air was still turquoise. I wanted to ask her about that. And about the Sun. More specifically, where was it?

And the Moon for that matter. But she'd said no speaking, so I refrained.

We made a few twists and turns until we reached a fire burning all by itself—except the flames were a bright sky blue at the bottom and a light pink at the top. It was the prettiest fire I'd ever seen. I stood there and stared at it.

"*Saffie, this way,*" Lukat whispered and gently tugged on my sleeve.

I turned and followed her between two more of those massive purple trees. We stepped into a clearing and the lighting was darker and much, much more blue.

Which reminded me of my questions. "So, Lukat, where are the Sun and the Moon—*oh my Goddess.*"

She'd stepped aside and my eyes landed on a whole lot of incredible. Those massive trees we'd walked around towered like the buildings in New York. At the base of each one was a wooden staircase lit only by flickering orange flames. I craned my neck back and shook my head. *Amazing.* The wooden staircases hooked around the trees and connected with each other, making bridges between the trees high up in the air. There were little huts built into the trees, with large windows and glistening flames for light. Even from down here, I saw people walking to and from, crossing the bridges, flying from hut to hut, and just hanging out inside them.

It's like Lookout Tower but better.

"Wow." I blinked and glanced around as my eyes tried to soak it all in. I knew I was here with every intention of destroying all of Seelie, but this was extraordinary. It made me realize perhaps there were parts of Seelie that deserved to survive. I hoped this was one of those parts. I cleared my throat. "Why are they in the trees? And why so high? I mean, I know we fly—"

"Do you?" Lukat frowned. "Fly, I mean. I don't see wings."

"Oh, yeah. I have them." I half turned and summoned my wings to pop out. "See?"

Lukat's jaw dropped. "I do not think I have seen wings like that. They are beautiful. So they just come out when you will them to?"

"Thank you, and yes, don't yours?"

She shook her head and turned—and then I realized that her wings were small and perfectly camouflaged into her hair.

"Oh."

"Well, now that I know you have wings, let's fly since we're going to the top?" Her wings flapped and her feet left the ground.

"After you." My wings were still a little weak, but I wasn't about to let anyone else in on that information yet, not until I knew if she could be trusted. So I let myself fly slow while looking around.

"The Sun and the Moon are far, far, *far* above the trees," Lukat said suddenly. She pointed. "The Sun doesn't hurt us like the Unseelies, but our eyes are sensitive, so we do not like it. The trees protect us."

"Oh."

"And we live up high because the creatures that walk the land are lethal, just the way the King intended them to be."

I didn't get to process any of this information because at that moment we landed on a circular ledge almost all the way at the top of this tree-hut village. Green grass that reminded me of Earth covered the floor of the ledge, and I wished I could wiggle my toes in it. Long strands of flowers hung from what looked like a wisteria tree but probably wasn't. There were little white glowing orbs hanging with them and swaying in a refreshingly cool breeze.

To my right, nestled against a tree-side, was a bookcase filled with massive books in glorious colors. On the left, there was one of those huts with large peaked windows and warm light spilling out. In the back, I spotted what looked like balcony railings. In front of me, nestled in the middle of the paradise, was a long pile of pillows and cushions.

I sighed and smiled.

I'd never realized Seelie could be so beautiful. I'd only pictured nightmares.

"Oh, oh, she's here!" An elder man with orange, oversized pointed ears and wild blue hair bounced in excitement. He sprinted away shouting, "Lloyd! Lloyd!"

I watched the short, elder man hobble around a corner, then I turned back to Lukat and my eyes widened. We were no longer alone. There were five other pointy-eared people standing by the cushions silently with their hands clasped in front of them. Almost like soldiers.

"Oh...hi...?" I glanced to Lukat.

She grimaced. "Sorry to startle you. These are my friends. Introduce yourselves."

"Hello," the one on the left said with a wide smile. He was a young male who looked like a walking bush. He had pale green skin and big dark green eyes. His wings, hair, and clothes seemed to be made entirely of leaves and flowers—I wasn't sure if this was an outfit or if he was born that way, but I wasn't going to ask. "I am Monek."

"And I am Rio," the fierce-looking female beside him said with a single nod. She had long hair that was such a dark plum purple it was almost black. Her skin held a beautiful olive tint and her dark eyes had sharp upward angles. She wore a long dress that matched her hair and golden bracelets that stretched from wrist to elbow. Two massive red lizards were hanging from oversized pockets in her dress, just watching the way her pale orange wings fluttered behind her. "These are Sol and Sal."

A petite female with glowing hair the color of cotton candy giggled. Her hair was tied in low pigtails on each side of her head. A red ring of flowers sat on top of her head like a crown.

She looked up with dark blue eyes and smiled. "I am Nexus." She waved and the motion made shimmery dark blue wings flap behind her back.

I turned to the last female and found she was the most strikingly pretty. Her hair was as white as snow, and it fell all the way to the floor. The fact that her eyebrows were black and her eyes were silver made her look dangerous. Where Lukat's *hair* was a rainbow, this girl's *body* was. Her feet were a soft purple that blended into a blue around her knees and then a green by her hips and up under her silvery dress. Her hands were a soft red that faded up to yellow shoulders. By the time the color worked its way to her face, it was as white as her hair. There was some kind of netting material draped over her arms and her legs that had colorful little flowers knitted into them.

"I usually get this reaction from young children. They always ask why my wings are only white." She smirked. "I am Glisa."

I blinked and waved. "I'm Saffie."

"I'd like you to meet The Circle," Lukat said softly and gestured toward the fairies I'd just met. "I sent them a secret message when we got to the village. We move fast."

I frowned as alarms went off in my head. "Wait, *what?*"

"So, this is why we were summoned," a deep male voice rumbled from my right side.

He stopped about ten feet away and nodded. Compared to the others, he looked almost human—despite the sharply pointed ears. But his skin tone wasn't much different than mine and his blue-green eyes could have been seen as human. His hair was almost black. He was tall and built like a Knight, or maybe that was the way he carried himself. His clothes looked like armor but made in shimmery dark gold fabric that was just cut to emulate armor. His wings were a dark gold. I did not miss the bow and arrows strapped to him.

But I *really* did not miss the gold lines on his face.

He had a soulmate.

I was so overwhelmed by all of their appearances that my brain was working slower. "*Wait*, why were you summoned? Who are you, besides your names?"

"This is Saffie," Lukat said and pointed to me. She then gestured to him. "He is Lloyd."

"And you summoned all of them here." I narrowed my eyes. "Why?"

"Because of the prophecy," Lloyd said softly.

"Excuse me?" The hairs on the back of my neck stood tall. "What?"

"Please sit and I will explain." He gestured to the pillows and cushions in front of me. When I looked, I found the other four had already sat down. "No need to waste energy while we speak."

I took a deep breath, then let it out. I knew the rumors about not eating and drinking in Seelie were just that, rumors. Just like their supposed aversion to iron. Still, it felt wrong to sit and chat while my friends needed me...but I could not do it alone.

And he said prophecy. That has to be important.

I nodded and joined the others, sitting on a surprisingly soft pillow. "Okay, I'm ready to listen. Please?"

Lukat cleared her throat. "First of all, may I inquire your age?"

"Three hundred and forty-two." Ever since I'd lost my memory and got it back, my own age blew my mind. I couldn't believe I'd been alive so long.

The others glanced to each other and then turned back to me.

"What?"

"We are The Circle. There are a few of us not present because I summoned at the last minute." Lukat smiled. She probably meant for it to be reassuring, but it wasn't. "Six hundred years ago, when Earth's war with Lilith ended, King

Atzaran went on a warpath here. He blamed us for Lilith's demise. Our already dreadful living conditions worsened, which is when we moved to only living in the trees."

My stomach tightened into knots. I already didn't like where this was headed.

"A short time after, the King's Seer entrusted a small group of us with a secret. She called us The Circle."

"What was the secret?"

"The prophecy," Lloyd said with an exhale. "The Seer, I believe earthlings would call her a psychic...well, she gave to us a prophecy that speaks of a single person who would bring down King Atzaran and save our world from his terror."

My breath left me in a rush. I was worried that was the prophecy they'd tell me. I'd never heard of it, but I wasn't surprised it was about overthrowing the King. "And why do you trust this Seer if she works for the King?"

Lukat growled. "King Atzaran is a brutal, monstrous creature. The Seer stays close to stay alive. She is the only Seer in this realm. The King had the others killed during the war."

Lloyd nodded. "And this Seer had two sons. The first was a traitor to our King in the war. His name was *Malachi*."

I gasped but no one noticed.

Lloyd continued, "The second has been Prince Thorne's right hand, his most trusted Commander. And he has just been sentenced to death for being as much a traitor as his brother. His name is—

"*Riah.*" My eyes burned and my chest tightened.

They gasped and sat up straight.

Rio narrowed her dark eyes. Sal and Sol flicked their forked tongues at me. "How did you know?"

I wanted to tell them, but there was one thing I had to ask first, just to be sure. "What do you think of this Seer and her two traitorous sons?"

Lloyd frowned and shook his head. "Commander Zachariah

has been in the dungeon for days. *We* have managed to stall his death. We're trying to rescue him, but we lack the numbers to combat the King."

"Malachi and Zachariah were good to us, even as Knights." Lukat gestured around us. "They went behind the crown's backs and aided us, built this secret meeting place for us. We mourn Malachi's death every day. That is why this prophecy is so important. The Seer said this person would save Zachariah—"

"We don't know that it means *him*," Nexus cried, twirling her pink hair around her fingers.

I do. I didn't even know what it said yet, and I knew with every fiber of my being it meant Riah...and the way they were looking at me, it made me wonder if they thought *I* was their savior. I wasn't sure what I felt about that.

I licked my lips and tried to act natural. "What does this prophecy say?"

Monek flew over to the wall of books nestled into the and tree then came back carrying a large purple one in his green hands. "Here, Lloyd. You read it to her."

Lloyd nodded, then flipped through the pages to where a gold ribbon was saving a page. When he opened the book, a soft golden light shined on his face. His fingers ran over the page in a gentle caress. He licked his lips and swallowed hard. "You should know, the Seer entrusted only a number of us and swore us to secrecy. We have told no others, for she warned us of imminent death if we did."

I pursed my lips and nodded. *Typical.*

Glisa was watching me with her sharp silver eyes. "How many prophecies have you heard before this? You do not seem frightened or alarmed."

My heart sank. "Where I come from, we have had many. Some have come to pass...others we still await."

They exchanged nervous glances.

Then Glisa leaned forward and her long white hair coiled in

front of her like a snake. "We are trusting you with our biggest secret."

"I do not know what you're about to tell me, or if I can be of any assistance." I sighed and crossed my legs under me. "But I swear on a sea of spider lilies that if I can help you kill King Atzaran, I will."

Their eyes widened.

"*She knows how we make oaths,*" Monek hissed to Nexus.

Lukat grinned. "Lloyd, read it to her. Let her know as we do."

"It is long, so prepare thyself and listen in completion before speaking." Lloyd's blue-green eyes were pleading with me to believe them, to trust them.

Or maybe I just felt it in his soul so strong that it showed in his eyes. Soul sensing as the Death Card was super overwhelming sometimes.

"I am ready." *Am I though? I'm not so sure.*

"*On the turn the tide shall carry, a blessed soul whose fire won't tarry,*" Lloyd chanted softly, his voice thick with excitement. "*She brings in hand a foreign power, for at her will, all life will flower.*"

All of them glanced quickly to me and then to Lloyd.

In the words of Deacon, I do not like the sound of this, I thought to myself.

But Lloyd continued on. "*With wings that sparkle like the stars, she'll burn it down to heal your scars. Watch the sacred for they shall know, to fall at her feet and heart to show. Marked in green then red to follow, gold hearted lines are not hollow. For by the throne a lie is hiding, between the lines their word is guiding.*"

The others leaned forward like this was also their first time hearing it, even though I knew it wasn't. Their souls were scared and tired—and desperate for help.

"*A cautious, careful, certain task, kills the first but not their mask. Strapped in gold his path his true, creation's son is over-due,*" Lloyd's voice grew softer, like this part was harder to say. "*Bound are the hands of healing touch, whose soul is tied to this glittered crutch.*"

My eyes widened. *RIAH.* My pulse pounded in my chest. *I knew it. I KNEW IT.* That had to be about him. He had the healing touch and his soul was tied to mine—and I glittered.

Lloyd didn't notice my panic, so he kept on. "*Wait for the night his life is thin, release him from his cage of sin. When crimson flashes by her hand, raise arms together, make your stand. To end this era you'll have to fight, stand your ground and hold it tight.*"

In the words of Jackson, bloody hell.

All of their eyes shot to me and stayed.

"*But lean on her and hear her plea,*" Lloyd said slowly. "*For if you do, she'll set you free.*"

I couldn't speak. I couldn't breathe. There were too many thoughts in my mind. Too many things to unfold in one prophecy. It was intricately detailed yet vague enough to mislead.

But they were all staring at me.

Watching.

Waiting.

I opened my mouth and then shut it. I cleared my throat, then tried again. "May I see it?"

Lloyd slid the book over to sit in front of me on the grass.

I leaned over and read the words for myself as a knot formed in my stomach. "And you believe this prophecy is about—"

"*You,*" they all said in perfect unison without hesitation.

I blinked and then nodded. "There is no suggestion of time in here. This could be any time, yet you seemed to be expecting me—"

"We know the war with Lilith is upon us. Could be any day." Lloyd sighed. "The King warns us—well, perhaps more like threatens us—daily. We believe *on the turn* means the turn of the new war."

I hate that I thought that too.

"The sacred refers to the vakinya." Nexus imitated antlers with her hands. "You saw them, yes?"

Lukat leaned over me and tapped beside one of the lines. "*Watch the sacred for they shall know.* The sacred animals chose you. They literally fell at your feet in the meadow. I saw."

My jaw dropped.

Glisa held one finger up. "Let us go through this one line at a time then? *She brings in hand a foreign power, for at her will, all life will flower.* Does she have foreign power?"

I cursed and held my hands out in front of me. Golden glitter sprinkled down to the grass and neon-colored flowers instantly popped up. The grass brightened and turned soft. *All life will flower...can that have a double meaning?* I was Death. That line could be about that, too. *Ah shit. Is this about me?*

"I understand, Saffie. I was not totally sure myself at first. I feared I wanted to believe it was you more than my observations found." Lukat tapped on my shoulder. "But then I saw your wings. Show them?"

I pushed my wings and they gasped.

It was only then that I realized none of their wings looked like *mine.* I'd always assumed the fae in Seelie would have wings like mine, at least some of them...but I'd yet to see any. Sure, I'd only met a few Seelies so far, but all of their wings seemed to be made of the same essence. They were shimmery and pale-colored and held the same basic shapes with minor variations. They looked like fairyfly wings—besides Monek.

"Have you never seen wings like mine?" I heard myself ask.

Their eyes were latched on my wings. They shook their heads.

My breath left me in a rush. With wings like the stars— that'd always been how we referred to them. Like little constellations on my back. I was born with these. Sure, they came out at will, but it was always *these*. At least until Prince Thorne cursed me—*OH MY GODDESS*. My heart stopped. Prince Thorne cursed me. Had he known about this prophecy? *Wait a second*. Riah himself told me his mother was Thorne's girl-friend. The King's Seer, the *only* Seer, was the Prince's girl.

For by the throne a lie is hiding, between the lines their word is guiding. The world spun around me as the missing pieces to the puzzle threatened to fall into place. Riah insisted Thorne and Sage were against the King. Those lines would suggest the same. *Kills the first but not their mask*. Malachi had to help the Coven in the war and it killed him, while Riah went on to be the spy. Butterflies danced in my stomach and a cold chill slid down my spine.

Holy shit. Is THIS why Thorne cursed me? Was helping The Coven with Cronos just a convenient cover? Was it really all about this prophecy? I didn't want to believe it, but the evidence was overwhelming.

I sighed and scrubbed my face and everyone gasped. I dropped my hands.

Glisa pointed to my right hand. "*Marked in green then red to follow.*"

"*Gold hearted lines are not hollow.*" Rio reached over and yanked the sleeve of my borrowed cloak up. "Look at her arm and her face."

"*Whose soul is tied...glittered crutch.*" Lloyd pointed to his face with gold lines. "You have a soulmate and your magic is glittery."

Monek frowned and tapped on his right hand. "Who is it? Your soulmate. Is he here?"

Glisa nodded. "He's in the King's dungeon."

The others turned to her.

She shrugged. "*Bound are the hands* and *release him from his cage of sin?* It has to be Zachariah."

"*Riah*," I breathed. "He likes to be called Riah."

They stared at me with wide eyes.

I nodded. "Riah is my soulmate. I came here to rescue him."

"Saffie?" Rio cocked her head to the side. "In Seelie, soulmates are marked only by the gold lines. What is this green crystal?"

I pulled my cloak aside and showed them the matching crystal on my chest. "I am half arcana. For that side of my bloodline, soulmates are marked with these glyphs. Once the ritual is completed, these glyphs turn colors to reflect emotions and warnings. Green means that his heart is racing. He is unwell and unsettled. He is in danger."

"*Marked in green then red to follow,*" Lukat whispered.

"Red means imminent life-threatening danger."

Nexus's face paled. "And when it flashes?"

Rio arched one eyebrow. "We fight."

My heart sank. This was too much. I was still coming to terms with everything I'd learned from Riah since my curse was broken. But this...this was too much.

"Saffie, can't you see it?" Lloyd leaned forward and squeezed my hand. "You are the prophesied one. You are the one to save us from the King."

I wanted to say I wasn't. I wanted to insist that that role belonged to someone else. Someone more worthy. Someone more prepared. Yet I couldn't. The evidence was too clear.

"An Earthling is our savior..." Glisa shook her head. "We should have suspected as much."

"Why are you here, Saffie? Why did you come? You could have died coming here."

"*Monek,*" Nexus hissed and swatted at him. "Her soulmate was taken. She came for *him*."

"I did come for Riah, but not just for him. They took others with him. So, we came to rescue them—"

"We?"

"Them?"

"Yes, I came with three friends. Willow, Lily, and Savannah." I grimaced. "We were separated right before Lukat found me. I need to collect all of them now."

Lloyd pursed his lips and tapped his fingers on the book. "Your other friends here are a young boy, two young girls, and a female with a thick accent?"

I gasped. "YES! Did you see them?"

"I am a member of Court, so I was there when they came in. The boy was discarded by Princess Sage. The female with the accent fed to the beast..." Lloyd's expression darkened and his voice dropped lower. "Then the dark haired young female went with the Queen, and the female with hair like sunshine was sent to be a toy for the King."

My stomach rolled. Rage rushed through my veins. *A TOY?* Golden glitter burst from my hands. I cursed and tried to reign my anger back in. I had to stay calm to think clearly. "The boy's name is Bentley. He was sent to the Wild Night. I know this because we were able to get him out and he taught us how to get back in to rescue the others. Paulina, Landy, and Amelia—I have to hope they're still alive."

Lloyd nodded and rubbed his hands together. "We can help you."

"Bentley told me to find someone named Ziva—"

Lukat grinned. "We know Ziva. She's one of us. She's in the Wild Night, but I can take you to her. And then we can find your friends."

I jumped to my feet. "Bring me to Ziva."

CHAPTER TWENTY-TWO

LILY

WELL, AINT' this some shit.

I sighed and pushed my hair back out of my face. Again. We weren't more than twenty minutes inside Seelie, and we'd already gotten separated. I didn't even know *how* it happened. The three of us had been holding hands, with Willow in the middle so we could be her eyes, and we were running below Saffie. She'd been right there above our heads.

Then *bam!* She was gone.

No warning. No indication. And no sight of her now. Or any of them.

There was no point in yelling their names, my voice was gone. I spun around in a circle yet found only darkness. The fae didn't like Earth Sun. I remembered Tenn saying that before. But I didn't want to play my cards too soon. I didn't want a Knight to see foreign sunlight and come running. For once, I wanted the cover of night.

I ducked behind a tree so that I'd blend into the shadows around me, then I pushed my magic out to feel for them. It was invisible. No one could see this little trick Cards could do, but it was convenient to say the least. Coven power was almost impossible to miss as a fellow Card, especially if you were looking for it. Civilian arcana's magic felt like a sunny day in early New England fall. Warm and strong, but not intense or overwhelming. Coven magic was mid-day cloudless skies in the heart of summer in Florida. It smacked you in the face. Some more than others. Willow's was subtle, as was the art of the Magician's illusions. But Saffie's was one of the strongest, even more so than Paulina's was before sacrificing her Mark.

Saffie's magic was like that tickle in the back of your throat you couldn't itch. There was no missing her as a fellow Card.

And yet I felt nothing.

No Willow.

No Saffie.

Savannah was a civilian. Those were easier to miss but I knew her well now. I'd been around her plenty. Her aura was intense and dark. It should have been thriving in these conditions, but I couldn't find her.

The only magic I felt was up ahead. It was faint and unfamiliar.

I'd been walking toward it for a few moments, yet it hadn't moved, which meant the person was injured or it wasn't a person. It was the only lead I had so I was going for it. I walked a little farther, ducking between trees, until I felt a wall of subtle, humming magic wash over me. I crouched down and narrowed my eyes, trying to see through the dark.

There was something up ahead, some form of structure. I summoned a small patch of light in my hand, then directed it forward. The air shimmered like glitter was floating through it—and then I saw it. A structure that looked like a smaller version of the Washington Monument. The tall, narrow, rectangular pillar had a pointed top that seemed to emit streams of magic. Down the center of the structure, six runes glowed in lime green. I didn't know the symbols, but I knew they were Seelie language. At the base of this phallic structure were a few stone steps with vines covering them and a small patch of golden light...and *magic*.

I glanced left and right to make sure I was alone. Then I sprinted for it. As soon as my feet grazed that light, a rope shot out and caught my ankles, then yanked me backwards. I screamed soundlessly and my back slammed into the dirt.

A woman stood in the shadows holding a rope in her hands —no, *a whip*.

She snarled and barked words at me in their language that I didn't speak. When I didn't answer, she stepped out from the shadow, the light from the lime green runes illuminating her body. She wore armor like the Knights but hers was black and covered her entire body, which I suspected was intentionally designed so she'd blend into the darkness. She snarled again in Seelie.

I grimaced and glanced down at the rope around my ankles. My dagger was in my boot. I wondered if I could get to it before she used one of the weapons hanging from her body. I was quick but not *that* quick. And not with this whip coiled around my ankles. *Maybe she'll set me aside like this and I can cut myself free then.*

She yanked on the rope and dragged me closer. Once my entire body was drenched in that green light, she sighed and shook her head. "Basel!" she shouted off to the side.

A male voice echoed from somewhere within the forest.

The woman glared at me. "New entry," she said with a growl.

"Half-breed or import?" he yelled back.

"Import."

Import? What does that mean?

The woman looked me up and down. "Drop off. Mark her now, then resume at dawn."

My pulse quickened. Something was about to happen that I knew I was not going to like. But before I could guess or figure out an escape plan, the woman turned—*and hauled me with her.* The whip squeezed my ankles so tight it sliced into my skin even through my boots. My back dragged along the dirt through the darkness. Rocks, sticks, and tree roots sliced into my skin. I hissed in pain, but no sound came out.

A hazy green light flashed up ahead where the pathway turned to the right. After the turn, I saw a man who looked like the actual Hulk standing there watching us. Two swords half the size of my body were strapped to his back. He shouted something to the woman dragging me and my heart stopped. That had to be Basel. The one who was going to mark me and resume at dawn—whatever that meant. *Don't think about that. You'll be gone before dawn. You'll escape.* I squeezed my eyes shut and concentrated on breathing and keeping my magic at bay.

There were two heavily armed Seelies and *me.* I was outnumbered. I wasn't foolish enough to assume there weren't more of them or that I could take them on my own. The two of them carried out a conversation and the snarls in their voices told me it was about me. *Play possum. Look weak.*

All of a sudden something wrapped around both of my wrists and I was pulled up off the ground. I opened my eyes just as fairy-Hulk stepped in front of me holding a tall crystal staff. He aimed it at my body and growled out words in Seelie. Green magic shot toward me. I sucked in a deep breath and braced myself. Ice-cold air slammed into my chest and then slid down over my legs.

I thrashed against whatever was holding me, Suddenly my clothes vanished. Instead of jeans and a long-sleeved shirt, I now wore a silky little gray dress that only hooked at the back of my neck and at each hip—that was it. There wasn't even a back to it. I was lucky my ass was covered. *What is it with the fae and nakedness?* I'd always assumed that was some rumor perpetuated by thirsty dudes but evidently not.

The woman snarled and yanked on the whip holding my

feet and my body was thrown face-first onto a stone slab. My cheek hit the cold surface and pain radiated through my head. I grunted but no sound came out. Black dots danced in my vision. Out of the corner of my eye, I watched a giant pink flower bigger than my car drop out of the sky like a UFO.

What the—

"Basel—" the woman snapped, then spit out words in Seelie.

He grunted back at her and flicked that crystal staff around.

The UFO-flower lit up like the Sun and my heart stopped. *OH NO. What is THAT?* I tried to ask, but my voice was still missing in action. I had no idea what was pinning my wrists down. It felt like concrete. No matter how hard I tugged they didn't budge. If I let my power out now, they could just kill me instead. I had no idea what their intentions were, but I didn't think it was immediate death—what with changing my clothes and all.

Dozens of glowing vines dropped out of the UFO-flower, looking like those crazy swing rides at carnivals. My heart skipped beats, then sent my pulse flying. My stomach tightened into knots. Each of the glowing vines had little Venus fly trap looking teeth things at the ends and they were headed right for me.

I closed my eyes, sucked in a deep breath, then clenched my teeth and braced myself.

But when those teeth things touched my skin, it was like being electrocuted. My eyes flew open on their own. Heat wrapped around my arms, across my shoulder blades, and down my back. My breath left me in a rush and my eyes watered. Every nerve ending in my body burned and tingled. Light flashed around me—and then it was over.

The heat, the pain, and the light were all gone. I sucked in ragged breaths of air. The woman's whip slid off my ankles. Whatever was holding me down lifted me up and then flung me into the darkness of the forest. I tried to scream but there was nothing, not a single sound. Cold air washed over me, rushing through my hair and over my bare back.

Everything was pitch-black, so I had no idea the ground was there until I belly-flopped into it. I coughed and a cloud of dirt exploded around me.

Basel yelled something.

And then there was silence.

I laid there, face-down in the cold dirt, just breathing for several moments. Something had just happened to me. They branded me for *something* and I didn't want to know what, which meant I had to be out of here by dawn. I pushed my magic out to see if by some stroke of luck Saffie, Savannah, or Willow were nearby, but nothing happened. I couldn't feel *anything*.

I was numb.

I scrambled up to my knees and glanced around. There was nothing in sight. It wasn't as pitch-black as I thought, but the only light was coming off of that phallic structure with the runes on it and *that* had to be a hundred feet away or more. The woman had snuck up on me before, so I had no idea if she was lurking somewhere watching, but there was only one way to find out.

Come on, Sun. Don't let me down.

I summoned my magic inside of me and almost cried as I felt that familiar tug of power in my gut. It was still there. This was a good sign. It wasn't full strength or even half. What should have been a bright yellow was a faint, hazy white. But it was light nonetheless. I held my hands up by my shoulders and pushed the light brighter—

Dozens of glowing eyes lit up all around me.

I gasped and fell back on my ass.

"Don't scream!" a young guy whisper-shouted. The dark bushes on my left rustled and then a *very* human-looking boy with sandy blond hair crawled out. He held both hands up and

stopped a few feet away, sitting on his knees like I'd been. "It's okay, we won't hurt you. Please just don't scream or they'll come."

I blinked and stared at him. *Who are you? WHAT are you?*

He smiled and it made the scar on his cheek stand out. "The marking is a bit jarring, but it won't hurt you now that it's on."

"Yeah, but *they* will," another guy hissed.

I looked to my right toward the new voice just as all of those glowing eyes moved into the little clearing I'd been tossed to. I glanced left and right, scanning each face. They all looked completely human, and it sent a chill down my spine. *Is this a fae trick? Some glamour or illusion? Why do they have humans? Where did they get them?*

"I'm Bobby," the first guy said and tapped on his chest.

"I'm Matt."

"Anthony."

"Cassidy."

"Kaitlynn."

"Trevor."

Names were being thrown at me left and right. I couldn't keep up. I could barely even tell who'd spoken. As each second passed, more of these people emerged from the forest. Each one looked as human as the others. Their eyes glowed but that could have just been a product of Seelie.

"*Guys, guys, guys!*" a soft feminine voice hissed from above us. "Lord have mercy."

I frowned. *Was that a southern accent?* I looked up and saw there was a girl perched on a tree branch with long dark hair and gray skin—*gray skin?*

"What?" Bobby asked up to her. I only remembered his name because he'd been first. "We're welcoming her."

The girl in the tree scoffed and jumped down. She landed gracefully on her feet at the base of the tree and then skipped over. She couldn't have been more than five feet tall, give or take. But as she sank to her knees in front of me and my magic illuminated her, I realized she wasn't gray at all. She wasn't even dark. That long hair was a soft sunny blonde that fell in loose waves. She had big green eyes on her little heart-shaped face. Her eyebrows were almost as dark as mine, like maybe she bleached her hair light. In the light of my magic, her skin was a shimmery pinkish-white tone.

She grinned and waved at me. "Hi. You okay?"

I exhaled and shrugged.

"Yeah, stupid question, right?" She rolled her eyes at herself. "I'm Bridgett, by the way. What's your name?"

My shoulders dropped. Of all the times to lose my voice.

Lily, I mouthed.

Bridgett frowned and leaned forward. "What was that?"

I sighed. It was too dark to read my lips and I didn't have a writing utensil, though there was definitely nothing to write *on.* I laughed to myself and raised my hands, then signed my name. *L-I-L-Y.*

Bridgett's eyes widened as she gasped. *"Is that American Sign Language?"*

My jaw dropped. *Holy shit.* I nodded and signed, *YES.*

She giggled and signed back to me, *I KNOW ASL.*

Traitor tears stung my eyes.

"You can hear us though, right?"

YES.

"Cool. That's good at least. *Y'all, she can't talk so move in closer and back off.* I'll translate what she says."

I snorted. She was definitely southern, but her accent was nowhere near as thick as Savannah's. *I wonder if she'll say ma'am soon?*

Bridgett's eyes sparkled with excitement. "Hi, Lily. So don't worry, none of us are going to hurt you. We're all in the same boat here. It's shitty and sinking, but we're going down together."

I frowned and signed, *WHERE ARE WE?*

I'd never been more thankful I'd learned American Sign Language. Easton knew it. He'd said, *how can the Lovers Card not be able to speak to everyone?* It was adorably sweet, and the only other language besides English and Arcana that he knew. But I'd made him teach me. I'd have to find a way to thank him when I got home.

Bridgett's smile vanished and her eyes turned sad. "This is the slave encampment."

My eyes widened. *SLAVES? WHAT?*

"Yeah, slaves." Bridgett pointed to her gray dress, then to mine. And that was when I realized we were all wearing the same thing, even the guys.

I must've made a face because Bobby chuckled, but it was a strangled sound. "Yeah, took some getting used to, wearing a dress, but they're surprisingly breezy and comfortable."

I AM CONFUSED, I signed. *YOU KNOW YOU'RE IN S-E-E-L-I-E?*

Bridgett translated for me, and they all grumbled and nodded.

I bit my lip, then signed a risky question, *ARE YOU HUMANS?*

After each thing I signed, Bridgett relayed it out loud to them.

They all shook their heads.

"Most of us are half-breeds, with one Seelie parent and one human parent, who either dug too far in their family tree for answers or were straight up given to the King. Ya know, the fae love to demand the first born child of humans seeking favors and all that jazz. They do that to have slaves. The King is a real twisted shit." Bobby turned his head to the side and showed off pointed ears. "I wanted to know who my father was. Bad choice. The rest of us, like Matt here, are arcana, which are—"

WITCHES.

"Witches, yes exactly!" Bridgett gave me thumbs up.

Matt's eyes widened. "Oh, you know about arcana? Wait, are you one? I can't tell at night because they numb our powers so we can't escape while not working."

I sighed. Of course they did. That explained a lot.

"Less than a quarter of the slaves are arcana now. Used to be more but I guess The Coven made it harder for the Seelies to get in and kidnap us."

There was a lot to unload in that statement, so I went with the most pressing question. *YOU KNOW WHO THE COVEN ARE?*

"Oh yes. We know *all* about The Coven." Bridgett shook her head. She tucked her blonde hair behind her ears to reveal they were pointed. "I'm a rare half-breed here. Half arcana, half Seelie. There has always been just enough witch blood in the slave encampment to keep the knowledge spread. Because we have to have a plan for the war."

THE WAR. It wasn't a question. And I didn't need to ask with who.

"Wait. you didn't answer the question. Are you a witch?"

"Matt, she has light coming out of her palms. She has to be a witch."

Matt frowned. "I'm a witch and I can't do that. Maybe she's Seelie half-breed?"

"I can't do that either," Bridgett said cheerily. "So, Lily? What are you?"

I sighed and held my left forearm out in front of me. Even in the dim lighting, the black *XIX* Mark was clearly visible.

There was a moment of silence and then a million questions firing at me at once. The people who'd been hanging back now rushed toward me. Their eyes all filled with a strange mixture of fear, excitement, and panic.

I held my hands up. *STOP. PLEASE.*

"One at a time, guys. Let me ask so I can also translate."

Bridgett bit her lip like she was trying to not smile and failed. "So, Lily, you're the Sun Card, right?"

I nodded.

"You know the Seelies hate Earth sunlight, right?"

I nodded. *I HAVE NOT WANTED TO PLAY THAT CARD YET. I JUST GOT HERE.*

She translated, then pursed her lips. "Okay, I get that. Sorry for all the questions, but we've all been praying The Coven would rescue us. Is that why you're here?"

I wanted to lie to her and give her hope, but I knew that'd be wrong. *TRUTH? WE DID NOT KNOW YOU WERE HERE. BUT WE DO NOW, SO YOU JUST HAVE TO GET ME OUT AND I'LL GET YOU OUT. OKAY?*

They turned to Bridgett and listened as she repeated me. Then they nodded.

Bridgett frowned and twirled her long hair around her fingers. "Lily, why are you here in Seelie? Did they kidnap you, too? Or did you go through the Land of the Lore like some of us did? Not me, but others."

This was not going to be easy to explain through sign language.

"You can give us a short version of the story since you're signing?"

I DID GO THROUGH THE LAND OF THE LORE, BUT I WAS NOT KIDNAPPED.

I waited to let her translate. A few people looked even more intrigued, and I suspected they'd come in the same route.

A boy in the back gasped. "Is that how you lost your voice? That's the price you paid to come in?"

I nodded.

They all cursed. I nodded and laughed silently, though it wasn't funny.

PRINCESS SAGE KIDNAPPED FOUR OF MY

FRIENDS. THE COVEN SENT FOUR OF US IN TO RESCUE THEM.

Bridgett translated in a hushed tone like someone else could've been listening.

The others moved in closer.

Bobby raised his hand like we were in class. "So you have three friends here in Seelie with you?"

Bridgett gasped. "OH, are they Cards, too?"

TWO CARDS. ONE CIVILIAN.

"Two Cards, one civilian..." Bridgett repeated me. She glanced behind me. "Where are they?"

WE GOT ATTACKED BY KNIGHTS. GOT SEPA-RATED. I DON'T KNOW.

Bridgett translated. "So you were looking for them and wound up here?"

I nodded.

"How is she supposed to rescue us if she's in here as a slave with us?"

"We have to get her out, obviously." Bridgett rolled her eyes.

She turned and said something to someone behind her, but my gaze latched onto her back. Her pale skin was marked with a glowing pale pink design. Down her spine were alternating small and large dots. On either side of those there were angular lines from shoulder blade all the way down to where her dress started at her hips. Her arms had a combination of lines and dots from shoulder to elbow. All of them glowing pink.

"Those our are slave markings," Bobby said softly. He grabbed Matt's shoulder and spun him around to reveal iden-tical glowing pink marks. "We all have them. Get them when we get here."

My eyes widened. I didn't want to look but I had to ask. *DO I HAVE THEM?*

"Yes, you have them too," Bridgett said with a sad sigh. "And I don't know if they're permanent if you get out of Seelie."

I scrubbed my face with my hands. Being marked wasn't my concern. All I cared about was getting our friends and getting home to Easton. These slaves were all victims, people stolen in one form or another. They weren't Seelie, they had no allegiance to the King, and they definitely hated him. They were my only hope for escape.

"Lily? Are you okay?"

I turned to Bridgett. *IS THERE A PLACE WE CAN GO WHERE THERE IS NATURAL LIGHT? WHERE MY SUNSHINE WON'T BE AS OBVIOUS?*

The others all looked to her, waiting for her to translate, but she just stared at me with wide eyes. I arched my eyebrow.

"There's only one spot but it's stupid close to where the masters stay. If you go shining your Earthly sunshine, they'll come running. And if they find out The Coven is in their hands —" She stopped mid-sentence and cocked her head to the side. "You think you can signal for your other Cards here, don't you?"

I nodded.

Bridgett rubbed her hands together. "Because if there are other Cards here *not* dulled by slave spells, then they should be able to feel and see *you*. We just have to get you to where that can happen."

Bobby was nodding. "If she shines light *here* where it's always dark, the masters will come right away. But if we take her to the valley, it might take them a minute to realize something is up."

EXACTLY. I snapped my fingers and pointed to Bobby. Then I gestured around to all of them. *I'LL TAKE YOU WITH ME.*

Bridgett narrowed her eyes. "Lily, you a runner?"

I smiled and nodded.

Bridgett jumped to her feet and nodded. "Lily, stay right behind me and put your lights out. Everyone else, fall in line."

Everyone lined up faster than I expected. Within seconds

we were running single file through the dark forest in perfect silence. The only light came off the soft glow of pink from our marks, which would have been pretty if they weren't slave markings. I had no idea how far or long we ran, but every few feet yards we'd all duck down and hide in the tall bushes.

Bridgett was the leader, and even though she looked young and innocent, I knew not to judge a book by its cover. No one would ever expect the shit Emersyn or Saffie did. Besides, she was both Seelie and arcana. That gave her a leg up on the others, so I understood why they followed her lead.

I tried to keep my thoughts clear and calm as we raced through the darkness. If the slave masters kept slave magic dulled at night, then I wasn't sure just how much power I'd have to signal for help. I just prayed that they weren't expecting The Coven's level of power. I just needed enough so that maybe Saffie or Willow would see me or feel me.

If not, these slave masters were going to get a whole new meaning of dawn.

Up ahead, light flashed and Bridgett dove for the ground. I dropped down beside her and watched as a few Knights in shiny gold armor with fluttery silver wings landed. They marched up to a tree and stopped.

I hadn't seen them coming or felt it. *This does not bode well.*

I leaned closer to Bridgett and signed *GOOD EYE.*

"Thanks, I used to be a tour guide at Disney." She gave me a wicked grin and tapped on her temple. "Gotta keep your eyes open or you'll get runover by cheerleaders in bows bigger than your head."

I chuckled and shook my head.

"*Nouma!*" one of the Knights shouted.

The side of the tree opened and six Seelies stepped out wearing that same black armor the woman with the whip had on. The Knights were speaking, but I couldn't understand a word.

Bridgett gasped and then leaned toward me. "They're looking for you."

My eyes widened.

She nodded. "They're saying four intruders came in through the archway and they're tracking all of you—*oh shit. They're tracking you.*"

My heart sank.

Bridgett gasped again. "Does one of your friends have wings?"

I nodded. *HALF-BREED.*

An evil smirk spread across her face. "Apparently, your friend with the wings killed two dozen Knights by herself."

YESSSSS. That's my girl, Saffie.

Then I realized that must have happened after we got separated. Which meant not only were they tracking us, but they'd be super freaking pissed. And if they caught me, they'd bring me right to the King...and I didn't think that'd help our odds in saving Riah or the others. No, I needed to get to Saffie.

"They said they haven't seen you...or anyone," Bridgett said softly. "Because right now they know they messed up in marking you and they don't want to be caught. The King is a monster."

Wonderful.

I tapped on Bridgett's shoulders, then pointed to my hands. *NOW.*

She nodded. "Follow me. We have to move over a bit."

The rest of the line hadn't said a word that whole time, but the second we started moving again, so did they. We made a sharp left turn around a tree and then went down a set of stairs carved into the ground. At the bottom, I discovered we were in a narrow valley that stretched far in front of us and behind. We were running away from where the Knights were, or I thought so. It was hard to tell. I looked up and my jaw dropped. The trees were parted right over this valley, showing off a gloriously colored turquoise sky with purple and pink clouds rolling in from the forests.

"Lily, can you pull light from the sky?" She pointed straight up and glanced back at me.

I nodded.

"PULL NOW! Make it brighter!"

Without hesitating, I reached up and called for the Sun. It didn't feel the same as ours, but it answered my call all the same. Those pink and purple clouds paled so much they were almost white. The turquoise sky became brighter than a neon Las Vegas sign, casting the entire valley in a turquoise glow.

FEEL ME, SAFFIE. FEEL ME!

Bridgett made a sharp left turn, which led to another stair-case carved into the ground. The second I got to the top, she dragged me back behind a big black tree and grabbed my wrist. Then pointed to our left. "Sunshine. Now. That light won't go unnoticed much longer. That way is out—the only place she'd be able to come in from."

I turned and blasted sunshine out of my palms like I was Iron Man. It answered with a soft golden glow. It wasn't full strength, but it was there. I watched my magic shoot through the trees and prayed she was out there.

Feel me, Saffie. FEEL ME.

Shouting erupted behind us, and my stomach dropped.

Bridgett cursed. "The Knights. They're coming. DOWN!"

We dove for the ground just as an arrow soared over our heads and impaled a tree. I glanced to our right. Six Knights charged for us. We'd been spotted. Two of them had bow and arrows. Bridgett pulled me back behind the tree, but the Knights had aimed their arrows down into the valley.

The slaves! I couldn't let them die like this. I lifted my hands and shot sunshine right into their eyes. They screeched and spun away. But the other four looked up and met my stare. And grinned.

"GET UP HERE!" Bridgett screamed.

The other slaves rushed up the stairs, but they weren't moving fast enough. The Knights had wings. *But they don't like our sunshine and you've got a winning hand.* I summoned every ounce of magic I could muster and funneled it right out of my palms. A wall of golden yellow mist slammed into them, pushing them back from the valley.

Out of the corner of my eye, I saw the last of the slaves emerge from the steps and dive behind the trees. We weren't safe, though, and I couldn't keep this up forever. Not here, not with my magic being dulled by these slave spells.

One of the Knights pushed through my magic and lunged off the valley cliff. His wings fluttered behind him. He lifted his sword—a thick black vine slammed into his ribs and poked out the other side. I gasped and flinched back, lowering my hands. The other Knights screamed like banshees and charged to their right. Vines shot up from the ground and sliced two of them in half. Tree branches swung down and wacked the other three like a baseball bat, sending them full speed into the valley wall.

"BASEL!" The female with the whip shouted from somewhere behind us. I couldn't see her, but I recognized her voice.

And then I felt it.

Coven magic.

It was a breath of fresh air that tingled against my skin. I jumped to my feet and shined my sunlight straight out in front of me and landed on a girl with long, wild red hair and eyes a similar hue to my own. The glowing gold lines on her face and arm were fierce looking.

SAFFIE.

She wore a crazy kind of outfit that looked like it was random pieces of green and purple silk stitched together by a kid for Halloween, but it only made her look more terrifying. Her stare was lava-hot as she glared at whatever forces were racing up behind us.

Then she lifted off the ground with those wings of hers that looked like a cluster of stars behind her back, or like fairyflies. She raised her hands and golden glitter rained from her palms. Light flashed by me. I spun around and my jaw dropped. Three dozen Seelies in black armor were sprawled on the ground. None of them moved.

I turned back to Saffie.

She arched one eyebrow and smirked a smirk I thought only Tegan could make. She was a tiny little thing, but right now she was tall and terrifying. She lowered back to the ground and then turned and our eyes met.

Saffie marched toward us. "One down, six more to go. Who are your friends?"

I sighed so hard I actually swayed on my feet.

Bridgett jumped up beside me. "She can't talk!"

Saffie stopped in front of us and smiled, but this one was her usual, friendly, not-a-serial-killer smile. "She doesn't need to with me. I can feel her soul."

I lost it. All of my composure vanished. I lunged forward and tackled her in a hug. She wrapped her arms around me and squeezed tight. We held each other for a few seconds before we pulled back.

Her eyes were glassy. "I thought I lost you."

I shook my head. Then I gestured to my new friends.

Bridgett waved. "To answer your question, we're slaves."

Saffie's eyes went cold. "Well, not anymore. You're with us now."

CHAPTER TWENTY-THREE

BETTINA

I LOOKED DOWN at my watch and my heart sank. It'd been forty-eight hours on the dot since the others left. Two days of waiting to hear from them yet greeting only silence.

The rest of us were about out of our damn minds.

Katherine had to use a sleeping potion on Constance because she was too stressed for the baby. I could've sworn more of Daniel's hair had turned gray. Kenneth was cryptic and quiet, which put me on edge. Royce just sat on the ground rocking while watching the screen. Braison hadn't moved from the rug on the floor in sixteen hours, despite Albert's attempts. Warner kept sending text messages to Lennox that weren't being responded to. Cooper's eyes were bloodshot, and he seemed to have lost weight since they left. His whole family had left except for Kessler, who hadn't moved from the barstool at the kitchen counter since sometime yesterday. I knew he was worried about the Bishops *and* my brother.

And Jackson...well, he was a silent, hovering shadow behind me. Every time I moved, he moved. I didn't blame him. I knew he was feeling what I was feeling...which was crippling, paralyzing fear. My best friend, my brother, and my uncle were all in there. None of them were going into Seelie, but in my gut I knew something was going to happen. Something *had* happened. It was Tegan. I could feel it in my bones. She was going to come back white as snow and unconscious. I knew it. I just didn't know how or why. Or how long she'd be down this time.

And my brother...Haven was a pillar of strength and reliability. Nothing shook him, nothing prevented him from being his non-human self...*except* for Tegan going white witch. It rattled him, broke him down, and left him like a statue frozen in his own fear.

My stomach turned. I groaned and hung my head, letting my dark hair fall between my knees. Jackson's warm hand landed on my back, then rubbed gentle circles. It was comforting but there was nothing he could do to ease this wretchedness until they came home. I'd just gotten my brother and uncle back after twelve years. I couldn't lose them now. And the Bishops, especially Hunter and Bentley, they'd been my second family since I was four.

Stop it, Bettina. Keep your shit together. They're fine. They're FINE. I couldn't lose control of my emotions now, not when I had to keep my ears open for Henley. I closed my eyes and focused on the sounds coming through the spell behind my ear. It was just a loud roar, like riding down the highway in a convertible. He was moving. Again.

"Hello, Heather," Kessler's deep voice boomed through the house.

I jumped and looked up. Kessler had his elbows propped on the counter and his head resting in his palms.

"The Knights just returned from Connecticut. They assure me the situation there has been contained." Heather's voice was firm even through the speakerphone. "And I just spoke with Major Ryan down in Philly. They're also settled."

Deacon's mother, Heather English, was one of the Majors of

New York City, but she was also unofficial spokesperson for the entire northeast. She'd been a huge help in the last two days, sending her own Knights out to the smaller cities the shadow demon was ransacking.

"Any fatalities?" Kessler said through clenched teeth. He still hadn't moved or picked his head up.

"No, but a lot of injuries. Mostly minor ones."

Kessler sighed. "Good. Thank you."

"I don't understand, Kessler. What's he doing?" Heather's voice dropped low like she was trying to whisper. "These attacks have just been a nuisance, nothing like we've seen lately."

That's what I'm worried about.

"That's what we're worried about," Kessler grumbled, echoing my own thoughts. "He's definitely planning something but we're not sure what yet. We're working on it. For now, get your Knights home, healed, and rested. We haven't seen the last of him."

"If you need anything, please don't hesitate to ask."

"Thanks, Heather. Someone will let you know as soon as Deacon is back."

Heather sighed. "Thank you. Good luck."

And then the room fell silent again. I felt everyone else's eyes on Kessler, yet none of us spoke.

"Cooper, anything from any of them yet?"

Cooper shook his head. "None of them have slept or I would have gotten through."

"I don't think time works the same there," Kenneth said softly. "Judging by what we know of it and what it's connected to."

"Are you saying they could all have aged?"

"Warner, don't say that—"

"It's possible, Cooper. Best to accept that potential

outcome." Kenneth scratched his jaw. "But if they haven't slept at all, then my gut tells me time works slower there."

"Speaking of sleep…" Cooper looked to the kitchen. "Uncle Kessler, why don't you get some rest? You've been up since they left."

"And I'll sleep when they return."

There was something different about *this* little quest. Something about it that left the rest of us crippled. None of us wanted to move from this screen. We needed to be here for Henley but also be ready to move if the others needed us. Heather had their plane ready and waiting for a call. *Our* pilot, Walter, was just down the street at the little local airport ready to fly us.

Because there was a danger and threat in the Land of the Lore we'd yet to experience.

"We're all running at half empty here, mates. If something went down, we'd be in piss shape."

"Jackson has a point." I rubbed my temple. The sound from the spell was so loud it gave me a migraine. I didn't know how Tegan did this for so long. "Where's Katherine?"

"Perfect timing. Here I am."

"Do you have anything safe you can give us —"

"So you don't need to sleep yet won't be zombies?" She shook her head. "Not quite like I give to Tenn and Tegan, but the soup I fed y'all a little while ago should help. I left it on the stove so just keep eating it as you can."

I nodded. "I was also thinking…what can we have ready just in case?"

She cocked her head to the side. "In case of what?"

My mouth went dry. I didn't want to speak the words into existence but I had to. "In case the others—"

I froze.

"Moonshine?"

"I don't hear anything."

"That's because you were talking, then stopped." Warner chuckled.

"No, no. Henley." I tapped on my ear. "I don't *hear* anything."

Everyone's eyes snapped up to me. There was a beat of silence and then we all jumped and scrambled over to the screen.

"What? It's just dark, like it has been for hours," Braison said breathlessly from the floor. "Nothing changed."

"Something did." I moved closer to the screen as if that would somehow help, but everything was black. "It's been a loud rushing of wind in my ear, but it stopped. Just let me listen."

I closed my eyes to try and let my hearing strengthen. At first it was nothing but then I heard a gust of wind rushing through tree branches. I heard twigs snapping like someone was walking on them. There was a faint chirp of crickets—and a hoot from an owl.

"He's in the woods," I heard myself whisper. Every nerve ending in my body was tense. My magic coiled in my gut, wanting to explode. "Kenneth, is that laptop still connected to Henley?"

"Yes."

Cooper cursed.

"Moonshine? What do you hear?"

I licked my lips and kept my eyes closed. "Whatever he's been planning...this is it. I can just feel it."

And then I heard the creaking of an iron gate and my heart stopped. "Daniel, wake Constance. Now."

Daniel cursed, but I heard his footsteps quicken as he ran for her.

"Bettina, it's still dark..." Warner groaned. "Are you seeing something I'm not?"

I opened my eyes and stared at the screen. My gut told me

exactly where he was. I just didn't want to be right. Then the darkness turned to gray, like smoke...or *fog*. My pulse quickened. *Please don't be right. Please don't be right.*

He moved through the fog—and a bright lavender-colored sky filled the screen.

Everyone cursed.

"Walter? It's Kessler, we need to fly. Now," Kessler growled into his phone. "On our way."

"Where are we going—" Constance gasped. "Oh *no. No.* The Old Lands?"

I just nodded as the shadow demon marched through the non-Earth-like colored forest of the Old Lands. "Kenneth, that laptop?"

"Up and running, see?"

I glanced over my shoulder and found the same image staring back at me as was on the big screen. "Go check it outside in the car. Make sure it works."

Kessler jumped into action, grabbing keys off the hook in the kitchen and a sword from the counter. "Load up. My truck. Let's go."

"C'mon, Albert," Braison said with a whistle as he charged for the door.

Warner bent over and scooped Olli up and chased after them.

"Bettina, you need to come with us."

"We need to make sure that screen is working before—"

"Bettina, screen is on in the car!" Jackson yelled from behind us.

I glanced over my shoulder and found only Kessler in the house with me. Without another word, we both sprinted out the door behind Jackson. Cooper was in the driver's seat with Constance riding shotgun. Braison's red hair glowed in the moonlight from the bed of the truck and Olli's long ears hung over the edge.

Jackson sprinted forward and leapt into the truck bed, then pointed to the door. "You two, inside."

The side door was open, so I jumped up and slid onto the backseat. Kenneth was behind Constance with the screen in his lap. I moved to the middle just as Kessler hopped in behind me and slammed the door shut.

Kenneth sat the laptop on my legs. "You watch."

"We have everyone? Cooper, Constance, Kenneth, Bettina...." Kessler turned in his seat to look out the back window that was open behind my head. "Jackson, Royce, Warner, Braison, Daniel, Katherine, Albert, and Olli. All here. Drive, Coop."

Light flashed on the screen like the shadow demon had walked into a patch of Old Land sunlight, but then he ducked under a fallen purple tree with hot pink leaves and the screen fell back into dark night. I hated the Old Lands for many reasons, but it's unpredictability might've been the biggest one.

"Do you recognize anything?" Kenneth asked as he leaned over to watch with me.

I shook my head. "If I recognize something we're in rough shape, considering the places I've been in—*what are those?*"

All three of us leaned closer to the screen as black creatures the size of English bulldogs ran towards him. Their bright beady red eyes shined like beacons in the dark. The shadow demon barked something at them in his demonic language and they took off running ahead of him.

Kessler cursed. "Demons."

"Timothy needs to learn demonic languages," Kenneth said with a sigh. "It doesn't come with the Card, but I fear it'll be needed."

"I might be able to help us with that, I used a spell to teach myself our ancient language."

The demon pushed through some orange bushes with nasty gold thorns.

Kenneth chuckled. "You are just like your mother."

Despite everything, *that* made me smile. "Thank you."

Kessler's finger pointed at the screen. "What is *that*?"

"You're the adult. You're supposed to know these things," I hissed as the demon stopped in front of a dark pond.

"Something about this water is *not* right. I know that."

The demon flicked Henley's hand and red flames flickered to life in a circle around the pond, illuminating at least a dozen black candles. Those small dog-sized black demons surrounded the circle and sat like good, obedient hounds. The demon waved his hands and the red flames turned gold—I gasped.

The pond water was *red.*

Blood red.

"HERE! GET OUT!" Cooper shouted and jumped out of the truck. "WALTER!"

His voice carried through the closed doors as Kenneth, Kessler, and I remained frozen in horror.

In the back of my mind, I heard a plane's engines roaring with life. I heard Albert and Olli bark excitedly. I heard footsteps hurrying away from us and our friends' voices getting farther away. But I couldn't move. I was glued in the seat, watching the pond full of blood.

The door beside us opened and fresh air rushed into the cab of the truck. "*GUYS!*" Cooper shouted.

Kenneth cursed and hopped out his door.

Kessler's large hand gripped my bicep gently and then I was sliding across the leather seat. My feet hit the ground, then instantly lifted up. I started to look up, but he growled, *"Keep watching! I've got you!"*

I refocused my gaze on the screen just as the golden flames brightened and flickered...and three skulls floated into view.

Human skulls.

"*Human skulls? WHAT?*" Kessler shrieked in my ear.

"There are human skulls in this blood pond," I said in a rush.

"*BLOOD POND*?" The others all shouted in unison.

I peeked up and discovered we were on the plane. Kessler had carried me all the way—*Strength Card, Bettina.* He literally carried me to a seat and sat me down, then buckled in beside me.

"Eden, Walter. Fast as possible," Cooper shouted. Then he turned and sat across from me. "What's happening?"

I felt everyone huddled around me. Kenneth and Kessler beside me just like in the truck, with the others either in front of me or leaning over my seat.

"Constance, do *not* look at this screen," I heard myself say. "In fact, don't listen."

"One step ahead of you," Katherine rushed by. "Ok, she's headphoned and eye masked. Joys of pregnancy. Daniel, sit beside her. She'll be calmest with you."

In the back of my mind I felt the plane taking off, but I was too hyper focused on the screen. *What is he doing? Where did this blood come from?* It didn't feel natural for the Old Lands.

"I have never heard of a pond of blood in the Old Lands," Kenneth whispered beside me.

"So where'd the blood come from?" Warner asked.

Braison groaned. "Don't ask that. There's skulls—"

I gasped as all the pieces clicked in my brain. "*Oh Goddess.* That's what he's been doing for two days!"

Their faces fell.

"He was getting blood. Those attacks were *distractions.*"

"*Bloody hell.*"

"*But to do WHAT with?*" Royce cried and tugged on his hair in front of me.

The shadow demon looked down. Henley's thin, pale fingers reached for the button on her black leather shorts and unhooked them. My eyes widened. But when she unzipped her fly, I cursed and covered the screen with my hands.

"*Boys look away!*" I shrieked. "*MOVE!*"

All of them fumbled and dove to get in front of me instead of behind.

"He's undressing," I heard myself growl. My stomach rolled. I knew what was coming. "Katherine, come here."

Katherine slid into the seat beside me that Kenneth had just vacated. She was the only other female on the plane that wasn't riddled with morning sickness.

"Just help me watch for every detail, okay?" I said as all of Henley's clothes dropped to the dark dirt at her feet.

"She's doing a blood bath ritual."

"Are you familiar?"

"Yes and no," Katherine whispered. "It's heavy black magic. Very, *very* demonic."

The shadow demon made quick work of peeling off every piece of jewelry from Henley's fingers, wrists, ears, neck, and ankles. *But he didn't touch the piercing on her face.* He must not have realized it was there.

And then she stepped *into* the pond. The water was thick, exactly like I expected a pond of blood to be. My stomach rolled with nausea. Once in, she submerged herself into the blood, leaving only her face above the surface and looking at the dark plum sky. Then Henley's left arm rose into the air, her *XVIII* Mark of the Moon Card looking red against her blood-stained skin. White magic glistened from her palm and shot into the sky.

The Moon slid into view the instant Henley called. It was full and pale green. But then the shadow demon hissed what sounded like a spell in demonic language and a black circle appeared in the center of the green moon. The black circle grew bigger and bigger until the green was a sharply pointed crescent —almost like an odd eclipse.

Those demon-hounds stuck their faces to the sky and howled. The Moon turned bright crimson red, like red from a paint bottle except it glowed.

And then the Moon began to bleed.

"*Oh my God...*" I waved at the guys to come look.

They leapt around the seats—and choked on their gasps. The Moon was glowing red and *bleeding*. Thick streams of blood dripped down from the sky and into the pond he was still submerged in.

"*What is he DOING?*" Royce gagged.

"This is a ritual for summoning." Kenneth sighed. "But it's a slow one. Takes time."

"So, what do we do?" Cooper said under his breath. "What's our plan?"

Kessler looked around at us. "We go in after her...and pray we're not too late."

CHAPTER TWENTY-FOUR

SAVANNAH

THIS IS what you get for running, Savannah Grace. I bent over and put my hands on my knees as I coughed hard enough to puke up a lung. *You know you're not a runner. You did this to yourself.*

I gasped for air between coughs.

You done been 'round these Coven folk too long, ma'am.

Goddess, when I die from this runnin', just tell my momma I picked the wrong damn friends.

Sharp pain pinched my side, so I squeezed it with my hand. But when I sucked in a deep breath, it made my stomach roll and yesterday's breakfast almost came back out.

Oh, this some baby back bullshit. Why you even runnin' when them bitches got wings? Ma'am? Tell me that. They gon' catch yo slow ass anyways. Let 'em. Why suffer twice?

I stood up straight and stumbled into a tree. My legs were wobbly like Jell-O. There was a throbbing ache in my knees and the left one definitely did not want to bend anymore. I smacked it. *Ain't nobody got time for that, ma'am. You too young to be this gaddamn old. The fuck is this?*

My cheeks were on fire and sweat dripped down my spine.

It was too hot. I wasn't built for heat. I was built for an ice age. *Damn it. Maybe I shoulda been a penguin.* I leaned against the tree and yanked my hoodie off, then tossed it to the dirt like a toddler tantrum. I'd get a new hoodie. *That* one had offended me.

Oh my Goddess, I am losing my damn mind here. She done gone. Checked out the door. And we signed a prenup, so she took all her shit with her.

I reached up to tie my hair off my neck, but my balance faltered and I stumbled a few feet away. My right foot splashed in a hot puddle. It felt like I'd stepped in whale piss. *Whale piss, Savannah? Because you're familiar with that?* I stopped and sighed in defeat. Then I frowned. My foot was wet. *Hold up. Why is my foot wet? I've got on waterproof boots.* I shifted my weight to my left foot and then lifted my right.

No shoe.

But there *was* a hole in my sock.

I stuck my foot back in the puddle and sloshed around. Still no shoe.

"*How the HELL did I lose a damn SHOE?*" I groaned and lurched over to the next big tree. "It was strapped on tight. I call bullshit."

So far, Seelie sucked bad.

THIS IS FINE.

I reached down and patted my satchel. It was still there at least. And a quick peek inside showed my journal. Lost my shoe, but I had the important thing. *Not that it's any use to me in this current condition, but I digress.*

I leaned against the tree, then slid down to the ground so I could take my other shoe off. Suddenly, someone yanked that tree out from behind me. My feet flew up over my head and then my own ass was in my face. I rolled backwards down what had to be a damn ski slope it was so long. When the world finally stopped moving, I flopped onto my back like an upside-down starfish.

Beneath me, the ground was a little soggy and wet, but it was cold so I did not even bother to get up. There was no point. I'd been running from those Knights for centuries it felt like. They were tracking me. I knew it with every fiber of my being. They were doing some sneaky fae shit and tracking me. Because I was a damn good hider. Sitting silent and not moving? Two of my favorite hobbies. Playing hide and go seek in the dark and hiding in the shadows? My favorite. I was built for that.

But these assholes had me out here *running*.

I was not built for that.

The only reason they hadn't caught me yet was because I kept tripping and eating shit as they zoomed over my head thinking I'd be farther along. I had no idea where Saffie, Lily, and Willow were. The last I saw of them, we were together running. Then I was falling off a tree in the dark by myself.

I sighed and lifted my hands up, but they were covered in some kind of gray mud. *This is fine.* I let my arms flop back into the mud but my right hand landed on something hard. I picked it up and inspected it. It was a black stone, like a river rock, with little white speckles on it that looked like a constellation. At the top there was a small hole that let you look right through it.

It's a hag stone. With stars on it. Cooper's face flashed in my mind. He'd gotten me such a nice gift. I had to start thinking about one for him. This stone wasn't much but I thought maybe he'd like it, so I carefully shoved it into my satchel. After that whole daddy debacle, I wanted to give him a thoughtful gift and not just a ribbon tied around a kiwi like Gigi had suggested when it first went down.

I lay there staring at the gray sky above me. Everything down here was a shade of gray. I chuckled. *Fifty shades of Grey.* I promised myself I'd leave out how hard I'd giggled about that if I managed to survive.

My body suddenly felt heavy, like a ton of bricks. A weight seemed to press on my chest, but it was oddly comforting. My eyes fluttered and then closed as fatigue snuck up and took me down.

I knew I was asleep instantly because everything went dark. I was still in a forest but this one reminded me more of home in Appalachia. The air smelled different, but I blamed that on being asleep. I was lucid dreaming, which wasn't new for me in any way, shape, or form. But this forest was. I spun in a circle and found nothing but darkness in every direction—a guy appeared right in front of me.

I screamed and jumped back before my eyes had time to recognize him.

"*SIR, NO!*" I groaned and pressed my hand to my chest where my heart was pounding. "*SIR, you do not just sneak up on people in their dreams like that.*"

Cooper grinned. "Well, actually, *I* do."

"No, ma'am." I bent over and put my hands on my knees again. "I can't with this day right now, y'all."

"Are there more than just us here right now?"

I narrowed my eyes at him. "I'm southern. This just how we talk when we're upset. *Y'all* and *ma'am* become interchangeable and gender neutral. *Errrybody knows that, Cooper.*"

"Is that a southern thing or a Savannah thing?"

I stood upright and put my hands on my hips. "Is now really the time to be tap dancing on my nerves like that? Boy, I will put you in the ground."

Cooper laughed and it sent warm fluttering butterflies through my stomach. "I'm sorry. I just...I needed to check on you. All of you. How are you doing?"

I groaned and hobbled over to the base of a tree. "What's it mean when I'm this tired in my sleep?"

Cooper shrugged. "I don't think you're really sleeping right now."

"Oh good. Failing at that too. That's fine. This is fine." I made sure to slide down the tree and not roll backwards down a hill. "Hey, look, still got my shoe here."

Cooper frowned down at the boots on my feet, then sat in front of me. "Talk to me, Savannah."

"Well, you ain't gon' like it." I threw my hands up and shrugged. "It's bad right from the jump. We come through the archway and Saffie has some weird tattoo on the back of her hand that means she probably owes Seelie something—which is never good. Willow was blinded. Lily is now a mute. And I can't remember a single bit of my magic."

His eyebrows shot up.

"Oh, and we got attacked by Knights and then separated and now I'm definitely being tracked by the Knights."

He nodded and pursed his lips. "Okay, so what are you doing?"

"I'm sitting here sleeping, evidently. I sat down to regroup and get a plan." *And that's the hill I'm gon' die on, okay?*

Cooper glanced around us like he could see what was really happening. "Shouldn't you be running?"

I slouched against the tree and shook my head. "If I have to run, just eat me. I'm done. Just eat me. It's fine."

He arched one eyebrow and smirked.

I gasped.

But Coop let that one slide. He chuckled and scratched his haw. "You've run before."

"I don't know who signed me up for cardio, but don't put me down for that no more. I'm done. I ain't doin it. I'm real tired of this." I waved my finger in the air. "Next bad guy is just gon' have to kill me. I wasn't built for this. I got bad knees, man. You just gon' have to kill me dead. D-E-D. Dead. I volunteer as tribute to be the sacrifice 'cause I'm sick of running. Unless you got some Hermes winged shoes, I ain't doin it. I can't do it no more."

He just stared at me with a goofy smile.

"Yeah, I do be on my bullshit." I sighed and nodded. "One day I'll get my shit together. It ain't gon' be today. Probably won't even be this year or this decade. Well, this decade is almost over and that's a lot of pressure to start a new one with—ya know, let's just say never. If your standards are low, you ain't gon' be disappointed."

"Listen to that accent. Thicker than your mama's sweet tea today." He laughed, like a deep in his gut kind of laugh that did things to me. "I tell ya what, you get your ass home alive, and we'll ask Tegan about some Hermes winged shoes. Deal?"

I cocked my head to the side. "Don't tease me with a good time, ma'am. But don't put me down for cardio."

"I didn't say you had to run. I said you have to return."

"Oh, then deal." I leaned away from the tree and looked around, then remembered this was a dream. "Well, I was hoping Saffie, Lily, or Willow would roll up on me, but I haven't seen them yet. Then you took me down."

He arched that damn eyebrow again and my face ignited like a bonfire.

Then he licked his lips and pointed to my satchel. "Look in your book."

"I can't remember my magic."

"But you do remember magic in general?" When I nodded, he asked, "Do you feel magic inside of you still?"

I opened my mouth and closed it. I did. I'd tried a few times to use it but all I got was some hot flashes.

"Savannah," Coop said softly and squeezed my shoulder. "The price took your memory of *your* magic—as in spells and shit that you knew and had learned. But you can still perform magic."

My jaw dropped. I just stared at him.

"Meaning if you read that journal of spells you carry, you might find something you can use to help you."

I gasped. *Cassandra left me stuff in there. She told me she did.* With everything that had happened, I'd somehow forgotten that part. *Did she know this was going to happen to me? She was the Hierophant not long ago. Is that why she did this?*

"Look?"

Cooper probably thought I'd lost my mind, and he'd be half right.

I pulled my journal out of my satchel and opened it up. Everything looked completely normal at first, but then I opened it from the back and found a note from her on the second page.

'Savannah, this isn't much but it might suit your needs in Seelie. If you like it, I'll teach you more when you get back. Xo Cassandra.'

Drawn in bold black ink below her note was a single rune. A rune I'd never seen before. It was both intricate and simple at the same time. There was a small triangle with an arrow above it and an intersecting *V*.

I flipped the pages but that was it. The rune was the only thing she'd left me. *That's confusing, ma'am. What am I supposed to do with this? It's pretty but*—my finger touched the ink and black mist billowed from the paper. Words flashed in my mind. I heard them echoed in my head in my own voice. Then I saw my dagger, the one Cooper had just given me, sitting in my hand.

"Savannah?"

I blinked up at him and met his stare. The words poured out of my mouth before I could stop them, *"Graceful and steady it moves without sight, the black abyss of darkness beneath the moonless night. Silent and lethal, an ally we call to thee, shrouded in shadow to blind our enemy."*

Cooper's eyes widened.

But I wasn't done. I reached to my hip and pulled the dagger he'd given me off the holster thingy Tegan had made. I smiled. It was a pretty, shiny silver dagger the length of my forearm. The hilt had gorgeous etchings and an antiqued finish. The blade looked untouched. Remembering what he'd told me back in his room, I pressed my thumb to the blade and grinned as it glowed in the dark like the North Star.

Like Cooper Bishop.

EW, brain. Not now, damn it.

Cooper's cheeks flushed but he said nothing.

I dragged the blade across my forearm, slicing my skin open. It wasn't much blood. I'd purposely gone for the fatty, non-dangerous part of my arm. Yet red blood gushed to the surface. Cooper opened his mouth and then shut it. I was about to explain what I was doing when the blood dripped onto the black ground of this dream forest and turned to an ashy gray fog. The fog shot up and covered my body, hugging every inch of me.

And then all the noise stopped. I hadn't even realized how much noise I was hearing until it was gone. It was *that* sneaky. Those damn Knights had manifested silence and that was what I'd been hearing. Fake silence. It was like a faint buzz and hum in my ear to feel real while it was really their magic tracking me.

Cooper's eyes widened. He glanced around, then turned back to me with a smile. "They're gone."

I scowled. "Could you see them before?"

"See? Not literally, no. But I sensed their auras." He gestured to the trees. "They're gone now. Whatever you just did removed the tracking, so they're not going to find you lying in the mud like an upside-down starfish."

I gasped and sat up straight, but we were still in the black forest. "How did—you know what, never mind."

He chuckled. "We all have our tricks."

"Yeah, like you creeping in people's dreams." I shook my head and started to close my journal. "Ya know, you should give people nightmares."

"I can't do that, not part of my gift."

"Well, it should be, nightmares are—" my finger brushed

over that rune from Cassandra as I was closing the book and a wave of black mist flashed in my mind, like staring at the ocean in the dark.

Cooper reached out and squeezed my hand, but I was lost to the new set of words in my head. Over Cooper's shoulder, I saw Saffie and Lily riding horses. Willow was sitting on a bench away from them. Except it wasn't a clear picture of them, it was more like a silhouette that I recognized the shape of. My mind was filling in the blanks that my eyes couldn't see. Behind them was a girl. I did not recognize her. She had wild hair and a dog was at her feet. I blinked and leaned around Cooper to get a better view, to maybe see where they were, and I saw two more people huddled close together and a third lying on the floor.

"Savannah," Cooper growled my name.

I gasped and looked up, only to find him *right* in front of me, mere inches away. His hand was cupping my face like he'd been desperately trying to get my attention.

"*Cooper,*" I breathed.

His eyes softened. "What is it?"

"*Hear my plea and greatest desire, from spirit, earth, water, air, and fire. Impart unto thee a power without pause, no sacrifice made with knowledge of cause. Magic and strength, bring forth from the core, to aid as needed until the empty cup pours.*"

The ground rumbled under our feet. Around us the forest darkened until we sat in only blackness. Cooper's Mark on his arm sparkled like starlight. The green of his eyes flashed and twinkled. The hand holding my face cooled and trembled.

"*S-Savann-nah?*" His voice cracked. He looked at me with confusion but no fear. "What is this?"

I pushed up on my knees and took his face in my hands. "*Freedom.*"

Then I pressed my lips to his and light exploded all around us.

I gasped and sat up—I was still in the mud. The forest was

still a foggy gray. Cooper was nowhere in sight. No one was in sight. My one shoe was still nowhere in sight. I looked down at my arm and grinned. The slice I'd made on my forearm was still bleeding. My dagger lay across my lap with my blood still staining the edge of the blade. I grabbed my satchel and dove for my journal. With muddy fingers, I flipped to the back and squealed at the sight of that note and rune drawing from Cassandra.

That was real.

I shoved my journal back into my satchel, then sheathed my sword.

Screaming erupted from all around me. Knights lunged from behind trees and bushes—all holding their heads like they were about to explode. Their eyes were wide but unseeing. Their faces paled like they'd seen a ghost, then they fled as fast as they could, their wings taking them up into the gray sky.

A split second after their screams faded to silence, the world turned dark around me.

Not like in my dream with Cooper, but like it was before I got separated from my friends. The trees were cast in shadows from the lack of natural light. And the nature was definitely not Earth-like in color. But none of that mattered.

Because Cooper had done it.

He'd given them *nightmares.*

Goosebumps spread over my body. I giggled. I couldn't wait to ask him what he made them see. And maybe brainstorm some ideas for future nightmares. I had a thing for collecting fears. It was important knowledge to have.

With a stupid smile on my face, I kicked off my other shoe and jumped to my feet. There was no way I was walking through Seelie unbalanced—that'd throw off my game too much. And I needed to get my shit together so I could find at least one of my friends.

"Savannah?"

I jumped and spun around—and froze.

Standing a few yards away from me was a spirit. It glowed that soft blue I remembered from Saffie's accidental summonings in Salem. This was probably a girl, though I couldn't judge just on the long hair and dress.

Then I realized she'd said my name. I cleared my throat. "Yes?"

"Are you Savannah Grace?"

I am a little bit creeped out. "Yes, I am."

The spirit grinned and hurried over to me. She grabbed my wrists and then we were flying back up that incline I'd fallen down. When we got to the top, she let go of me and hopped back.

"Wait here, please?"

"Um, yes, ma'am." This was the most polite spirit I'd ever seen.

She nodded then flew away from me. I leaned against the tree—this time carefully—and waited. My mind was still processing whatever I'd just done in that dream with Cooper.

A few moments later the ground rumbled under my feet. I pushed off the tree and put my hand on my dagger hilt. A soft yellow light burst through the trees. A herd of animals I'd never seen came prancing toward me. They were huge, white wolf-doggies with large antlers covered in red flowers.

That same spirit girl was running ahead of them. She pointed at me and then looked over her shoulder to something behind her. She was smiling. "SEE! I found her!"

A petite little face with long, wild red hair poked up from behind the flowery antlers.

I gasped. "SAFFIE!"

The majestic creature she was riding carried her over to me and then stopped. Saffie sighed and her shoulders sagged. She looked down at the spirit and smiled. "You did it. Thank you so much, Patti. Be at peace now."

The spirit closed her eyes...and faded away.

One of the other animals strolled over with Lily on its back. She grinned and waved. *FINALLY,* she mouthed.

"*MA'AM,*" I said with a relieved laugh. "What did you do?"

"I think I'd have to ask you the same question." Saffie winked. "Where are your shoes?"

"Long story. Just call me John McClane now."

Lily threw her head back and laughed silently.

"I don't get that reference, but you will tell me later." Saffie nodded to one of the fluffy wolf puppies beside her. "Two down, five to go. Hop on, *ma'am.*"

CHAPTER TWENTY-FIVE

SAVANNAH

"GO, GO, GO!" Saffie helped the last of the boys in silver dresses onto the backs of the fluffy wolf puppers. "TAKE THEM AND GO!"

"Glisa, lead them! FAST!" a fae girl with long rainbow ombre dreads shouted from behind red flowered antlers. Then she turned to us. "Saffie, what about you three?"

I had no idea who these people were, but we'd come across them stumbling through the forest in a panic. Saffie had leapt off her wolf-pup without hesitation and started throwing people on them. Within mere seconds, each the three-dozen white fluffy animals had at least three people riding on their backs. A fierce fae girl with long white hair and intense silver eyes whistled and then shouted in what had to be Seelie language. And then they were sprinting away, leaving me, Lily, and Saffie standing alone.

"Don't worry about us. We can't fail them *now*," Saffie shouted back, her cheeks flushed. "Get them to safety. They need The Circle now. GO, LUKAT, GO!"

Lukat, the chick with the sick dreads, grumbled but turned the animal around and chased after the others. Lily spun to face Saffie with sharp lavender eyes and black hair braided straight down her back. Now that she was standing next to me, I saw she was wearing the exact same dresses as all the others had been.

"Safferella? What are *we* doing? What's your plan?"

Saffie held her head high and narrowed her eyes on the forest in front of us. "*Bait. RUN.*"

Lily and Saffie took off, gracefully leaping into a run.

DAMN IT. I groaned and chased after them as fast as I could. Saffie was making a liar out of me. I'd told Cooper I wasn't running anymore yet here I was *running.*

"*BAIT?* For what? What's happening?" I shouted as soon as I got within a few feet of them. "Who were those people?"

"SLAVES!" Saffie yelled over her shoulder. "We just freed them! I may have killed a lot of Knights in doing so!"

"*SLAVES?! Ma'am.* How did you find slaves and free them already?" All I'd done was dream with Cooper. I felt seriously under accomplished.

Saffie pointed to Lily who was running in front of us and my eyes landed on her bare back...with glowing pink marks all over it. My breath left me in a rush. Then it hit me. The matching gray dresses. The panic. The hurry.

"Did they do that to you, Lily?"

She held one thumb up but didn't slow her pace.

Those sons'a bitches! Rage exploded inside of me.

Saffie gasped and her face snapped to our right. She threw her hands out and golden glitter exploded out of her. "LILY, SUN. NOW!"

Bright golden sunshine burst from her palms. Without slowing down, Lily thrust her arms out and blasted all of Seelie with sunlight. Then it clicked. *BAIT.* Saffie was drawing the Knights to *us* by using our magic and revealing our location. They'd think the slaves were with us and by the time they got here it'd be too late.

THIS IS FINE.
THIS IS FINE.

"They're here," Saffie growled like a damn lion with a sick smile on her face that made me both very concerned and horribly excited.

The trees swayed over our heads.

THIS IS BAT SHIT CRAZY.

WHAT ARE WE DOING?

"Stay behind me," Saffie shouted to us and flew up in front of Lily.

Knights landed in a straight line in front of us, looking like the elves of Rivendell with their matching gold armor and elegant wooden bows. Lily's sunlight shimmered against their armor.

Saffie's eyes glowed like diamonds under a spotlight. "They're *mine*."

Another line of Knights lowered to the ground with a thud behind us. Then two more lines, one on either side of us. They had us surrounded. They'd boxed us in. It was like in the movie the Gladiator except I was not Russell Crowe. The three of us stood in a triangle with our backs to each other. Except they'd trapped us in a small clearing in the forest where there weren't even trees to use as shields. *Oh my Goddess.*

I pulled my dagger out and held it up. "I'm taking you fishing when we get home. I don't think you knew what bait meant."

Saffie chuckled and it sent a chill down my spine. "Works for Tegan."

Lily's head snapped toward Saffie like she wanted to scream.

"*MA'AM*, you are not Tegan!" I shook my head and eyed the several dozen heavily armed, highly pissed off Knights surrounding us. "Tegan would have a plan. What's yours? Because I don't have any magic right now. Tell me you got something."

"They don't want to kill us outright, or they would have already."

"That is not reassuring, ma'am."

In perfect unison and Legolas-like grace, the Knights drew back on their bows and aimed them at us.

"The King wants us. Two Cards and a black magic witch? They want to bring us to him and be rewarded for it. Killing us won't do them any service." Saffie's voice was calm and sure, like she'd done this a million times. "And they want their slaves back."

I sighed and shook my head. *That does not sound like a plan,* I whispered.

"Lily, on my cue, duck behind that tree. Blind as many as you can," Saffie whispered in our ancient language just loud enough for us to hear. *"Savannah, guard her back. Don't let anything get near you."*

Lily and I looked to each other and then around the clearing.

"Ma'am, there ain't no damn tree."

Saffie chuckled and twirled her wrists. "Oh, there will be."

Gold glitter rained from her hands to the ground. I looked down and found vines slithering through the neon purple grass. About two feet in front of me, the ground was splitting, like something was trying to come *up.*

Since when can she do THAT? You sneak little shit, Safferella.

"I know we're pretty but are you just going to stand here all-night staring at us?" Saffie yelled out in a calm voice. "You don't talk to women often, do you?"

Lily's eyes widened and locked on me. *What is she doing?*

I shook my head. I thought she'd be stalling until she could get this tree out she'd mentioned, but it sounded like she was damn taunting them.

"Who's in charge here? I mean, besides the guy I killed a

little while ago." Saffie shrugged. "I'm sure you've replaced him by now."

Jesus, Mary, and Joseph, she's gonna get us killed.

Lily exhaled and wiggled her fingers like she was ready to move.

Out of the corner of my eye, I saw one of the Knights step forward with only a sword in his hand. No bow. In the back of my mind, I wondered if Tolkien had been to Seelie because these dudes looked *just* like the elves of Middle Earth.

"See, I knew it." Saffie brought her hands up and *clapped.* As in literal applause. "That wasn't so hard, was it?"

Who IS this girl? I liked stone-cold Saffie, but I wasn't sure where this persona was coming from. I knew she dreamt of vengeance for Riah and for what the Seelies did to her, but that passion was fiery and hot. This was cold and calculating. It was fearless—*oh no. OH SHIT. I did this.* That spell I'd done to unlock Cooper's magic so he could make nightmares affected Saffie, too. I'd even seen the silhouette of her and others when I did it.

I heard Kevin Hart's voice in my head say, *It's about to go down.*

"Is this about Zachariah?" the Legolas-wannabe asked with a twisted smile. "Yes, we've all heard how he fell for the half-breed Earthling and betrayed his own kind."

Saffie cocked her head to the side. "Which part of that bothers you most? The half-breed, Earthling, or betrayal?"

Tennessee is going to KILL me.

I just wanted to make Cooper stronger. I didn't intend to make Saffie mouthier.

Mr. Legolas-wanna snarled. "You might as well give up. You're too late. Zachariah is already dead."

I knew it wasn't true, but a lead weight dropped in my stomach.

Saffie snickered. "Then I've got nothing to lose, do I? Let's see if he wants to play."

She threw her hands straight up and glowing green spirits rose from the ground. They surged on the Knights, tackling them to the ground. Bows and arrows went flying in pieces. Knights screeched and cursed. *OH NO SHE DIDN'T!*

In front of us, a massive oak-looking tree that was about five feet wide pierced through the ground and shot up to the sky. I grabbed Lily's arm and dragged her toward cover while she blasted the Knights' eyes with sunshine. We crashed into the tree and spun around to look for Saffie, but vines sprung from the dirt, rising up to form a wall taller than me. We spun in circles, looking for a way out, but the vine-wall wrapped all the way around the tree. She'd trapped us. It was to keep us safe, that was obvious, but she'd trapped us all the same.

Damn. Maybe she IS Tegan.

"Can you see anything? You're taller."

Lily turned to me and arched one eyebrow.

"Hey, a couple inches is still taller—"

The ground trembled and then one of the trees *moved*. A split second later, Knights screamed and then there was a heavy splat. Lily and I looked to each other, then dove for the wall, climbing up the vines until we could peek over the top. Lily already had her hands out and was blasting people with sunshine like she was Cyclops with laser beams.

Around this clearing was mayhem like I'd never seen before. Saffie stood tall and terrible right where she'd been swinging her arms around like an orchestra conductor. She was *vicious*. Vines and roots flew left and right, seizing arms and legs and hoisting Knights in the air.

The soulmate crystal on the back of Saffie's hand was emerald green. Riah was definitely still alive, but these Knights were going to die for taunting her with it. This was brutal ruthlessness and I was enjoying every second of it—even though she'd put baby in the corner and out of play.

It was worth the show. I wanted to pull my cellphone out and videotape it, but I didn't want to look away. My phone was buried somewhere in my satchel after Saffie changed my clothes into this flimsy silky dress contraption.

Lily smacked my shoulder and then pointed up. I followed her finger just as a lone figure lowered from the sky. At first all I saw was orange. Saffie looked toward it but didn't attack. The figure, I couldn't even tell if it was a guy or a girl, held a glowing yellow sword in each hand. Pale orange wings flapped behind their back. They landed right on top of a Knight and sliced their sword right through his neck.

The newcomer looked up and I saw a beautiful dark-skinned girl with big dark eyes and a wide self-satisfied smile. She had sharp cheekbones and an angular jaw that made her look fierce. Her hair fell in wild waves down to her hips and glowed a pretty orange. "Lloyd sent me."

Saffie grinned. "Take the back?"

This new girl nodded, then darted away from Saffie and off to our left where the Knights were trying to fight off swinging tree branches. She leapt right into action. Her moves were insane. There was no doubt this girl was a warrior. A few Knights lunged for her, but Lily shot sunshine into their eyes. They hissed and shielded their faces and then fell to the new girl's blade.

I turned back to Saffie just as vines dropped down from the trees and coiled around Knights' necks, yanking them up and snapping sickeningly. Their legs dangled and swayed lifelessly. Blue fairyflies swarmed three of them and knocked them to the ground like something straight out of Jurassic Park—*don't underestimate the little guys!*

A dozen knights charged for Saffie from out of nowhere, like they'd just landed. They screamed like banshees, and it made me shiver. She flicked her wrist and sent puffy little yellow flowers that looked like dandelions flying right at them Knights and slammed into their faces. They gasped and dropped to their knees. Black veins stretched across their faces. Blood gushed from their eyes and noses. They face-planted in the dirt and didn't move.

I looked around expecting them all to be dead, but there were more coming.

Saffie raised her hands and seeds lifted off ground. She flicked her wrist and the seeds shot *straight down the Knights' throats*. They coughed and then leafy vines burst from their mouths and ears. They choked and tripped over their own feet. Screams echoed up their throats around the vines. Thick tree roots pierced through their bodies and shot out to the ground. They were being impaled from the *inside-out*.

GNARLY.

HOLY SHIT.

That second spell I'd done with Cooper *had* to have worked. Saffie had been vicious when we got here, but *this* Saffie was a stone-cold assassin. She just turned in a slow circle, using their own land to literally rip them apart. Those lavender eyes were fiercely sharp and the rage burning inside of them could have froze hell over.

I am here for it, ma'am.

Tennessee is gonna be PISSED, but I don't care.

While I just stood there like a useless lump clinging to a wall made of vines.

And then they were gone. Quicker than they appeared. I glanced around us but the land had already claimed the bodies, clearing them from our sight. Saffie spun to face me and Lily and just nodded. Blood was splattered on her fancy green and purple fairy outfit.

To me, it made the look even more sexy than it already was, but maybe I needed therapy.

The unknown girl walked up and chuckled. "That was a joy to watch."

"It was a joy to do." Saffie grinned. She waved her hand and the vine wall trapping me and Lily vanished. "Well, maybe not *that* part. Sorry, friends, I had to be careful with you."

I snorted. "I am one hundred percent here for assassin Saffie, please and thank you."

The girl frowned.

Saffie shrugged and held her left hand out. "I'm Saffie."

"I'm Quoya." She looked to me.

"I'm Savannah. This is Lily, but she can't speak right now."

Quoya pursed her lips. "The archway?"

Lily sighed and nodded.

"Lloyd sent me once the first set of slaves arrived to the village on the vakinyas—"

"*Vakinyas?*" I frowned. "Wait, those fluffy wolf doggos?"

Lily hung her head.

"Yes, they're called vakinyas. They are sacred to Seelie," Saffie's voice was soft and warm when she spoke of them. She turned back to Quoya. "Thank you for your help."

She smirked and eyed the pool of blood at her feet. "Not that you required such, prophetess, but happy to provide. Lukat instructed me to take you where you sought to go—"

"Why are you helping us?" I narrowed my eyes on her. "Pardon me, but I've known my whole damn life to not deal with the fae or trust them...so why should we believe you're genuinely helping us?"

Saffie arched one eyebrow and crossed her arms over her chest.

"Such is a fair accusation, sad as I am to admit." She pointed into the distance with her sword. "But the only Seelies who have ever made it to Earth are Royals and Knights. *They* cannot be trusted. They are monsters from the very depths of Lilith's soul. Everything they touch withers and dies, including this world we call home. The King only keeps us alive to play with us for entertainment. He steals young Earthlings to be his slaves, doing with them whatever he pleases both in and out of his chamber."

Lily shuddered.

Quoya's dark gaze dropped to Lily's arms and her face fell. "I heard they got to you. I am sorry, but I must say I am glad they did."

"*Excuse me?*"

Saffie's expression softened. "Lily's kidnapping is the direct reason we were able to free the slaves as we just did. We are just lucky no further harm was done to her in the process."

Lily pushed her shoulders back and nodded, then gave two thumbs up.

"I know you're tough." Saffie winked to her. Then she turned to our new friend. "Did all the slaves make it to The Circle?"

"As I was leaving, I saw Lukat arrive with the last of them. They should be safe by now...for now. Though I fear that will only last as long as the palace is distracted by their new visitor." Quoya smirked. "Lukat suggested there was somewhere specific you needed to go? She didn't say where."

"To find Ziva."

Quoya's eyes widened. "Ziva? She was taken by the Wild Night as a youngling, but I can bring you to her."

Ziva's a little kid? Well, Bentley was a kid when he went. Makes sense he'd befriend another child. I wasn't sure what assistance a young fae could give us, but I'd learned already not to doubt or question Bentley.

I cleared my throat and raised my hand. "Will we be running again? How far is this place?"

"Far enough yet too near," Quoya said under her breath. She rolled her shoulders and her shimmery wings fluttered. "I suggest we fly. Saffie, can you carry one of your friends? I can take the other."

I wanted to protest. I did not have wings. I did not like the idea of flying high in the air without wings. But I loathed running. More importantly, I trusted Saffie.

Saffie shook her own wings out, but hers looked so much different than Quoya's. Saffie's were just a cluster of stars, basically, whereas every other fae I'd seen so far had solid formed wings.

Lily glanced back and forth between the two girls with one arched black eyebrow. She pursed her lips and then walked to stand beside Quoya. They were about the same height. Lily nodded and pointed to their heads. *Taller,* she mouthed.

I chuckled. "That's fair. Aight, how you want me, Safferella?"

Saffie held her arms out like she wanted a hug so I gave her one, hooking my arms over her neck. She wrapped her arms around my waist and pushed off the ground. Cold air rushed over me, blowing my hair into my face. I wasn't about to let go, so I closed my eyes and pretended like I was in a convertible.

"Savannah? Are you okay?

"Yes, ma'am. Just not looking."

Saffie chuckled in my ear. "Okay, just checking."

"Lily okay?"

"Yep, Lily is good. She's right next to us. You'd know that if you opened your eyes."

"I'd know a lot of things if I opened my eyes...like how far down the ground is...how your wings don't really look like wings at all....what kind of monsters or hellscape is below us," I said with a shrug, enjoying the darkness of having my eyes closed. "I'm good. Ignorance is bliss."

"We can't fly right into the Wild Night," Quoya shouted over the rush of wind. "But I'll bring us to the edge. It's going to be a treacherous journey inside, so I hope you're ready."

Why do I feel like Samwise and Frodo heading with the one ring into Mount Doom? This Quoya chick just better not be a Gollum, or I will melt her ass in lava.

Goddess, I hope there's no lava.

I'm not built for heat.

Just to be sure, I started going over every word and action Quoya had made thus far in my head—I was an overthinker, it was par for the course. But then I realized something I had just blown right over before because of the chaos.

"Saffie, did she call you a prophetess?"

She sighed in my ear. "Yes. There was this intense prophecy given to them by the Seer at the end of the One Hundred Years' War with Lilith that stated a specific person would save them."

"And we trust this Seer?"

"She's Riah's mother."

At that, I opened my eyes but kept them locked on Saffie's face. "I feel like I might have known that already. But damn. Okay. And they think this person is you?"

Her face fell. "When we get back to the village, I'll show it to you. The evidence against me is substantial."

My chest tightened. I licked my lips and my hair got stuck in my mouth. "Saving people isn't a bad thing."

"I know," she said softly. "And I want to save them..."

"I may not know this prophecy, Safferella, but I know in my gut there is no way you aren't supposed to save Riah first."

Her eyes glistened with unshed tears. "I just have to get to him."

"That glyph is still green—"

"For now—"

"*Saffie.*" I waited until she looked at me. "I'd bet money the King wants to use Riah as bait to lure you right into the palace. Where they'll outnumber you. Especially after you just slaughtered a shit ton of them."

"Does that not concern you?"

"Of course it concerns me. But any chance to save him is better than no chance, no matter how treacherous." I nodded to where Lily was holding on to Quoya. "We're with you. And I think you've already made friends."

Silence.

"Saffie, this ain't Riah's first rodeo. He can handle it." *Goddess, please let me not be lying.*

"I know. I just have to keep telling myself that." Her voice was soft. "I know we have to do this smart, it's just killing me more and more with every passing second."

"Good thing you're the Death Card, then. Eh?"

She snorted. "I should drop you for that."

I gasped. "SAFFERELLA, ma'am."

"Okay, follow me!" Quoya shouted, distracting Saffie from whatever prank she was about to pull on me.

I squeezed my eyes shut because I had zero interest in watching us land. I felt air rush by and my stomach dropped like we were on a rollercoaster, but I didn't open my eyes up until my feet were planted firmly on the ground.

And then my jaw dropped.

I didn't know what I was expecting but *this* was not it.

Quoya sighed and gestured in front of us. "This is the Wild Night. The land of death and fire."

The Wild Night was fire and brimstone. It was Ragnarök. It was a Christian's view of Hell. Everything was on fire. It was like standing across a lake and watching a mountain burn. It was a wildfire raging in perpetuity.

We stood at the base of a mountainscape with a river of lava between us. Our feet sank in black dirt. I glanced around us but the forest was more than a football field away, like it was trying to separate itself from this travesty. Smoke and ash billowed into the sky as trees burned, fully engulfed in flames.

Suddenly, Bentley's return to us on the beach made sense. We'd pulled him from *this*.

My heart sank. We weren't even inside and I couldn't fathom it. My thoughts went to Bentley, and a million questions I didn't really want to know the answer to flashed in my mind. I was thankful none of the Bishops were here with us to see this. I was going to have to try and block Cooper from seeing this memory in my dreams and nightmares—because it was definitely going to haunt me.

I knew Saffie and Lily were thinking the same thing without even asking.

All we did was stare in horror.

Bentley lived there for seven *years*.

"It never stops burning," Quoya whispered. "Those sent here never return."

"Except for Ziva?"

She grimaced. "Yes and no."

The river of lava that had been perfectly flat rippled, and waves rolled toward us. Quoya cursed and unsheathed her swords just as flames burst from the surface of the lava. I dove backward to dodge getting hit, but the lava rushed toward us. Behind us the land shot up into a steep cliffside, like it was alive and forcing the river back. But it was coming right for me. I scurried back but I was running out of space. Something gripped my waist and then I was lifted off the ground just as lava covered the spot I'd been in.

Saffie held both Lily and I off the ground but not very high.

"Safferella—"

"There's nothing *alive* for me to use here," she said in a rush. "I already tried."

"No. I was going to ask you how long you can hold us like this."

The ground shook and rocks jumped out of the lava. Quoya cursed and dove for it with her yellow sword. My breath caught in my throat as this rolly-polly rock unfolded into a monster from a nightmare. It was made of stone, ash, and flame—eyes and a mouth with literal flames flickering out. It swung for Quoya, *just* missing her. With her pale orange wings and orange hair, she blended in with the fire, so it was hard to track her.

Quoya was skilled, but each slice of her sword only slowed the monster down. Each time an arm or leg was chopped off, it just re-formed in the lava and grew back, like an evil cousin to a hydra.

Saffie's magic flickered and we sank down a few inches before she caught us.

Two shadows cut across the lava and my heart stopped. I opened my mouth to yell for Quoya when the two shadows parted and turned to flame. The smaller one jumped up and landed on top of the monster's round head, then sank its teeth into the monster's head. I couldn't tell what it was under that flame ball.

The other shadow-turned-flame slid like a baseball player across the lava. A long sword made of flames swung through the air and sliced the monster's legs clean off. They splashed and sank into the lava. The monster roared and tried to fight back but then their arms were just suddenly *gone.* There were too many flames, too much lava and fire, I couldn't tell where one thing ended and another began.

But then a person flipped up and slammed the tip of a fire-sword right into the chest of the monster...then all three of them plummeted down into the lava river.

I gasped and leaned forward—to do what, I had no idea.

A split second later that person pushed up out of the lava river and arched their back, flipping their hair made entirely of fire over their head like the Little Mermaid wishes she had. My jaw dropped. Thoughts failed to function. None of us made a sound or movement.

The person strolled out of the lava and I saw the tale tell hour-glass outline and figure of a woman. She sauntered across the black sand with a big black dog marching beside her. Both of them were drenched in flames, like someone had dumped gasoline on them and then lit 'em up. Their bodies were both solid black, like charred charcoals. Like a house after it has burned to the ground.

She looked up and flames danced from her eyes. She waved her hand and the lava receded back into the river and away from us. Saffie's grip dropped and my feet crashed onto the dirt with a heavy thud. I braced myself for heat, but the sand was cool to the touch.

There was so much to say, yet all I could do was stare.

The girl walked toward us, and with every step the flames extinguished. Her charred black skin with fire clinging to it faded into a glorious brown color a few shades darker than Lennox or Warner's. Actually, it was the same pretty color as Quoya's. If there'd been any doubt as to whether this was a girl or not before, that was gone now. She wore a sexy little black number to rival a belly dancer's outfit—because apparently in Seelie being mostly naked was ideal.

As she walked, the high slits on her black skirt parted to reveal long, lean legs that had gold chains wrapped around them. More gold chains were wrapped around her waist and covered her chest. Her hair was tied up in a high tight bun and it was neon-pink, yet the few strands hanging by her face were lilac. A gold chain covered in diamonds was coiled around her bun and then laid flat down the middle of her face until it attached to her nose piercings.

My jaw dropped. *Who is this Goddess?*

For a moment, I wondered if she was *the* Goddess, but then I realized that was highly unlikely. It was just a jarring reveal. One second she was a charred and flaming nightmare, and the next she was flawlessly beautiful.

I was so distracted by her that I somehow paid no attention to that prancing dog at her side that was now a fluffy reddish color—almost like a golden retriever but darker and definitely not an *Earth* dog.

The girl stopped in front of us and looked Saffie up and down with big hazel eyes. "Bentley was right. You do look like one of them."

Saffie narrowed her eyes and cocked her head to the side. Golden glitter danced around her fingertips. "Who are you?"

Quoya smiled and shook her head. "*Ziva.*"

CHAPTER TWENTY-SIX

SAFFIE

THE GIRL STOPPED in front of us and looked me up and down with big hazel eyes. "Bentley was right. You do look like one of them."

I narrowed my eyes and cocked my head to the side. I felt my magic tingle in my fingertips, and it flashed in my peripheral vision. All I felt in her soul was rage and sharp determination. "Who are you?"

Quoya smiled and shook her head. "*Ziva.*"

"*You're* Ziva?" Savannah shook her head and blinked. "I thought Quoya said you were young—"

"When she was taken, yes." Quoya shrugged like this was obvious.

"I was a young girl when I was sent to the Wild Night, but time does not work the same in there," Ziva said with a smoky kind of voice, gesturing to the wildfire behind her. "But you know this already from Bentley, otherwise you would not be here with us now."

Savannah cleared her throat. "What did you mean she looks like one of them?"

Ziva gave us a small smile, then walked up to me and held

out her left hand. Gold chains and diamonds sparkled as she moved. "I am Ziva. For the last seven years, Bentley has been my best friend. And *you* are Saraphina Proctor."

"You can call me Saffie." I shook her hand and smiled. "It's nice to meet you. Bentley was rather adamant about us finding you. I think he was worried."

That rage in her soul lightened and I felt a shimmer of happiness for a fleeting second that was replaced by sadness. "I miss him. I am not quite sure how long it has been since he was here. I come in and out of the Wild Night. Time is a strange thing for me."

"That sounds overwhelming, I hope we can keep you out of there now." I smiled. "These are my friends Savannah and Lily."

The reddish-brown dog sitting by her feet decided he'd waited long enough, apparently, because he barked and shoved his face into my hand. I giggled and ruffled his ears. He had big black teddy bear eyes and his fur was silky soft despite him being covered in flames a moment ago. The coloring of his fur was actually the same color as my Olli. It made my heart heavy to think about what he was doing.

"Hello, puppy. Who are you?"

"This is Squishy."

Savannah chuckled. "Squishy?"

Ziva shrugged. "He's Bentley's. Bentley and I were kids when he found newborn Squishy. He'd said, *he's so squishy I could die,* and the name stuck."

I thought about Olli and how much I'd missed him. I knew Bentley had to be torn up over his Squishy. I crouched down and gave him a hug because I sensed he wanted one. Then I pulled back and smiled. "Well, Squishy, we're gonna have to get you home to Bentley, then."

He barked and licked my face.

When I stood, Ziva was smiling. "You've been busy already,

Saffie. Freed the slaves and eliminated a lot of Knights. I think we'll be good friends. Where's your other companion? Bentley said he saw you coming in with three females—the Sun, the Magician, and the Queen of Swords. I see your Sun and your Queen. Where is your Magician?"

My jaw dropped. "He knew the four of us were coming?"

Ziva nodded. "One of the last things he saw, but yes."

Savannah whistled under her breath and shook her head. "Willow was blinded when we came through the archway. Lily here lost her ability to speak, and I lost my memory of my magic."

My heart sank. "We got attacked by Knights and were separated. We're trying to find Willow still and then we need to get to the palace."

"What was your price?"

My stomach tightened into knots as I lifted my hand up to show her the marking of my abstract butterfly. "This."

Her hazel eyes flashed, and I knew she knew what it was. She met my eyes. "I do not dare speak of what I think that means. Let us get your Riah and he will for sure know."

I nodded. It wasn't reassuring but I didn't blame her. And getting Riah was my main priority. "Do you know where they're keeping him? And how to get there?"

"In the dungeon." Ziva sighed. "And I know someone who might be able to help get you inside the palace."

"Do you need me?" Quoya twirled her sword around. "I'd like to get back to assist and prepare."

"Go ahead, Quoya. Thanks for escorting them to me. I'll take it from here. Ensure The Circle is ready."

"Goodluck, Saffie—and friends. I hope to see you soon." Quoya waved and then shot into the sky like a rocket. In seconds, she was out of sight.

"Come, we need to keep moving. Follow me." Ziva waved for us to follow her.

Squishy pranced beside her like she was taking him out for an afternoon walk for fun. Savannah, Lily, and I fell into line behind her. My legs were so short I was practically jogging to keep up. We followed her along the edge of the lava river and then around a mountainside that jutted out.

"Um, Miss Ziva, ma'am?" Savannah cleared her throat as our pathway turned into a narrow valley between mountains. "Prepare for what?"

Ziva glanced over her shoulder with furious, sharp eyes. "You do not yet know the impossibility it is to reach the palace. We're going to need help and a whole lot of luck. But I've been preparing. We all have."

Knots formed in the pit of my stomach. "Ziva, do you know of the prophecy?"

"Yes," she said softly, her voice rough and low. "Bentley knew it as well. He warned us, The Circle, that it was you and that we should prepare—for your arrival was imminent."

My breath left me in a rush. Bentley had known and he hadn't told me. Hadn't warned me in any way. Part of me wanted to be furious with him for it, the other part of me knew deep down that it was better I didn't know. Riah was more than my heart could handle.

"The question is..." Ziva stopped and turned to me. "What do *you* think of the prophecy?"

"I will destroy anything that comes between me and Riah, prophecy or not."

"I kind of hope it comes to that." Ziva grinned. She pointed behind her. "For those without wings, try not to look down."

Look down?

"Ma'am. No," Savannah drawled out the *o* like it was three syllables long.

Ziva waved us on as she rounded the edge of the mountains —and right to the edge of the cliff where a narrow, one-person wide rope bridge stretched over a deep canyon. Without pausing or missing a beat, she skipped along the bridge like it didn't dangle hundreds of feet off the ground by only ropes and vines. Like *she* had wings. But she didn't. I eyed her back and found no trace of wings whatsoever.

"*Oh, this some baby back bullshit,*" Savannah mumbled. "I take it back. I'll run."

Lily gripped the vines and leaned over the edge. She shuddered and then leapt onto the bridge. Up ahead, Ziva and Squishy were already to the other side, standing at the opening of a glowing turquoise cave.

"Go ahead, Savannah."

"I'm workin' on it," she hissed.

I chuckled. "Savannah, *I* have wings. And I'm a fast flyer. Even if you fell, I'd catch you before you hit."

She whirled around with wide blue eyes. "*You're fast? That's what you've got for me?*"

I shrugged. "I outflew Tennessee once."

"Well...shit." She turned back to the bridge where Lily was finishing the last few steps. "Imma run, okay?"

"Go for it."

She let out a battle cry and sprinted over the slabs of the bridge like there was an enemy to slay at the other side. I chuckled and flew behind her. It was true. I *had* outflown Tennessee once. Back before the twins arrived in Tampa. Before he knew that he knew me. Before he knew he had wings of his own. And I knew he'd barely been trying to keep up. If he'd wanted to catch me, he would have. But Savannah didn't need to hear that.

Oh, I sounded like Bentley or Tegan there.

Even though I did have wings, I didn't look down as I flew over. I kept my eyes on my friends so I didn't lose any more of them. Savannah lunged onto the cliff and practically hugged the mountainside while mumbling something about being dramatic. Ziva nodded and then continued on, leading the way into the cave. I was expecting wilderness and a tough climb, but inside the cave was merely a staircase carved into the mountain.

Lily scowled and glanced over her shoulder, then tapped on Ziva's shoulder.

"This is The Circle's passageway. Not many Seelies will risk this side of the Wild Night. They don't like to get close and the land is untamed out here, so the Knights don't know this exists."

Savannah cursed. "I am a little unsettled right now, so I'm going to distract myself by asking personal questions that I don't have the right to ask so just lie to me if you must. Wait, can Seelies lie?"

Ziva smirked over her shoulder. "Fortunately, they cannot."

"Why is that a good thing?"

"Because the King has no idea he has an enemy in his own lands. He will not know what hits him when we finally strike."

The stairs seemed to descend straight into Hell with how far down we were going. I understood Savannah's unease and I knew by the faces Lily was making she did too.

"How is it you've fooled him if you cannot lie?"

At that, Ziva half turned and gave me a wicked grin. "Because *I* am not full Seelie. I can lie as well as you can, Saffie."

I opened my mouth and then shut it. "Half-breeds can lie here?"

She chuckled. "Yes, but do not tell the King that. Would hate to ruin the surprise prematurely."

Savannah snorted. "I like you, ma'am."

"Thank you?"

"You're welcome." Savannah frowned. "Why don't you have wings if you're a half-breed? Saffie does."

"I asked my father that once. He was arcana, and he said, *genetics is a bitch.*"

Savannah threw her head back and laughed. "Ain't that the truth. Where is your father now?"

Ziva took a deep breath and then exhaled slowly. "Earth. Though I cannot say for certain where. I have not had contact since he left."

I frowned. "Have you been to Earth, Ziva?"

Suddenly, we reached the bottom of the stairs and were in front of another opening. This one was an octagon shape made of gray stones. That same turquoise glow illuminated the way.

Ziva sighed. "I was born there, lived there as a child before a Knight found me. The Knights are instructed to bring back all half-breed Earthlings to Seelie. My father put up enough of a fight with his magic that that Knight decided to take him as well."

Lily held her arms out and pointed to the soft, glowing pink markings.

"The King has a penchant for young Earthlings. They're all delivered to his chamber upon arrival and then he decides what to do with them. I was never a slave, but the Wild Night was torture enough." Ziva shook her head. "My story is one for another day. Though I can lie, I promise on a sea of spider lilies that I will always be truthful to you."

I nodded. "Thank you. We trust you."

It wasn't a lie, I did trust her, but I wasn't about to make the same oath back. It wasn't one to make lightly. If she was bothered by this omission, she didn't show it. She just smiled and turned for that octagon opening.

On the other side sat a lake that glowed a brilliant turquoise —the same light we could see from the top of the staircase. There was no bridge to cross the lake nor was there any other way to go, but there was a line of big gray stones sitting in the water. Squishy charged across the stones and to the other side with Ziva hot on his heels. This time, it was Lily who seemed the most nervous, while Savannah was smiling. She grabbed

Lily's hand and dragged her across the stones. I sighed and followed after them.

We caught up with Ziva just as the pathway curved around a cliff and then under a waterfall on our left. After the waterfall, the pathway turned and opened up into a dark lagoon. The water was that same glowing turquoise, but it held streaks of blue as well. Everything else around us was black. The dirt, the stones, the trees hanging over the lagoon—all black. It was like one of those blacklights I'd seen in Salem that only lit up the glowing parts.

Savannah gasped but kind of hissed a little at the same time. Her jaw dropped and her feet slid to a stop. She stared straight ahead. Lily frowned and skipped over, then her eyes widened. Ziva and Squishy walked to the edge of the water and let the glowing color wash over their feet. I hurried to catch up—then did a double take.

The lagoon was full of mermaids.

Like that movie Chutney had watched with me in Lookout Tower in the fall called *Peter Pan,* there were about a dozen of these females lounging on the shore and stretched out on stones. They weren't the bright colored kind like in the film. Their skin was a pale gray with dark veins or splotches on them. Most of them had long black hair and eyes that were entirely yellow, like no pupils or irises, just yellow. And the scales on their tails were in varying shades of gray.

It was a little bit creepy but still beautiful and fascinating. I'd never seen a—

"*Mermaids,*" Savannah whispered.

"Dauvotai," Ziva corrected her. "But yes, essentially the same."

The *dauvotai* noticed us but didn't move. They did throw some fish-like things over to Squishy for him to eat. The lagoon opened up on the far side to a river that seemed to wind a bit. Trees hung low with vines falling into the water.

One of the females closest to us smiled, then looked over her shoulder and shouted something in a language I had never heard, "...*Ziva.*"

The shadows on the far side of the lagoon moved and the water rippled. A silvery fin splashed above the surface. Lily and Savannah took a step back. Squishy walked in deeper. I stood still beside Ziva.

Suddenly, a girl emerged from under the water with long brown hair—*brown?* I had not seen any brunettes since arriving. It was such an Earthly color. In fact, this female's skin held barely any trace of gray and there were none of the dark lines. Her brown hair was a pretty, chocolatey brown and hung in waves down over her bare chest. She perched up on a stone and curled her shimmery silver fin around Squishy's body, pulling him into her lap for cuddles.

"This is Shannon," Ziva said softly. "She's a half-breed as well."

Shannon looked up and smiled, her light eyes reflecting the neon color of the water. "Hello, you brought me new friends. Earthlings?"

Ziva nodded.

"Hi, I'm Savannah!" she said excitedly from suddenly right beside me.

I smiled. "I'm Saffie. My friend here is Lily, but she cannot speak."

Shannon frowned. "I am sorry to hear that, but I do love your name. Have you seen the spider lilies yet?"

I gasped. "*No.* I'd love to."

"I'll show you." Ziva turned to Shannon and her eyes sharpened. "We come to you for more than one reason. The first, they have lost a friend they came into Seelie with. A blind witch. Have you seen her?"

"She's about our height with brown eyes and blonde hair."

Savannah tapped on her left forearm. "Has a black *I* on her arm."

"Blonde hair? *OH*, hair like sunshine?" Shannon smiled like she was proud of herself for figuring that out. But then her expression faltered. "Sorry, no, none have come by here by that description. What is the other reason you come?"

Savannah cursed.

I sighed and scrubbed my face with my hands—

Shannon gasped. "ZIVA. Her hand! And her WINGS!"

At this, the other females' attention snapped to me and stayed.

"With wings that sparkle like the stars," Shannon whispered as her eyes drank in the sight of my wings. *"Marked in green then red to follow, gold hearted lines are not hollow*—Ziva, is this her?"

Ziva nodded. "Yes, our prophetess has arrived. That is one of the other reasons we have come."

Shannon grinned but it looked mischievous. "We are in."

"We're not doing anything just yet—"

"When crimson flashes by her hand," I said and tapped on my glyph which was thankfully still green. *"Raise arms together, make your stand."*

All of them looked to each other and grinned.

And I felt their desire for revenge.

It almost made *me* smile.

I hadn't expected so much assistance here in Seelie, but I was prepared to burn it all down. If fate brought me a prophecy and an army to do so, then I wasn't going to turn it down.

Ziva said something in that foreign language and gestured to the river behind them. "Watch for my cue."

"We are ready. He must pay."

Savannah and Lily high-fived.

"There was one more reason we came—"

"Wait for the night his life is thin, release him from his cage

of sin." Shannon nodded and then tapped on her face. "Your soulmate?"

Sharp pain shot through my chest.

"He is in the dungeon," Ziva said softly. "We seek the path."

"I can escort you, though I have need of your assistance as well. This night we found two other land strays. Will you take them with you? They cannot stay here much longer."

Ziva nodded. "They'll have to go with us, but after, yes, I will bring them to The Circle."

Shannon sighed with relief. "Thank you. Wait here. I shall retrieve them."

Ziva turned to us and grimaced. "Sometimes the King will dispose of a body he has finished with but they're not quite dead...or they are thrown out by the Queen...or if they're lucky, sometimes people escape the palace and wind up by the river where the dauvotai take them until one of us can bring them to the village."

"That's a whole lot of fucked up to unpack in one statement," Savannah grumbled.

Lily shuddered but then her eyes widened and locked on the lagoon behind me. Her jaw dropped and tears glistened on her eyelashes.

I frowned and spun around—and gasped. "AMELIA?! LANDY?!"

CHAPTER TWENTY-SEVEN

TENNESSEE

"THERE!" Bentley screamed and charged ahead of me. "DON'T STOP!"

I clenched my teeth and dug my heels in harder, pushing my legs faster. Tegan's snow-white hair swung side to side over my arm with every one of my steps. I was trying to focus on fleeing this Goddess-forsaken hellhole but the way her arm flopped all lifelessly like that was short-circuiting my brain. My pulse was flying so fast it was almost one steady stream.

And I had Chutney hanging on my back, held up by half-assed magic I threw up there on the fly. She was unconscious, but I wasn't sure how bad of shape she was in. All I knew was the fresh scent of her blood dripping onto my shoulder.

Easton cursed violently from my left side. *"I'M FINE. I'M FINE."*

Except he wasn't fine. None of us were. Too many of us had gone down on the way *in.* Easton's right arm was mangled with a bone protruding from his skin. If there were any blood-eating creatures out here, we were one hell of a beacon for them. Poor Lennox, the first one of us to go down, was draped over his left shoulder like a ragdoll. Her arms flopped and her indigo hair swayed.

"*Razzle dazzle, razzle dazzle,*" Deacon growled under his breath from right behind me. Red lightning and mist shot out like a tidal wave all around us. "*Stay back, stay back, stay back.*"

Chutney slipped down my back so I stopped short, but with Tegan in my arms I couldn't reach for her. *SHIT.* My magic was just *not* responding. *Come on. WORK.*

"*Haven, move!*" Uncle Tim yelled.

"*Dropping—*"

Chutney sank. I summoned a gust of wind to catch her, but this damned place was affecting me, or maybe it was my unconscious soulmate in my arms. Or both.

"*Tim, get us closer!*" Hunter yelled and I felt magic hitting my back.

"*This is gonna hurt—*"

Hunter roared in pain. "*Just...keep...MOVING.*"

"Haven, freeze," Uncle Timothy barked in my ear. "Hunter, grab her."

I couldn't see what they were doing behind me, but Chutney's arms coiled around my neck. Magic flashed in my peripheral vision, then Chutney's legs hooked over my hips. Uncle Tim leaned in front of me and fired magic *under* Tegan.

"*MOVE, MOVE, MOVE!*" Deacon screamed and his voice cracked. "*NOW!*"

He flew past us, looking a lot like me. He had an unconscious Devon draped in his arms and was firing his Devil magic out from under her. His left hand was as white as snow and had gold lightning-shaped streaks across it from when Tegan burned him. As he moved, it flashed like a rainbow. Emersyn was hanging on his back, except she was awake in her hypnotic state, so Deacon just *made* her hold on.

"GO, HAVEN!"

I charged forward without hesitation. Chutney was re-secured on my back so I could run, but even my speed was slower. I should have been miles ahead of the others. I should have gotten out and called for help. But the Land of the Lore was trying to claim me, to drag me in and never let me out. Every step felt like quicksand. It was affecting me more than the others.

"*TIM, DRAG ME, DAMN IT!*"

I glanced over my shoulder just as Hunter bellowed in pain. Poor guy's leg was broken and hanging in unnatural ways. Uncle Tim had one arm hooked around Hunter's waist and was literally dragging him, but they weren't moving fast.

"SILAS, BURN!" Bentley emerged from the shadows and sprinted back to his father. He used his fiery sword to point to our right. "BURN!"

I didn't look. I kept my focus on the road *ahead*. On our pathway *out*. It was right there, too. I saw it. I *felt* it. The light at the end of the tunnel was calling us home. We just had to get there. It would've been easier to carry all the injured if Bentley and Silas helped but then we would've had no free hands for defense, and that was the only thing keeping our path open.

Bright orange flames surged all around us. The heat stung my skin it was so close.

A huge dark shadow flew over my head. I gasped and looked up—and found a massive light gray dragon blocking the night sky. *SILAS*. He spit streams of fire in every direction. His tail whipped and my eyes widened. *Bentley* was hanging from the tip of his tail. He swung his legs forward, then let go and flew like Tarzan. In my peripheral vision, I saw him firing magic and using those fighting skills I hadn't gotten used to yet—but I kept my eyes on the prize.

The exit.

Silas landed about thirty feet ahead. He whipped around and lowered his head, spitting rivers of fire behind us. The spikes on the back of his head and spine were menacing as hell when he ducked down like that. His gold eyes shined like pure sunshine.

The tunnel opening was right behind him. We were almost there.

Red lightning streaked across the sky and then Deacon appeared at the opening. His violet eyes were wide with fear and locked on something behind us. "RUN!"

My heart stopped. I pushed even harder.

Deacon cursed and leapt through the opening that was now looking literally like a tunnel, like this magic fog of death was trying to lock us inside. He slipped out of sight but then a split second later he leapt back in without Emersyn or Devon. He charged right toward us, his face pale and eyes wide. Without a word, he sprinted by me—Hunter screamed in agony.

"GO!" Hunter wailed.

A cold chill slid up my spine. The gold bands around my arm flashed like strobe lights. My stomach tightened into knots. Something was coming. Something *bad*. Something my grandfather's sword wanted to fight. But I had no hands to—

Bentley slid up beside me out of nowhere. He fired his orange magic at my back and then Chutney slipped off of me. In a smooth, seamless motion, Bentley dipped down and threw her over his shoulder, then took off for the opening. He glanced over his shoulder and those golden eyes widened. "MICHAEL!"

I cursed and slid to a stop. Dirt flew up in front of me. I tossed Tegan in the air, then ducked down and let her drop to hang over my shoulder. Time seemed to slow down around me, everything slipped into a blur. My gold bands were glowing like spotlights. I flexed my left hand and Michael's sword flashed into my palm. *Michael*, Bentley had yelled. Not *Tenn*. But Michael. Because whatever was behind me needed a certain kind of enemy.

Bentley kept running with Chutney. Easton chased after him, carrying Lennox in the exact same way. I tightened my grip on my grandfather's sword, *my* sword, and pushed off the balls of my feet. Deacon and Uncle Tim hobbled by me, clutching Hunter's body between them.

And then I felt it.

A wall of dark force pulsing with black magic. A vile and evil power unlike anything I'd ever felt. I clenched my teeth, raised my sword, and spun. All I saw was black nothingness and the bright glow of Heaven's sword slicing through it—and then fire and smoke exploded all around me.

My feet shot off the ground. I flew backward so hard and fast my gold wings curled in around me. I yanked Tegan down and squeezed her to my chest. Ice cold air rushed over me, head to foot—and fresh oxygen filled my lungs. Over the top of my wings I saw the edge of the tunnel opening as I flew through it, leaving that damned place behind. My magic surged with a vengeance. My wings flew out and flapped, flipping me right-side up. My boots slammed into the ground and the earth trembled around me. But my strength was spent. My body collapsed and my knees crashed to the dirt. Pain laced up my thighs. I sighed with relief. *We're out.*

Silas flew over our heads, flipping head-over-tail and out of control. I threw my right hand up and pushed my magic. It responded *instantly,* catching Silas's free fall and gently lowering him to the ground. He landed half a mile away and shook himself, then shot back into the sky. A split second later, he landed in front of me.

I lowered Tegan into the cradle of my arms and let my gaze scan over her, but she seemed to be breathing just fine. Her hair was still snow-white, which meant her eyes were no doubt white and gold still too. My stomach turned. But she wasn't the only one down. I glanced over my shoulder in search of the others.

Uncle Tim knelt beside Hunter. Deacon was a few feet back crouched in front of Emersyn, who stared blankly ahead with an unconscious Chutney in her lap. Bentley carried his mother over to lay her on the ground beside Hunter—who instantly sat up to check on her. But she looked as lifeless as she did before. *She's alive.* I could still feel her magic. That had to be a good sign.

"*Help...please...take...*" Easton groaned. "*Help.*"

I glanced over my shoulder and found him sheet-white with a heavy stream of blood running down his body. Bentley cursed and sprinted over. He reached up and gently slid Lennox off Easton's shoulder, then lowered her to the ground. Easton exhaled a stream of obscenities and hopped around. I knew that dance. That was the *holy hell that hurts but I can take it* dance.

"*Nine...ten...eleven...and me. That's twelve,*" Silas said with a heavy sigh. "We're all here."

For some strange reason, I chuckled. "I think that's the most I've ever heard you speak, Silas."

He bent over and rested his hands on his knees. He chuckled and shook his head, then looked up at me with an *actual* smile. "Pot calling the kettle black, angel boy?"

I sank back on my heels and laughed.

The others chuckled with us.

"*Goddess,* we have a twisted dark as hell sense of humor," Uncle Tim said with a grin.

We all nodded.

Easton coughed then pointed behind me. "Are we in the clear now, B? We're out of that place?"

"Yeah, we were already out but Tenn using Michael's sword pushed the Land of the Lore away from us." Bentley rolled his neck. "It will be hiding from us at this point. So we're safe from it at least."

"What was that thing? At the end?" Silas growled.

Bentley shook his head. "I only saw that Tenn had to swing."

Everyone looked to me.

The word *Lilith* bounced around my mind, but I didn't dare

say that out loud. Mostly because *I* didn't want to believe that that was her. I cleared my throat. "I don't know, but I've never felt something as dark as that."

"*I don't like the sound of that,*" Deacon whispered. He waved his hand in front of Emersyn, but she didn't react. His purple gaze shot to mine. "I need to get her home. I'm afraid to release her myself. I'm just...I'd rather be careful. I need Katherine."

I nodded. Tegan seemed to pulse in my arms, as if I needed the reminder of her having gone white witch on me again. Although this time, I couldn't even be upset with her. Devon was going to die, of that I was *absolutely* positive. And I knew my soulmate recognized that too. She had to use her magic to save her mother...it just came with one hell of a side effect.

"Dad, you breathing down there?" Bentley crouched over his parents. "Dad?"

"Um..." Hunter grumbled and lifted his right hand. His soulmate crystal was red but then changed to green as we watched. "Not really. We have to get home. Now."

"Um, my dudes?" Easton gestured around us. "Anyone notice it looks exactly the same as when we went in? How long were we in there?"

Bentley grimaced. "From what I heard, time works slower in there than normal. So..."

Uncle Tim stood and stretched his back. "Only one way to find out."

And then I realized our ride was unconscious. Tegan felt like lead weight in my arms. Sure, she was light for me just by weight, but every time she went white witch it impacted my magic more and more.

"I can fly you back."

I looked up to meet Silas's eyes. "Sorry. We should have planned for this problem."

Silas smirked. "I do believe the Goddess *did*. She did instruct me to come, didn't she?"

"Touché." I nodded and got to my feet. "Fly us to Eden?"

"Eden? Not Tampa?" Deacon frowned.

I looked down at Tegan in my arms and then the others who'd gotten hurt. "Let's just get them all to Eden, where we *know* they're safe on holy ground. Then we'll call the others, okay?"

Once Silas shifted, it took us a few moments to get all the injured situated on his back. Easton was up at the front holding Lennox with his good arm, because the ride was a tad smoother up there—like any good rollercoaster. Deacon sat Emersyn directly in front of him so he could hold on to her shirt while using his magic to pin her down. Chutney was draped across his lap. Bentley held his mother behind them. Hunter was having the hardest time getting in place with his messed-up leg, but Uncle Tim had him wrapped in a bear hug from behind.

Which left me in the back with Tegan against my chest. As we flew over the clouds and across the night sky, I couldn't help but think about our first dragon ride together. I clung to that memory as tight as I could to keep myself from spiraling into a panic attack. Thing was, I *felt* her in my arms. Her magic was stronger than ever. I didn't understand what this was or why it kept happening, but the fact that it happened when spirits or heavenly power were involved terrified me to my core.

I wrapped my arms around her tight and just breathed her in.

Come on, kitten. Wake up. Come back to me.

Silas spit a fireball and growled. Without Chutney, I had to guess what he was saying. But we all must have assumed the same because we all gripped the spikes on his spine a split second before he dropped beneath the clouds. The first thing I saw was the magical barrier of Eden, and then the outline of

Edenburg. The second thing I saw was a small airplane lowering into Eden beneath us.

I gripped Tegan tight in my arms, then flew off Silas's back. My gold wings flapped in the cool breeze. "Hold tight, guys. Silas, let me see who that is before you land, okay?"

Silas nodded.

With Tegan pressed to my chest, I pulled my wings in and dropped like a torpedo. It was dark, so it was difficult to see the details of the plane from way up there. At the last second, I flipped and then landed on my feet on the wing of the plane.

Everyone *inside* the plane screamed and jumped.

My father's face filled one of the small windows. His eyes widened and he slammed his forehead into the glass. *TENN!* He yelled, though I couldn't hear him. A pair of pale green eyes in a familiar face popped into the window in front of that. Cooper sighed visibly and shook his head. My father leaned back and then Hope was in the window with wide, mismatching eyes that matched mine. I pointed above me and mouthed *SILAS*. They nodded. Behind them I spotted Jackson, Warner, Kenneth, Daniel, Constance, Katherine, and Braison.

And then they spotted Tegan in my arms and they panicked.

I lifted her legs to cradle her in my arms and her long *white* hair swayed in the wind.

NO! Cooper yelled.

My father shook his head. *DAMN IT!*

I KNEW IT! Hope growled and cursed.

I pointed to the ground and mouthed, *NOW*. My father leaned the other way and shouted to Walter, or I was assuming Walter. I leapt off the wing and landed on the nose. Walter leaned forward, grinned, and gave me a big wave. I pointed to the ground. He nodded and gave me a thumbs up. To give them space to land, I pushed off and flew back up to where Silas was flying above them. Everyone looked to me with expectant, worried eyes.

"It's them. Everyone is there. Alive and well from what I can see." I glanced down. "Silas, give Walter space to land so you don't give him a heart attack and then you're good to go. Okay?"

Silas nodded.

By the time I got down to land, Walter had already parked the plane and my Coven-mates were pouring out of it. Hope was the first one off, followed by my father and Cooper.

"HAVEN!" Hope screamed and charged for me. She tackled me and Tegan in a hug, then pulled back. "I knew it. *I bloody KNEW she was gonna do this!*"

My chest tightened. "Well, this time she had to."

"Son?" My father squeezed my shoulder. "What do you mean? What happened?"

Cooper rushed up behind them. "Is everyone okay?"

I wanted to lie, to play it cool and not panic them...but I didn't have it in me. "No."

The others had all caught up just as I said this. They gasped.

"Tenn? Who? Who's hurt? How bad?" Katherine's face was pale. "Oh *no*, Tegan."

I opened my mouth and then closed it. "Katherine, you're about to have your hands full. Get to Headquarters and call Myrtle. I'll be right there so we can treat Tegan as needed. Daniel, can you call Mona and make sure she's there. We're gonna need her."

His face paled. "Of course." Then he took off.

Katherine eyed the sky. "Timothy—"

"Uncle Tim is fine."

She sighed and then nodded. Without another word she turned and sprinted away.

Cooper frowned. "Tenn, what happened?"

I looked at the ground and shook my head. There was no way I was talking about that yet. If ever. There were some things that just haunted a person. I heard Silas land behind me, and I remembered the injured on his back.

"Brace yourselves," I whispered. Then I turned and led the way over to Silas.

Hunter screamed out a list of profanities I'd never even thought to combine.

Hope tugged on Tegan's arm and I hissed. Like I actually *hissed.*

"STOP," Hope snarled. "Give her to me right now so you can help them down."

I growled and carefully lowered my unconscious soulmate into her best friend's arms.

"*Wait, wait, wait,*" Hunter roared. His face was contorted and red. "Just...wait."

I flew up so he could see me. "Easy, big guy. Let me?"

He nodded.

I summoned a nice gust of wind to lift him straight up, then lowered him down. "Dad?"

"I'm here." He moved into position. "Which leg is it?"

"Right," Uncle Tim answered.

"Got it. Go ahead, Son." He held his arms out. "I'm going to carry you, little bro. Don't be a shit."

Hunter grumbled but he let his older brother pluck him out of the sky. My father was only an inch taller than Hunter and twenty pounds heavier, so it looked rather goofy to see him cradling the guy. But he was the Strength Card, so there was literally no one else who could have attempted it. Well, there was a chance I could have but with my father around there was no reason to risk it.

Hunter gasped. "Devon!" He threw his right hand out and his crystal was red.

I cursed and shot up to where she was in Bentley's arms. He lifted her up for me.

"Give her to me, Tenn," Cooper yelled.

I used my magic to lower Devon into her eldest son's arms. "Hurry, get her to Katherine *now*. Bentley, follow and explain what happened?"

Cooper and Bentley spun and sped off as fast as they could. A red soulmate crystal will do that.

"Kessler, go. Please," Hunter begged, his eyes tracking Cooper's fleeting form.

"Right, sorry." Dad cursed and charged after them.

With a flick of my wrist, Bentley, Uncle Tim, and Deacon were on their feet on the ground. "D, she gonna attack me?"

"No, she's out of it." Deacon grimaced. "More so than I intended, actually."

I moved to Emersyn, but her gold eyes were unseeing. It was unnerving. I flicked my wrist, and she gently flew to the ground, where Deacon promptly caught her. Then I turned and found Easton slumped over Silas's spike and Lennox with blood gushing out of his arm. "*DAMN IT. EASTON?*"

He groaned. "Did I throw up or is that blood?"

"Just hang on, dude." I carefully lifted him and carried him down myself.

"Come here, easy E." Uncle Tim hooked his arm around our Lovers Card and led him toward help.

I turned back to Silas and lifted both hands. Chutney and Lennox were still very much unconscious as they floated down to us. Warner caught Lennox while Braison caught Chutney.

"Thank you, Silas. We couldn't have done that without you. Go back to Issale. Let Koth know I'll be in contact soon?"

He nodded, then shot up into the night sky and vanished.

"What the bloody hell happened, mate?"

I shook my head. They deserved an answer, but I was incapable of anything until I got Tegan back in my arms. "Hope? Give her to me."

She didn't fight me. She just let me take Tegan back. The moment she was back in my arms, my pulse calmed a little. As much as possible. "Come on."

The others followed along with me. They didn't speak but I felt their eyes on me. I felt their questions. I sighed. *Answer them, Tenn. Don't lock up.* I cleared my throat. "Lennox went down the second we entered. We got attacked and Chutney went down. And then...Devon. Her projections were compromised. She started having seizures, violently. She was going to die, we all knew it, so Tegan knocked her unconscious—"

"*Oh no.*" Hope scrubbed her face.

I nodded. "Spirits dragged her into this lake. I dove in and got her but Easton and Deacon tried to help...when they touched her...it burned Deacon's hand and broke Easton's arm."

They hissed and groaned.

"We got attacked again and Hunter couldn't fight back while holding Devon...broke his leg." I looked up and found we'd already walked all the way to Headquarters. Constance had the door open and waiting for us. I smiled at her. "How are you feeling?"

She grimaced. "As decent as expected. Bentley filled us all in on what happened. You tell them?"

I nodded.

Katherine flew into the foyer and snapped her fingers at me. "Get Tegan upstairs. Now. Get Lennox and Chutney downstairs. Mona is waiting."

My heart skipped beats as panic resurged. I'd managed to distract myself on everyone else, but it was back tenfold. I flew up the stairs to our room on the third floor, then gently laid her on our bed. I quickly took her shoes off, though I had no idea what made me do it. I just needed to do *something* for her. Not being able to help her gutted me.

"Okay, get out," Katherine yelled as she ran into the room. "Your panic doesn't help. Myrtle, you ready?"

"I'm ready," Myrtle's voice was warm and strong through the phone. "Haven, Grandson, leave the room. You can come back soon."

I shook myself, then flew to the door. I paused to take one last look at her lying there with white hair. My chest tightened so hard I had to gasp to breathe.

"OUT, TENN!"

Right. I closed the door behind me and hurried back down the stairs. I needed distractions. I needed tasks...but as I entered the living room, I knew something was wrong. Hope and Kenneth were huddled in front of a laptop. Jackson and Warner were strapping themselves with weapons.

"What's going on?" Then I remembered *Henley.* I cursed. "SHIT. Where is she? What's she doing? Update me."

"Come here," Hope ordered without looking away from the screen. "She's in the Old Lands doing a ritual."

What? I hurried over to sit beside her and then fought the urge to break something and scream. The shadow demon had Henley on her knees in the dirt, drawing an inverted pentacle in blood on the ground. Demon-dogs growled around her. Black candles switched from red to gold flames rapidly. In front of her was a circular pond...my stomach turned.

"Is that *blood*?"

"Yes," they said in unison.

"Shit, shit, shit." I jumped to my feet and started pacing the living room.

"Haven, we have to go into the Old Lands to try and stop her—"

"I know, I know. I'm trying to decide who to send." I pinched the bridge of my nose and cursed again. "All right, we don't have a lot of options here. Uncle Tim, Dad, Lancaster, Warner, and Hope. You're going in."

Royce raised his hand. "What about me?"

I shook my head. "You're too emotional, Royce. You lose it. I get it. But you need to sit this out. Braison, you're too distracted by Paulina. Just hang tight with me in case I need you both. I'm keeping Cooper too."

"You better send Deacon," Bentley said in that soft, calm voice of his. "They're going to need Lonan if they want to get there fast enough. And they don't have Chutney to call him."

Deacon cursed.

I turned to him. "D? How's Em?"

He scrubbed his face roughly. He held his hand up to show their soulmate crystal was yellow—*calm*. "She's fine. Katherine and I released her from her hypnosis, but Cooper has her sleeping it off. Besides, Bentley is right. They need me. Just check on her for me?"

I nodded. "Okay. Go. Now. Or you've got no chance."

They sprinted for the door without hesitation.

Except for Hope, who paused on the threshold. Her gaze met mine. "Do not let her paralyze you, Haven. She's going to pull through this like always, and we might need you."

"I know. I'm trying. Go." I exhaled in a rush. "And Hope?"

"Hmmm?"

"I swear if you don't come back—"

She smiled. "Love you too, bro. Team no dying for the win!" She saluted me, then disappeared into the night.

"Royce, Braison...go down and help with the others. Please?"

They didn't question me, they just turned and headed down to our infirmary in the lower level...and then it was just me and Bentley. I collapsed onto the couch and buried my face in my hands.

Bentley cleared his throat.

"*Oh, Goddess, no.*" I looked up at him to find him staring into space. "What is it?"

"You better call Koth and send him to Manhattan."

Son of a bitch. I did not like what that suggested. But I pulled out my phone and dialed his number anyways, because I knew better than to question our Hierophant.

"Tennessee." Koth answered on the first ring. It wasn't a question. "Talk to me."

CHAPTER TWENTY-EIGHT

BETTINA

As we charged for the gate, I couldn't help but be overwhelmed with déjà vu. Jackson was a few feet ahead of me, leading the way just like last time. Uncle Tim was beside me, fiddling on his phone. I knew it was different because Deacon, Kessler, and Warner were with us this time, but the emotions were weighing me down. Because as I saw those memories fresh in my mind I had the new knowledge that he was my uncle, which meant the memories of his death hurt even worse.

But I couldn't focus on that. Not when I heard Henley's voice in my ear. She was chanting in that demonic language, her words coming out faster and faster every time. My pulse quickened along with it. We needed to hurry.

Jackson took my hand in his, the warmth in his skin instantly calming me. "We need to hurry."

"Deacon, take the lead with Jackson." Kessler pointed to the gate in front of us. "Warner and I will take the back."

"Let's hold hands, peeps." Warner grabbed Uncle Tim's hand, then held his other out to Kessler. "I've been lost in this forsaken place once. I ain't lookin to do it again. So grab on. And let's not run. Bitches get lost when they run through this hellhole."

We all grabbed each other's hands without hesitation. Warner was right. We needed to stick together.

Deacon looked down at all our interlocked hands and nodded. "Don't let go until we get to Lonan."

He waited for us to nod, then turned and led the way through the black iron gate. As I crossed over the border I felt my magic surge to life, like it also recognized where we were and was *not* happy about it. That damn fog wall was up ahead. I tightened my grip on Jackson and Uncle Tim.

Without another word, we pushed through the fog. I wanted to close my eyes and let them drag me through blind, but I just didn't trust these lands. To not look gave it the upper hand. Instead, I focused my gaze on the rose tattoo on Jackson's thumb. We had to start this journey slow, entering the Old Lands was one of the trickiest parts. It was like its magic tested new visitors upon entrance to see what hell it planned on unleashing.

The fog cleared and the air shimmered like golden glitter— and my chest tightened. It reminded me of Saffie. *Goddess, please let them be okay. Let them save the others in time.* Red light flashed in the corner of my eye. I looked up and saw red lightning bolts streaking across the green sky.

Deacon raised his free hand and flexed his fingers. Red mist poured from his palm. "Come to us, Lonan."

I hated being in here without Chutney. Her communication with the animals was a real game changer. I glanced around us, bracing myself for an ambush. A massive black shadow shot across the sky, slicing through Deacon's red magic, then landed a few feet in front of us. The ground trembled and leaves fell off tree branches.

Lonan was as intimidating as ever. He picked his head up and big red eyes sent a chill down my spine. *He's not a demon.*

Those are just his eyes—wait, what if he's part demon? What if that's why he was banished? Oh, shut up, Bettina! Doesn't matter. He's our friend and we trust him.

Black shadows wrapped around his body and then Lonan stood before us in his human form. "You here for Henley?"

"YES!" We all shouted.

Hope flared in my chest. "Do you know where she's at?"

"She's been possessed by a shadow demon," Kessler said in a rush.

He snarled. "Damn it. I knew I should have attacked. There's a bunch of demons. Where's Chutney?"

Deacon's face fell. "She got hurt but should recover."

Lonan cursed and backed away. "We have to hurry. Hop on."

In the blink of an eye, he was a black dragon again. He sank down low so we could climb on. We all hurried over then paused, like we suddenly all realized Tenn or Tegan usually got us up there. Kessler grabbed my hand—*then threw me up.* My legs flailed in the air. I dropped down roughly onto Lonan's back, nestled between two spikes. I glanced over my shoulder and found the others getting the same assistance. We were all loaded up within a few seconds. Lonan rumbled and then shot like a rocket straight into the sky.

This time, I let my eyes close. I focused on my grip on Lonan's spike and the feel of Jackson's arms coiled around my waist. The wind was warm rushing over my face, but it did nothing to ease the chill in my bones. Thunder rumbled in my ear. The chanting began to echo, and it sent goosebumps racing across my skin. Something growled and it felt like it was breathing down my neck. The hairs on my arms stood tall.

"Hurry, Lonan," I shouted over the rushing wind.

Lonan growled and it rumbled through my body. He dove for the ground. The sudden drop sent my stomach rushing up my throat, knocking the breath from my lungs.

I opened my eyes just in time to watch us plummet straight into a patch of pitch black. Lonan dropped beneath the tree line. Up ahead, red glowing light flashed like a strobe, casting trees in black shadow. Lonan didn't slow down or miss a beat. He expertly wove a path straight through the forest.

"*RISE!*" Henley shouted.

I gasped. "*Go, go, GO!*"

Golden light flickered from the ground. Jackson cursed in my ear. Lonan sank lower until he was flying just above the ground. The red light was getting closer. The clearing was *right there.* Lonan growled and lunged between two trees. Dozens of little black demons leapt off the ground and charged for us. Lonan spit bright orange fire and slid to a stop in the dirt.

"*OH MY GOD,*" I whispered as my eyes took in the horror in front of me.

Henley was back in her clothes and kneeling on the ground with her back facing us. "RISE!" The shadow demon shouted through Henley's voice.

SHIT. SHIT. SHIT.

Blue flames rushed through the clearing, mixing with Lonan's. "What the hell is that?"

"*How?*" Uncle Tim whispered.

"WE HAVE TO STOP IT!" I screamed and threw my leg over Lonan's back, then jumped off. Pain laced up my legs on impact, but I was trained for this. "GO!"

Jackson, Warner, Uncle Tim, and Kessler charged ahead of me with swords slicing through demons as they ran. Deacon cursed and then sent a red lightning bolt right into Henley's spine. She bellowed and her back arched.

But it was too late. *We* were too late.

It was already here.

I thrust my hands forward, shooting ice from my left and pink magic from my right. Pink mist illuminated the clearing— my stomach sank. This demon was growing *out of* the blood pond. It was *made of blood*. Nausea bubbled up my throat. I flung my hands out and sent a stream of ice, freezing its entire body. The damn thing towered over even Lonan. It was some kind of worm-like monstrosity with long arms, giant pointed horns, and a face that I would never, ever get out of my memory.

Henley was chanting under her breath, but I heard her clear as day in my ear.

Deacon lit her up with one red lightning bolt after another.

"FALL BACK!" Jackson shouted as he sent his blue flames right into the blood-demon. "TOGETHER!"

We all sprinted for him while firing everything we had at this thing.

"*What the hell is that?*" Warner shrieked.

"A greater demon!" Uncle Tim sliced his ice-sword through a small demon's face. He looked up at the nightmare and his eyes widened. "DUCK—"

The greater demon swung his tree branch-like arm through the air right for us. We all dove to the ground. But Kessler reached out and grabbed the demon's hand and pulled. The demon snarled and spit blood onto us. The scent of maple syrup was suffocating. The blood hit my arm and burned *through* my jacket.

"We can't send it back." Kessler bit out as he tugged on its arm. "Not just us."

"Kill it!" Uncle Tim leapt up and sliced his sword through the demon's arm, chopping it in half.

Lonan sent a river of fire into Jackson's blue flames, and both coiled around the greater demon's body. The demon shook its severed arm and it regenerated instantly. I covered its body in ice. None of this was working. The greater demon swung his arms side to side, just missing us by inches.

Henley was on her knees, drawing runes of blood in the dirt and chanting under her breath. Warner cursed and dove for

Henley, tackling her to the ground. They rolled in the dirt and blood.

Warner pinned her on her back. "*How do we kill it?*"

Henley wiggled her arm free, then yanked Warner's dagger off his hip and slammed it right into Warner's chest.

"NO!" We all screamed and dove for him.

Henley cackled and leapt to her feet. She turned into shadow and vanished—only to reappear *right* in front of Jackson. He slid to a stop but he was too close. Henley swung her arm. Jackson leaned back, but fresh blood splattered right across my face. Jackson balled his fist and punched her straight in the nose. She staggered back just as Deacon slammed her with red lightning. I covered her body in ice. It was hard to fight a target you didn't want to hurt.

She gasped and then vanished and reappeared on the other side of the clearing, behind the greater demon. White magic sparkled from her hand. A large, ornate, silvery gate glistened into existence.

"NO!" Deacon screamed and sprinted after her, firing his magic.

I chased them. I didn't know what he did but I trusted that reaction. I shot my ice in rapid succession. Henley pulled the gate open, and light sparkled and flashed in the opening. She shouted a few words in that demonic language. The greater demon *laughed* and then dove right through the opening... vanishing faster than it had appeared.

Henley had ice covering her legs and arms and red mist smothering her. Yet she met Deacon's eyes and grinned—then turned to shadow and disappeared.

The silvery gate slammed shut in my face. The ground was littered with chunks of ice.

"Where does that lead?" I pushed my hair back. Bile rose up my throat. My heart was racing through my veins, drowning out the sounds around me. The sound of squealing tires and horns honking blared in my ear. Police sirens wailed in the background. "Where is she?"

Deacon yanked the gate open and leaned forward. His face scrunched up in agony. "New York City. I can *smell* it from —WARNER!"

I gasped and spun on my toes. Kessler was on his knees, pushing his hands into Warner's body. Uncle Tim bent over and —*administered CPR*. My heart sank. *NOOOO*. Jackson was holding Warner's wrist and checking for a pulse.

Warner lay motionless on the ground, blood gushing onto the dirt.

"Deacon, *HIT HIM!*" I pointed at our friend.

Deacon cursed and dove for them. He held his hands over Warner's chest, then fired bright red lightning right into him. Warner's arms and legs flopped—"

"PULSE!" Jackson cried. "GOT IT!"

But Warner wasn't moving. His eyes were still closed. Words rushed through my mind. Like always I had no idea where it was coming from, but I stopped fighting it ages ago. I slid to my knees beside him. The wound was too far to the left to be his heart, but it was close enough. I had no idea what my spell was about to do.

Shrieks of terror ripped through my thoughts. There were explosions and metal crashing. Glass shattered. Screams rang out in surround sound.

"Deacon, Kessler, and Uncle Tim—go through the gate!" When they flinched I shook my head. "Just GO! The greater demon is in Manhattan! Get out and call for help!"

Kessler cursed violently but he leapt to his feet and dragged Deacon and Uncle Tim onto theirs. "She's right. Let's go."

"GO!" I screamed and then held my hands over Warner's chest. It was hard to concentrate with Henley in my ear.

"*Bettina,*" Jackson groaned and squeezed Warner's hand.

Lonan sank to his knees beside us in human form and

grabbed Warner's other hand. He looked to me with calm eyes. "Just close your eyes and let it out."

"Right." I closed my eyes, took a deep breath, and then exhaled—and the words poured out of my mouth. "*Seek the source, stop the pain. Seize it, fix it, make it drain. By the wound, hold it tight, just a temporary fight.*"

I felt my magic rush out of me and tingle in the air. I opened my eyes to find a sparkly pink cloud hovering over Warner's body. The gold bands on each of my fingers glowed in the dark.

Warner gasped and his eyes flew open.

"WARNER!" We all shouted.

He sat up straight and then swayed. "Am...I...dead?"

"Not yet," Jackson breathed. "Take it easy."

"This won't hold forever. We have to get you home to Katherine."

"Help me up," he grumbled.

I stepped back so Lonan and Jackson could hoist him to his feet—but my gaze landed on that blood pond. The greater demon had come from *within* it. "Lonan...*Lonan*. Is this where the Gap is? The one we just learned was here?"

"*Yes,*" Lonan growled right behind me. "The nature of the Old Lands allowed for the Gap to be on the ground. She used blood to open it, though I do not understand *how*."

"I don't either." Jackson hobbled over to us with Warner leaning into him. "We can't just leave it like this. Anything could come through, right?"

"I don't know about that. I don't know how this works. I wasn't involved in the closing of other Gaps." I pushed my hair back and stared at it. "But Kessler said we can't close it ourselves, and there's less of us now."

"I'll stand guard," Lonan said in a rush, black scales starting to cover his body.

"By yourself? That's too bloody much."

"Bettina...bubble," Warner mumbled.

297

I frowned—and then his words clicked. *BUBBLE.* Warner and I had used one of my bubbles to our advantage before. "The Gap is in this blood pond on the ground. I can put one of my bubbles on it as a barrier."

"*OH.*" Jackson's eyes widened. "Yes. Brilliant. Do that?"

I pulled my dagger out of my boot and raised it over my head. "*See this Gap within thy veil, by my blade thy shall not fail. Bind the ground, bind it now, seal this land with my vow.*"

With a battle roar and all the magic I could muster, I slammed the blade of my dagger into the ground in front of me. A massive bright pink bubble covered the Gap with a dome, like trapping a bug under a bowl.

Lonan whistled under his breath. "Impressive. Now leave. Fast."

"Lonan—"

"I'll stand guard here until someone from The Coven returns to close it. The animals will assist me. If there's trouble, I'll send for you." Black smoke coiled around his body and his massive tail whipped behind him. "Just focus on that greater demon and getting Warner healed. GO!"

CHAPTER TWENTY-NINE

SAFFIE

"AMELIA?! LANDY?!"

Gliding across the glowing blue river was a little black rowboat with Amelia and Landy sitting inside. At the same time, Savannah, Lily, and I all stepped toward the boat. but Ziva's long fiery sword flew in front of us, stopping us in our tracks.

"That water is dangerous for you," Ziva said in a rush, though I only barely registered it.

I was reeling. Emotions swirled inside of me too fast to even process. Butterflies danced in my stomach. *Amelia and Landy. AMELIA AND LANDY. They're here. They're ALIVE.* Tears stung my eyes. None of us spoke. We all just stared at each other while their boat drifted to shore, like we were afraid if we looked away, they'd vanish again. *Four down, three to go.*

I wished I could pull out my phone and call Deacon. To call Koth and Maddox.

Amelia and Landy were gripping the edge of the boat so hard their knuckles were white.

It wasn't until Landy scrambled out of the boat that I realized something was off. She looked the same but *different*. She was taller and leaner, and her face had lost the baby faced, innocent look. She was still in the same black skirt she'd been in for the birthday party. Before it had gone halfway down her thighs, *now* it barely reached her thighs. She had to be taller than me, not that that was difficult to do. The seams on the waistband had been cut on the hips, like she'd done that so the skirt would still fit her bigger body. She had on that black hoodie still, though it was missing sleeves and was now a crop top.

"Is this real? Are you really here?" Landy asked, her eyes watering. Her voice was deeper and thicker than before. Her brown eyes were colder, sharper.

But her soul was still *all* her, I recognized it immediately. This was Landy. She was just...older.

All I could do was stare. It was Bentley all over again.

And then Amelia carefully climbed out of the boat and stopped beside Landy.

I gasped.

"*AMELIA?!*" Savannah shouted. "WHAT?"

Lily grabbed my arm and squeezed. I felt her pain and fear inside of her.

The only part of the girl in front of me that I recognized was her face, and even that had changed. There was no sign of baby fat on that face. Her cheekbones and jawline had sharpened like a grown woman. Ziva cursed violently and muttered something about the King. I didn't pay attention. I couldn't. My eyes had to have been playing tricks on me. Landy looked just like a bigger version of herself, but Amelia was all grown up.

Her hair that used to be sandy blonde like Deacon's was now platinum and swinging down by her hips. There was so much skin showing it felt wrong to even look at her. Sweet, innocent little Amelia was gone. Gold chains were wrapped around her hips with swoops of diamonds hanging over a white skirt—if you could even call it that. The slit on the right side went all the way up to the waist. And there were more gold chains and diamonds coiled around her right thigh. She was wearing a little black crop top that definitely was not given to her at the same time as the rest of the ensemble, because there were strings of diamonds covering her chest and sticking out the top of the shirt.

My stomach turned and tightened.

What happened to you?

Amelia's violet eyes filled with tears that spilled down her face. She swayed and leaned into Landy, then covered her mouth with her hand.

For a moment, the five of us just stood there, staring in shock.

I didn't know if we ran to them or if they ran to us, or maybe we met in the middle, but the next thing I knew we were holding on to each other in a big group hug. Amelia sagged into Lily's arms and let herself be held as she sobbed. The brokenness in the sound hurt my soul to hear.

"*I can't believe it. I can't believe it,*" Landy kept whispering over and over as she hugged me and Savannah. "You came for us. You came."

I pulled back and found Landy and I were about the same height. With shaky fingers, I wiped her tears off her face. "*Of course* we did. It took us four days to figure out how to get here, but we spent the whole time working only on that."

Amelia finally peeled herself out of Lily's arms to give Landy a hug. "I told you they'd come, didn't I?"

That did it. My heart broke. These two little girls had been waiting and praying we wouldn't abandon them.

"Is everyone okay at home?" Amelia sniffled. "Is everyone... alive? Deacon?"

"Everyone is alive. A few injuries trying to get into Seelie here, but I have faith they'll make it. Deacon is fine." I shook my head. "Henley is...the same."

Amelia nodded solemnly. "Did you say it's been four days at home?"

"Yes," Savannah and I said at the same time as Lily nodded.

"That's *it*? Landy pushed her hands through her hair. "Feels like I've been here forever."

Amelia closed her eyes and sighed. "Feels like I just got here. It happened so fast."

Savannah cleared her throat and wiped under her eyes. "So, um...uh...what happened to your clothes?"

It was obvious they'd both grown, but Amelia had definitely grown *more*.

Landy grimaced and tugged on her micro-mini skirt and cropped hoodie. "I just outgrew mine, and since I've been with the Dauvotai, they didn't have any other clothes."

And then we all turned to Amelia.

She squeezed her eyes shut like the memory hurt. Her face paled. I didn't want to read her soul, but I didn't get a choice. It felt like someone standing on the beach just screaming as loud as they could. There was pain, sadness, a ton of fear, and a shit load of anger.

Amelia was sent to the King's private chambers, that was what Bentley had said.

"Amelia..." I reached out and took her hands in mine. "You don't have to talk about it, but are you hurt?"

She shook her head and sniffled. "I don't think so. Nothing...happened."

My heart sank. I felt in her that that wasn't true. Savannah and Lily reached out and squeezed her shoulders.

"You don't have to—"

"Yes, *I do.*" She opened her eyes and anger burned in the violet. "Deacon's going to ask. Aunt Heather and Uncle Sebastien are going to ask. I might as well get used to talking about it. In the Court, the Queen requested Landy go with her and the King had me sent to his room. His *play*room, with no

302

doors and a retractable staircase that kept main door three floors up—a room made of stained-glass walls that had only a bed in it."

My stomach turned but I didn't let go of her hand.

"I tried to escape but couldn't, so I hid my wand under the mattress," her voice was thick like she was trying to keep her emotions in check. "He finally came in and then took one look at me, I mean ten seconds most, and said that I was too young. So he used his magic on me and then *voila* here I am with this new body. A body of *prime age,* as he said."

Lily gagged.

"He put me in...*this,*" she gestured to her clothes. "I had a different shirt-like garment that he removed rather quickly. We all know what he wanted of me, but he did not get it. At least not for the most part. There were some things I had to let happen in order for me to take him by surprise and escape. That's all I'd like to say on the matter for right now."

"That slimy scumbag piece of shit," Savannah shouted. She balled her hands into fists and her face flushed in anger. "I'm gon' kill him. I'm gon' rip his soul right up out of his nostrils mummy-style. I will tear his throat out with my teeth."

"He's the Seelie King," Amelia said softly.

"And I'm a black belt in *I wish a bitch would,*" she shouted back. "Come at me. COME. AT. ME. You don't touch little children like that. No, no, I don't care what happens to me. That piece of maggot breath has to die and imma be the one to deliver him to Jesus."

Ziva chuckled.

Amelia actually smiled just a little. "Thank you, Savannah. It was horrible, but in the end he didn't get the opportunity to do what he wanted and that's what matters."

I groaned and gestured to her body—her *grown up* body. "So, he aged you? Just like that?"

Amelia nodded. "He said I was fifteen now."

"FIFTEEN IS PRIME AGE?" Savannah shrieked. "You tellin' me this ancient ass dried up mongrel meat thinks FIFTEEN is the prime age—oh imma kill him. IMMA KILL HIM."

"Well, fifteen isn't too bad. Just, what, three years older?" When she nodded I turned to Landy. "And are you fifteen as well? What happened with the Queen?"

Landy shuddered. "The Queen said she was disgusted by me. She said animals belonged with animals and dropped me off by the river."

"That's where I found her." Shannon, who'd been listening quietly, finally spoke up. "The closer you are to the palace, the less predictable time gets. In the palace, time moves slow but the river moves swiftly. I would say she has aged two years."

"Two years." Landy wrapped her arms around her waist and shuddered. "I guess I was here a little while before Amelia showed up with Shannon's sister. Topless."

Amelia tugged on the little black tank top. "Landy gave me her shirt."

Lily gestured toward Amelia.

Savannah growled. "Yeah, I'm not seeing a whole lot down there either. Safferella, help her out?"

I glanced down and saw they meant under her skirt. I cursed and pushed some magic at both of the girls, giving Amelia some little white shorts under her skirt and growing Landy's skirt down to her knees.

Then I sighed. "We have to try and blend in so we're not blatantly obvious if spotted. So, this will have to do for now, that okay?"

Amelia nodded. "As long as I'm with you guys, I'm okay."

Tears pooled in my eyes and a hot lump formed in my throat. "You're with us now. And we've made friends here already."

Landy's eyes grew worried. "Have you found Bentley yet? What about Paulina? They tortured her."

"Bentley is home. We were able to do this ritual that allowed us to pull him out. Long story, but he's safe with his family."

They both sighed with relief.

"But he's...like...the same?" Landy's voice was tight.

"He came home sixteen years old." I frowned. "So he's older than you both now."

Amelia shuddered. "As long as he's okay."

"I doubt he is *okay,* but physically he was fine," Ziva grumbled under her breath. "At least when he left."

"And Paulina?" Landy whispered.

"We have not yet found Paulina. We were told she was fed to the beast."

Amelia flinched. "What does *that* mean?"

Ziva growled. "The reason no one gets to the palace uninvited."

Shannon pursed her lips and twirled her fin. "He was just fed some last nightfall, before the new arrivals, so if your friend has any chance of being alive, you'll want to go for her now."

"I do not dare to put favor in our odds." Flames danced over Ziva's body. "But we must try, and you must see what we're up against."

"Let's go," the rest of us said at the same time.

Shannon tapped on the boat. "I can escort you down the river to the entrance nearest the palace, but you'll have to move fast once inside."

Ziva gestured to the boat. "Get in."

Squishy barked and leapt inside the boat first and then sat up at the front with his face hanging over the edge. I chuckled and hopped in behind him, which earned me a face lick. Landy giggled from the seat across from me, on the other side of Squishy. She ran her fingers through his reddish-brown fur and he slid into her lap. I looked to my right just as Ziva was climbing in the back. Savannah, Lily, and Amelia were already in.

"Everyone stay *inside* the boat until I say. Do not touch the water," Ziva warned.

A few of the dauvotai pulled the boat back into the water and then pushed us forward. Shannon and another dauvot, who I was assuming was the sister, held on to the front while we moved into the river current. I glanced behind us and found all the dauvotai escorting us down the river and that warmed my heart. Of all the things I'd planned and prepared for mentally, help from within Seelie was not one of them.

The river was peaceful but eerily quiet. A complete absence of noise. The water glowed a bright neon-blue, and because the forest was black I could see the river winding in front of us. Vines and branches swooped low over our heads. When I looked up, I found only darkness, not a single hint of light of any kind.

I found myself relaxing and slouching against the side of the boat.

It was so beautiful, I could've sat all night just watching—I gasped and sat up straight.

"*Close your eyes!*" Ziva, Shannon, and I all yelled at the exact same time.

Which sent my pulse flying. I spun to look at my friends and found them already covering their eyes. Except for Ziva, whose hazel eyes were now flickering like flames. Her pretty brown skin had turned into that charred black with streams of lava covering her body.

"They're looking for us," Ziva growled, and it sounded smoky. "Saffie, take no chances. Close yours too."

I nodded and squeezed my eyes shut. It was always a toss-up on which of the Seelie's tricks would work on me or not. I supposed it was a product of being a half-breed. Shannon and the dauvotai had kept both Amelia and Landy safe. Ziva was Bentley's trusted friend. These were all good reasons to trust them, yet there was still that flicker of doubt in the back of my mind and pit of my stomach.

Squishy growled so loud it sent vibrations through the boat.

I concentrated on my own pulse pounding through my limbs and took deep breaths.

"Shannon, *faster*," Ziva said in a low voice.

The boat lurched forward, and warm air rushed over my face, blowing my hair back. I kept my eyes closed, yet I could still see the glow of the river. No one else spoke. I wasn't sure they were even breathing. It felt like forever before the boat suddenly stopped.

"Okay, you can open."

I opened my eyes and my jaw dropped. We were still tucked under the cover of the black forest, with the glow of the river shining behind us. The river had come to an abrupt fork that was more like a *T* shape where you had to go left or right only—yet we'd slid right up to the edge. Directly in front of us, not more than two or three feet, was a sharp cliff. I flew out of the boat and over to the edge to look down. The cliff dropped at least five stories down to a dark, creepy desert. There were no trees or plants of any kind. It was just cold, vacant land.

My magic rushed out to see what was there...and found only pain. Intense, torturous pain. A severe sadness clawed at me, like nails down my spine. It choked me like it wanted to bring me down with it. My chest grew tight and my heart seemed to beat even harder. *RIAH?* I raised my hand, but the glyph was still green. That feeling wasn't him. Relief rocked me so hard I fell backwards.

"*Whoa,*" Savannah whispered as she caught me and dragged me back from the edge. "What just happened?"

"I thought that...feeling...was Riah." I held my hand up and stared at the glyph. "It's not."

"What feeling?" Landy whispered. "I don't feel anything."

"Because you're not of this world." Ziva walked up beside me. "Be thankful you cannot feel anything, for I am sure it not desirable."

I shuddered.

Lily nudged me, then pointed to the sky. I looked up and smiled. It was still night, but I knew that in this spot there would be sunlight come dawn because there wasn't a single tree above. The sky was a cloud array of colors so beautiful it took my breath away. Turquoises, blues, pinks, and purples all swirling together and perfectly blending. Little blue stars twinkled through the darkest colors.

I followed the pattern of the stars, searching for a constellation I recognized, when a tall, gleaming structure broke into my view. I flinched like it'd slapped me. It was massive and impressively built from stone and colored stained-glass. There were narrow pillars that sparkled like crystals and intimidating towers with sharp pointed spikes sticking out the side. It was far in the distance and yet still towered above us, which meant it had to be overwhelming up close. Even from afar, I spotted large terraces with vines, trees, and flowers a plenty. There were bridges and cliffs that stuck out and lowered to the ground.

There was no question of what this place was.

The palace.

Which meant Riah was in there somewhere.

We just had to get there, and the only thing standing in our way was this lifeless dark desert.

Amelia let out a loud breath. "Did I come out the back side? I do not recognize any of this."

Ziva nodded and pointed to where a soft blue glow radiated from the back. "The King's private chamber for...*guests*...is on the backside of the palace."

Amelia swallowed hard and wrapped her arms around her waist. "I did not see this vacant land back there?"

"You landed far away from it," Shannon said softly from behind us. "But it is there, stretching far on each side."

Ziva narrowed her eyes on Amelia. "How *did* you get to land without dying?"

Amelia bit her bottom lip and shrugged. "I had my wand, so I gave myself wings like from a costume? They worked but I lost my wand in the landing."

"You lost an Earthly wand *here?*" Shannon hissed. "Near where my sister found you?"

Amelia nodded.

"Go look for it, Shannon." Ziva's eyes flashed with fire. "Find it and destroy it."

Amelia whined.

"I am sorry, Amelia. But such a thing being lost here cannot be trusted." Ziva glared at the palace. "If found, it would have been tampered with and left so you could reclaim it."

Amelia nodded. "I understand. I'll just get a new one when I get home."

"Ziva."

She turned to meet my stare. "Your Riah is in there, deep in the dungeon—as far as I know."

My pulse quickened and every muscle in my body tightened. "How do we get there?"

She pointed down to that dark dead desert. "Through *that.*"

"*That?* Looks like the dead marshes down there." Savannah groaned. "*Orcs don't use it. Orcs don't know it. They go round for miles and miles.*"

I frowned. I knew that was a movie reference, but I was not making the connection.

Lily snapped her fingers. When Ziva looked to her, Lily tapped on her Sun Mark and then held two fingers up.

Willow and Paulina.

We still hadn't found them.

Ziva's face fell. "I had hoped we would encounter them on

the way, but at this point I fear they must be within the palace or with the Knights."

"The beast," I heard myself say. "She'd been given to the beast."

For the first time since we met her, Ziva looked afraid. "That may look like open land to you, but it is a death trap. Beneath it lie tunnels home to the beast. There are holes and cracks on the surface to ensure the beast is frequently and properly fed by all those who attempt to enter the palace uninvited."

Silence.

"This beast is—"

"Fast, cunning, and brutal." Ziva rolled her shoulders. "And your weapons will not hurt it, so do not waste a chance for escape on an attempt to kill it. The beast can cross these tunnels in the blink of an eye. Just because we cannot see it does not mean our presence will go unnoticed."

Fantastic. I'd known our biggest issue would be the palace, but I had not expected this.

"*Come hobbitses, soft and quick as shadows we must be,*" Ziva whispered. We must've made weird faces because she shrugged. "My father's favorite movie. We used to watch it when I was a kid, before I was taken." She winked and waved for us to follow her.

Savannah snickered under her breath and raced after Ziva. "I like her. I think we should keep her."

Lily grinned.

I motioned for Amelia and Landy to go in front of me so that I would know for certain they were still with us. Ziva and I were the best weapons here, so we had to be at the ends of the line. Ziva led us through a narrow path between the black trees, then stopped in front of a short stone wall with a big hole in it.

Savannah groaned. "Don't tell me we have to—"

"Slide. Yes. I'll go first." Ziva moved into position and then glanced back. "It goes quick and smooth, as The Circle uses it often. Make haste."

And then she jumped into the black hole and out of sight.

Lily rushed over and leapt inside after her. A split second later, soft yellow light illuminated the tunnel from the inside. Amelia grabbed Landy's hand and dragged her to the hole, then they went down one after the other.

Savannah grimaced and pulled her satchel tight to her chest. "Of all the times to be forced into a dress."

I laughed as she slipped into the hole and slid down. Without hesitation, I raced in after her. She had a point. I was also in a dress but thankfully Ziva had not been lying. The tunnel was smooth and I zipped through the faint yellow light rather quickly. In any other circumstance, I might have even enjoyed the rush of speed. The second my feet hit the ground, several hands hauled me upright.

And then I just stared. *The palace isn't that far, I could just fly—*

"Don't." Ziva placed her hand on my shoulder. "It looks closer than it is. It's more than a mile away and you would be spotted easily. The only way we're getting to Riah while he's alive is if they don't see us coming."

Cold dread filled my soul. *While he's alive.* She was right. I knew she was.

"Come, quickly, and let us pray this works."

The dark and colorful night sky cast the dead desert in shades of blue and green, so as we ran alongside the edge of the cliff we were barely visible. After about thirty feet, Ziva stopped and pointed to another hole in the ground.

"Drop and be ready to move," she whispered. "Do exactly as I say if you want to survive."

We all nodded.

My heart lodged in my throat.

Ziva took a deep breath, then jumped feet-first into the hole.

I had to give my friends credit. I felt their fear raging inside of them, but they did not hesitate. The second Ziva was down, they each followed, one by one, until it was my turn.

I slipped through the hole and landed with a sickening crunch.

Ziva held her finger over her mouth and then glanced around with narrowed eyes.

The air down here was hot and sticky. It was damp against my skin. There was a stench I did not even want to try and identify. I glanced down and found that the crunching sound had came from a pile of small bones that might have belonged to a bird of sorts.

We'd just entered the beast's tunnels, and I already knew this was a terrible idea.

Ziva waved for us to follow her. We did without hesitation, but there were so many bones littering the ground our steps crunched and cracked. The tunnel walls were made of dried out dirt and chunks of rock. It was brown, dingy, and smelled like death. Along the base of the walls were full skeletons cleaned of any meat. Some were animals, but most were humans, or human-looking. There were skulls in piles. Even though they held no expression, each one seemed to scream at me.

I tried to ignore all the glistening silver swords and daggers lying around as Ziva's warning echoed through my thoughts. Above us as we ran were teeny tiny cracks that let more hot air and blue-green light in. None of them were big enough for a person to fit through.

How the hell are we getting out of here?

Hopefully through the palace and then Riah will know what to do.

Suddenly, the tunnel walls shook like a train was coming.

Ziva gasped. "RUN!"

"*What is that?*" Landy hissed as we sprinted.

"THE BEAST!"

A loud ear-splitting roar erupted behind us, and the walls shook so hard dust rained down on us. Ziva cursed and yelled for us to run faster. Hot energy slammed into my back like lasers. I glanced over my shoulder just as a massive, pale creature slid into the tunnel far behind us. *The beast!*

"GO, GO, GO, GO!" I screamed. "HE'S HERE! GET US OUT!"

"ALMOST THERE! KEEP RUNNING!"

I watched over my shoulder as I ran as fast as I could. The beast was almost the same size as the tunnel itself. He looked like a giant, pale blue lizard—

"*Is that a fucking iguana?*" Savannah shrieked.

"Something like that!" Ziva screamed. "Follow me! HURRY!"

Hurry? Oh Goddess, this was a terrible idea. Unless there was an opening right in front of us, we weren't going to make it. Squishy snarled and barked and it made the hairs on my arms stand tall. The beast was closing in on us. Large talons almost as tall as me dug gouges into the tunnel floor. Bones and swords flew up around him like a wave. Rocks and dirt fell in sheets off the walls.

We're not gonna make it.

"SQUISHY, GO!"

I pushed my magic out and tried to summon for something to use, yet there was nothing. Everything in the tunnels was dead. I tried to call for spirits, but they were too slow to rise and the beast soared right by them. I threw my hands out and fired golden glitter magic behind me.

The beast growled and hot breath drenched the back of me.

I glanced back and screamed. The beast lunged, but I jumped up and his snout passed under me. I grabbed the tunnel ceiling and yanked—stones and dirt crashed down on the beast's head. He snarled and shook it off, but it gave me just enough time to get a few feet ahead. I looked up and almost cried when

I saw Ziva *throwing* Amelia up into a hole in the ceiling. Landy was next. Savannah and Lily were watching me with wide, terror-filled eyes.

"*GO!*" I waved my hands in front of me and red light flashed in my face.

I gasped and my feet slowed. My eyes locked on to the bright *red* glyph on my hand.

RIAH!

Sharp teeth sank into the silk of my dress and yanked me back. My face slammed into the tunnel floor. I cursed and rolled onto my back just as the beast opened his mouth above me. I threw my hands up—

A dark object tackled the beast from the side. The beast roared and flicked its head back and forth to shake off whatever had landed on it. Long dark hair whipped through the air, followed by a string of curse words growled in *Spanish*.

I gasped.

PAULINA!

She climbed over the beast's spikes and dove on top of its snout, wrapping her long tan arms around its mouth—*wait, no.* It was a VINE. She pulled the vine up and forced the beast's mouth closed.

"PAULINA!" I screamed.

She looked up and her brown eyes met mine. "GO!"

"I can't leave—"

The beast thrashed and part of the vine snapped. He was breaking her hold.

"SAFFIE, GO!" She looked up and screamed. "RUN!"

CHAPTER THIRTY

SAFFIE

I HATED LEAVING PAULINA, but I didn't have a choice. I spun and flew as fast as I could for the opening. Ziva and Savannah were lifting Squishy, but he was as tall as them and probably equaled both their weights. I cursed and dove for him, wrapping my arms around his fluffy body and using my wings to lift us up.

Amelia and Landy grabbed his paws the second they poked through the hole, yanking him onto the surface. I dropped back down into the tunnel, gripped Savannah's waist, and lifted her up to the hole. The girls were dragging her out when I heard the beast roar.

"*NOW!*" Paulina screamed.

Ziva jumped up and grabbed my legs. "FLY!"

I pushed as hard as I could through the opening while Ziva was hanging from me. Hands grabbed my arms and pulled. My body dragged over rough pebbles and dirt. As soon as I was up, I spun and at the same time we all dove for Ziva.

"UP! UP! UP!" Paulina shrieked from below us. Her voice was moving closer.

It was a mad dash for Ziva's legs. Lily and I reached down into the hole and grabbed the tops of her boots. The beast lunged with its sharp teeth out. Lily blasted sunlight right into his eyes. It hissed and shook its head *and Paulina was tossed side to side.* She was holding onto his spikes like she was trying to ride a horse.

It was a split second, but it was all we needed to pull Ziva out of the tunnel. The beast lunged for the hole and slammed into the ceiling, then flicked his long, pale tongue out.

"Paulina!" I dove for the opening and tried to reach for her.

Our fingers grazed but the beast took off running, carrying Paulina with it.

"SAVE HIM!" She yelled and her voice echoed down the tunnel.

"I'LL COME BACK FOR YOU!" I screamed as loud as I could. *"Please just hang on."*

Lily punched the ground with her fist and let out a silent scream. Her lavender eyes were tearing up. My breath left me in a rush. We'd found her. She was alive but would she stay that way? I didn't know and it didn't look good.

I promise I'll come back for you, Paulina, I silently vowed.

Behind me, Squishy snarled and barked.

Ziva looked up and her eyes widened. "Of all the luck..."

"Umm...*guys?*" Amelia said under her breath.

Savannah cursed. "We're gonna need a new plan. Stat."

I spun around and my breath left me in a rush. We'd made it out of the tunnels, but we'd come out at a different location—one I hadn't even seen by the river. Instead of a black forest, there was a village made of stone. There wasn't a towering cliffside but open staircases that led into this village. Purple trees with hot pink leaves surrounded the stone village. Up on the stairs and on the edge of the village, I spotted males and females in those pale gray dresses with glowing pink lines on their backs. *Slaves.* Somehow we'd missed some of them.

But they weren't the concern at the moment.

Because between us and the stone village had to be five dozen Knights in shiny gold armor.

Ziva cursed. "This is the Knights' barracks. I did not realize we'd come this far."

They had us surrounded. We had nowhere to go.

And they each aimed their bow right at us.

We needed a way out. We needed a shield. I pushed my magic out in desperation, but there was no nature I could call on, everything was dead. Spirits roused at my call, but these were slow, for reasons I did not understand. They would need a minute to get warmed up and I wasn't sure there was enough of them to take *all* of the Knights.

Think, Saffie. THINK.

But all I could see was Riah's face. Pain raced up and down my body and I tried to convince myself that it was *my* pain and not his. I felt his pulse racing erratically. The glyph on my chest glowed such a bright red it cast everything in crimson shades.

There were too many of them.

One of the Knights in front of us shouted something and nodded. I frowned and glanced over my shoulder to find a dozen Knights flying down behind us. We were surrounded. We couldn't even—a large, pale blue tail whipped up out of a hole in the ground and curled around two of the Knights. They screamed and thrashed to break free, but the beast dragged them down into the tunnel. The beast roared and then their screams were stomped out. Metal crushed and slammed into the walls. The was a beat of silence and then the sickening crunch of bones.

Bile shot up my throat.

Well, we can't go back that way.

The other Knights flew over our heads and landed on solid ground up with the others.

We still had nowhere to go. Knight village was out of the question, but they'd also blocked off both directions down on this level. Lily threw her arms up and sunlight shot out of her. All of the Knights hissed and covered their eyes. I flexed my fingers and pulled for the spirits. *COME ON!* I'd never felt such resistance from the dead before, and I had a horrible suspicion it had something to do with the King.

Savannah gasped and dropped to her knees, then words poured from her mouth, "*Life once followed, and now is dust. As weathered iron turns to rust. Take from the bonds of spirit to ground, as strife and evil does surround. Where water has fled, few remain. Hold protection true until battle does wain. We take fire, fierce and loyal as our ally, to guard from within the threat from the sky.*"

The air shimmered like glittery dust.

"Squishy!" Savannah pressed her hand to his back. "FIRE CIRCLE!"

Squishy snapped to attention. His ears flopped and then stood tall like a police dog's. His whole body turned jet black, that same charred color he'd been when he'd first emerged from the lava with Ziva. Flames danced around his body and smoke billowed from his snout. He lowered his head to the ground.

I heard the flick of the Knights' fingers on their bows as they fired their arrows. I curled my fingers, using all of my physical strength to drag the spirits from the ground. *Come ON. NOW.* Time seemed to slow down.

The arrows flew in a perfect arc right for us. There were too many, hundreds of them. There was no way we could dodge them. There was nowhere for us to run. The arrows sped through the sky.

Fire burst from Squishy's mouth. He whipped around, throwing flames to the left and right until a ring of fire surrounded us. As the flames connected behind us, a silvery mist shot up and covered us like a dome.

The arrows pierced through the dome—*and turned to dust.*

Squishy pranced on his paws in place like he was dancing. His tail wagged wildly.

The Knights let out a battle roar and charged for us with their long silver swords.

"Will this dome keep *them* out, too?" Amelia asked in a tight voice.

"Let's not give them the chance," Ziva growled.

"Just hold them off for a second..." I said through clenched teeth.

Ziva summoned fire to her palms, then threw it at the line of charging Knights. The flames spread out, taking down three Knights with each hit. Squishy fired more from her side. Lava burst from the ground like a raging river rapid. The Knights slid to a stop and pulled golden shields off their backs.

Green, glowing light finally shot through the ground as the spirits broke through whatever hold was on them.

"Finally." I threw my hands out and screamed, "KILL THEM!"

In a glowing green tsunami, the spirits attacked the Knights.

I spun to my group. "RUN!"

"LEFT!" Ziva shouted and pointed toward the purple trees. "CIRCLE!"

We dove over the ring of fire and sprinted to our left as Ziva ordered. The Knights' barracks were now behind us, but we weren't moving fast enough. I didn't know how long those spirits would hold them.

"There's stairs!" Ziva pointed ahead. "In the cliffside, sticking out."

I dug my heels in harder and my legs screamed in protest. I could have flown but my friends couldn't, and I was not leaving them behind. I held my hand up and my heart stopped. My glyph was still red. It hadn't gone back to green. *Marked in green then red to follow.* Tears stung my eyes and a hot lump formed in my throat. It wasn't going to.

Riah's life was in danger *now,* and I was running away from the palace.

Squishy howled and his fur stood up. He snarled at something to my right and charged for it.

I looked just as a large, dog-sized, black creature was falling out of the sky and flying right for me. It had webbed wings that stretched from leg to leg and fangs that dropped out of its mouth.

"SAFFIE!" Ziva screamed and slid to a stop, but she was too far in front of me. "NO!"

She wasn't going to make it. The creature was right on top of me. I shot golden glitter into its chest, but it bounced right off. I lunged to the side *and it followed.* There was a flash of movement and then something dove in between me and the creature. But the creature had been so close that all three of us crashed to the ground.

All I saw was red hair sticking out of a large, gray hooded cape—and then I was thrown into the air. I flipped and somersaulted, then my shoulder slammed back down, but momentum sent me rolling several times before I stopped face-first in the dirt. I scrambled to my feet and looked up just as the creature sank its fangs into my savior's shoulder.

We all screamed and rushed for this person. This stranger who had just saved my life. I couldn't see his face under the creature, but a muscular arm shot out and plunged a dagger into the creature's throat. The creature hissed and then collapsed dead on top of the man.

I rushed to him and slid to my knees. "Oh Goddess, oh my, *get it off!*"

Squishy lunged forward and sank his teeth into the dead creature, then dragged it off of the man.

"Good boy, Squishy," Ziva said in a rush and dropped down on the other side of the man. "Saffie, I'm sorry. Those things are invisible *right* until they attack."

"I beg your gaddamn pardon, ma'am?"

"Sir? *SIR?*" I shoved my hands into his wound to put pressure on it. "Sir?"

The man choked on a cough. He was buried under his own hair and hood.

"Sir, thank you so much. I can't believe you did that for me—"

"*Of course,*" he whispered.

"We need to get him help. Do you have healers? Doctors? Medicine? Something?"

Ziva nodded. "The Circle can heal him if we move fast."

"The Knights are coming!" Landy shouted.

Amelia cursed and dove down beside us. She gripped one of his legs. "We have to move. They're coming!"

Lily shined sunshine out of her palms and nodded for us.

"Landy, get his other leg next to Ziva!" I yelled and slid my hands under the man's injured arm. "We have to carry him."

Landy took his other leg and her face paled. "Oh Goddess! He's bleeding bad from here, too!"

Ziva shook her head. "We won't make it far—"

"*Get me in a forest and I'll be fine!*"

Ziva cursed and copied my position. "Three, two, one, *lift!*"

We picked him up off the dirt and he groaned. He was heavier than I expected and my body was worn out. My strength was already fading. We weren't going to make it to The Circle like this, but if we made it to the forest, I knew I could protect us. I needed the living to make them dead.

Squishy trotted in front of us, his head snapping left and right, up and down, like he was scanning for enemies in every direction.

"*Graceful and steady it moves without sight, the black abyss of darkness beneath the moonless night,*" Savannah shouted all of a sudden from where she jogged beside us. "*Silent and lethal, an ally we call to thee, shrouded in shadow to blind our enemy.*"

She swung her dagger across the back of my left arm, then did the same to the others. Before we could react, she spun and nicked Lily with her blade as well. Lily flinched.

"Savannah, *what*—"

Gray smoke lifted from the ground and shot over our heads. It moved like a snake in the wind, slithering between all our bodies and covering every inch of us.

"Lily, STOP!" Savannah swatted at Lily's hands, stopping the sunlight from shining. "That was a shadow shield spell. The Knights can't see us or track us now. I don't know if it's permanent or not yet."

Ziva whistled under her breath. "I'm going to need that written down later."

We were losing speed. Every few feet we had to stop and fix our grip before the man slipped to the ground. Going up the stairs took forever, and my muscles were so tight I thought they'd pop. Just as we approached the forest, the purple trees rustled and then a herd of vakinyas stepped out in front of us, their red flowers pulsing with life and color.

I sagged with relief and tears stung my eyes. *"Thank you.* Guys, load up."

"On the pillows!" Ziva shouted and nodded her head.

The fae who'd met us at the bottom of the village and carried this man up to the top followed Ziva over to the pillows that sat directly in the middle of the circular terrace. Amelia, Landy, Lily, and Savannah all gasped at the beauty of it all. I didn't blame them. I'd reacted the same way my first trip up. But I had to focus on this man who'd sacrificed his own life to save mine. Blood was gushing from his shoulder and leg. The skin I could see under his cape was sickly pale and a bit blue.

"NEXUS!" Monek shouted over his shoulder, then screamed words in Seelie I didn't know.

"Healing products," Ziva whispered.

Rio and Glisa flew in and stopped beside the man. They reached down at the same time and pulled back his hood. They gasped. I couldn't see his face yet, but I saw theirs.

"*Hetron?*" Rio hissed in alarm.

Ziva scowled and hurried over and then sank to her knees beside Glisa. Her face fell. "*Where the hell were you?*" She growled under her breath.

He chuckled and lifted one hand in a shrug.

Glisa shook her head, then tossed her floor-length hair over her shoulders. "We should have known. You always do this."

The Circle members had all crowded around him. Everyone was talking over each other in panicked tones. My friends were being asked a million questions. One of the elder ladies wrapped a big blanket around Amelia and Landy.

They were fine. I needed to know who this man was. I needed to make sure he was healed. I pushed through the small crowd and then sank down in front of him. A jolt of energy rushed through my body. *I know you.* I'd never seen this man's face, but I knew him. I felt it in my bones, and it did not make any sense.

His eyes were a pale blueish gray, and his skin was dewy soft. His face was all sharp angles and he had perfectly shaped eyebrows that I knew Savannah would say gave him *resting bitch face.* His hair was red, not like mine but more like Squishy's. Reddish-brown. And it was braided really intricately like the Vikings used to do.

"*Move, move, move!*" Nexus hissed and swatted everyone out of her way. She crouched in front of me with a big bowl full of flowers, crystals, dirt, and pink leaves. "Give him some space. He'll be fine if you let me work."

Monek leaned over and pulled her long pink hair back out of her face, carefully and gently braiding it. Nexus was doing...*something.* I wasn't even sure. But there was magic coming from her palms and spells leaving her lips. She worked on his leg first and I watched in amazement as the wound sealed itself up.

My eyes widened.

"He heals faster than anyone I've ever seen," Rio said softly from beside me, her voice thick with worry, like a sister upset with a brother who put himself at risk constantly. "*That does NOT mean you continue this!*"

He gave her a sideways grin and it reminded me of Tegan or Tennessee.

Squishy wiggled through the crowd to sit beside Ziva but then lay down and rested his big face right in the man's hand.

He smiled and immediately ran his fingers through the reddish-brown fur. "Good boy."

"What is she doing to him?" Amelia whispered.

"Nexus is our healer. She's quite gifted." Monek's face shined with pride and admiration. His green, leafy outfit fluttered.

Savannah cleared her throat. "So, what was that monstrosity? The one that got him?"

Ziva shuddered. "Taliveru."

"Anything that makes *you* shudder will haunt my nightmares," Savannah grumbled under her breath. "And I like nightmares."

Ziva grinned up at her. "Thank you?"

Nexus flew around to work on his shoulder wound.

Rio shook her head. "The taliveru are one of the most lethal, treacherous creatures here in Seelie. They are invisible at will, blending into their surrounding until they attack—and by then it is usually too late. Death is imminent, depending on the strength of your blood, which isn't usually strong enough for everyone except him.

My stomach tightened into knots. I reached down and squeezed his hand. "Why did you take that hit for me?"

"It would have killed you," he said with a gravelly voice.

I let out a strangled whine. "And why won't it kill you?"

"That is a long story for another day." He glanced down at the shoulder Nexus was working on. "It may eventually kill me. We cannot be sure."

I huffed. "Why did you risk yourself for me when we have never met?"

He smiled. "I am old. You are young and have a war to fight."

I shook my head. "You don't even know me. Besides, we *all* have a war to fight."

"I am Seelie," he said with a sigh. With his other hand he gestured to himself. "I knew the chances were high my body would heal from a taliveru wound. However, you are a half-breed, and I know for certain you would already be dead."

"Why do you think I'm half-breed?" I'd never met this man, yet he seemed so sure of me.

And I felt like I knew him. There was more he wasn't saying.

"I know you—"

"*How?* How do you know me? I don't remember meeting you."

"*Ah, you wouldn't.*" His pale gaze soaked me in for a long moment, then he smiled softly. "Because, Saraphina, I am your father."

I gasped. My heart stopped. The world around me ceased to exist.

The entire crowd froze.

"*My FATHER?*" I shrieked.

"Yes, I am your father." His smile widened. "And we have met. You just did not know it."

Tears pooled in my eyes. This was my father. My *father*. The man who was the sole reason I was half Seelie in the first place. A million thoughts and even more emotions rushed through my mind. I'd both dreamed of meeting him my whole life and dreaded the day it would come. All my centuries of torture because of being a half-breed, because of *him*. It wasn't right to blame him. He hadn't been the one to do those things to me...but it was an irrational anger inside of me all the same.

My father.

He's my FATHER.

I wanted to call my mother and have her confirm it, but there were no phones in Seelie and certainly no facetime.

He sat up and our eyes were level. "When I found out you'd entered Seelie, I went looking for you. I knew you'd be in danger. I knew they'd taken your soulmate."

"You knew that?"

"The Seer told me, after your birth, that you were the one the prophecy spoke of," he said softly. He reached out and wiped a tear from my cheek. "I knew I had to help prepare for your arrival. I was already a member of The Circle, so I've been waiting for you. When I heard about Zachariah, I knew he had to be yours. I knew it would be any moment. And then there you were. Prophecy or not, I was not going to let my daughter die at the hands of a taliveru. Whether it finally did me in or not."

I opened my mouth, but words failed me. Tears streaked down my face. Three and a half centuries of wondering and he was sitting right in front of me. I sniffled and wiped my tears, and the red glow of my soulmate glyph lit up my whole face.

My heart sank. I had so many questions and comments for my father, but I had a soulmate to save. Those things would have to wait.

He reached out and took my hand with the glowing red glyph into his own. "I'll be here. And even if I don't survive this war, you are Death and you can summon my spirit until you get all the answers you need. Put our past aside for now. I am here to help you save your friends and soulmate."

A broken sob slipped up my throat. I crumbled into his chest. His arms wrapped around me, holding me tight.

Savannah, bless her heart, cleared her throat pointedly. "So...war, huh? Sounds fun. What are we doing for it?"

Ziva chuckled. "Well, she has a point. We need a strategy."

"The prophecy states, *when crimson flashes by her hand, raise arms together, make your stand,*" Rio said in a cold voice.

"To end this era, you'll have to fight, stand your ground and hold it tight."

I sniffled and pulled back to look into my father's eyes. "Don't you even dare die on me now."

He smiled and nodded. "Then we ought to have a plan."

"We attack."

Everyone turned to me.

I held my head high. That rage I'd been feeling ignited tenfold. I pushed to my feet. "The King has reigned too long. It's time we reclaim this land and send him to his grave. I've seen many of you in action already. You are weapons more than you know. You have the slaves. A furious tide is begging to be released in them. They want vengeance. They deserve vengeance. You all have been oppressed and abused. You have been left for dead with no help from the palace, and many have died by their very hands. You owe them no honor, no sympathy, and most of all, no mercy."

Everyone nodded and jumped to their feet, their eyes sharp and clear and burning.

The glyph on my hand tightened with sharp pain. The red glow illuminated everything around us as it flashed in quick pulses. *RIAH.* My heart stopped. I looked up at them with tears in my eyes. "Your revolution begins now. We ride for the palace."

CHAPTER THIRTY-TWO

CAROLINE

"THIS IS by far my favorite spot on campus. Follow me." I smiled over my shoulder at my little tour group as I pushed open the wooden door in front of me. Bright mid-day sunlight slammed into me, and I felt myself get happier. I stepped inside the room and grinned as the group gasped behind me. "I know, right?"

With a happy grin, I walked through the student lounge—heading right for the far wall opposite the door that was made entirely of glass and had the most spectacular view of Central Park. The two walls on the side were also made entirely of glass and I knew from personal experience that their views of the city lights at night were breathtaking. The mahogany hardwood floors creaked under our feet as we walked, just the way real wood floors should.

"What is this room for?" One of the mothers asked with an adorably confused expression on her red freckled face.

"Absolutely nothing at all, which is why it's so great." I chuckled, as did some of the other students within earshot. I gestured around us. "This is the grand student lounge. As I showed you on our tour, each of the dormitories have their own lounges for the residents of those towers. But *this* lounge is open to everyone. It's where we can all hang out together...and not worry about making too much noise or disturbing the cats by the fireplace."

I'd taken on a new job here at SOMA since Christmas... school tour guide.

It happened by accident the first time after Headmaster Muller scheduled too many in one week to handle herself, so I'd stepped in...and did the tours *my way*. Which was much more fun and a lot less stuffy. I showed perspective parents and students our school and gave them all the information they wanted. We wanted our school to continue to grow and it was.

I always saved my favorite room for last. It was my favorite because the old Caroline never would have hung out here, but the new and improved me cherished it. The room was full of all types of couches, floor pillows, and fluffy rugs—whatever the students whipped up with their magic to suit their needs.

One of the twelve-year-olds in front of me looked around with wide eyes. "What is everyone doing?"

"Hanging out. Chilling. Showing each other new tricks they learned in class. Really, whatever they want to do—within reason, of course." I shrugged. "We want every student at SOMA to feel comfortable and at home, and to have all kinds of friends. The faculty uses magic to alert them if inappropriate behavior happens here, otherwise they leave us be."

Behind them, the wooden door swung open and Headmaster Muller walked inside with a smile on her face. Her blue eyes were bright and sparkly, and her black hair was tied up in her standard high ponytail. As she stopped at our group, her grin widened. "Good morning, everyone. Is it still morning?"

"It's noon." I chuckled. "Well, everyone, this is where we part ways. This is Headmaster Muller and she's going to finish off the last section of the tour—the part with all the logistics that you parents want to ask a million questions about. Enjoy your visit to Manhattan and I hope to see all of you on campus soon."

We quickly said our goodbyes as they each turned and followed Headmaster Muller back out the door.

"Who are you and what have you done with Caroline Davenport?" A familiar male voice rumbled from my left.

A girl I knew without looking scoffed. "My, my, what a performance."

I sighed and turned toward them. My smile dropped and I hated the new reaction to two of my oldest and best friends—or who used to be my best friends. Olivia and Oliver Jr. The Fitzgeralds. They both looked chic as hell with their black clothing and matching brunette hair, their hazel eyes holding identical cruel expressions. They'd been on my tour just now, lingering in the back silently.

Ignoring their snide remarks, I forced a smile. "Olivia and Oliver, I haven't seen you since Christmas. Where have you been?"

At *that,* Olivia grinned and rolled her eyes. "Where *haven't* we been?"

"More importantly, where are we going next?" Oliver wagged his eyebrows and rocked back on his heels. "Where's Noah? We have so much to talk about."

My cheeks flushed. "Oh, he's doing some kind of experimental art class with the elementary school kids. He'll be out soon. So, what did you think of the tour? Going to start school here soon?"

Olivia scoffed. "No, thanks."

"Yeah, we'll pass. We just promised our parents we'd take a tour and *consider* it."

I frowned. "Why won't you attend SOMA?"

Olivia arched one eyebrow. "Why won't you attend the Valentine's gala in Paris with us? I know you saw our texts."

"The Paris Majors are opening up Headquarters to the

public for the gala. It's *the* place to be this year." Oliver leaned against the floor-to-ceiling window overlooking Central Park. "Perfect place for you and Noah to spend your first Valentine's together as a couple."

"Noah and I are going to the Red Ball in Edenburg, and we're *very* excited about it."

Olivia cringed. "Since when does Caroline Davenport want to go anywhere near *Edenburg?* Since when are you such a bummer?"

"Since Liam and Scarlet died," I snarled loud enough to make half the lounge turn towards us. "Since I almost died. Or did all the drugs and alcohol erase those memories already?"

They rolled their eyes.

Rage bloomed inside of me. "You know what? You're right. I'm not the same Caroline Davenport you knew. I've changed. I'm a better person now and I promise you life is better because of it. I have drive and passion for things I never had before. I have purpose now. I don't sit around partying and acting like I'm better than everyone else just because I have money. Because in case you forgot, being rich doesn't prevent you from dying when demons roll into town. Noah and I haven't texted you two because we no longer have room for your toxic ass selves in our lives anymore. Evolve or get out because you are not taking me back down to—"

A loud roar like thunder rumbled through the glass wall. The entire room jumped and turned to the window. It sounded like thunder except the sky was a perfect cloudless blue. Hundreds of birds shot up from the trees at once, like a black tidal wave.

What the hell?

Bright orange flames burst through the tree line and into the sky—one after another. The world shook so hard people on the sidewalks dropped to their knees and cars swerved. The building trembled and lights flickered. Even from five floors up,

I heard the screaming from outside. I stumbled away from the windows as the glass rattled. My mother's protective spells were supposed to be strong enough to protect the school, but every instinct inside of me was screaming *RUN*.

"*Is this an earthquake?*" some kid shrieked from the back.

"*New York doesn't get earthqu—*"

A demon rose up from inside of Central Park, looming out from the trees like a nightmare straight out of an Avengers movie. I gasped and my body locked in place. I'd never seen a demon like this. It looked like a giant worm-cockroach, with big horns on its head and long branch-like arms. The demon turned toward the school and spit a stream of fire straight for us. It swung long arms through the air, taking whole sections of trees down in one swoop while setting others on fire.

"OH SHIT!" I screamed and spun on my heels.

I wasn't the damsel in distress I was before. I had a job now. I had a damn plan for this. I clenched my teeth and sprinted out the door, but the building shook so hard my balance faltered and I crashed into the far wall. I cursed and leapt toward the big red button on the wall and slammed my palm into it. A loud siren ripped through the speaker system, wailing over and over. Red lights flashed from the ceiling.

"*CODE RED. DEMON ATTACK,*" Deacon's voice echoed down the hall. It was a recording, yet even still I felt his Devil's magic wash over me. "*STAY CALM AND SEEK SHELTER IN DORMS OR BASEMENTS. STAY INDOORS UNTIL CODE BLACK.*"

Doors up and down the hall flew open instantly with students and faculty running for cover. This was the plan. The school was protected with barriers and spells. But after the New Year's Day attack, we'd established emergency protocols so everyone knew what to do. And that was *nothing*, except to seek shelter. Within milliseconds, the hall was flooded with hundreds of fleeing students. Deacon's magic kept the panic at a manageable level, but there was still screaming and everyone was running.

I had to get outside.

Noah was out front with the little kids.

Gus-gus and Zeus were in the lobby by the fireplace.

I weaved my way through the crowd, sprinting for the stairs. Deacon's recording started over but my pulse kept rising. "GET BELOW GROUND!" I shouted over the screaming and rattling walls.

Dear Goddess, what's happening out there?!

My legs and feet burned as I flew down the stairs.

"CAROLINE!" Professor Wallace shouted.

I waved her off. "GET THEM BELOW!"

The students were all taking the back staircases to the basement, so as I made a sharp left turn I found the front hall completely swarmed with students coming toward me. I was swimming upstream.

A warm hand gripped my arm and yanked me back. "CAROLINE!"

I spun and gasped. "NOAH!"

"Where are you going? We have to get down!"

"Gus-Gus and Zeus! They won't leave without me!" I grabbed his face and kissed him quick, then shoved him back. "GO! TAKE THE KIDS!"

I didn't wait for his reaction, I had to get to my fat blue cats. My babies. The Old Lands kittens I'd saved months ago. Our school played home to about two dozen of these cats and as I sprinted in the opposite direction of everyone else, I noticed the students were carrying the cats with them to safety. It brought tears to my eyes.

But I knew *mine* wouldn't be there. They would hide and wait for me.

I sprinted past student services and down the grand wooden

stairs. The main lobby area was empty, with only a fire crackling in the background.

"GUS-GUS! ZEUS!"

They flew out from behind a sofa and I almost cried. They rushed to my open arms, and I pulled them to my chest—the floor trembled and groaned. My legs buckled and my knees slammed into the wooden floors.

"CAROLINE!" Noah shouted. And then his hands were in my view. "Give one to me!"

I handed Gus-Gus to him and jumped back to my feet just as the world rocked. Every window rattled. Noah and I froze, gripping each other and the cats. Outside, car horns honked and police sirens wailed in every direction. Screams echoed left and right.

A cloud of bright orange flames slammed into the windows. The walls groaned. The front door swung open and slammed into the wall—*and I spotted SOMA kids out front. LITTLE kids.*

"OH SHIT!"

Noah and I sprinted for the door.

Outside was chaos and mayhem. Taxis and cars were crashed into each other and buildings. Steam and smoke rose through the grates from the subway. People were scrambling in every direction.

And a dozen five-year-old SOMA students were crying and running straight towards us.

"The field trip!" Noah cursed and leapt forward. He waved his arm. "COME ON!"

Professor Kline took the kindergarten class to the park today. I knew it, but I'd forgotten. Now they were racing for their lives. Their little legs couldn't carry them fast enough. Behind them, Professor Kline's face and half her upper body were covered in blood. She was dragging her left leg and losing steam.

The demon reared back and spit fire in a circle around it.

Those long tree branch-like arms swung side to side, plowing down every tree in a direct path behind Kline.

"They're not gonna make it," I heard myself whisper. I thrust Zeus into Noah's arms. "GET THE KIDS INSIDE!"

And then I took off with my heart lodged in my throat and absolutely no idea what I was doing. Behind me, Noah screamed my name but I ignored him. I had to. This demon was coming for Kline and the kids and I couldn't just do *nothing*. Everything was happening too fast. The Coven hadn't arrived yet. My parents hadn't arrived. Hell, even the Knights weren't there yet. I knew they would come, but for now I was the only help these kids had.

"TO NOAH!" I shouted as I passed them.

Professor Kline and five kids were still up ahead.

The demon's massive, glowing red eyes narrowed on them and then he *grinned*. My stomach dropped. I dug my heels in harder. The demon swung his arm right for the last five kids. I dove and tackled them to the ground like dominos just as the demon's arm swept over my head. I rolled and scrambled onto my hands and knees—

Professor Kline cried out agony.

I looked up and my breath caught in my throat. The demon had scooped her up in his hand and lifted her up. It opened its mouth and fangs the size of my body dropped down, venom dripping down to the sidewalk and burning through the pavement. Professor Kline wailed. Red blood stained her short blonde hair.

Oh my Goddess. It's going to EAT her?

OH GODDESS.

THINK, CAROLINE, THINK!

I had to do something. Anything. Except I didn't know battle spells. I didn't know how to fight or kill a demon. But she was about to die so I thrust my wand up and did the only thing I *did* know.

I wrapped a giant scarf around the demon's mouth.

The demon growled but didn't drop her, so I flicked my wand and covered its hands in silk mittens and then put dark sunglasses over its eyes. The demon hissed and swatted at its face—*and dropped Kline.*

She dropped to the grass in a motionless heap, but at least she wasn't lunch. The demon slashed through the garments I'd given it in a split second and roared like a dinosaur. Its glowing red eyes focused on me and then it charged.

I grabbed the kids' arms and hauled them behind me. I held my wand up and tried to think of a single spell to stop the demon, but my mind went blank.

"CAROLINE!" Noah yelled.

Rocks slammed into the demon's face, but it wasn't slowing down.

"RUN!" Noah cried.

But it was no use. I wouldn't make it. And I had to protect the little kids. The scent of maple syrup slammed into my face. It was right over us, close enough to see the drops of venom sliding down its fangs. I braced myself—a stream of fire shot over my head *into* the demon's face.

I dropped to my knees, covering the kids with my body just as a huge orangish-brown dragon flew over us. He roared and slammed into the demon, covering its eyes with his dragon wings.

STEVE!

I gasped and leapt to my feet, dragging the kids with me. "RUN TO NOAH! NOW!"

They scrambled and charged toward Noah across the street. He was running for us. His eyes widened and his jaw dropped. *Oh no!* I pushed my legs harder.

Steve bellowed—then landed on the front steps of the school in a tangle of limbs and covered in blood.

"STEVE!" I ran for him. "NOAH, THE KIDS!"

Noah cursed and scooped the last three kids up and sprinted back for the school. I rushed to Steve and slid to my knees by his face. His eyes were half open and his body trembled. There was blood *everywhere*.

"Oh, Goddess. *Steve*." I pressed my hands to his neck to search for a pulse, but I didn't know where a dragon's heart even was. His scales were almost too hot to touch. "Shift back so I can—"

The demon roared and spit fire into the walls of the school.

Something hard slammed into my feet and then I was lifted into the air upside-down. I screamed. My mind flashed back to that night in Times Square with the morpher demon—when I'd almost died. My body locked up. This was it. This was how I was going to die.

A dark red dragon flew by me from out of nowhere, shrieking and spitting fire.

The pressure on my ankle vanished and I plummeted toward the ground, but at the last second a greenish-brown dragon caught me. My breath left me in a rush. The dragon dropped me a few feet to the ground beside Steve, then dove for the demon.

"NOAH!" I screamed and wrapped my arms around Steve's big dragon shoulders. "NOAH!"

I tried to drag him myself, but he only moved an inch before my legs gave out under me.

"CAROLINE?" I heard footsteps and then Noah slid in beside me. "Oh, Goddess, Steve. We'll never move him. I'll get his tail."

Noah cursed and moved down to pick up Steve's tail.

"PULL!"

We both turned white from the exertion of trying to drag a dragon, but we'd only gotten a foot closer to the door and we still had to get him up *stairs*. But I was *not* leaving him.

Noah's face paled and his eyes locked on something behind me. He dropped Steve's tail. "What is *THAT*?"

I glanced over my shoulder, then did a double take. A horde of demons was charging right for us from inside Central Park. My heart stopped. If we left Steve, the demons would be on him like ants. Tor and Kiev would be outnumbered and overpowered in seconds.

But the front door to the school was wide open.

I looked to Noah. "THE DOOR!"

"THE COVEN IS HERE!"

I gasped and spun around. The Moon Card, Henley, was headed toward us—*wait a second*. She was strolling. Like this was a casual walk in the park. *Hold on, is that blood?* Her pale skin seemed to be stained red.

And then her glowing red eyes met mine and a cold chill slid down my spine.

"THAT'S A DEMON!"

"STEVE, SHIFT!" Noah screamed.

We dove for him and tried to drag him, but he was barely moving. He was just too heavy for us. I cursed and looked to the open door of the school. *Damn it.* I pointed my wand toward the school crest and shouted the spell to lock the school down.

Without us inside it.

The door slammed shut and magic shimmered over the walls.

The ground trembled under my feet. The demons were close enough to hear their ragged breaths and growls—to smell their rancid breaths and the scent of maple syrup.

Just then the side emergency door of the main building flew open and people rushed out. People dressed in black with weapons raised in the air. *The Swords!* With a battle cry they charged past us. I glanced over my shoulder just as the two front lines clashed—demons vs Swords students.

A black leopard, a mountain lion, and a massive grizzly bear charged into battle. The mountain lion leapt over our heads and tackled three demons right behind us. *Marcy!* The grizzly bear sliced demon throats as he ran through the lines of them. *Chris!* The black leopard slid up behind me and planted his feet. *Professor McCallis!*

"They're not gonna last!" Noah shouted, his voice breaking. "There's too many of them to win!"

"We just have to stall—"

"DUCK!"

I dropped down just as white magic shot over our heads and slammed into the walls of the school. The magical barrier flickered and flashed. The spells weakened and windows instantly shattered.

Noah gasped. *"That's not supposed to be possible!"*

"That's Coven magic!" My eyes widened. We'd never prepared for an attack from The Coven. We didn't have spells strong enough to fight *them.* "What do we—"

"DEACON!"

I gasped and spun around and found red lightning streaking across the sky. *DEACON!* Tears stung my eyes. *The Coven. They're here. They came.* Red mist flowed live a river from behind the demons. I didn't know what Deacon was forcing them to do but each demon stopped moving the second the mist touched them.

Henley shrieked and her eyes flashed bright red. *But her feet stopped.*

The red mist washed over me, and I felt Deacon's magic ordering me to stop moving. My body locked in place. Above the red fog, Kiev and Tor, the young dragons, were dive-bombing the big demon's eyes like they were trying to pluck them right out. This demon was apparently immune to Deacon's persuasions and that made my body turn to ice.

Kiev sliced the demon's face open with his talon, but the demon swung his arm and slammed it into Kiev's body. The red dragon flew into the building next door, then slumped to the ground. Tor dodged the demon's swings by hanging onto its horn. The demon snarled and snapped his head down and Tor rolled right off the horn and onto the horde of demons below.

Timothy, the former Judgement Card, emerged from the burning trees of Central Park behind the demons. He sliced and diced a path through them with a sword that looked like it was made of pure ice. He thrust his arm out and I spotted IX on his left forearm.

Timothy is the new Hermit?? How is that possible? He was already a Card before?

I wanted to move, to help them or to move Steve, but my body was still locked in place from Deacon's magic. All I could do was stand there and watch and wait.

Timothy charged for the big wormy-cockroach demon, then leapt into the air and swung his sword down—*and sliced the demon's hand off.* I gasped and started to cheer but the hand began to reform.

The giant wormy demon screamed words in a language I'd never heard and in a voice that was *definitely* not human. More demons appeared from out of nowhere, like they popped up from the cracks in the tree trunks. *Since when can demons speak?!*

The giant demon roared and swung its arm and then Deacon and Timothy were soaring straight up into the air. The demon craned his neck back and opened his mouth wide *right as Tim and Deacon began to drop back down.*

"KESSLER!"

Kessler, the Strength Card, appeared way in the back. He charged forward and grabbed the demon's tail *and swung.* The demon flew backwards and crashed onto its back beneath the trees. Kessler tackled Henley—and disappeared in the sea of demons and Swords students.

But Deacon and Timothy were several stories high and free-falling for the ground.

That damned nightmare demon had gotten back to its feet and was charging for us again.

Shadows slid over my head like a dark thundercloud. My stomach tightened. I held my breath, expecting it to be another one of those wormy-cockroach giant demons, but then six massive dragons flew like missiles right for it. I recognized Silas instantly. He dove for Deacon and Timothy. At the last second he flipped upside-down, and the two Cards landed on his stomach.

The other five dragons slammed into the side of the giant demon at the exact same time, sending it crashing to the ground. Dirt and dust billowed into the air. The ground rumbled and trees toppled over. It was only in that moment that I realized half of Central Park seemed to be on fire. My heart sank.

As the big one fell, the other demons turned and charged to its defense.

Koth emerged from the chaos of the demons and flew right for the school. His violet eyes spotted Steve lying at my feet. He landed, whipped his head back and forth, and then stuck his snout in the air and *sniffed.* His violet eyes widened *and then he was gone,* shooting into the blue sky and out of sight faster than my eyes could track.

Movement in my peripheral vision made me turn—all of a sudden a long strip of ice formed across the street. I opened my mouth to shout when Deacon and Timothy came sliding down the top of it while shooting magic as they went. Smaller demons flew into the air like someone had thrown them and then turned to ice before crashing back down.

The monster nightmare demon roared and stood up straight. It had black blood dripping from its body, but it didn't seem to care. It swatted at a brown dragon with three spikes on the tip of his tail that flew between its horns. A bright green dragon fired flames into its chest. Two other dragons—one ivory, one charcoal-gray—were scorching its stomach. Silas was on the ground, burning demons left and right.

"LANCASTER!" Kessler shouted from somewhere within the battle.

A lone figure cut through the chaos with a sword in each hand and blue flames coiled around his wrists. He was shouting out orders to the Swords students in a beautiful British accent. *That's Jackson Lancaster!* The dude was a living legend. I'd only gotten glimpses of him at the Yule Ball, but this wasn't any better. He moved so fast. The Swords followed his orders without hesitation. He moved them into formation and attacked like he led armies every day. The nasty gash across his chest looked painful, but he didn't seem to notice it at all.

The fact that the Knights of New York had not yet arrived told me that this whole nightmare had only been going on for a few minutes, even though it felt like an hour.

Red lightning shot up from the ground, splitting a narrow pathway between the demons just big enough for a tall girl with long black hair to half-drag a guy toward the school. The guy had a cloud of pink magic clinging to his body and a huge bloody wound in his chest. I recognized him from the Yule Ball because I remembered loving the way his tattoos looked on his beautifully dark skin. The girl looked up and I spotted mismatched eyes—*that's Hope Proctor! Bettina Blair! Tenn's sister!*

My pulse quickened. The Coven was arriving, though I didn't understand where the big hitters were. Where was Tenn, Tegan, and Emersyn? It wasn't like them to be absent.

"HOPE!"

She stopped and fired ice behind her without looking. Gold light flashed from her fingers.

Timothy raced up behind her and took the injured tattooed guy from her. "HENLEY!"

Hope, aka Bettina—I wasn't sure what we were supposed to call her now—cursed and disappeared back into the battle. There seemed to be an endless flow of demons from inside Central Park. It made no sense. The big demon was only temporarily preoccupied by the dragons. We all knew it wasn't going to last long.

We were losing this little war.

Koth dropped down out of the sky, appearing from out of nowhere with four people on his back. I narrowed my eyes and spotted Cooper, Royce, Braison, and—I gasped. *TENN!* Big, golden angel wings flashed behind his back and then he was *gone*. Tennessee moved faster than any living creature I'd ever seen. All I could see was the glow of archangel Michael's sword streaking across the sky.

The wormy-roach demon roared and then light flashed. It hissed and shivered. Its tail flicked in the air. Tennessee was everywhere at once, slicing Heaven's sword into the monster with lightning speed.

Koth swooped down and plucked five demons off the ground, then bit their heads off—and spit them back into the other demons like bullets. Fire raged left and right. Demons, dragons, and Swords were lost to a cloud of dirt and smoke.

Royce stumbled out from within the smoke, half-carrying Deacon with him. Deacon was bleeding and not using his right leg, but he was striking Royce with red lightning every other second—like he was forcing him to move.

"*Deacon!*" Noah shouted from behind me, making me jump.

Deacon looked up and cursed. He flicked his wrist and my body unlocked. I stretched my legs and arms, then charged for them.

Royce draped Deacon's arm over my shoulders. "Get him out!" He turned and charged back into the battle.

"What the hell is that thing, D?" I grumbled and hobbled us both back towards the stairs.

Deacon groaned. "Greater demon. Bad, bad, bad—oh SHIT, WARNER!"

I looked up to find Timothy and Noah sitting Warner on the stairs next to Steve. Timothy said something under his breath and then raced back into battle. Noah carefully rested Warner against Steve's tail, but even from here I could see the pallor of his skin was *not* good. The wound in his chest was gushing blood—even if the pink magic was keeping it in a bubble around him.

"What the hell is going on here?" I cursed and sat Deacon beside Warner.

"NO!" Royce screamed so loud we all jumped. "COME BACK! DAMN YOU!"

Noah and I spun around to see what Royce was yelling about but my gaze landed on Tenn. He was whipping around the greater demon, flashing green and blue magic while stabbing it.

Deacon groaned. "I could do that if I had wings too."

Warner chuckled, then winced. "Don't make me laugh while I'm trying not to die."

Deacon patted Steve's tail. "Hang in there, panda boy. We'll get you help."

"Why isn't it dead yet?" Noah pointed to Tenn. "How can it survive *that* sword?"

The greater demon hissed *and then vanished.*

Tennessee growled from where he hovered in the air far above Central Park. He raised his right hand and water shot up from the ground. With a flick of his wrist, the water rained down on the fire scorching the trees. The flames hissed and smoked as the water snuffed them out.

Then Tenn spun around and lifted his right hand again. Except this time the final dozen demons still alive lifted up off the street and hovered in the air. The dragons covered them in bright orange flames instantly.

And then New York fell silent.

"Every time," Royce cried and tugged on his hair. "Every damn time she just vanishes!"

"We'll get her, Royce. *We will.*" Braison wrapped his arm around Royce's shoulder and led him toward us on the front steps.

Cooper hurried over with a deep scowl. "D? Warner? We still alive?"

They both held their thumbs up but didn't speak.

Noah looked down at his watch and sighed. "That was literally the longest eight minutes of my life."

Eight minutes?

Koth flew over and then mid-flight shifted into his human form. He crouched down in front of Steve and pressed his hand to his snout. "You did good, kid. Real proud of you. Just rest until we can get you some help."

"Are we flying him home, my Lord?" I didn't know this dragon dude's name, but I recognized him from the Yule Ball—he was the brown dragon with the scary tail.

Koth cursed. "Greater demon wounds are going to be tricky. *Silas?*"

"I'm here," Silas grumbled.

"You and Yaluk get Steve home to Elan." Koth frowned and looked over my shoulder. "Tor, how's Kiev?"

"Sore, but nothing the infirmary here can't handle, if that's okay with you?" Tor pointed behind him. "Kessler is carrying him over here now. He hasn't shifted back either."

Koth nodded.

"Warner? D?" Jackson Lancaster shouted in his pretty accent as he slid over to us. "You alive?"

"Yeah," Cooper answered for them.

Jackson nodded but then he scowled. His aquamarine eyes narrowed and bounced around the group. "Bettina. Where's Bettina—BETTINA?"

Tenn landed beside me with sharp eyes. He spun toward Central Park. "*HOPE?*"

"She's fine!" Braison shouted from the street, his red hair wildly tangled.

Timothy used his sword to point into the park. "She's over there."

We all looked to where he pointed and found Bettina, aka Hope, walking down the dirt path like she was on a mission. She held her phone up to her ear as her eyes were locked on the ground. Then her mismatched eyes widened and she bent down. She picked something up, then cursed. "HAVEN!"

Tenn, aka Haven, rushed over to her side. He took one look at whatever was in her palm and then cursed violently. He scrubbed his face and marched back toward us. He flicked his wrist and Bettina, Timothy, and Braison all flew over to the stairs. Once we were all in one place, Tenn sighed. He pinched the bridge of his nose. "Okay, damage control time. Dad...can you get Manhattan cleared up and secure? Like, can just you take the reins on that and not make me think about it at all?"

Kessler smiled. "Of course, Son. Leave Royce, Braison, and Lancaster, and I'll have this resolved quickly."

"Done. Deacon and Warner, you're going to Katherine immediately. Don't fight me." Tenn snapped his fingers and pointed behind him. "Oh, I saw the Majors cars headed this way. They should be here any second to help you control the situation."

"No problem, Son."

Tenn nodded. "Hope and Uncle Tim, come with me. Cooper, take Caroline and Noah and get SOMA calmed and secure. Koth, can you fly me back to Eden? And then go back to Issale, I don't want you out of home country right now—not to order you around."

Koth chuckled. "It's all right. I can do that. Silas and Yaluk are going to fly Steve home to be healed."

Tenn grimaced. "Elan knows what to do for greater demons?"

"I think so, but if not, I know a good healer in Eden to call."

Tenn nodded. "Good. Don't hesitate to ask Katherine, or any of us."

"Will do." Koth pointed to the green dragon behind him. "Finn can be of service if you need him."

Finn nodded.

"Thanks. Finn, can you stick around here and then fly them back to Eden?"

Finn nodded.

Tenn rubbed his hands together. "Okay, everyone, get to work. Call me if absolutely anything else goes wrong."

Koth took a step back and then in the blink of an eye he was a massive black dragon again. Tenn flicked his hand and Warner, Deacon, Bettina, and Timothy flew up and landed on his back.

I cleared my throat and raised my hand. "Pardon me, Tennessee?"

He looked to me and arched one eyebrow.

"Um...should we be concerned that greater demon is coming back here?"

Tennessee growled. He looked up at the school and cursed. "Keep everyone inside for the next few days. Full lockdown."

My stomach dropped. I did not like that answer at all.

Before I could ask anything else, Tenn hopped onto Koth's back and they vanished out of sight...leaving the rest of us on the steps. The dragons got to work on Steve immediately. Kiev hobbled forward while leaning on Tor.

Kessler cleared his throat. "All right, Cooper, take Caroline and Noah and get the school settled. We'll handle the rest."

CHAPTER THIRTY-THREE

SAFFIE

LLYOD'S EYES about popped out of his head. "*THIS* is what you've been working on when you disappear?"

"Hetron..." Quoya blinked and shook her head. "What did you do?"

Hetron, also known as *my father*, looked up with a grin from where he was crouched. "We all knew the prophecy. We all knew her soulmate would be in the dungeon, and we all knew we'd have to attack. We've also all been preparing for this war in our various ways. *This* has been my project. It's a trap."

He stood, pulling his project up off the ground with him. It was a net made of vines, twigs, and branches—and it had to be a hundred feet long. He'd had it laying in the dirt, just waiting to be lifted.

I reached out with my magic and felt the life still in this net, so I grabbed ahold of it. With a flick of my wrists, the net shot up into the trees far above us. Everyone gasped and jumped back. I twirled my fingers, forcing the net to attach itself to the trees, then I dropped my hands. And the net stayed in place, dangling from the branches down to the ground like a wall.

Savannah gasped and snapped her fingers excitedly. "I saw

this on Shark Week. They put the long nets out in the water and then wait for the sharks to come swimming and *BOOM. GOTCHA.* Brilliant, Paparella."

My father frowned at her. "*Paparella?*"

"Safferella. Paparella." She gestured between us. "You get it, right?"

He opened his mouth, then chuckled and shook his head. "I've been called worse, I suppose."

Glisa, who was finishing up braiding that long white hair of hers, narrowed her silver eyes on the net. "I understand the concept of a trap and a net. But how is this going to help us with the Knights? They will see it. And it is so long, how will we—*did you—*"

"Yes, we did. Monek has been helping me." My father grinned rather smugly and walked up to where I'd hung the net. "Saffie, thank you for that assist. Now, watch this..."

He turned and *walked through the net.*

Monek flew over and also flew right through the net without getting caught, like it wasn't there at all. Then he spun and flew back to us with a shit-eating grin. "Hetron used his secret special magic that the crown does not know about."

"Secret special magic?" Savannah and I repeated at the same time.

"Without taking the time to explain the *whys* and *hows,* you just saw it." My father gestured to his magical net as he walked back through it. "I do not use this often as I do not want the King to know of my ability."

"He used it around our village. If any Knights or Royals try to come in, they will be caught and we will have time to react." Rio said with her eyes locked on the net. "But those are hidden from the eye—"

"Ah. Yes, that is part two." My father turned and wagged his eyebrows. "My friend?"

Ziva marched up to the net and placed both palms on the

vines. Purple magic billowed from her palms and swirled around the net, stretching left and right. The magic coiled around her own body, changing her hair from that pink and purple combo to dark blue. The gold chains and diamonds on her face and hair sparkled.

And then the net vanished.

I gasped.

Lily shined sunlight out and it faintly lit the outline of the net. She grinned and nodded.

"That's some Tegan level espionage shit right there," Savannah whispered under her breath. "I can't wait to tell her about it."

Butterflies danced in my stomach like pinballs. My magic was roaring and begging to be set free. My pulse was flying so fast it was basically one solid beat. My feet kept lifting off the ground because my wings were trying to carry me away. To Riah. That red flashing light on my chest and hand were short circuiting my brain and taking over more and more with every passing second.

We'd gotten over here to this part of the forest surprisingly fast thanks to the vakinyas. My father had led us here. He'd said he'd been scouting and planning for the perfect point of attack for when this day came, which I was thankful for since time was of the essence. We had the entire village with us, most of the fae here I'd never even seen before this moment. And we had more freed slaves than I realized.

Everyone was talking over each other, trying to formulate a plan.

But none of their ideas were what we needed.

I shook my head. "STOP!"

They all gasped and turned to me.

I took a deep breath. "We don't have time to bicker and debate. I have a plan. Listen, because I can only say it once. On Earth, there was a war between humans. A war between the crown and the people. Just like you, the people had right to revolt but the crown had the powerful army, weapons, and skills, and the people had no way of combating that."

"*Guerilla warfare,*" Savannah whispered and pumped her fists.

"The American Revolution," Amelia and Landy both said at the same time.

Rio cocked her head to the side. "We're listening."

"What is it?" Glisa asked with wide eyes.

I turned away from them and pushed my magic out, then lifted my hands up to the sky. Huge trees burst from the ground, filling the open spaces. Behind me, everyone gasped. I spun back to face them. "You cannot beat them head on, so you lure them into your trap and then you ambush. You will have to be patient. But this has worked many times in history on Earth."

Rio pulled two swords off her back. Her red lizards flicked their tongues from her pockets. "What do we do?"

"I will lure them in. Once they get inside the forest, you attack without mercy or hesitation. If you have wings, get up in the trees and hide in the shadows." I turned to where the arcana and wingless half-breed slaves stood. "No wings, hide behind the trees and in the bushes."

And then I noticed none of them had shoes on. They were probably used to it, but there was no reason to risk it. So I threw my hands out and shot my magic right at their feet while picturing Riah's boots. In the blink of an eye, everyone had boots on. Bridgett tugged on her little gray slave dress.

"Let them die while you wear their slave dresses. Let it be the salt in their wound and the very last thing they see," I said with a growl, then I turned to The Circle. "Rio, Glisa, and Quoya, stand out in the open. Let them see you. Let them think you are unaware of their arrival. You are our bait."

They nodded and pulled their swords out.

"Lloyd, you're a Court member and they do not know

you're a spy. We don't want to spoil that prematurely. Get out of here. Now. Get back to the village and fortify. Make sure that when we return, the Knights can't get to you."

He nodded and then spun and flew out of sight.

"Nexus and Monek." I turned to them and pointed in the direction Lloyd flew. "Go to the vakinyas. Guard them and keep them ready. When our wingless friends flee, they will need a ride. It is your job to make sure this happens. Once they're loaded up, Nexus, get back to the village and prepare for healing wounds as I am sure there will be some. Monek will accompany the others back. Lukat, where's Lukat?"

"I'm here." She stepped out from behind Quoya with her rainbow hair. "I am not a fighter—"

"Which is why I have a special job for you." I pointed to the net. "You are the cue. The eyes. Your job is to signal to everyone else when to attack and then when to flee."

"Not all commanders wield swords," Savannah said behind me.

Lukat's eyes sharpened and her cheeks flushed. She backed up to the net. "I can do that. Everyone, watch for my cue."

Everyone nodded.

Lily snapped her fingers until I looked to her. She tapped on her Sun Mark, then pointed to me.

I thrust my left hand out and curled my fingers, summoning every *arcana or human half-breed* spirit. They instantly rose from the ground in that familiar glowy blue form. They looked to me and saluted, like they knew I was calling them for battle. "You're on offense. See a Knight, kill a Knight."

They nodded.

Then with my right hand, I summoned every *fae civilian* spirit in the area. They popped up even faster, glowing green with wings fluttering and swords in their hands. "You are defense. Guard our living. Stay with them, and keep them safe and alive."

They nodded.

"All spirits, when they flee, you flee. Stay with them until I return for you. Stay with them no matter what. Keep them alive. Guard them. When I return, I will give you peace. But I need your help until I can get back, got it?"

All the spirits nodded and bowed in gratitude.

Bridgett, who was sitting on a tree branch right above me, cleared her throat. "Um, Miss Saffie? How are you going to lure them in here?"

"I'm going to give them what they want."

Quoya frowned. "What is that?"

I grinned and gripped my citrine bracelet. My golden armor stretched over my body and my sword formed in my hand. "*Me*."

Savannah squirmed and giggled. "Don't tease me with a good time. Roll tide, ma'am. Let's go."

Everyone got into place, and I almost cried at their trust in me.

"I'm going to the palace to get Riah. I will be back to finish this war with you, but I do not know how long it will take. Stay as safe as possible. Keep to the village and watch for my return." I turned and headed toward the edge of the forest, to where the tunnels started. "Ziva, Squishy, Father, you're with us. Let's go."

We were silent as we sprinted for the wall, but I felt everyone's cold determination. They were as serious about this as I was. I glanced down at my hand. It was still flashing red. It'd been going on too long. Riah needed a distraction.

As I slid to a stop at the edge of the cliff, the sight of the palace made my stomach turn. I summoned my magic into my palms until it formed glowing gold glitter balls the size of my head. I took a few steps back, then ran and used all my body weight and power to throw my magic straight for the palace. I fired over and over, rapidly and mercilessly.

My glitter magic bombs shot like shooting stars and slammed into the walls of the palace.

My father laughed a deep belly laugh behind me. *"MORE! They can take it!"*

Each hit sent tremors through the palace. Stained-glass walls shattered and exploded.

Savannah gasped. "IT STOPPED FLASHING! IT'S JUST RED! IT'S WORKING! MORE, MORE, MORE!"

I fired several dozen more magic bombs at the palace, but my gaze was locked on my glyph. It wasn't flashing anymore. She was right. Whatever they'd been doing to Riah had stopped because of my attack. Tears stung my eyes.

I'm coming Riah.

I wondered if he could sense my presence. If he could feel the fire flowing inside of me. He'd been through hell to save and protect me for three centuries. I would tear down an entire kingdom in return. And then I'd watch it burn.

"They're coming," Ziva said in a rush, pointing to the ground by the palace.

"Lily, blind the barracks. Savannah, hang on to Amelia and Landy and don't let them out of your sight so we can focus on the fight." I glanced over my shoulder just as Amelia and Landy dove for Savannah, wrapping their arms around hers. Savannah grinned and gave me two thumbs-up. "Ziva and Squishy? Give me fire. Shoot them out of the sky with fire like you did by the barracks. Can you make lava whereever you want?"

Ziva's body turned jet-black with orange flames streaking up and down her limbs. Fire balls flickered in her palms. "Where do you want it?"

I pointed down to the tunnels. "The beast can't possibly like lava, and we need a way across."

She nodded and moved to the edge of the cliff, then shot streams of fire straight down to the surface. Glowing orange rivers of liquid fire rushed like river rapids heading toward a waterfall. Within the flash of an eye, it was pouring over the edge of the holes and into the tunnel.

The beast roared.

The tunnels shook and I could see which way he went... right for the palace.

"I know the pathway down to the surface, but we'll need something to throw to the beast while we run across," my father said in a rush. He pulled a bow and arrow off his back and fired arrows into the wall of oncoming Knights. "We need to catch a few."

The Knights were flying straight for us. They had bows *and* swords.

"I'm going to break their bows. You capture a few and I'll tie 'em up?" I waited for him to nod. "Do you know where they're keeping Riah?"

"In the dungeon," Ziva yelled over her shoulder as she threw her arms up and shot fire balls into the oncoming Knights. "I escaped from there once."

My father's eyes darkened. He leaned in close. "I know a secret passageway into the palace that only the Royals use. I found it once by accident while escaping. Once we get by the beast, I'll lead you there."

I had so many questions about that statement, and Ziva's, but now wasn't the time for backstories and sharing traumatic experiences. This was war and the Knights were almost here. I glanced over my shoulder and spotted Glisa, Rio, and Quoya standing together like they were just relaxing. *Perfect bait.* Behind them, Lukat leaned against a tree and held a flower up to her nose. I grinned. They understood this game more than they realized. *Go figure, the Seelies are good at tricks.*

A spirit popped up behind me. He grinned. "I'm their heads up so they know they're coming."

I nodded and then turned back and almost cackled. Lily was blinding the barracks so bad that they were literally falling off the wall to get away from her light. Savannah still had Amelia and Landy clinging to her, but now they were off to the side next to my father and hiding behind a tree.

He pointed over the cliff. "There's no way down here. I'll carry these girls down. You get Lily?"

Ziva looked to me. "Squish and I will ride the lava and meet you down there."

Squishy's fur stood tall. His ears and tail perked up. Fire danced around his now charred, jet-black body. He growled and spit fireballs into the air. I turned my eyes to the sky and summoned magic to my palms. The Knights were getting really close. They were mostly dodging the fire, which I expected. But the few they hit plummeted down into the tunnels.

And I never heard them hit the ground. Heavy crunching echoed in the air.

The beast was having one hell of a night.

"Guys, hide. I'm going to make them chase me and then I'll be right back."

Lily, Ziva, and Squishy kept throwing their magic out while they hurried to hide behind a tree next to the others.

I fired magic at the Knights, knocking them right out of the sky. There had to be six or seven dozen of them, at least. And these were just the ones at the palace. I knew when I came back to finish this war, we would need extra power. The King had one hell of an army. It was going to take more than just me and Riah.

"YOU!" One of the Knights seethed and pointed at me.

I grinned. "Come and get me, boys."

They screamed and dove for me. I spun and sprinted into the pretty purple forest. The spirit flew ahead of me, flying right for Lukat. Rio, Glisa, and Quoya turned and looked to me.

"THERE'S TOO MANY!" I screamed in a fake panicked voice. "THEY FOUND US!"

Knights cackled behind me.

"There's only four of them!" One of them snarled. "EASY KILL."

I leapt in the air, then rolled over. My wings held me in place, hovering upside-down over the ground as the Knights swarmed. I threw my hands up and fired my magic. Golden glitter shot straight for the bows made of tree branches and snapped them into pieces. The Knights hissed and looked down to their broken weapons—

"NOW!" Lukat screamed.

Seelies dropped from the trees and crashed into the Knights. They slammed their daggers and swords into their spines. I shot straight up and tackled three Knights. I forced them into a huge tree, and they each slumped unconscious and plummeted to the ground. I flew down and rolled them onto their stomachs, then summoned vines to bind their arms and legs together like I once saw at a rodeo.

I flicked my wrist and two spirits popped up immediately. "Take them to my father at the cliff!"

They took off. I spun to see if my rebellion needed help, but these Knights were not prepared for guerilla warfare. Rio, Glisa, and Quoya were fierce as hell. They reminded me of my Coven-mates in battle, moving skillfully through a battlefield and delivering death. The spirits were doing exactly as I told them. The fae rebels were tackling Knights out of the air left and right, then throwing them to the ground before moving on to the next. The rebels on the ground were slicing and dicing on the run. Blood splattered in every direction.

It was gore.

It was hell.

It was beautiful.

I looked up and met Lukat's gaze.

GO! She mouthed.

I nodded and spun around, flying as fast as I could for the cliffside. My father waited until he saw me, then wrapped his arms around Savannah, Amelia, and Landy and flew off the side of the cliff. Ziva and Squishy dove for the lava, riding down it like they were surfing a wave. Lily lunged out right in front of me—I basically tackled her and took her down over the side of the cliff with me.

We all landed at the bottom and regrouped.

"Beautiful work, Saraphina," my father said with a twinkle in his eye. "*Saffie,* I mean."

"Thanks." I smiled and tried to ignore the rush of emotions inside of me. I'd have to process all of them and *my father* later. "Anyone hurt?"

They all shook their heads.

Amelia grinned and pointed to the ground behind me. "Except for them."

I glanced back and my eyes widened. There were eight Knights tied up on the ground. My father had caught more than me. And they were all awake. Somehow that just made it better. I'd never been a cruel person. I'd never been cold and lethal. I'd never wanted to make my enemies suffer before I killed them.

But then they took what was *mine.*

And now they would feel every ounce of my pain.

Those same two spirits I'd told to carry the captured were still standing there. "Spirits? Carry the bodies ahead of us. Lead the beast in the opposite direction. Got it?"

One of the spirits whistled and two more spirits came rushing out of the cliff wall. Each of the spirits grabbed two Knights and then took off across the tunnel surface. The tunnel shook under our feet and a loud growl rumbled up through the holes. The beast smelled dinner.

"Ziva, lead us across. Father, fly over us to make sure he's not coming. Girls, hang on to each other and don't let anyone fall. I'll take the back." I pointed straight at the palace. "On your cue, Ziva."

She nodded and rolled to the balls of her feet. "Squish, you know the drill."

Our lovable fire dog put his snout to the ground and moved to the edge of the tunnels.

The beast's pale blue tail flicked out of a hole and snatched a captured Knight right out of a spirit's hands. Squishy leapt forward.

"*NOW!*" Ziva whisper-shouted and charged after Squishy with both swords drawn.

Lily took the lead with the girls next, then Savannah at the end, like they wanted to book-end them for protection. My father shot into the sky and narrowed his eyes in the direction of a scream. I sprinted after my crew but glanced over to find three of the captured Knights had already been eaten.

"HURRY!" I whisper-shouted.

I flew instead of walking so I could keep my eyes locked on my friends and not the ground. If one of them slipped, I was going to dive after them. Every other second, I peeked up to the palace to make sure more Knights weren't coming. None were. Then I remembered that spell of Savannah's—the shadow one that made them not able to track us. The Knights hadn't seen any of my friends on the cliff and they hadn't seen *me* until they got there, which meant they had only seen my magic.

And for all they knew, I was still in the forest battle.

I grinned. My plan was working. We just had to get to Riah. The palace loomed over us, and I wasn't foolish enough to think our toughest battles weren't going to be inside. I still wasn't sure if Thorne and Sage were on our side or not. But even if they were, I wasn't sure if they'd play that card this soon. While in Seelie. My gut told me they'd keep that secret a little bit longer. Not that it mattered. The King would be there. He would be waiting.

And I had no idea what that fight would look like.

My father flew down beside me. "We're almost to the passageway. Another twenty feet—*something's coming. Look!*"

I followed his point to where a dark object was moving inside the tunnel. It was too small and too dark to be the beast. And then I felt it. Arcana magic. I gasped and dove for the nearest hole. It was barely bigger than my head. "PAULINA!"

"SAFFIE!"

I threw my arm into the hole at the same time as she jumped up. Our hands clasped. Lily was suddenly beside me, digging at the tunnel surface to make the hole bigger. Because there were two holes fairly close together, we could just open them up into one. Savannah, Amelia, and Landy dropped down and started clawing at it. I pushed with my magic to try and force it open but the land was dead, there was nothing for me to grab ahold of.

"Lily, stop!" Paulina shouted, "GIRLS, STOP!"

We all froze.

"Paulina, we have to get you out—"

"You can't!" Paulina cried. I could barely even see her face. "Stop. It's no use from here. Trust me. I know now which areas I can fit through. It will take too long to dig through this, and the beast will be back. You have to leave me for now."

Lily reached into the hole and grabbed Paulina's hand.

"I only stopped you to tell you they took Willow." She shook her head. Her voice was dry and raw. "That's how I knew you were in Seelie. That's why I knew to follow the beast. She's in the palace...with Sage and Thorne."

My heart stopped. I glanced up at the palace. I had suspected we'd find Willow in the palace, but I hadn't really accepted it. I had hoped otherwise. I growled and punched the ground. *"Which damn side are they on?"*

"I don't know. I know what Riah said but...don't trust it." She licked her cracked lips. "Saffie."

I cringed. "Don't say it with that tone."

"Riah is still alive. You can feel it. But you don't have long. Forget me for now. *Get to him.*"

"We can't forget you!" Savannah cried.

"The King already has," Paulina said sadly. "He thinks I'm dead. Nothing survives the beast. Let him think that. Save Riah. Get these girls out of here. We both know this war you started is only the beginning."

"Damn straight," Ziva growled.

My father landed beside me, then slid a dagger through the hole. "This will cut through the tunnel. Dig by the river."

"I will. Thanks." Paulina grabbed my father's dagger and looked back to me. "Saffie, get Riah home and healed and then let him help you burn this palace to the ground. The King MUST be killed."

I pulled my arms out of the hole and nodded. "I will come back for you."

Paulina smiled. "I know. Now, HURRY!" Then she dropped and sprinted away from us.

"Come," my father said softly. "The passageway is right there. Prepare for trouble inside."

CHAPTER THIRTY-FOUR

SAFFIE

THE SECOND I dropped down into the secret tunnel, I froze.

I opened my mouth and then closed it. For a moment, my mind went blank. All I could do was stare. The passageway was a dark tunnel made of little glowing gold lights. The tunnel stretched on as far as I could see in either direction, yet there was no light at the end—only solid darkness.

"What are we looking here, folks?" Savannah whispered.

The lights began to move around me. They swirled and coiled around my legs, then shot up to swarm around my whole body.

"*Fairyflies.*" I giggled and held my hands out. Fairyflies danced around my fingers, their little legs and wings brushing against my skin like they were trying to hug me. My breath left me in a rush. I giggled again. Fairyflies had always been drawn to me, but this was something else. "They're *fairyflies.*"

Lily smiled.

"Those things love you, ma'am." Savannah chuckled. "You might need to start naming them."

I felt a wave of raw emotion, both of happiness and sadness.

I looked toward it and found my father standing at the opposite end of the group. His pale eyes glistened with unshed tears.

"Why do they love me so much, Father?" I walked toward him and the fairyflies followed me as if I'd summoned them, the way they always did.

He sighed and I felt something shift inside of his soul. "You were born here."

I flinched. "What? No, I was born in Salem—"

"You were born right here, in this very tunnel, in the very spot I stand," he said softly. He stared at me like it had just happened. "Your mother had been captured by Knights. The King was angry about Althea's snooping around. The Knights went for Althea but grabbed Myrtle by mistake. The King did not trust that she wasn't Althea in disguise, so he kept her in the dungeon until Althea herself attacked the archway gate in a desperate attempt to destroy it. At that point, he decided Myrtle was not Althea but was sentenced to death anyways, for he could not send her back and make himself look dumb. I was already in the dungeon before her, so together we escaped."

I tried to speak, but my words came out as air.

"They stole a pregnant woman?" Savannah shrieked.

My father's cheeks flushed. He eyed the ground. "No, they did not."

"I don't—*ohhh.*" Savannah's eyebrows shot up.

Ziva's jaw dropped. "*Hetron.*"

Lily covered her mouth with her hand.

"There isn't much else to do in a dungeon. We were alone and Myrtle is a remarkable woman." He shrugged and smirked. "With Myrtle's magic and mine combined, we managed to escape. That's when we found this tunnel. We tried to get out in time but alas...Saraphina refused to wait."

Tears stung my eyes. My mother had never told me that.

"Saffie was born here and then we went running. The Seer found us just beyond this tunnel. She had her son, Commander

Zachariah, personally escort them back to Earth because no one —and I mean no one—would've dared to question the King's favorite Knight."

Riah. Tears streaked down my face. All I could do was stare at my father. There was too much and not enough to say. *Riah saved me, all the way back then?*

"When Zachariah returned, he told me that you were in a little town called Salem and if I ever wanted to go be with you and your mother, he would escort me there. The Seer, his mother, soon told me you were the prophetess, and I knew I could not bring any more attention to you." He walked over and wiped the tears from my cheeks. "Let us save this for a moment when your soulmate's life is not hanging by a thread. I will answer all your questions once we get him back to Earth. For now, take a deep breath and summon that fire I've been seeing inside of you, because we're going to need it to rescue him."

I took a deep breath, then exhaled and shook myself. Riah had been saving me since the very day I was born. I owed him the same risks and sacrifices in return, soulmate or not.

"Don't you dare die before I get my answers," I said with a growl.

He smirked and backed away. "Wouldn't dream of it."

"Good. Now bring me to my Riah."

"You winged folk don't wait on us." Savannah bounced on her toes. "Imma run, but y'all just get to him."

My father smirked. "Let's run, then."

With that, we turned and sprinted down the tunnel of fairyflies. They moved from the floor in front of us, clearing the path so we didn't step on them. It was really a remarkable tunnel—probably the prettiest sight I'd ever seen. When I burned the palace down and tore every stone from its structure, I would be sure to save this part.

After all, this part was *mine.*

We'd only been running for about twenty feet or so when

suddenly the fairyflies lifted us all off our feet and carried us down the tunnel. I had wings, but that didn't stop them from giving us a ride. There were hundreds of them on each of us, literally flying us down the tunnel. They moved so fast the tunnel was a blur of golden light.

It was impossible to tell how long the tunnel was, but finally it tapered down to one doorway. The fairyflies sat us on our feet while others flew ahead and into the doorway—illuminating a stone staircase.

My father put his hand over his heart and bowed, then whispered something to the fairyflies in Seelie language. They swarmed around him like they were hugging him, then shot over to me.

I smiled and held my hands up. "Thank you, my friends. We'll see you again."

When I turned, I found my group crammed into the staircase with my father holding the handle to a white door. "I'm ready."

"This door leads directly into the palace and close to the staircase that'll lead us to the dungeon." He pointed to his right. "Once inside, we move quickly and we move *quietly*. If I say run, *run*. Ziva, you know where the dungeons are."

"I do." She pushed her shoulders back and her blue hair turned red.

"I'll lead us to the stairs, then you guide them down." My father pulled a sword off the holster on his hip. "If we encounter *anyone* from the palace, you let me handle them. Riah cannot wait any longer. Got it?"

My whole body tightened into knots. My stomach turned so hard I thought I was going to be sick. I couldn't do this any longer. I couldn't wait one more minute to go to him. It was making me sick.

"Three...two...one—" He pushed the door open, and we all rushed out.

At first all I saw was white light. Almost like sunshine was pouring in. But it wasn't coming from Lily. The palace looked both nothing like what I expected and exactly how I expected at the same time. Everything was pristine white. The floors were white marble. The walls were white stones. Every few feet there were thick pillars that held paintings of landscapes. The trims on the pillars were a shiny gold. It was beautiful, unfairly so.

We walked in a huddle with me up at the front and my father and Squishy in the back with Ziva. I knew if anything went down, those two would rain fire on the world, and it made me feel better.

Because with every step I took in this palace, the weaker my body felt. It felt like I was growing lighter. My feet lifted off the floor. My wings sparkled brighter. The power in the air here was doing something to me. My father grabbed my wrist and held me down. He frowned and looked me up and down, but he didn't say a thing.

I couldn't worry about that just yet.

"*Are those clouds?*" Savannah whispered.

I glanced up and my eyes widened. They *were* clouds. I hadn't noticed them before.

"*The ceiling is bewitched,*" Landy whispered.

"*I read about it in Hogwarts, a history,*" Amelia finished the movie quote.

I couldn't blame them. It popped into my mind as well. Savannah looked rather proud of them. Suddenly, Lily grabbed my arm and yanked me to a stop. I looked to her, but she thrust her arm out and pointed. I frowned and followed her wide-eyed stare—and gasped.

On the opposite side of the wide hallway, through a half-shattered stained-glass wall, was a wide terrace overlooking the front of the palace. In the distance, I could see Ziva's lava river and flashes of magic in the air.

But standing at the edge of the terrace was a girl with strawberry blonde hair.

WILLOW.

We all froze. I knew what they were thinking. Willow was right there. The desire to rescue her was overwhelming, but Riah had to come first. He was the one in the dungeon. He was the one sentenced to death.

But also, Willow wasn't alone.

Princess Sage and Prince Thorne stood on each side of her, dressed in matching black cloaks and holding Willow by the arms. Sage's long blue hair blew in the breeze. Thorne stood tall and unmoving. Sage was saying something to him, but I couldn't hear. Then she glanced over her shoulder and spotted us. She said something else and Thorne snapped around. His fiery orange eyes narrowed, his long red hair whipping around like a cape.

"*Oh shitttttt,*" Savannah drawled.

"Why aren't they attacking?" Ziva hissed.

Because maybe Riah was right. Maybe they ARE on our side and that's why they've got Willow.

"Maybe they're stalling while more Knights come," Savannah grumbled. "Time to fly, witches."

My father's grip on my wrist tightened and then he was running, dragging me away, farther into the palace. I glanced over my shoulder just as Sage burst through the terrace doors. My heart stopped. My friends were all right behind me.

"Ziva, go!" My father hissed and threw me. "NOW! I'll meet you!"

I flipped upside-down and then hands seized mine and dragged me back down. It was Lily and Savannah. They didn't let go of me. They just dragged me with them. I had no idea why gravity was no longer working for me, but my wings just wanted to carry me *up*. Savannah and Lily's hold on me was tight as they followed Ziva around a corner and into an open foyer with a wide staircase of white stone. It zigzagged across the space.

But as we rounded the corner at the bottom of the stairs, my feet touched the ground. That weightlessness was gone. I gasped and leapt forward to catch up with Ziva as she took a sharp turned and headed into a dark hallway with a narrow spiral staircase made of rough stones. These stones were not polished or pretty. They were raw and rugged. Which meant one thing...the dungeon.

My pulse fluttered. We were close. I knew it. I glanced over my shoulder, but my father had yet to catch up. But he was on his own. He had to be, and he knew it. Whatever he was doing was buying us time, because even if Sage and Thorne were on our side, they clearly weren't ready to act on it *here*.

At the bottom of the winding staircase, we came out into a dark, narrow hallway. The walls were dark gray stone and the floor was made of even darker cobblestones. Every ten feet or so a torch hung from the wall with a flame flickering. Even still, there wasn't enough light to fully light the hall. Even with the vaulted ceilings.

Lily walked up beside me and held her palms out. Soft golden light spilled out, illuminating the hall. My heart stopped. Between each of the torches was a doorway, except the doors were made of solid stone. There had to be ten on each side. At the end there was a set of stairs. I couldn't see where it went, but the pounding in my soulmate glyph beat harder.

Riah was up there. I knew it with every fiber of my being.

I heard Ziva whisper something, but my mind didn't register it. All I heard in my head was *RIAH, RIAH, RIAH.* I flew as fast as I could down the hall. Each stone doorway I passed, I felt a rush of fear from inside. My stomach turned. There were people inside of those cells. I wanted to save them, but I couldn't yet. I had to save Riah first.

My friend's footsteps thundered behind me.

I looked up and choked on a scream. My body locked in place and turned to ice. My heart stopped in my chest. Black dots swarmed my vision.

There was no stone doorway in front of me. Just a short foyer that led to a rounded room with a tall, vaulted ceiling. Silvery light streamed down from skylights in the ceiling. There was a staircase of about a dozen steps that ended at the base of an oversized stone dais that had to be ten feet wide and fifteen feet tall.

At the top...was *Riah.*

Chains hung down from the ceiling and were hooked to each of his wrists, holding his body in the air. He was *hanging* by his arms. His legs hung straight down but his toes just barely grazed the top of the dais—he could touch but he couldn't at the same time.

His shirt was gone but there was so much blood on his skin that I could barely see the gold lines of his soulmate glyph. If not for the glowing red light from the crystal heart on his chest, I wouldn't have realized what the lines were.

Blood trickled down his arms from the chains on his wrists. His dark jeans were torn in several places. His head was slumped forward with his long, blood-stained white-blond hair hanging over his face. Fresh blood trickled from what had to be his nose or mouth. I couldn't see his face to know which.

I needed to go to him, but the sight of him broke my brain. My body was locked. My heart felt like it was going to shatter worse than that stained-glass. My chest was so tight, I thought my ribs were going to break. I sucked in gasps of air, but none were getting in.

Behind me, footsteps thundered close and then they slid to a stop. Amelia and Landy gasped. Savannah cursed under her breath. Lily's sunlight flickered from her palms and then went out. Squishy whimpered. Ziva said something and shook my shoulders.

And I snapped.

I charged forward as fast as I could, flapping my little starlight wings faster than they'd ever gone until I was up there in front of him. He didn't look up. He didn't move at all. I could hear his heart pounding and saw the heavy beat in the veins on his arms. I took a deep breath and it smelled of burning embers, like smoke on a campfire. Like *Riah*.

My mouth opened but nothing came out. Words died on my tongue.

I reached forward with shaking hands and pulled his hair to the side. He flinched and his muscles tightened, like he was bracing himself for pain. He couldn't even tell it was *me*. He didn't even look up, like he was resigned to his fate. I slid my hands forward until I felt his face in my palms, then I tipped his head back and gasped.

His face was hollowed and bruised. The skin stretched over his cheekbones and jaw was dark purple. Black veins streaked out from the corners of his mouth and eyes. His lips and eyes were black and blue. Weird, shimmery gold splotches highlighted his face on the bridge of his nose, the curve of his bottom lip, and right above his eyelashes. That fresh blood I'd seen dripping came from his nose. Dried blood was caked into his cheeks and forehead.

He *still* had not reacted to me.

I gently ran my thumbs over his cheeks—

His eyes flew open.

My heart stopped.

They were bloodshot and black at the edges, which scared me to death, but the gold color shined bright. For a moment he just stared at me like I was a dream. I kept my eyes on his, but a broken sob ripped up my throat.

He flinched and that dreamy haze vanished. His gaze sharpened like he was seeing me for real, like he just realized I was actually there. "*Saraphina?*"

I sobbed and cupped his face tighter. Before I could stop myself, I pressed my lips to his. They were dry and tinged with blood, but he tasted like *him*. I cried against his mouth, then pulled back.

His eyes sparkled and followed me. "Saraphina...you're here."

"I came for you," I said between sobs. I pushed his hair back off his face. "I came to save you."

His eyes watered and his lips quirked up like he wanted to smile. But then he looked over my shoulder and frowned. "*You?*"

"My turn to save you, kid," my father said in a rough voice. He flew up beside us and then tugged on the chain holding Riah's arm. "Don't speak. Save your strength. We'll need it for the escape. Let's get you out of here."

I nodded and flew over to his other hand and tugged on the chain. "Do you have any ideas for getting him out of these? What about Ziva's fire—"

"No, no. The King controls fire. He would not line the dungeon with torches if fire could break these chains—even lava for that matter." My father sighed and looked up at the ceiling where they were attached. "I did not expect him to be in *this* chamber. Damn it."

"Okay, okay, well there has to be a key, right?" I glanced to the walls around us.

"*No,*" Riah whispered.

"No key?"

He shook his head ever so slightly.

I pressed my hand to his chest and nodded. "I'm pretty good with nature, especially here in Seelie, but I feel nothing living in here."

My father's eyes snapped to me. He grinned and then dove for his pockets. He dug around then pulled out two pieces of vine. "What can you do with these"

I gasped and snatched one from his grip. "What are these—"

"Pieces that fell off my net. I just shoved them in my pocket."

My eyes widened. "These are your magical vines."

Riah frowned up at my father.

"Later," he said softly to him.

That must've been a sufficient answer because Riah's gold eyes turned to watch me as I stuck the vine between his skin and the chain around his wrist. I bit my bottom lip and pushed my magic into the vine, telling it to grow longer. Golden glitter coiled around it and then the vine was growing rapidly, stretching out in both directions.

Wind through the chain to the top.

"Saffie, this one."

I looked over and found my father had gotten the vine ready for me on his other hand. In a few seconds, I had both vines crawling all the way up the chains to the vaulted stone ceiling where they were fastened. I had no idea if this was going to work or if it even made sense, but once the vines coiled around the fasteners up top, I grabbed the bottom and *pulled.*

Nothing happened.

The chains rattled and metal creaked, but it wasn't enough strength.

"Spirits," my father whispered and blew his reddish-brown hair out of his face. "Many have died here. Call on them. That is something the King could never do."

RIGHT. Come on, brain. Stick with me a little bit longer. I know he's in rough shape, but we have to get him out of here to heal him.

I held my hands out and wiggled my fingers, pushing my Death Card magic into the dungeon around us. Blue and green glowing figures rose from the ground. There were so many of them they were overlapping shoulder space. They all had wings.

My stomach turned. My father cursed violently. Riah squeezed his eyes shut.

"Spirits, break these chains."

The spirits flew up and grabbed the end of the vines. I reached up and pushed my magic, forcing more strands of the vines to stick out all the way up the chains. The other spirits dove for them immediately.

"Break them," I ordered, pushing my power into my voice.

The spirits pulled while I pushed my magic through the vines. The chains groaned. The metal stretched until each and every ring snapped in half.

Riah gasped and dropped—my father caught him by the waist before his knees slammed into the stone dais top. Riah coughed and blood burst from his mouth. His arms hung by his sides like he couldn't move them.

The man with a healing touch cannot heal himself.

The spirits, without me telling them to, reached for Riah. They pulled him out of my father's arms and gently lowered him to the ground in front of Savannah. Amelia and Landy leapt forward and caught him before he slumped forward. My father and I rushed down there.

Landy looked up at me with wide eyes. "Do we tell the spirits to carry him out of here?"

"*No,*" Riah whispered. He looked up and those broken golden eyes met mine. "*Free...them...*"

I wanted to do as Landy said. I wanted their help to get him out. But Riah's wishes had to come first. And I hated the idea of abusing my power with the dead. Just because I could ask them to help me, it didn't mean I *made* them. I already felt guilty about all those spirits I'd left to help The Circle in my absence when I could have sent them to peace.

So, with a heavy heart, I held my hands out and let my magic soar. "Thank you. Be at peace now."

The spirits sighed with relief. They all reached out and touched Riah before fading away to nothingness.

"Okay, that was creepy with the touching," Ziva said under her breath. "We need to go. We've been here too long."

I dropped to my knees in front of Riah and cupped his face. "Still with me?"

He smirked and nodded once. I felt his weakness like it was my own. It was a heavy weight on his soul, like just being in this body was too much for him. His soul was begging to be set free. I'd never felt anything like it. A soul shouldn't have felt trapped, like it was bound in a cage. I didn't understand what I was feeling, but I was definitely not going to listen...yet.

"We're going to have to carry him, Father."

"I know." He dropped to one knee beside Riah and threw his bloodied arm over his shoulder. "Get the other side. We can't go the same way we just came—"

"Why not?" Ziva hissed.

"Whatever was happening to her up there will be worse when we go back." He grimaced. "I also may have caused some problems on my way down. Long story. We have to go the other way."

Amelia moved away from Riah so I could drape his heavy arm over my shoulder. She frowned. "There's another way?"

Ziva growled. "I don't like it, but we have no choice. I'll go get the door open. Hurry."

As her and Squishy dashed out of the cell, Landy scowled. "What does she know?"

Riah sighed. "*Queen's...chamber.*"

My stomach tightened into knots. I understood Ziva's reaction now. "You're sure it's the only way?"

"Yes, but we have to move—"

"*Wait!*" Savannah yelled. It was only then that I realized she'd been digging in her satchel. She yanked her notebook out, then flipped it open from the back to a page with an unfamiliar rune drawn in black. She pressed her fingers to it and she gasped. Her eyes widened. "*Upon the elements I bid you hear my desire, with spirit, earth, water, air, and fire. Guide me until this journey is complete, with strength and bravery to face this feat. Ground me in magic ancient and right, help me overcome my fears this moonless night.*"

Riah gasped but his breath came out more even on exhale. His eyes shined a smidge brighter. His pulse beat a little slower. He smiled, like an actual smile. "*Thanks. GO.*"

I had no idea what Savannah had just done or what that rune was, but I would ask later. At the same time, my father and I hoisted Riah off the ground. He was so tall that we had to fly fairly high to get his dangling legs off the ground.

"*Landy!*"

There was rushed footsteps and then Riah's weight got lighter. I glanced over his shoulder and found Amelia and Landy each holding one of his legs off the ground while we dashed toward Ziva.

Just as we were catching up to her, there was a pop and then a secret door opened from the side of the dungeon wall. Lily rushed forward with sunlight shining from her hands, lighting up a stone staircase. Thick, bushy green vines clung to the stones all the way up. Little torches lined the walls.

It took all of us to carry Riah up the steps, but Squishy was up at the front on guard. At the top of the stairs, those bushy green vines moved up and over a circular archway. Small torches hung inside the arch, tucked between the ivy. Strands of bright white flowers hung down from the top. It was actually stunning.

But the sweat dripping down my spine and the shaky ache in my muscles was not.

I took a deep breath. "GO."

Together, we marched forward with Ziva and Lily in the front and Savannah in the back. Amelia and Landy were still carrying Riah's legs. We hobbled under the archway that turned out to be about ten feet long. I watched Ziva and Lily, waiting for reactions of an attack. Surely the Queen would sense us in her chambers. But as they walked out of the archway and into the room, their eyes widened in awe. Their jaws dropped.

Warm golden light poured into the archway.

I had no idea what caused such a reaction until we stepped out from under the archway. And then I saw it. Every inch of the room was filled with nature. The room itself was like a greenhouse. The walls were clear glass that curved into a dome shape. I knew it was still dark outside, so this warm sunlight must have been made by magic. Green vines and colorful flowers hung from the ceiling, draping down all over. There was a cobblestone pathway that curved into the center of the room and under another archway—one made of pink and red flowers. On one side of the pathway was a little field of wildflowers. On the other side was a waterfall made of big gray stones. Clear water rushed over them and into a little pond that had floating lilies.

It was gorgeous, but that wasn't what caught our attention.

It looked like *Earth*.

Everywhere we'd seen in Seelie so far had been in different colors than we were used to seeing on Earth. Back home trees weren't purple and blue like they were in Seelie. Leaves weren't neon-pink. Water wasn't glowing neon blue. Out in Seelie, as beautiful as it was, it was alien and foreign. But this room felt like home.

"Anyone else really fucking creeped out by this?" Savannah said in a rush under her breath.

"I sure am," an unfamiliar female voice purred from out of sight.

We all jumped and turned toward the sound just as green magic slammed into Lily's chest. She gasped soundlessly and her eyes widened. Her back arched and her feet lifted off the ground. The world stood still, ceasing to move in time at all. My heart caught between breaths, between beats. My body was locked in place.

A woman stepped out of the shadows of a flowered vine where she'd been perfectly hidden—basking in the opportunity her chamber had given her by distracting us. I knew exactly who she was in an instant.

The Queen.

She wore a white cropped top and long white skirt that dragged the ground. Over that, she wore an intricate golden armor piece that stood tall at her neck and then ran down her chest in thin strips that hugged her body in ways that felt inappropriate to look at. The armor dangled around her hips just like Amelia's did. She wore golden arm bands and a shiny golden diadem across her forehead. Her hair was long and red, the exact shade of Prince Thorne's, yet her eyes held a small violet galaxy like her daughter, Princess Sage's. A circular golden crown clung to the back of her head with golden bars sticking out like a halo. Like a drawing of the sun.

In her hand, she held a tall golden staff. In her other, a steady stream of green magic aimed right at Lily. It glowed bright and thicker, coiling around Lily's body like a snake.

Lily screamed but no sound came out. I felt her panic and fear and it broke my heart.

NOOOOOO!

We all tried to dive for her, I felt it inside them, but none of us could move.

"STOP—" my father groaned out. The muscles in his body flexed and then he lunged forward.

"No." The woman twirled her staff and my father crumbled to his knees. The Queen chuckled. "Nice try, youngling."

He trembled and rocked back and forth. His wings fluttering behind him.

She smiled down at him, like his effort made her happy. Then she turned those violet eyes on us. "I am Queen Eithne."

Enya? I'd seen it written before but clearly the spelling and pronunciation did not match.

"I move time at my will." She was beauty and terror wrapped into one. "*Your time...*is up."

WHAT?!

She arched one eyebrow and snarled her upper lip. Then she yanked her arm back and Lily flew toward her. I tried to move again but it was no use. My body was not my own to control. The Queen had frozen time around us, locking us in place to watch. That green magic slithered over Lily's entire body, then exploded like a firework—*and Lily vanished into golden smoke.*

NOOOOO!

The Queen chuckled and twirled her hand. The golden smoke slammed into the Queen's chest and flashed. When the glow vanished, a net of brown vines was draped over her chest and around her throat like a turtleneck sweater.

Lily was gone.

The Queen looked down at it and then back up to us and grinned. "Who'd like to die next?"

Tears formed in the backs of my eyes. A hot lump burned against my throat. Lily was gone. She was *gone*. I tried to search for her, but I found no magic. There was a hint of her soul, but it was too weak—trapped in those brown vines.

The Queen took a step toward us and then flinched. "What?"

Blue light flashed and then something leapt across the path and tackled the Queen to the ground. Someone with wild strawberry blonde hair and a *I* Mark on her left arm.

WILLOW.

The two of them rolled across the cobblestone pathway. As Willow flipped them over so she was on the bottom, she fired

379

blue magic into the Queen's chest and used their momentum to throw the Queen straight across the room.

Willow jumped to her feet and blinked. "You're there, right? I still can't see!"

Suddenly that hold on our bodies vanished.

Savannah tackled Willow in a hug. "We're here!"

"Let's go!" My father leapt back and scooped Riah up. When he looked up, he flinched. "There's no saving Lily now. Let's go before she wakes and we're all dead."

CHAPTER THIRTY-FIVE

SAFFIE

As Ziva led us out of the Queen's chambers, the rest of us were sobbing.

We were racing through the palace corridors as fast as we could carry Riah, but there were too many tears in my eyes. My vision was blurry. I blinked and wiped my face on my sleeve to clear my eyes, then found we were back in that same corridor we'd first entered. Ziva was guiding us back to the fairyfly tunnel.

The hall was empty.

My feet lifted off the ground like before but the weight of Riah hanging on me kept me down. Except my legs weren't quite working, so I had to fly. I'd never realized just how heavy my soulmate was—

A cold gust of air slammed into us from the right. We all slid across the white stone floor and crashed into the wall with a bang. Amelia and Landy crumbled to the ground between our legs. Riah's body pressed me into the wall, covering my body like a shield. He tried to fight it, to move off me, but the wind was too strong. It was stronger than any hurricane I'd ever felt. And ice cold. My eyelashes fluttered.

And then *he* stepped out from behind a pillar.

There was no questioning who he was. Not because of the crown on his head or the whimper from Amelia, but in the menacing cold energy radiating out of him. *King Atzaran.*

He smirked and strolled out with one hand flexed, then it hit me. The Seelie King could control air. I hadn't known that. Found out a bit too late. He wasn't even trying hard. His long blue hair was hanging in waves down his back. Those fiery orange eyes that matched his son's blazed with fury and hatred. He wore a long white cloak that was open at the chest, revealing a lot of bare skin.

I knew his power was greater than ours. I knew the attempt was futile, but I refused to not *try.* My hands were pinned to the wall under Riah. I couldn't use them. So I summoned my magic into my mouth and then spit golden glitter like a sprinkler.

"*Aw,* aren't you cute." The King chuckled and danced through my magic. Then he turned and looked down to Amelia. A disgusting grin spread across his face. "Look who's back. I won't make the same mistake twice, little witch."

He flicked his wrist and then Amelia and Landy were upright and standing beside me.

The King purred and his eyes flashed. "And your little friend is here. My Queen let you go, but since that resulted in such a nice growth, I think I'll forgive her. *Prime meat.* What a sandwich you two will be once I kill your friends."

No, no, no, no, no. I tried to get more magic out. I felt my friends doing the same, but the wind was too strong. King Atzaran sneered and thrust both hands toward us. Big thorns the size of my fingers shot right for us. I took a deep breath and pushed my magic out of my hands. The thorns froze mid-air. I flicked my fingers and sent the thorns flying backwards at the King.

He deflected them with a wave of his hand and wagged his eyebrows at me.

"You're fun." He curled his hands in. "What else can you do?"

Without pause, he threw streams of fire right for us. Squishy howled and the fire moved backwards. Ziva summoned flames to her palms and shot them at the King but they floated slowly, like they were being pushed back.

The King threw his head back and cackled.

Willow hissed. *"I can't see. Too much wind. I can't."*

The King's maniacal laughter echoed up and down the halls. I glanced left and right, waiting for his Knights or the Queen to show up, but they were nowhere in sight. If there was ever a time for Thorne and Sage to prove which side they were on, this was it. Yet something told me deep down they weren't going to rescue us here. We were on our own...against the Seelie King.

Who apparently had elemental magic. So far, it was only air, earth, and fire—

I spoke too soon. I jinxed it. The King lifted his hands up over his head and neon-blue water rushed out of his palms like a tsunami. The water swept us off the wall and into the middle of the hall. We were in an ocean of water up to our chests and it was filling the entire hallway behind us. The King just kept cackling. Another gust of wind crashed into the water. Waves rippled and rolled on the surface, splashing into our faces.

A current pressed into my body, digging into my skin. I clenched my teeth and tried to push against the current and water, but nothing was giving. My legs were stuck in place. We didn't even have to tread water. He kept us anchored in place as he taunted us nonstop. I glanced to my friends and found them struggling as much as I was. Our hair whipped behind all our heads like we were flying. The skin on our faces trembled. It was a rushing roar in my ears. We were helpless to stop it. I couldn't get any of my magic to work under this level of attack.

We'd lost.

We were going to die.

"Just what I needed today," a deep female voice purred in the distance, just louder than the wind.

The King lowered the wind a tiny bit and glanced over his shoulder. I felt the desire in his soul shift. Whoever this woman was, he wanted her more than he wanted us.

The King purred something in Seelie and licked his lips.

Footsteps clacked against the stone floor and then a breath-taking creature stepped out behind the King. She was gorgeous in a way I couldn't put words to. Her skin was a dark, deep brown. Her hair was white as snow and hanging in elegant waves down to her hips. She wore an intricate white and gold cutout dress that showed off her beautiful skin tone and the curves of her body.

She sauntered up to him like a jungle cat on the hunt. Her gold eyes sparkled. She walked up and pressed her body to the King's back, then wrapped her arms around his waist, pressing her hands to his chest. "Well, maybe not *just*."

The King looked over his shoulder to her.

She *kissed* him and spun his body around so they were chest to chest. The King went into her embrace with passion. She dragged his body down onto hers until he had her nearly bent over backwards. He reached down and gripped her thigh, lifting her leg up. She must have read his mind because she wrapped her arm around his neck and hooked her legs around his hips. The King growled in hunger, then ducked his head and nibbled on her neck. She giggled and fisted his long blue hair.

Riah groaned like he was going to be sick.

That is NOT the Queen. Who is this? Are they going to make us watch?

The woman looked over the King's shoulder while he nibbled on her throat. Her golden eyes looked right at us with a sharp, clear expression. I felt determination in her soul. And anger. I gasped. This was a distraction. My pulse quickened. I nodded.

GO! NOW! She mouthed, and then with her free hand she reached down between their bodies—the King hissed.

His hold on the water snapped.

That current he'd been pushing against us had nothing to stop it or hold it in place. The raging river carried us down the hallway in a flash. The King glanced over his shoulder and frowned just as the water whipped around a corner and washed us right out onto that terrace and over the edge...headed straight for the beast's tunnels below.

CHAPTER THIRTY-SIX

NADIA

THE SNOW CRUNCHED with every step I took, the sound echoing between the cliffs on either side of me like a pinball. Despite it being noon, there wasn't a single person in sight because I was apparently the only Canadian willing to come out here.

The Northwest Territories were a bitterly cold tundra, at least in early February. Hay River had long since frozen over with ice and now had a thick blanket of snow on top of that. I walked right down the center of the frozen river with my arms wrapped around myself. There was enough sunlight shining through the cover of gray clouds to make the snow sparkle like diamonds. But there wasn't any sunshine to warm me up.

I glanced left and right, spotting rows and rows of snow-covered pine trees.

Everything was white...and freezing.

It was negative thirty-five degrees Celsius outside, which was about negative thirty Fahrenheit. Each of my breaths burned down my esophagus like I'd swallowed acid. My eyelashes were starting to frost over from the cold.

As I walked, I just reminded myself why I was out there in the first place.

For Aunt Dora.

I lifted the dried bouquet of dead, dried out flowers and tried to search for meaning. This bouquet meant a lot to her. She'd saved it for a long time, just for this purpose...so that after her death, her family would take it to the spot she designated and set it back into the earth. My younger sister Annie and I were set to do just that today. We had the instructions drawn out on paper by Aunt Dora herself. I was just waiting for Annie to arrive.

"MISS?"

I jumped and spun around—and found a person on a snow-mobile flying right toward me. I frowned and waved to whoever it was. They were covered in winter gear so I couldn't see anything but big goggles, yet I knew it wasn't Annie. The person was too tall to be my sister. About fifty feet behind them were four other people on snowmobiles, just waiting and watching us.

"MISS? ARE YOU OKAY?"

Their voice was muffled but I thought I recognized it. Definitely a woman. I nodded. "Yes?"

The woman slowed to a stop, then pulled her goggles up onto her forehead. I recognized her in an instant. Her face was flushed from the cold but her smile was warm and friendly. Dark red hair that was braided in pigtails popped out of her hood. Her eyes widened. "*Nadia?*"

I smiled. "Hi, Tanya."

"Nadia, what the hell are you doing out here?" She looked around like the answer was visible somewhere. "It's freezing."

"You're out snowmobiling..."

"*I'm dressed for it.*" She sighed and pointed to my jacket. "That's not enough clothing. What are you doing?"

She wasn't wrong. It wasn't *technically* enough clothing for the negative thirty-degree temperature...for a human. But as a witch, I had spells to keep me warm without all the extra layers. Not that I could tell Tanya that. She was a human, a kind one too. I used to babysit her kids.

Instead, I just lifted my aunt's bouquet and grimaced. "Aunt Dora's last wishes."

Her face fell. "Oh. I see. Okay, well is your car nearby?"

I nodded.

"Don't stay out here too long, Nadia. You'll freeze to death."

"I promise I'll be leaving in a minute. I just got out here."

She looked me up and down with her eyebrows scrunched down low like she was having reservations about leaving me, but after a long moment she slid her goggles back down over her eyes and nodded. "All right, well I'm going to call you in twenty minutes. If you're still out here, I'm going to pick you up. Consider yourself warned."

I grinned. "Fully warned. But I'll be gone. Just waiting for Annie or I'd be done already."

"Well, it was nice to see you." Tanya smiled wide, then held her hand up to her head like it was a phone. "Call me and let's make plans, eh?"

"Will do." I gestured to her waiting group. "Go ahead, Tanya. I'll be fine. Promise. We'll have dinner soon."

She waved and nodded, then took off in the opposite direction back towards her group. I watched them vanish into a cloud of white dust as the snow kicked up off the ground. No one else emerged. The river was silent but for the wind whistling through the trees.

I sighed. "She's not coming."

Holding Aunt Dora's dried out flowers in one hand, I pulled my cellphone out of my zipped pocket, praying I had missed texts or calls from Annie—but there was nothing. My stomach tightened. I quickly dialed her number and held my breath as it rang.

A little voice squealed, "Aunt Nah-nah!"

I grinned at the sound of my little three-year-old niece's voice. "Hi, Kylie. Is Mommy there?"

"Kenny!"

There was shuffling and then another little voice answered, this one a few years older. "Hello?"

"Hey Kenny-ken."

"OH! Aunt Nadia!" Kendall giggled. "Where are you? Mommy is leaving."

Just now leaving? Great. Thanks, Annie. I'll just freeze my ass off out here. But a five-year-old didn't need to hear that thought, so I forced a smile into my voice. "I'm out on the river with Aunt Dora's flowers. Can I talk to Mommy?"

"Okay, hold on," Kendall said with a heavier sigh than a little girl should have had reason to give. Which meant my sister was on her bullshit again. I heard the bedroom door creak open and then the sound of Beyonce singing in the background. "Mommy? Mommy? *Mommy?* ALEXA, STOP."

The music cut off instantly.

"*Excuse me, young lady?*" my sister screeched in the background. "Did I say you could just turn that off? I was listening to that."

Kendall sighed. Again. "I *was* calling you, but you couldn't hear me over it."

"You were not calling me."

"I said, 'Mommy', three times—"

"What did we talk about last night?"

"To call you Annie from now on so no one will know you're our mom and they'll give you a record contract?"

WHAT? Nausea rolled in my stomach and I tasted bile. I saw red all around me. If I had been there in person, I would have snapped and put hands on my sister.

"Exactly. Remember that or we're stuck in this shitty ass

snow town forever. Now, what's so important? I'm busy," Annie snapped and I about screamed. *"Well?"*

"Aunt Nadia is on the phone," Kendall whispered.

"OH, well why didn't you say so from the beginning?" Annie scoffed and then her breath rumbled in my ear. *"Nadia, girl, wait 'til you hear this!"*

I clenched my teeth and took a deep breath. Yelling at my younger sister only made things worse, especially when I wasn't there in person. *"Annie—"*

"I'M GOING TO LOS ANGELES!" Annie squealed in my ear. "That guy I met last week, you know the one I told you about with the Porsche and the long hair? Anyhoo, I was singing for him last night and he wants to introduce me to a producer friend of his in LA—*tonight.* We're meeting him in this club in Hollywood at like midnight."

My jaw dropped. *"What?"*

"Why you taking that tone with me?" Annie whined.

"Are you serious right now?" I threw my arm out and spun in a circle. "Well, for starters, YOU WERE SUPPOSED TO MEET ME ON THE RIVER, ANNIE."

Annie hissed. "Oh shit. That's right. To do those stupid flowers, eh?"

"Stupid —" I slammed my mouth closed to stop myself from screaming. "Yes, Annie, to carry out our aunt's last dying wish."

"Oh, whatever. She's dead. She won't know if we wait a few days to do it until I get back."

Tears stung my eyes. I never would have thought it was possible to hate your own family member, your own flesh and blood...but Annie warranted the emotion. The only reason I stuck around was for her little girls and for Aunt Dora. My nieces didn't deserve what my sister did to them.

"Are you listening to me, Nadia?"

I rolled my eyes. *I'm trying not to.* "I'm hearing that you let me walk all the way out to this river when it's negative thirty degrees out without bothering to tell me you weren't coming—all so you can be played yet again by yet another schmuck."

"Brad is not playing me!"

"Brad does not know any music producers, Annie!" My pulse quickened. Heat rushed through my veins. "That Porsche is twenty years old and barely runs. He's gonna fly you down to LA to stay in some cheap ass motel and pretend to introduce you to some producers that will end up being random club DJs just so he can get some ass—which we both know you'll give him. And then I'll end up with yet another niece to take care of since you can't."

Annie huffed and puffed like the wolf about to blow my house down. "You know what? You're just jealous because you don't want anything in life and *I do.*"

I closed my eyes and shook my head. All the things I wanted in life flashed through my mind like one of those emergency news reports on the bottom of the screen.

I wanted my parents to survive that accident.

I wanted to attend Edenburg.

I wanted to move out of this frozen hellhole.

I wanted my sister to graduate high school without getting knocked-up. Twice.

I wanted my nieces to have a mother that acted the part and loved her daughters.

I wanted Aunt Dora to pull through witch's flu.

My heart was heavy in my chest, like an anchor sinking to bottom of the ocean floor. My life back in Toronto hadn't been perfect, my parents hadn't been perfect, but the life I had was perfect for me. Aunt Dora did her best raising two big city girls out in the middle of nowhere. She'd even told us if we behaved ourselves and got good grades, she'd move us down to Eden in the United States and let us get proper magic school training.

But Annie had ruined that for both of us by getting pregnant at fifteen.

I could have left after I graduated, but by then Kendall was a year old and I just couldn't. So I'd done what I always did...I set my own desires aside and stayed. And then Kylie had been born a year after that. *Kendall and Kylie.* Named after the youngest Kardashian-Jenner sisters, because they were Annie's idols. Aunt Dora kept telling me to go, to live my own life. She used to say, "one of these days you'll sacrifice yourself too far."

And then *she* died after getting witch's flu from driving Annie all the way to Vancouver for some pathetic excuse for a gig—without working heat in her car.

Maybe it's good she leaves. It'll just be you and the girls. That'll be better.

"SEE, YOU DON'T LISTEN TO ME EVER!" Annie screamed.

I sighed. "How long are you going?"

"I don't know, *duh.* However long it takes to get a record deal." Annie scoffed. "Can you just come home and watch the girls until I get back? Like feed them or whatever?"

"When are you leaving?"

"Brad will be here in five minutes."

You gave me five whole minutes warning before leaving two toddlers alone? I bit my cheek to stop myself. It was pointless to yell at her. I cleared my throat. "Put Kendall on the phone."

"Why?"

"Just do it."

"*Fine.*" She scoffed, then her voice was farther away. "*KENDALL.*"

"Yes, Momm—I mean, Annie?"

"Aunt Nadia is on the phone," she all but growled.

There was a beat of silence, then a little voice spoke softly in my ear. "Aunt Nadia?"

Tears pooled in my eyes. *Damn you, Annie. Damn you.* I licked my lips and swallowed through the hot lump in my throat. "Hi, princess. Listen, your mother is going out of town, okay? But she didn't give me enough time to get there before she leaves, so I need you to take Kylie and go across the street to Miss Carol's house. Make sure you both have on your jackets, hats, and boots, okay? Can you do that for me?"

Kendall sniffled. "Yes, I can."

"I'm going to call her right now so she knows you're coming. Stay with her until I get home. I will come and get you, okay?"

"Okay," she whispered.

"Okay, I'll be back as soon as possible. I love you, Kenny."

"I love you too."

"Put *Annie* back on the phone, please."

There was another beat of silence and then my sister was back. "What did you say to her?"

"You lost the right to ask that when you demanded your daughters call you by your first name," I snarled. "Now you listen to me, Annie, and listen carefully, because if you don't do as I ask—so help me Goddess—I will have The Coven arrest you."

"You don't know anyone in The Coven or how to call them."

"*TRY ME,*" I growled.

"Fine, tough guy, what do you want me to do? Your laundry or some shit? Want me to wash your car or something—"

I screamed. I actually screamed. "I WANT YOU TO ESCORT YOUR DAUGHTERS TO CAROL ACROSS THE STREET. I want you to hold their hands and literally walk them over there and not leave until Carol herself has Kendall and Kylie. And then I want you to pretend like you care about them for five minutes and give them each a hug and tell them you love them."

Silence.

"Did I stutter, Annie?"

She sighed. "Fine. I'll do it. Whatever. But I'm not hurrying back from LA."

"Just text me when your task is complete." I hung up the phone and threw it as hard as I could into the snow covering the river. There was like two feet of it, so no harm was done to my iPhone, but throwing something felt good. Once I picked it back up and took a few deep breaths, I dialed Carol's number and waited for her to answer. "Hey, Carol. It's Nadia."

"*Hey there!*" Carol's sweet, chipper voice was so damn bubbly. "I thought the girls were coming over so you and Annie could put out Dora's flowers?"

I sighed and hung my head. "I'm at the river. Annie stood me up. Listen, I just got off the phone with her...apparently that Brad guy is taking her to LA—"

"*Oh, God.*" Carol groaned. "To do what? Beg for money on street corners?"

"*Oh, he's gonna make her famous.*" I snorted. "I'm at least an hour from home and Brad is picking her up in five minutes—"

"I can go get the girls right now, eh?"

"I threatened to have her arrested if she didn't escort them directly to you. But thank you. I'll hurry home—"

"Don't worry about it, sweetheart. I was expecting them anyways. My boys are excited for their play date." She chuckled. "My house is warm, lunch will be ready in five minutes, and there are fresh cookies in the oven. Your girls will be perfectly safe and cared for in my home until *you* return."

"You're an angel, Carol. Thank you."

"You are too, Nadia. Don't forget that. Now take your time honoring your aunt—OH, look at that, little miss priss is strutting over here now. Oh, lord, *Bill.* Look at this. Two feet of snow and she's wearing sky high stilettos. Go on, Nadia. I got these little munchkins."

"Thanks, Carol."

I heard Carol calling out my nieces' names in the background before she disconnected our call and it eased my fears a smidge. Not a lot though. I shoved my phone in my jacket pocket and zipped it closed. I needed to do these flowers and then get back.

Call her Annie? I squirmed and felt the need to Hulk-smash the ice covering the river.

Our parents would be so disgusted in the person Annie turned out to be, and part of me wondered if they would blame me for it. For not stopping her. An ice-cold gust of wind slammed into my face. I sighed and looked down at the dried out, dead flowers Aunt Dora left behind.

I didn't understand the significance or the reason for the request. All I knew was it was personal to my aunt. And for that, I never pushed the issue. She did her best by us, so I would do my best by her. Even if it made no sense to me. I dropped down to my knees and pressed the bouquet of dried flowers into the snow.

Aunt Dora's note was in my pocket, so I pulled it out to review her instructions. She'd written this before she ever got sick, maybe even years ago. I wished I'd been allowed to read it before she passed so I could have asked the significance...but that was a futile dream. I carefully opened the piece of parchment and double checked I was in the right spot.

Stand on the river beneath the Y tree.

I glanced back up to the cliff to my left, where a line of trees stretched along the river. Directly up from me was a single birchwood tree with no leaves that was almost invisible against all the white snow around it...it was shaped like a capital Y.

The next part of the note was a detailed drawing of what she wanted me to do. I took my time to carefully copy it without messing it up, then I was to draw a pentacle around it, with the bouquet of flowers in the middle of the star. At each of the five points, she'd drawn a different rune. I had no idea what they meant, but they were beautiful to look at. They felt nice to draw in the snow.

Not for the first, or millionth time, I wished I knew more

magic—more of my own species. But Mom had been terrified of demons, so she ran far away from Eden and married a human. Dad knew we were witches—me, Annie, and Mom—but Mom only taught us the bare minimum. The basics. Then Aunt Dora had taught us more once we arrived in the Northwest Territories. Or taught *me*. Annie never cared to learn.

But I made sure Aunt Dora taught Kendall and Kylie.

In the snow, above the rune at the top of the star, I drew the only rune I *did* know. The rune for the Goddess. The mother of our species, the one who created us and gave us life. The moment my finger finished carving the rune into the snow, all the runes glistened and sparkled with a faint purple glow.

I gasped. It took me a moment to compose myself to finish the ritual.

Read the spell, Nadia. That's the last part.

I cleared my throat and then read the words from the paper, "*I call thee, Goddess, please come near, I'll speak my words ever clear. The soul of one who lost the fight, sends this token for a peaceful night.*"

The snow glowed a pale purple. The bouquet of flowers blossomed with life, the colors brightening like it was spring. The snow melted away beneath it—and then the ice vanished. Aunt Dora's bouquet dropped into the dark water of the river under all this ice and snow. I scrambled back a few feet in fear that the ice was breaking, but the hole sealed itself right back up. Snow spread back over the section as if nothing had ever happened.

The bouquet was gone.

I stared at the empty, clear snow with my jaw dropped and my heart pounding in my ears. I'd never witnessed the Goddess react that way. Excitement fluttered through my veins. I looked up into the gray clouds over my head and smiled.

"Thank you, Goddess," I shouted.

As my voice echoed down the frozen river that didn't have a

single other person in sight, my thoughts went back to my family. To Annie's peak selfishness. To sweet little Kendall and Kylie who were smart enough to know their mother didn't care about them. It wasn't fair.

I looked back to the sky and held my hands to my chest. *Goddess, if you can hear me, I need your help. Kendall and Kylie deserve a better life than this, than Annie. My sister isn't suitable to be a mother, she doesn't even want them. I don't know what to do, Goddess. Please help me. Give me a sign, a signal—anything. Just tell me how to get them away from her. Please, I'll do anything to get them a better life...just give me a sign. Please.*

Sharp, burning hot pain shot through my arm. It scorched a path over my skin and grew stronger. I screamed and swatted at my arm but there was nothing there, just my jacket. The pain grew stronger and stronger. My vision blurred. I tried to gasp for air but nothing was getting in. I was on fire. It was invisible yet melting me from the inside-out. I cried out. Tears streaked down my face. My whole body was trembling. I tugged my jacket off and dove for my arm and hissed.

My skin was hot to the touch and deep red like I'd been burned. My whole body warmed. Sweat dripped down my spine. I hunched forward and tasted vomit in my mouth. Somehow the pain intensified. It felt like a serrated knife was being dragged through my body. I hissed and slammed my right hand over the spot on my left forearm. Heat exploded out from me in a wave. Snow melted away in a big circle around me.

Bright golden light poked through my fingers and shot straight into the sky. I gasped and pulled my hand off only to find a huge glowing, golden circle on my forearm. The light pouring off my skin was too bright to look at, so I turned away. The clouds parted over my head and a bold blue summer sky appeared in full view. Massive streams of golden light shot out of the sky and slammed into my chest.

I gasped and flew backwards. My feet lifted off the snow

and my back arched. The pain and light grew stronger and stronger until I was lost to it completely. The world vanished around me. It was like I'd crawled into the Sun and now my body was melting. My eyes burned. Hot liquid slid down my face. Every muscle in my body convulsed.

The Goddess was punishing me for begging her for help.

That had to be it.

Nothing else could have caused this much pain.

Just when I thought my heart was going to stop completely, a dark object sliced through the glowing golden light. My vision was blurry, but it looked like the outline of a person. White light flashed—and the glowing light dimmed. I blinked and blinked, each time the light was fainter. Each time my vision cleared a bit more.

"*Breathe,*" a strange voice purred through the wildfire raging inside of me.

Yet I gasped for breath all the same.

Darkness crept in all around me.

This is it. This is how I die.

Cold hands wrapped around my forearm—*and then it was over.*

Gone.

Like it never happened.

No aftermath. No phantom pain. Just gone.

I closed my eyes and focused on breathing. My pulse was flying high.

"That's it, just breathe," a soft feminine voice called out gently. "Keep your eyes closed and count down from ten. Then open."

I had no idea who this person was, but the advice sounded good enough. I counted, taking a deep breath with each number...

Ten.

Nine.

Eight.
Seven.
Six.
Five.
Four.
Three.
Two.
One.

I opened my eyes and spotted a girl with pale skin and black hair leaning over me. Behind her, the sky was cloudy and gray just like it'd been all day. I braced myself for the pain or light to come back...but it didn't.

The girl leaned into my view. "Hey there, supernova. How we doing?"

I blinked and tried to focus on her face, but it was still blurry.

"Here. Sit up. That should help." She reached down and grabbed my hand, then pulled me up into a seated position. "This better?"

I blinked and looked around. I was still sitting on the snow on the frozen Hay River.

"Disorienting, isn't it?"

I jumped at the sound of the girl's chipper voice. I turned toward her—and my jaw dropped. The girl was nothing like I expected. She had black hair hanging straight down to her shoulders. Her lips were painted a bright candy apple red and her eyes had the most intense black, smoky style going. Her eyes themselves were the most alluring part.

They were red.

Like glowing Christmas lights in the dark kind of red.

For a moment all I could do was stare. My eyes were a boring hazel. *This* girl had won the lottery. She was even rocking a black leather crop top and shorts—a look I never could pull off.

"Hi, I'm Henley Redd." She held her hand out in front of me. "And you are?"

"I'm..." I coughed. "I'm Nadia Bowen."

"Nice to meet you, Nadia." Henley pursed her red lips. "Do you know what just happened to you?"

I shook my head. "No, but nothing has ever been more physically painful."

Henley held her left forearm out in front of her and pointed her black painted fingernail at a row of letters inked into her porcelain skin. *XVIII.* "Do you know what this means?"

"Roman numeral eighteen? Or The Moon in the—" I gasped and looked up into her red eyes. "THE COVEN."

Henley grinned. "Very good. That's right. I'm Henley Redd and I am the Moon Card in The Coven."

I blinked. "How did you find me so fast? Did I do something illegal?"

"No, you're fine." Henley chuckled. "I found you because the Sun and the Moon are connected, and as such, we can sense each other."

I frowned and looked up at the sky. "The Sun?"

A cold finger tapped on my arm. I looked down and my jaw dropped.

On my arm, in the exact same spot as Henley's and in the same exact font, were the letters *XIX.*

The Sun.

"Welcome to The Coven, Nadia Bowen." Henley jumped to her feet and brushed snow off her black leather shorts. She winked down at me. "You're lucky, you know. The Sun and Moon are the only two Cards that can sense each other like this. So I felt you get Marked and was able to pinpoint your location. Glad I did because you blew up the entire river."

My jaw dropped. "I'm in The Coven? Like for real?"

She nodded. "We'll have to initiate you later, but yes, for real. I think you'll like it. We're quite the little family."

"So...I mean...what does...how..." I shook my head and pushed my blonde hair off my face. "What now?"

Henley grinned. "Well, I bring you home to Eden to meet the others. *But* before we do that, I need your help. We were on our way to do a special ritual for a fellow Card, but we could use your help. What do you say?"

CHAPTER THIRTY-SEVEN

TENNESSEE

I WASN'T sure I'd survive another episode of Tegan the White Witch. I was barely surviving this one. I felt like I was dropping the ball, like I was letting everyone down every step of the way. She needed to wake up and not ever do this again.

As Koth dropped beneath the clouds and gently lowered to the front yard of Coven Headquarters in Eden, my soulmate was all I could think about...except it was the rare moment when I hated that. My Coven-mates needed me. My civilians needed me. *Henley* needed me. But my mind was only on Tegan.

It took every single ounce of self-control I didn't know I had to stop myself from rushing up there the second my feet hit the ground.

Instead, I carefully helped Deacon, Warner, Hope, and Uncle Tim down.

Koth shifted into human form and met my gaze. "I will return to Issale now but only to check on Steve and to gather Silas and Maddox. Then I will return. We both know you're going to need us soon."

I sighed and nodded. "You can bring Steve and Elan here if you need to."

He nodded, then leapt into the air, shifting on the fly and zooming out of sight.

"There's a hole in my chest, dudes," Warner said suddenly.

Uncle Tim hooked his arm around Warner's waist, throwing Warner's tattooed arm over his shoulders. "Come on, Cinderella, let's get you to Katherine before your carriage turns back into a pumpkin."

Warner's head rolled on his shoulders and his eyes drooped closed. He grinned. "Cinderella...I get it."

Deacon sighed and stared at the front door. "Hey, angel boy, how 'bout an assist?"

He probably expected me to use my magic, but I was feeling shaky this close to Tegan. Instead, I followed my uncle's move and supported Deacon's weight to carry him in. Up ahead, Warner's legs gave out from under him and he dropped. Uncle Tim caught him before he made it to the steps but not before I caught sight of the fresh blood gushing from his chest. My stomach turned.

"Set me down here. Help them," Deacon ordered, and I noticed he put a little bit of his magic into his words—not something he ever tried with me.

Which meant Warner was in bad shape. I cursed and hurried around them to open the front door. As it swung open, eight pairs of eyes with anxious expressions snapped toward me. Mona was the closest to the door as she paced the living room in her tank top that revealed a fully grown out soulmate glyph—that was currently green.

Her purplish-brown eyes snapped up to me. "Where is he?"

"Dad's fine, just handling clean-up for me." I started to say something else when I spotted Constance curled into a ball on the couch with a bucket beside her. My pulse fluttered. "Constance?"

"I'm fine," she groaned and picked her head up to look at me. "Just a little morning sickness—don't worry, it's not contagious."

Daniel cringed and pinched the bridge of his nose.

Constance frowned. "Who's bleeding?"

I stepped back and helped Uncle Tim carry Warner over the threshold.

"WARNER?" Lennox shouted.

I did a double take as she hurried over and pressed her hand to his forehead. "Lennox, welcome back. Nice work back there, by the way."

She gave me a soft smile. "Thanks, Tenn. May I take him down to Katherine?"

"Immediately, please."

"I'll help you," Mona said softly.

I moved out of their way and my gaze shot up the stairs.

"Tenn?"

I jumped and spun toward my name—and found the others watching me with blatant concern in their eyes. Well, Bentley was staring into space and that made *me* concerned. I cleared my throat. And then I realized who all was in the room. Easton sat on the sofa with a cast on his arm. Beside him, Chutney had bandages on her head but was otherwise fine. Emersyn stood like a statue in front of the fireplace. I couldn't tell if she'd come out of her hypnosis or not.

"*I said* I'm fine. I just need one of Katherine's little juice boxes," Deacon mumbled as Uncle Tim helped him through the front door. He smirked but then he must have spotted his soul-mate because his eyes widened and he forced himself upright. "*Emersyn.*"

She whimpered and darted across the room, then all but tackled him. Her arms coiled around his neck tight. The back of her right hand showed a green glyph. "Goddess, my glyph went red, D. Don't do that to me again."

He chuckled softly and ran his burned hand through her hair. "Don't run off into the Land of the Lore on *me* again, eh?"

She groaned and buried her face in his chest.

I nodded to him. "Do you need Katherine?"

"Let her focus on Warner for a minute. I'll be all right."

Bentley jumped to his feet. "What happened?"

"The shadow demon somehow managed to summon a greater demon into the Old Lands Gap. Hope managed—" I frowned and glanced around. My sister was nowhere in sight, yet she'd arrived with us. "Hope? *Hope?*"

Uncle Tim and I jumped out the front door and found her standing on the porch, staring into space.

"Hope?" I yelled. She didn't answer. "*BETTINA.*"

She flinched like I'd slapped her. "Don't call me that."

"Then answer when I call you three times, *Hope.*"

She grimaced. "Sorry, I was listening to Henley."

Uncle Tim wrapped his arm around her shoulders and led her into the living room...and all the way over to sit on one of the big comfy chairs next to the fire.

Bentley nodded. "Greater demon. What happened?"

Uncle Tim quickly and efficiently filled them in while I stared at the stairs. Every bone in my body was begging me to go up to her.

"*She's okay,*" Emersyn whispered beside me. "*I was just up there. Still white witch.*"

I groaned.

"So, what's Henley—the shadow demon—doing now?" Easton asked and tapped his ear.

Hope scowled and shook her head. "I'm having a hard time hearing. He keeps talking to someone in that demonic language, but I've got to concentrate."

Uncle Tim pursed his lips. "Could you perhaps create a spell so that the audio is on a speaker, so to speak?"

Hope sat up straight. "Like a speakerphone?"

Easton nodded. "Maybe we can help you listen?"

"That's brilliant." Hope licked her lips. "I can probably do that."

"Better include something about being a spell by the Aether Witch," Bentley said with a sigh. "You'll need to tap into that to access it."

Constance raised her hand. "And something about being on command, for obvious reasons."

Hope nodded and pressed her hand to the spot behind her ear where Tegan's spell was placed. "*On my command, when I call. In this room, bound by the wall. Marked by Aether on mine ear, make the words for all to hear.*"

The room filled with a soft roaring sound and the chirping of birds. Dogs barked in the background while cars honked. There was a soft male voice whispering a chant just barely loud enough to be heard, but it was not in English.

"*Patience,*" Henley snapped. "I know what I'm doing."

My stomach turned. Everyone in the room was concentrating on Henley, but my whole body was in knots. Deacon reached out and tapped my forearm, then nodded his head toward the stairs. My gaze shot over to Uncle Tim, but he just nodded and smiled.

Right. I'm a mess.

I spun and flew up to the third floor, to where our penthouse suite sat alone on the top floor of the house. I carefully and quietly pushed the door open and then slipped inside. The room was quiet but for the faint crackling of a fire in the fireplace on the far wall. It was a perfectly comfortable temperature, yet my bones felt like ice.

Tegan's white hair blended in with the white sheets on our bed.

My chest tightened and my breaths grew short. It felt like someone was squeezing my heart and twisting it, crumbling it between their fingers and draining my blood. I forced myself to take a deep breath, then crossed the room toward the bed. My legs felt like jelly. There was a wooden chair sitting beside the bed, probably for Katherine to heal her from, so I collapsed onto it.

The room was so quiet I could hear the air she breathed in and exhaled.

I sat there in the silence for a few moments, then groaned and buried my face in the blankets and screamed. Once I couldn't breathe anymore, I pulled back and stared at her beautiful face. The gold and yellow eyes creeped me out, but I would gladly take those over this unconsciousness any day.

This was driving me over the edge into madness.

I reached out, taking her hand in mine and lacing our fingers. My skin was always much more tan than hers but now we looked like two different species. The crystal rings on her fingers did look nice next to the silver ones on mine. I leaned forward and cradled her hand against my face, needing to feel closer. Her magic was strong as hell. It radiated around her like a forcefield. There was no doubt that she was alive. I just didn't understand why she was unconscious or why any of this happened.

Unable to stop myself, I reached out and pressed my fingers to her throat. Her pulse beat strong and steady. I sighed and ran the backs of my fingers over her cheek. "Tegan?"

Silence.

"Tegan, please wake up."

Silence.

"Kitten, we need you to snap out of this now." I sighed and hung my head. "The shadow-demon took off Keltie's jewelry in the Old Lands and her dermal piercing with the camera is gone. Hope found it on the street in New York. All we have is Hope's listening...but something big is about to happen. There's a greater demon here. I don't even understand how he managed to summon it. We can't do this without you. *I* can't do this without you."

I stared at her beautiful, restful face and willed her to wake up with everything I had.

But she didn't even flutter.

"I need you, babe. Come back to me."

Footsteps thundered up the stairs. I braced myself just as the bedroom door flew open.

Uncle Tim slid inside with wide eyes and a pale face. "Downstairs. Now."

I nodded and stood as Uncle Tim turned and fled back down the stairs.

"This is it, Tegan." I turned back to her and leaned over, then cupped her face in both of my hands. Then I did something I never thought I would...I willed my body to glow and pushed my magic into her. All of it. "Babe. I know you can hear me. Something big is about to happen. I haven't told anyone else this, but I think I saw Lilith in the Land of the Lore. I felt her... and I'm terrified. So, wake up...because I can't do this without you."

CHAPTER THIRTY-EIGHT

NADIA

I DIDN'T REMEMBER RESPONDING to Henley, but the next thing I knew we were surrounded by a black wall of fog—or maybe it was smoke. Everything was a blur, both in my mind and around me.

I'm in The Coven? I'M in The Coven. Me? How did this happen? Why me?

The black tornado of smoke around us vanished and bright light shined into my face. I cringed and started to shield my eyes when I realized it didn't hurt. I looked straight up at the Sun, *and I could see it.* Like the whole thing. I saw the swirls around it and the sparkles—

"Easy, tiger," Henley said with a laugh and gently pushed me. "You may be the Sun Card but let's not overdo it until you've been initiated. We need those eyes. 'Kay?"

I nodded and then blinked several times. It was so strange. My eyes didn't burn at all. There weren't even dots in my vision from staring at bright light. *Weird.* I looked up again and found bright blue skies without a single cloud in sight.

A gust of wind slammed into my face. It was hot, like someone was pointing a hair dryer at me. That was when I noticed the heat. It was oppressive. It felt like an attack. It felt like I'd get a sunburn even through my jacket—*wait a second, I'm wearing a jacket. Why am I not melting or having a heat stroke? Where are we? How'd we get here?*

Snap out of it, Nadia. You need to ask questions.

I turned to Henley to ask where we were, only to find her hiding under the shadow of a palm tree. A *palm* tree. I hurried over to her just in time to hear her speaking in a weird language on the phone—*is that the ancient language?* My mother never taught us because she thought it would be rude for us to speak it in front of our human father. If only she'd known I'd end up in The Coven.

I'm in The Coven. I'm the Sun Card.

Me...the Sun.

The girl from Canada who loves blizzards and ice hockey.

Suddenly, that black smoke wrapped around us again. It lasted for a split second, and when it vanished, we were inside a hospital...standing in the hallway by the emergency exit in an oddly dark corner. The hallway was quite busy, with the nurses' station just up ahead and people sitting in chairs outside of rooms. Yet no one seemed to notice our sudden arrival. *Is THIS what magic is supposed to be like? What is happening right now?*

A million questions raced through my mind at once. *How am I supposed to compete with this? What are The Coven going to think of me and my lack of magic knowledge? What are they going to expect of me? What do I even DO?* It seemed like there should have been some prerequisites before being Marked for such a job. I didn't have any fighting skills, yet I knew The Coven killed demons—that was like one of their main jobs. I'd never even seen a demon. As a kid, I thought my mom had made them up just to scare us into behaving and not missing curfew.

Wait...ARE they real? If I rolled up to Eden and started asking about fighting demons and demons weren't real—I shuddered. My stomach tightened into knots. This Marking was a mistake. Someone made an error in judgement. I needed to find a Karen to ask to speak to the manager and get this reversed.

My phone vibrated in my jacket pocket, making me jump, so I pulled it out only to find a text message from Annie. I opened it up and wanted to scream when I saw her message. *Girls are with Carol. I know you called her so calm your tits. I'm at the airport. Don't know when I'll be back. Don't pester me while I'm gone or I won't give you any money when I'm rich and famous.*

Bright, shining, sparkling golden yellow light pierced through my skin *from inside of me.* Rays of literal sunshine shot out of my palms and lit up the walls like spotlights calling for Batman. My pulse skyrocketed but that only made more spotlights pop out.

I squealed and swatted at it. "Oh, God. Oh, God. Oh, God. Stop, stop, stop."

"Hey, hey, just breathe, girl." Henley's pale hands gripped mine and held them together. White clouds of glittery mist coiled around our hands, blocking out the magic coming out of me. Once it was gone, she winked one pretty red eye at me. "See, no big deal. All gone."

"What was that?" I stared at my hands in horror.

Henley giggled. *"Nadia.* You're in The Coven now. You have real power, real magic. It responds to your emotions, so you'll have to learn control. For now, just stay calm and your magic will too. I promise, you'll get the hang of it in no time. It'll feel natural."

I sighed and nodded. Then I took a deep breath. "Okay. All right. I'm fine. Right. Totally cool. Thank you, Henley."

She winked and gave me a playful smirk. "We're family now, Nadia. I've got you. Come on. We've got to help our friend."

I started to follow her down the hall when a door opened and a little blonde girl came rushing out, crossing my path. Her parents apologized to me as they hurried after her. I smiled and watched the girl chase after a bouncy ball while her blonde hair swayed. She reminded me of Kendall and Kylie with all that light blonde hair. My chest tightened. I couldn't remember the last time I saw my nieces smiling like this little girl was. *I need to get home.* I was in The Coven now, Henley said that came with power—I gasped.

I'm in The Coven now.

I have power.

I have help.

I looked up at the white ceiling of the hospital, but I wasn't seeing it. My thoughts went to the Goddess. *You heard me, didn't you? This is the sign. This is how I help them, isn't it?* Tears pooled in my eyes and my pulse quickened. *Breathe, Nadia. Stay calm or your new magic comes out.*

But I *was* emotional. I'd asked the Goddess to help me and she'd answered. Immediately.

"Nadia?"

I pulled my cellphone back out and started to dial Carol's number.

"Nadia?" Henley appeared in front of me. She reached out and lowered my phone. "Nadia?"

I looked up and grimaced. "Sorry. I just need to call my neighbor who is watching my nieces. My sister left town. I'm supposed to be watching them now. But I'm here with you. I just need to tell Carol I'll be later than expected—wait, how long until I can go home? I can't leave them there all night—"

"*Nadia.*" Henley smiled and her red eyes sparkled. She took my phone out of my hand and slid it back in my jacket pocket, then zipped it shut. "I already called our Coven Leaders. They went to pick up your nieces and are probably on their way back to Eden with them now. They're perfectly safe."

My jaw dropped. "*Really?*"

She grinned and hooked her arm through mine, then pulled

me into a brisk walk. "I told you, Nadia. The Coven is a family. We take care of our own. That now includes you, your sister, and your nieces."

That now includes you, your sister, and your nieces.

A hot lump formed in my throat. *The Coven is a family,* she'd said. A family. There were twenty-two Cards...if they considered each of their respective families as their family...a wild wave of emotions rushed through me. I'd never had a big family. It'd just been my parents, me, and Annie—and Aunt Dora, though we rarely saw her. I didn't know what to expect or to think.

"Henley?"

She looked over at me and arched one black eyebrow. "Yea?"

"Thank you."

She grinned. "You'll settle in. Trust me."

Why do I doubt that? I groaned and let Henley lead me down the hallway in silence while I focused on breathing and *not* bursting into a ball of sunshine inside of a human hospital.

"Wait, why is she *here?*" I whispered so no one would hear. "In a human hospital?"

Henley grimaced. "Long story, but one of our healers has been taking good care of her here."

"Oh. Okay." I had no idea what that meant, yet it wasn't really my place to ask. Not while I didn't know anyone. The last thing I wanted was to annoy my new Coven-mates from the jump.

A door opened on the left side of the hall in front of us and a tall man wearing a black hoodie pulled low over his face strolled out. He walked over to the nurses' stand and started asking something about pudding for his grandmother. It struck me as strange, but then I realized I was still in my faux-fur-lined winter jacket.

"In here." Henley tugged on my arm and pulled me through a doorway.

I shook myself and followed—then slid to a stop. I didn't know what I was expecting to find, but *this* wasn't it. The room was your basic hospital room with one bed, but the person in the bed was completely covered head-to-toe in white bandages. Even their face was covered up. I couldn't tell if it was a guy or a girl. All I could see was light pink hair sticking out under the bandages.

"Who is *that*?" I whispered.

"Her name is Frankie." Henley walked over to the girl's left arm and pulled a small portion of the white bandages off to reveal big black letters inked into her skin just like ours. *XVI*. "Frankie is our Tower Card."

She's in The Coven, too. Which was a stupid delayed thought. Henley had told me that already. But still, the poor girl had to be miserable. "What happened to her?"

Henley grimaced. "She blew up a car while trapped inside of it. Should have died but she's strong. That's why we're here. We need to do a special ritual to help heal her faster."

"Is she awake? Will it hurt her?"

"We've got her in a magic-induced coma to keep her calm, but it needs a little boost."

"And I'm gonna help?" *I have no idea what I'm doing here. This can't be a good idea.*

"Well, I was going to go grab one of our other Coven-mates —my little brother Royce, to be specific—but he's a tad emotionally unstable these days." She shrugged. "Besides, the Sun and Moon are always stronger together. And with the strength from the Tower in the mix, we should be able to do big things."

I nodded. "Okay. Sure." *That doesn't make sense to me, but I feel like it should.*

"Are you experienced with magic, Nadia?"

I shook my head. "Not at all. Mom's parents died before I

was born and then she married a muggle. She only taught us bare basics, and then she died when I was sixteen. My aunt Dora has taught me a little bit more since then but...well, you saw where we live."

"Covered in snow? Yeah, interesting choice."

"The Northwest Territories of Canada. It is quite pretty but remote as hell." I sighed. "Magic wasn't used much. Annie doesn't like it either. So no, I know very basic and specific things."

She picked up a black leather bag that was sitting on the chair beside Frankie's bed and pulled out a black candle that had to be six inches tall. "Ever worked with candles?"

My eyes widened. *Candles? Worked with? Oh, Goddess. What have I gotten myself into?* "Never. I didn't know candles could be used in magic."

"Oh, candles *are* magic." Henley's bright red lips spread into a wide smile. She sat the black candle on the bed in front of her, nestled against Frankie's hip. Then she immediately reached in and pulled more out. She made quick work of lining the perimeter of the bed with these black candles. "How about I take the lead and you just let me tap into your new magic?"

Relief washed through me so hard I actually swayed. "That sounds great. Just tell me what to do."

"Do you speak any other languages?" She walked over and yanked the curtains closed. "More specifically, our ancient language?"

"No, I only speak English. Maybe little fragments of French."

"No big deal. We'll help you learn. In the meantime, don't freak when I recite the spells because the language can sound intense." She pulled a black lighter out of her bag and lit the candles in front of her. Each one flickered with a *black* flame. "Here. Light those for me?"

I caught the lighter she tossed and went to work lighting the four candles on my side of the bed. As each one danced with its own black flame, I felt a cold chill on my spine, like fingers running down my back. *This isn't Hocus Pocus, Nadia. We aren't the Sanderson sisters. This is real magic.* I was trying not to ask a million questions. Henley seemed so chill and laid back, and she was so nice. I didn't want to be annoying. I didn't want to be seen as naïve and stupid.

"Okay, done. Here's your lighter—what is that?" My eyes widened.

Henley held a dagger in her hand with a blade as black as her hair. She held her other palm out to me. "Lighter, please?"

I dropped it into her hand and just stared.

She took the lighter and clicked for a flame, then traced that flame down the edge of her dagger while whispering something. When she was done, she shoved her lighter back in her bag and then looked up to me. "Healing rituals for this level of injury require blood spells. It's no big deal. I do these all the time."

"Oh—um...okay..." I glanced to the door, then back to her. "Isn't someone gonna come in?"

"Nope. My magic is repelling them as we speak." She held her left palm out and pressed the tip of her blade to her skin and sliced into it. Deep red blood welled up to the surface more and more as she dragged the blade through her hand. When she finished, she held her hand out to show me the strange symbol she'd carved into her skin. "We have to use special runes with the blood."

"*We?*" I shrieked.

"Yup. Watch." She switched the blade to her left hand and held up her right palm—then carved the exact same symbol into her other hand. Without missing a beat, she reached down and carefully carved the rune into both of Frankie's palms. "See? Easy. Now, you do yours."

The black hilt of the dagger mocked me.

I had to be tough enough for this job. For the girls.

Pain could not be a deterrent anymore. I took the dagger by the hilt, then brought the pointed tip to my left palm. I took a deep breath and cut into my own skin. My eyes locked on Frankie's so I didn't mess it up. I hissed and shifted my weight around to try and ignore the pain. It hurt, but it was nothing like being Marked. The rune was not one I'd ever seen. It looked like a fancy version of the pie symbol, like from math or an upside-down stylized *U*. Intersecting it straight down the middle was a *Y* shape that had a small *x* and an arrow at the bottom. It was intricately simple.

"Okay..." I held the hilt between two fingers and handed it to her. Then showed her my palms. "Is this right?"

Henley grinned. "Perfection. Now, we're going to hold hands. It's imperative that you do not let go until I say so."

I nodded and held my hands out over Frankie's unconscious body. Henley grabbed my right hand and squeezed so that our bloods mixed between our palms. Her blood was hot against my skin, or maybe that was my new magic. I had no idea. Henley reached down and held Frankie's hand. *OH. Duh.* I copied her and took Frankie's right hand in my left. We were now in a sort of circle.

Henley took a deep breath, licked her lips, then started chanting in a language I'd never heard before. Probably the ancient language. The big florescent light over my head changed to a soft golden color like afternoon sunshine through a cloud. Above Henley, the light turned a blueish white. *Sun and Moon.*

Her chanting grew louder and faster. The black flames shot up a foot in the air. They flickered black to red, red to black, over and over again. The other lights in the ceiling went out, leaving only the ones above our heads. The corners of the room were drenched in darkness and my pulse skipped beats.

Yellow light erupted from between my hands. Henley's were white. Our feet lifted off the ground until Frankie's arms were stretched out as far as they could without our hands pulling apart. Sharp energy prickled along my skin like being poked with needlepoints. Blood dripped from our clasped hands, but the drops floated in the air, connecting with each other to make a circle of blood.

My pulse quickened. This was getting weird. I glanced to Henley, but her face was calm like she'd done this a million times.

Black smoke seeped under the door and billowed into the room. It crept across the floor like a rushing river, like it was a living, breathing entity. Within seconds the smoke completely covered the floor and was rising higher. It coiled around my ankles like hands reaching up and grabbing me. Everywhere the smoke touched me, my body *burned*.

Thin tendrils of the smoke slithered up my body, sending electric shocks through my muscles. Henley's chanting grew so loud she was shouting now. The heavy pounding of my pulse drowned out the beeping of the machines in the room. *This isn't right. This can't be right. I don't like this.* I tried to open my mouth to call out to Henley to stop when a smoke tendril wrapped around my face.

My jaw couldn't move.

I couldn't open my mouth.

Violent tremors ripped through my body and I started to tremble.

I tried to yell but my lips felt glued together. My voice came out in a hum.

For the first time since I met Henley...I was afraid.

Petrified.

This can't be right.

Healing someone shouldn't hurt. I didn't know a lot of magic but that seemed obvious. Something inside of me told me I'd made a huge mistake. *Who are The Coven?* I tried to recount every story my mother and Aunt Dora had taught me about them but now I didn't trust my own memories.

I'd never been more terrified in my entire life.

I didn't want this. I didn't want to be in The Coven if *this* was the kind of magic they did. Something was wrong here. Henley's chanting was so loud it sounded like thunder. I didn't know what she was saying but now I was questioning if it was the ancient language after all. It felt...dark. Sinister. It felt wrong.

Oh, Goddess, what have I done? Who have I trusted here?

I squeezed my eyes shut and my heart stopped.

Everything was *red*.

And then I heard a man's deep, rumbling voice chuckle in my ears. My body went ice cold. Electricity shot up and down my limbs like my magic was trying to fight back, but I was locked inside of my own skin. Something brushed through my hair. That chuckle grew darker and hungrier—and then hot breath brushed over my neck, right behind my ear.

My eyes flew open.

NO. Stop this. STOP! But my mouth wasn't working.

Red light flashed inside of the ring of blood. The black smoke slithered over to the circle and went inside of it, swirling like a whirlpool, then it shot straight up to the ceiling. A glowing green orb floated up out of the circle. Streaks of its light flashed across the room like lightning.

I didn't want to watch.

I couldn't look away.

What have we done?

Light flashed. I squeezed my eyes shut again—and glowing green eyes were staring right at me. Bolts of glowing green lightning shot out from the corners of his eyes. Even with my eyes closed, everything was red. Blood red. Darkness crept in all around me, casting him in shadow but for his eyes. Even though his eyes were in front of me, I felt his breath on my neck and hands on my waist.

"*Open,*" he purred in my ear.

My eyes flew open—and a scream died in my throat.

Those same green eyes I saw when my eyes were closed were now shining out of the face of a man...a man emerging from the black smoke inside the circle of our blood. The black smoke pinning me in place slithered off my body and rushed toward the man like he'd beckoned it.

In the blink of an eye, he was out of the circle and standing at the foot of Frankie's bed.

Every single fiber of my soul told me to RUN.

But I couldn't.

He was *beautiful*. Dangerously so. He had long dark hair except for two white strips around his face. Tall black horns stood from the top of his head. They seemed to be made of a crystal, like hematite or onyx. A scruffy beard covered his jaw and the curve of his mouth. He wore a long black tunic, black pants, and black boots. Glowing green orbs that matched his eyes were strung and draped over his chest and shoulders.

Power radiated off him in waves, pulsing through the air.

He was unnervingly beautiful. And absolutely *terrifying*.

Henley bowed her head, then looked up at him with wide, glowing red eyes. She licked her lips and smirked. *"My Lord."*

My eyes widened. *MY LORD? WHAT THE HELL?*

The man grinned, revealing glistening white teeth. He looked to Henley and I saw pointed ears sticking out of his dark hair. He reached out, pressed his finger under her chin, and tipped her face up toward him. Then he spoke to her in that language she'd been chanting, his voice both a growl and a purr.

Henley *beamed*. "Thank you, my Lord."

He glanced over his shoulder to where Frankie lay motionless under all those bandages...and he laughed. A deep laugh. Without taking his eyes off Frankie, he nodded toward her. "I told you this one had enough power for us. She's strong...for now."

Henley's red eyes sparkled. "What now, my Lord? What with these two?"

"The next phase as we planned. We'll come back for *this* one." He turned around and his glowing green eyes landed right on me, just like when my eyes were closed. His gaze slithered up and down my body and then he closed the distance between us and took my jaw between his thumb and pointer finger. He tilted my head back, then he leaned close and whispered in my ear. "But the Sun comes with me."

Inside, I was *screaming*. But when I opened my mouth, my voice came out as a shaky whisper, "W-w-wh-who are you?"

CHAPTER THIRTY-NINE

TENNESSEE

I HAD JUST REACHED the top of the stairs when Easton screamed.

The ragged, broken sound made my heart stop and my steps falter.

No, no, no. Please. A million horrible scenarios ran through my mind as I rushed down the steps with my heart lodged in my throat.

"Her name is Frankie." Henley's voice carried up the stairs. "Frankie is our Tower Card."

I gasped. *Frankie? What's she doing with Frankie? Shit, shit, shit.*

Our new Tower Card was still in a magical coma. We didn't even know her yet and I felt protective of her. But Easton's pained scream didn't make sense. He didn't know Frankie either. He'd only be that upset about—my heart stopped. *OH no.* Lily wasn't here. Lily was in Seelie with Saffie. They weren't back yet. It couldn't be about her. *Please don't let it be her.*

I sped down the rest of the stairs and slid into the living room just as Easton's legs gave out and he crumbled to the ground. Royce and Braison dove for him. I looked around the room and my voice died on my tongue. Hope's eyes were wide and her mouth hung open. Uncle Tim leapt up and hurried over to Easton. Chutney sat on the far edge of the sofa with bandages on her head and tears pooling in her eyes.

"What happened to her?" A girl whose voice I didn't recognize came through Hope's speakerphone spell.

"She blew up a car while trapped inside of it," Henley said in a voice that sounded almost natural and sent a chill down my spine. "Should have died but she's strong. That's why we're here. We need to do a special ritual to help heal her faster."

"WAIT WHAT? What ritual? What are they doing?" I glanced around the room to my Coven-mates. "What's going on here?"

Everyone turned to Easton with sad, broken expressions.

Deacon and Emersyn clung to each other so tight their knuckles were white. Deacon's eyes were closed, but his face was scrunched in pain. Emersyn turned her face away from Easton and I saw tears made of fire flames slide down her face.

My heart sank. I didn't understand what I'd missed. Wasn't sure I wanted to.

Bentley held the Hierophant's locket tight in his hands and pressed to his forehead. Orange magic flickered all around it. His legs bounced like he was running in place while sitting. Jackson stumbled over to my sister and grabbed her shoulder, fisting the material of her sweater between his fingers. She reached up with shaky fingers and gripped his hand.

The door beside me flew open and then Cooper and my father came rushing out.

"Is she awake? Will it hurt her?" That unfamiliar girl asked, she sounded scared.

"What happened?" Dad barked.

"Who screamed?" Cooper frowned but then his face paled. "Easton? What?"

"We've got her in a magic-induced coma to keep her calm,"

Henley's voice was cheery and chipper like nothing was wrong. "But it needs a little boost."

"And I'm gonna help?"

Help with WHAT?

"Well, I was going to go grab one of our other Coven-mates —my little brother Royce, to be specific—"

Royce gasped and fell *into* Easton.

"But he's a tad emotionally unstable these days," Henley continued.

Royce's face paled. His hands that were holding on to Easton trembled.

"Besides, the Sun and Moon are always stronger together. And with the strength from the Tower in the mix, we should be able to do big things."

"*SUN AND THE MOON?*" I shouted as my worst fears were coming to life. *Lily. NOT LILY. No, no, no. HOW?* "WHAT—THE SUN?"

"SHE'S NOT DEAD!" Easton cried and pulled his knees up to his chest and started to rock back and forth. "*She's not dead. She's not. She can't be. She's not dead!*"

Cooper cursed and sprinted over to him, then sank down in front of him between Uncle Tim and Braison.

"Are you experienced with magic, Nadia?" Henley asked.

Cooper glanced toward Hope. "Who the hell is Nadia?"

Hope closed her eyes and shook her head. "From what we can hear...our new Sun Card."

NOOOO. The world rocked and I felt my body sway. My father reached out and steadied me by gripping my shoulder. His hold was tight, like maybe he too was holding on for support. The girl was still speaking but the pain rolling off Easton drowned out her voice in waves.

Lily can't be dead. She went into Seelie. Anything could have happened.

"*What?*" Easton's head snapped up and the pain in his eyes

took my breath away. He looked to me with those baby blues that were red with tears about to crash down like a hurricane storm surge. "You're right!"

Oh fuck. I said that out loud.

"The Northwest Territories of Canada—"

"THAT'S NOT EVEN HENLEY! WE DON'T KNOW! THAT DEMON COULD BE LYING!" Easton pushed to his feet, shoving the others off him. He staggered toward me, his eyes locked on me like I was going to tell him his girlfriend wasn't dead. *"She could be lying. Right Tenn? We can't see anymore! We don't know if there's a Mark!"*

"Easton...I don't know, man." I didn't know what to say, what to think. My body was numb. But I knew if it were Tegan, I would need proof before I believed she was gone. "Maybe? I don't know. We need to find them..."

"Maybe she gave up her Card to survive like Paulina and Kenneth did? Or like Evaline?"

"Ever worked with candles?" Henley purred.

My body went cold.

Oh no. A demon with candles doing a ritual. "They're summoning something," I heard myself growl. "Is Koth back yet?"

Uncle Tim looked up to me and shook his head.

"Never. I didn't know candles could be used in magic," this Nadia girl said softly.

"Oh, candles *are* magic." Henley's voice was almost a giggle. It may have been her voice, but it didn't sound like her at all. "How about I take the lead and you just let me tap into your new magic?"

My stomach rolled.

Easton whimpered and stumbled—Cooper snaked his arm around Easton's body to catch him. But he didn't let go. Easton leaned *into* Cooper. Both of their eyes were locked on Hope.

"Do you speak any other languages?" Henley asked. I could

hear her footsteps moving around Frankie's hospital room. "More specifically, our ancient language?"

"They're summoning something," I said again. This time everyone looked to me with wide eyes. "Another greater demon, I assume. We need to get there. Emersyn, go see if you can get her up—"

"No, *you*." Flames danced in her golden eyes. "You have the strongest connection. Use it."

I cursed and flew up the stairs and back up to my room. In seconds I was bursting through our door, but Tegan hadn't moved. She was still in the same spot and entirely unmoving. I flew over and crouched on the bed beside her, then pressed my hands to her chest, right over the crystal heart of our soulmate glyph that was pulsing green.

"Tegan Bishop, hear me right now," I said while pushing my magic into my voice. I let my body light up once again until I glowed brighter than the North Star. Green and blue magic billowed out from between my palms and her chest. "*Tegan.*"

Her white hair shimmered and seemed to turn *more* white. The black lines of our soulmate glyph flashed in a rainbow swirl, then shot out to cover her entire body. The gold lines on my arm shined like spotlights. I felt the power of Heaven in my arm—the same power I felt when I used my grandfather's sword. I clenched my teeth and focused on *that* power, then I pushed it into Tegan's chest.

Her body lit up in that same glow mine had. Her rainbow magic shimmered all around her body—electricity slammed into my palms and suddenly I was airborne. My wings popped out and caught me from flying back. I hovered there for a second just watching. Waiting. *Hoping.*

Something had just happened.

She'd thrown me.

Me.

She was still very much in there and her magic was ready to kill anything that touched her.

"TENN!" Someone screamed for me from downstairs.

I cursed and dove for my soulmate. In a panic, I cupped her face and kissed her. "WAKE UP!"

Then I spun and flew back down to the living room. "What—"

I choked on my words as a roaring sound filled the room. It sounded like a tornado destroying everything in its path.

"Koth isn't back yet," my dad shouted over the rushing wind sound.

Henley was screaming a chant in what had to be a demonic language.

SHIT. I tugged on the braid in my hair that Tegan attached that leather strip to...the one to call Koth in an emergency. He'd said he was coming back but he wasn't here yet. They were no doubt trying to heal Steve, but we had no one else to call. Frankie was in a hospital in Tallahassee, Florida. Of all the moments to have lost our visual, this was *not* it.

They were inside of a hospital room, but it sounded like they were outside in a hurricane. Henley's chanting voice made my blood boil. I had no idea what was happening but with every passing second my stomach tightened into more knots. A cold breath seemed to brush over my skin.

And then it stopped abruptly.

Silence.

"*My Lord,*" Henley whispered.

LORD? Oh, Goddess. No, no, no, no, no. This isn't happening. I wanted to be wrong.

A man's deep voice rolled like thunder, but there was an edge to it that I knew was not in any way human. He spoke in that same language Henley had just been using to summon him.

"Thank you, my Lord."

My Lord. That's not a good sign. It has to be a greater demon.

Holy shit. How did she get it through?

The guy, whoever he was, laughed deep laugh. "I told you this one had enough power for us. She's strong...for now."

My chest tightened. He was talking about Frankie. He had to be. I'd felt her magic myself.

"What now, my Lord? What with these two?"

"The next phase as we planned. We'll come back for *this* one." There was a brief pause and then the man's voice came out like the purr of a tiger, "but the Sun comes with me."

Easton cried out and half collapsed into Cooper's arms.

The front door flew open. Koth, Silas, and Maddox stormed inside. We barely turned to look.

"W-w-wh-who are you?" Nadia stammered.

"I am Asmodeus."

Everyone rushed toward the sound of his voice, yelling and raising weapons as if he was in the room with us. The wind was knocked right out of my lungs. My knees buckled and I staggered back until I crashed into the wall. My father stood still like a statue. Uncle Tim's face fell. Constance sprinted out of the room while covering her mouth with her hand. Daniel chased after her.

My Coven-mates were shouting, yet I couldn't hear them over the heavy pounding of my heart against my ribs. *Asmodeus.* My mind spun. I didn't know how this was possible or what the hell we were going to do against him. *Asmodeus??*

Bile rose in my throat. I was wrong. They hadn't summoned another greater demon.

This was a fallen angel.

An actual, breathing angel who'd fallen from Heaven into evil and darkness.

The controller of demons on Earth.

And he was *here.*

There was shouting, screaming, and all kinds of other sounds. I only registered them in the back of my mind. Everything else was just...blank. I was the grandson of an angel, but I wasn't an angel myself. I had an angel's sword yet *still not an angel.*

How are we supposed to defeat HIM?

"Wait, is this LA?" Nadia's foreign, soft voice broke through my downward spiral. "Yes, it is. That's the Chinese Theatre!"

"*LA?* They moved already? How does he DO that?" Royce cried.

"The city of dreams," Henley's voice sounded like sandpiper.

I shoved all the panic, fear, and *what-the-fuck-are-we-gonna-dos* to the back of my mind and spun to Koth. "Fly—"

"Outside," Koth growled, then leapt back out the front door.

He was a full-blown black dragon before he left the porch. His long black tail whipped across the foyer. Silas and Maddox raced after him, waiting until they hit the grass before shifting.

"LET'S GO!" I shouted and waved them out the door like a third base coach when the bases are loaded. "*Go, go, go, go.*"

No one hesitated even a fraction of a second. They raced out the door and charged for the dragons. Hope's speaker-phone was still blasting the sounds of Los Angeles through our living room. In my peripheral vision, I saw Silas and Maddox take off with my Coven-mates on their backs, but the screaming from LA held my steps. Things exploded like bombs going off. Cars crashed and glass shattered. Police sirens wailed in the distance. It sounded like Manhattan all over again.

"Henley, wait!"

Hope and I froze on the threshold. There was something in the edge of Nadia's voice.

"Why are we attacking innocent people?" Nadia screamed. There was blatant panic in her voice. "This can't be right. No, this is wrong. Stop this!"

"*GO!*" I grabbed Hope's arm and my wings carried us over

to Koth. We landed on his back right behind Jackson. I tapped Koth's back. "GOOD!"

I knew I flew fast, but even I was never ready for Koth's takeoffs. In the flash of a second, we were flying through the clouds.

Hope gasped. "HE TURNED ON NADIA!"

Jackson glanced over his shoulder. "*Who* did?"

"The shadow demon!"

My stomach turned. This was too far. This was too much. We had to get Henley free of him before there was nothing of Henley left. Yet we had no idea how to kill the shadow demon, and Henley wanted to stay until we did. My pulse was flying faster than Koth was.

We dropped out of the clouds and two dragons appeared just in front of us with the rest of my Coven-mates on their backs. Koth zipped between them and then snorted and nodded his head.

"*GOING DOWN!*" Chutney yelled from Silas's back. She looked over her right shoulder to me. "Plan?"

I jumped up so I was crouched on Koth's back, then peered over his wing to the ground below. Los Angeles was on fire, literally. Even from this high, I saw the destruction already happening. With every second we got closer and closer to the ground until I saw the demon outbreak stretching a few blocks.

"Silas, take the far-left end." I turned to my right and pointed to the other side. "Maddox, y'all take the right. Everyone, work your way to us in the middle. Got it?"

"You're shorthanded!" Uncle Tim shouted over the rushing wind as we sank lower.

I cursed. He was right. We were. Both in general and literally. I had to think quick. Down below, the big old bug-greater demon towered over the buildings and green lightning flashed from the center of the street—*Asmodeus*. They were in the middle of the destruction, right where Koth was heading. I needed more backup. I needed *specific* backup.

I threw my hands out and pulled a gust of wind toward me from each side. Chutney screamed as she lifted off Silas's back and shot to Koth's. My father's eyes widened as he floated over, thousands of feet above ground, to land behind me on Koth's back. I glanced back and forth between Silas and Maddox, then flung Braison off of Silas, over my head, and onto Maddox's back.

"D, move 'em to the middle. Em—*BURN*. Royce—"

"*Poison Roycy!*"

I chuckled and nodded. Then looked to my right. "Maddox's crew, kill everything you see! Chutney, stay with Koth for translation. GO!"

The dragons were fierce warriors. They took their orders instantly, shooting toward the ground like torpedoes. Silas and Maddox took sharp turns in opposite directions. I prayed this plan was going to work, or at least not get anyone killed. We were still shorthanded and about to face our toughest opponents yet.

"HOLD ON!" Chutney screamed from up behind Koth's head.

We flew through a black cloud of smoke and ash—and into a nightmare. My mind flashed memories from Samhain when thousands of demons were unleashed on top of us. There were demons *everywhere*. It was hard to even see humans scrambling up and down the street. Koth spread his wings wide and dropped, spitting fire left and right and melting demons in a flash.

"TENN!" Chutney thrust her hands up. "LIFT!"

Shit. I jumped up, pushing my magic and lifting Jackson, Hope, and my father into the air with me. Koth zoomed out from under us, Chutney riding his back and firing flaming arrows from a wand I didn't know she had.

The four of us landed on our feet and immediately turned our backs to each other.

Hollywood Boulevard was a bloodbath. It was late morning, but I couldn't have said what day of the week it was. There were people *everywhere*. Cars were crashed into the buildings and each other, but all of them were now vacant. Red and black blood stained the stars with celebrities' names. The famous Chinese Theatre was straight ahead of me with demons crawling over every inch of it. To my left, the Roosevelt Hotel had orange flames bursting from nearly every window.

A loud Godzilla-like roar ripped through the chaos to my left and windows shattered in the buildings behind us. That big bug-greater demon flew back and slammed into the wax museum, crumbling it to pieces. Koth hovered over it, shooting a river of fire into its face. Silas was dive bombing it, ripping its arms off as fast as they grew back. A wall of fire and red lightning moved toward us from a few blocks down, along with the heavy stench of maple syrup and fleeing demons.

All of this happened in *seconds*.

But I was looking for Asmodeus.

Bright golden spotlights flashed in every direction. I spun toward it just in time to see a blonde girl fly backwards and flip head-over-heels before crashing to the ground. Warmth and magic radiated out of her.

"JACKSON—NADIA!"

He made it ten feet when Henley—*the shadow demon* —pounced on our new Sun Card.

"Dad, Hope!" I pointed to my left. "Demons!"

"SHAKE AND BAKE!" Hope screamed and charged ahead of my father, already shooting ice.

There was a sea of demons scrambling in every direction. I tapped my golden bands and felt the sweet relief of my grandfather's sword in my hand. Heavenly power pulsed unlike anything I'd ever felt. I glanced left and right, up and down. *Where are you?*

I moved into the street, pulverizing demons with my glowing six-foot-tall blade.

Then I saw *him*.

I knew it was him instantly.

He had long dark hair except for two white strips around his face. Tall black horns made of hematite stood from the top of his head. He wore a long black tunic, black pants, and black boots. Glowing green orbs were strung and draped over his chest and shoulders.

My pulse quickened. I knew damn well whose job it was to fight this guy. Grandson of an angel versus an ancient fallen angel. *No big deal.* I was six-foot-five now and Asmodeus was at least half a foot taller than me, not counting the horns. But I couldn't let myself think about it. There was no one else. This was *my* job. I charged for him, slicing smaller demons into ash as I moved.

And then he turned and our eyes met. He frowned. His eyes were the same glowing green as the orbs on his necklaces, but they had lightning bolts shooting out of them. "*Michael?*"

I froze.

"Oh, it's *YOU*." Asmodeus shook his head and grinned. A sword suddenly appeared in his hand, and he pointed it at me and then chuckled. "My, my, did you have parents or were you a straight clone?"

I clenched my teeth and raised my sword. *Shit, shit, shit, shit, shit.*

Fear was not something I felt often during a fight.

But I felt it now.

"Have you met him yet?" Asmodeus taunted me with that grin that sent chills down my spine. "Have you seen just how identical you are to him?"

I kept my mouth shut. I didn't know his angle here, but I wouldn't let him get to me.

"My, my, and with his sword?" He pressed his hand to his chest. "If I didn't know better, I'd say you *were* Michael."

I arched one eyebrow. *What's your play here, dude? Why is this your angle? What are you doing?*

A group of demons charged for me, but Asmodeus barked out words in that demonic language and they froze mid-step and scrambled away from me.

Asmodeus lifted his hands out to his sides and demons popped up through the cracks in the sidewalks like weeds. He grinned and shouted to them. And then he pointed his sword back at me. *"This one is mine."*

I tightened my grip on my sword—*and then he was there.* His glowing green blade swung down right at my head with blinding speed. My body took over, instantly blocking his attack with Michael's sword. White and green light flashed and sparkled. Electric sparks buzzed up my arms.

Asmodeus spun away, then stopped a few feet back. He cackled and clapped his hands—his sword *gone.* "I see you've got his speed, Little Michael. But what about—"

A wall of green and black swirling magic rolled for me like a tsunami, crumbling the asphalt in its wake. I cursed and pushed my own magic into it. Green and blue collided with his darkness. I planted my feet and forced as much of it as I could. I sent hurricane-force winds into him with whatever debris was in my path.

Green lightning sliced through the storm of my making, so I called it back—not because I needed to but because I wanted him to think he'd gotten the best of me. He didn't need to know the extent of my abilities.

"*OH.* You've got his power all right." He threw his head back and cackled, then shook his hands out. "Haven't felt that in a while. This is going to be fun. Tell me, Little Michael, do you have his skill, too?"

I didn't have time to answer or to think before he charged for me. I rolled to the balls of my feet and willed my body to glow for an extra boost of power. Long, glowing green blades formed in his hands a split second before he swung for me.

The world disappeared around us.

All I saw was the flash of his swords clashing against mine. We moved up and down the street through clouds of black smoke and streams of fire. He charged for me over and over, but I knew it wasn't his full strength. I didn't think I was *that* good. And then it hit me, were we both just distracting the other while holding our best back. I knew the longer he fought me, the less my Coven-mates would to. I also knew better than to show all my cards right away. I didn't know what Asmodeus was capable of, but I didn't want him to know that for me either.

We were playing the same game.

And I didn't know what that said about me.

Asmodeus was *cheering* and whistling. He cackled while he attacked me. "Lilith underestimates you, *but I won't.*"

Our swords clashed over our heads, magic pulsing and crashing together.

Heat filled my chest so fast I hissed.

Asmodeus's eyes flashed with excitement. He opened his mouth—

Rainbow magic exploded all around us.

I gasped.

TEGAN?!

The black smoke and fire evaporated in an instant. All of the smaller demons burst to ash and dust the second the rainbow mist touched it. Over Asmodeus's shoulder, I saw the big giant bug-greater demon narrow its eyes and snarl—then vanish into shadow.

I knew I needed to keep my eyes on Asmodeus, but my head

turned on its own volition—turning until my gaze landed on a girl dressed in all black with hair as white as freshly fallen snow. Her gold and white eyes blazed with fury and pure, raw power. A red heart-shaped crystal glyph glittered from the center of her chest. She hovered above the ground with her arms spread out to her side and magic pouring out of her palms.

TEGAN.

My heart flipped in my chest and kicked into overdrive.

Asmodeus growled and it sent vibrations down my arms from where our swords were still touching. "*YOU.*"

Tegan snarled. Her whole body lit up as white as her hair and then she thrust her arms forward. All I saw was a flash of white and then Heavenly power slammed into my back. It shot through my body like I'd been struck by lightning—except it didn't hurt. It tingled and burned the same way Michael's sword did. The Heavenly power raced up my arms and into Michael's sword—

Asmodeus hissed and yanked his arms back. His body was smoking up in a white cloud. He pointed at Tegan and growled *—and then he was gone.*

"NO!" Henley screamed bloody murder from behind Tegan.

She turned to shadow and slipped around Jackson—*who I realized had been fighting the shadow demon the entire time* —and charged for Tegan.

My eyes widened. I pointed. "*Babe!*"

The look in Tegan's eyes were ice cold and lethal. She spun and slammed Henley right in the face with a beam of rainbow-colored magic. Henley flew up in the air and flipped. Tegan's magic coiled around Henley's ankles and yanked her back down to the rainbow-painted ground. She landed in a cloud of magic. Henley—*the shadow demon*—jumped up and fired magic at Tegan, but *he* was no match for her there. Her rainbow magic literally swallowed it whole.

The shadow demon tried to turn to shadow to get away, but Tegan was merciless and vicious. I had to focus on the glistening red eyes in Henley's face to stop myself from interfering. Tegan would never hurt Henley but each hit of magic made me flinch nonetheless.

"HENLEY!" Royce screamed from somewhere behind me.

I didn't look for him. My eyes were locked on Tegan.

That white hair whipped around like a cape. The power radiating off her made the hairs on my arms stand tall. My golden bands were flashing even with Michael's sword in my hand, like they wanted *more*.

Henley screamed and I heard several people gasp.

It sounded like *Henley*.

But it wasn't. Those eyes were still red.

Lightning shot down from the sky, striking the street all around Henley. Magic slithered like snakes along the asphalt. A rainbow-colored arrow pierced right through her chest. Henley gasped and lifted off the ground, her back arching. My stomach rolled. Every nerve ending in my body tightened. I wanted to look away, but I didn't want to miss anything.

I'd never seen *this* Tegan.

It reminded me of the night when she borrowed all our magic and locked us in a—

Glowing magical bars dropped down on top of Henley, melding with the sheet of magic beneath her...trapping her inside of a cage.

Henley's body hit the bottom and didn't move.

The street fell silent, but I felt each and every one of my Coven-mates behind me.

Tegan spun around and smirked. "Sorry I'm late?"

CHAPTER FORTY

TENNESSEE

My breath left me in a rush. I bent over and rested my hands on my knees as the tsunami of relief destroyed me. My heart thundered in my veins.

Tegan's black, studded, filthy combat boots appeared in front of me. Her fingers pressed under my chin and forced me to look up. She grinned at me with those creepy gold and white eyes sparkling and that white hair swaying in the California breeze. "You were right."

I stood up straight and shook my head. "About what?"

"I *could* hear you."

Tears I did not welcome stung the backs of my eyes and a hot lump formed in my throat. She jumped up and coiled her arms around my neck. I sighed as the warmth of her body chased away those last few chills of fear. I groaned and squeezed her to my chest as hard as I could, digging my fingers into her body. If I was hurting her, she showed no signs. I felt her fingers grab fistfuls of my hair.

"Thank you for pulling me out," she whispered in my ear.

A broken half-groan, half-sob slipped from my mouth. I closed my eyes and buried my face in the crook of her neck.

No one said a thing around us, but I felt their eyes on my back. This was not the moment to lose control of my emotions. I took a few more deep breaths, soaking in the scent of her, then forced myself to pull back...and slowly release my hold on her.

She slipped out of my arms with a grin on her face. She winked to me and then turned, leaving a hand pressed to my chest. "Anyone hurt?"

Jackson scoffed and gestured around. "In general, or just bloody now?"

"I don't like that answer." Tegan chuckled softly. "Nice chest, Lancaster."

Royce let out a strangled cry and sprinted for Henley's cage.

Without looking, Tegan flicked her wrist and Royce slammed into an invisible forcefield around Henley's cube of magic. "Don't touch it, Royce. I'm not hurting her. I promise. But it *will* hurt *you* severely if you touch it."

"WHAT DID YOU DO?"

At that, Tegan looked to him. "I'm done playing this game. She's going to stay in there until we figure out how to kill that damn demon. We're not risking her another second longer."

Royce sank to his knees and scrubbed his face. Deacon limped over to his cousins, and I noticed his limp had definitely gotten worse. *What the hell just happened to him?* At that, I glanced around for the first time myself, silently taking a head count. It appeared everyone was present—of those who came with us. Everyone seemed to be in good condition, apart from Easton's cast, Chutney's head bandages, Deacon's limp, and Jackson's chest gash.

Hope pushed between Cooper and Braison and sprinted for Tegan. She pulled her best friend in for a hug, but only held it for a few seconds. Then she stepped back, gripped Tegan's shoulders, and literally shook her. *"Damn it, woman!"*

Tegan giggled. "I second the feeling. Trust me."

Movement out of the corner of my eye made me jump—but it was only my father.

Carrying a cute, sandy blonde girl with wide hazel eyes. His hands were gripping her biceps, holding her feet a foot off the ground. She was wearing one of those puffy coats that went down to her knees and had a fur-lined hood. In Los Angeles. For some reason, my mind focused on this strange detail.

Easton charged for her but Cooper, Jackson, and Uncle Tim all caught him and stopped him a few feet back. They held on to him while he whined and fought against their hold. "*Please, let me—*"

Tegan held her hand up and Easton's mouth slammed shut. Her creepy gold and white gaze was locked on the new girl in the winter coat. My heart skipped beats, but I wasn't sure why I was suddenly so nervous. Maybe it was because this was the first moment we'd had her in front of us. This was our moment to find out if it was true...if she'd been Marked.

My soulmate walked to my father and stopped. "Let go of her, please, Kessler."

Braison shook his head, his red hair flying. "Tegan, she could—"

"I'd like to see her *try*." Tegan cocked a wicked smirk. She snapped her fingers and my father's grip on her dropped. She arched one eyebrow at the girl. "Name?"

"Nadia B-B-Bowen."

The girl was trembling from head to toe. Her face was pale and her eyes wide. But I couldn't feel bad for her fear, not yet, not until we knew whether or not she was innocent in her role of summoning the fallen angel, Asmodeus—a true Prince of Hell.

I moved to stand beside my soulmate, wanting to get a closer look at her.

"I'm Tegan Bishop, the High Priestess. Take off your jacket, please?"

Nadia's eyes somehow got wider. She stared for a second, then nodded and yanked her long puffy coat off. I felt my Coven-mates' magic tense. I knew what we were all looking for. But Nadia had on a long-sleeved shirt.

Tegan wiggled her fingers and Nadia's left arm floated up. She then reached down with her chipped black nail-polished fingers and slid Nadia's gray sleeve up to her elbow.

There on the inside of her left forearm were three black letters.

XIX.

The Sun.

My breath left me in a rush.

"NO," Easton screamed but his voice was ragged. "*Nooooo. No, no, no, no.*"

Deacon hobbled over just as Easton collapsed and sank to the ground. Emersyn was suddenly there, pulling him into her arms as he broke. Everyone near him reached out and grabbed ahold of him as he fell apart. Bentley crouched down and slipped his hand around to press to his chest—orange magic coiled around his hand and he frowned.

Easton sobbed and tugged on his hair while he rocked back and forth.

Tegan's face fell. She flicked her wrist and the white portal box of hers opened up directly beside them. "Deacon, take him to Eden. He doesn't need an audience...and you need that leg healed."

Deacon nodded and dragged Easton through the portal.

As the white light faded, Nadia's eyes widened. "What did I do to him?"

I cringed and rubbed my chest to try and ease the pressure. *Lily is dead. I can't believe it. How did this happen?* My mind didn't want to believe it.

"His girlfriend has been the Sun for over a decade," Chutney said softly with tears in her eyes. "She went into

Seelie. We haven't seen her or heard from her…and then you got Marked."

"*She died?*" Nadia shrieked.

"Maybe she didn't though?" Chutney squeaked. "We don't know! No one has heard from them."

Cooper grimaced.

My eyes widened. My heart stopped. "Cooper Bishop. Start talking."

He sighed and pinched the bridge of his nose. "A while ago I was able to connect to Savannah's dreams—"

"*AND?*" We all yelled.

He shook his head. "I don't think it's good, guys. She told me they'd been separated, she was lost, and the Knights were tracking her. I helped her try and get them off her back, but I haven't heard anything else."

"So she might be—"

"Might is not a word we need right now. But speaking of *right now…*" Tegan raised her left hand and curled her fingers. "Jackson."

He hurried over to stand between me and her. "Ready."

"Okay, Nadia, here's the deal. This is Jackson Lancaster. He's the World Card. He's a lie detector, so I'm going to ask you a few questions and you're going to answer them. Got it?"

"Yes," Nadia breathed and wrung her hands together.

I couldn't imagine this was an easy moment—with all of us pissed off, scared, and circling around her.

"Is your name Nadia Bowen."

Nadia nodded, and then Jackson nodded.

"Were you told you are the new Sun Card?"

Nadia nodded. Jackson nodded.

"By who?"

Nadia licked her lips and glanced over Tegan's shoulder to where Henley lay unconscious in her magical cage. "Henley did. Or, that girl there with the red eyes."

"Truth," Jackson whispered.

"What were you doing when you were Marked? Where did she find you?"

"I had walked out onto the Hay River—I live in the Northwest Territories of Canada." Her gaze bounced around. "Everything is frozen and covered in snow, so I was way out on the frozen river to...to...well, to do a special funeral ritual for my aunt."

I frowned. "A funeral ritual? What kind?"

"Um, I'm not entirely sure. My Aunt Dora had written down the instructions—oh, wait." She fumbled in the pocket of her jeans, then pulled out a folded up piece of parchment and handed it to Tegan. "This is it. I followed what she wrote exactly, and I used the dried flowers she'd been saving for it."

Tegan unfolded the paper and I saw writing and sketches on it. Tegan smiled. "Her husband died on the river—"

"*What?*" Nadia paled.

Tegan shrugged. "This is a ritual for widows. It's quite old magic so I'm not surprised your aunt who lived far from thriving society still used it. Short answer, a widow will take necessary steps like this to prepare for their death and then their family will act out the final wish. The ritual tells the spouse who died first that their partner has joined them in the afterlife so they could let themselves go. It's quite sweet, actually. Totally harmless, too."

Jackson shook his head. "Sometimes I'm glad I can tell when you're lying or not. That's cool."

Tegan winked at him with her creepy eyes. "So, Nadia, you were Marked right after this?"

She nodded. "I finished the ritual and then...well, I don't know if She listened or if it was coincidence, but I prayed to the Goddess to ask for help—and instantly my arm burned."

"Is the help you need a personal matter?" Tegan asked softly.

Nadia nodded.

"Will you tell me later in private?"

Nadia bit her bottom lip and glanced around, then looked back to Tegan and nodded.

"Now, what did you know about The Coven before Henley arrived?"

Nadia let out a frustrated sigh and ran both hands through her sandy hair. "Not much. I know what you're trying to figure out, but you don't understand. My mom married a human. She taught us bare basics of magic, and really only to control and conceal what we have to protect the species. We weren't even taught the ancient language. We, as in my younger sister and I, were basically humans...and then our parents died and we were shipped off to our aunt in Hay River. She lived a simple, quiet, small town life. She taught us magic for surviving her lifestyle, which was only a tiny bit more than my mom taught us. *I didn't even know you could use candles!*"

Jackson nodded but didn't speak.

I sighed. "Take a deep breath, Nadia."

She sniffled and wiped the tears out of her hazel eyes. "I was only taught that The Coven ruled our kind and killed the demons—so they had extra magic and power. I knew about the Cards but not in detail. And I wasn't even sure if demons were real. I'd never seen one. My sister and I thought my mom made them up to scare us into behaving. When I was Marked, I was afraid to ask if they were real because I didn't want anyone to make fun of me. Or to think I'm weak. I just...I didn't know they could look like that. She said...Henley...she was so nice to me."

"What did she say?" Tegan narrowed her eyes. "When she took you from Canada, what did she say?"

"She said the Sun and Moon have a connection and can always find each other—"

"*Is that true?*" Emersyn hissed.

Tegan nodded. "Yes. Their dirty little secret. Go on, Nadia."

"She said that was how she found me so fast. She said she was on her way to do a special healing ritual for the Tower Card —" she gasped. *"Oh my God. Frankie! Did we hurt her?"*

My stomach tightened into knots. "I was going to ask you the same."

"My magic is protecting Frankie as best it can. I think he just needed to tap into Coven power. We'll discuss her later. What else, Nadia?"

"I swear on my life, she told me we were helping Frankie. But then the magic was hurting me and I knew something was off, but it was too late. I couldn't control my own body. I don't know how to use my magic. Then it ended and *he* was there." She shivered and cringed. "Then we were suddenly here...and that big bug arrived...and then he just...I tried to stop them and she attacked me. Then you all showed up."

Tegan was silent a moment, then looked to her right. "Jackson?"

"She's telling the truth."

"Okay." Tegan flicked her right wrist and Bentley flew through the air and then stopped beside me. "Benny?"

He smirked and rubbed his palms together. Orange magic sparked to life like flames on a bonfire. Orange crescents flashed in his golden eyes. He took a step toward her. Nadia paled and jumped back but slammed into my father's chest. He held her shoulders to steady her.

Bentley pressed his palm to Nadia's chest. Tegan reached out and wrapped her hand around his left forearm. Orange lightning bolts streaked across his back and down his arms, shining even through his dark shirt. Thick black smoke billowed from under his palm, flickering through his fingers into the air around them. Orange magic flashed and sparkled. Nadia's hazel eyes were wide, and I could hear her teeth rattling from where I stood.

Bentley dropped his hand and stepped back, his magic fading as fast as it came. He looked to Tegan and then nodded.

Tegan sighed. She grabbed Nadia's jacket from where it'd fallen to the ground, then unzipped the pocket and pulled Nadia's phone out. She handed it to Nadia. "Call your neighbor and check on your nieces."

Nadia gasped. "*W-wh-what?* How do you—how did you—"

"I heard everything."

"Wait, what?" Hope shrieked. She put her hands on her hips and arched one black eyebrow. "Like that whole time? Since you went down?"

Tegan pursed her lips and shrugged. "That's debatable, but I definitely heard everything from the blood bath on."

"*You son of a bitch,*" Hope said with a laugh and a smile.

"So, you heard about the other greater demon she summoned?" Jackson used his hands to imitate having horns. "Because we don't know what the bloody hell that thing is."

"Leviathan."

The ground shook and I actually swayed on my feet. Weight crashed down on my shoulders and on my chest.

My father's face fell. "That can't be possible..."

"That's *Leviathan?*" Uncle Tim practically shouted. "You're sure?"

"Positive."

Cooper frowned and pointed to where Asmodeus was last standing. "And that dude was—"

"Asmodeus." Tegan nodded. Her face showed no emotion whatsoever. Like we weren't talking about two Princes of Hell. Two fallen angels fighting for Lilith. "I know. And he's not done."

Hope narrowed her eyes. "Leviathan? I recognize the name but....?"

"He was an angel, born in Heaven. His wrath and rage consumed him and turned him into a beast," Tegan said quietly, her voice dangerously smooth. "He's the creator of beasts."

Jackson put his hands on his hips and hung his head. "So we've got *two* fallen angel demon wankers here? Asmodeus and Leviathan. And now we've lost the only thing left to track them?"

"What about *her*?" Chutney growled. "Maybe she can track them?"

"That's not how that works, Chutney. She can't lead us to them. And she's the Sun Card, whether we like it or not, which means she's with us now." Tegan turned to Nadia. "I'm sorry I had to be so harsh just now. Even though I heard the whole thing, I had to do my job just in case."

"I am so confused," Nadia cried. "I didn't know...I don't know...what's going on?"

I sighed and pointed to Henley. "*That* is technically Henley Redd, our Moon Card. However, she was possessed by a shadow demon not too long ago."

"Fun fact: red eyes typically mean demonic presence." Tegan winked and handed Nadia her jacket. "I thought I was human until last August. I understand not knowing what's going on. And to be honest, I trusted these guys faster than I logically should have. I simply got lucky they were good."

"So...so you're saying the Coven Leaders didn't go to pick up my nieces like she told me?"

I shook my head. "As one Coven Leader, I assure you we did not."

"I'm the other Coven Leader. Sadly, I've been a little unconscious for a bit, so I didn't either. I don't think they're in any danger but call to make sure." Tegan held Nadia's phone out higher. "Take it. Call Carol. Say whatever you want but just make sure she keeps the girls until we can get to them...because it won't be today."

Nadia's jaw dropped and tears filled her eyes. "Am...am I in trouble?"

I glanced to my soulmate.

I believe she is genuinely innocent, so I say no. What do you say, babe?

I wanted to be mad at Nadia. I wanted to blame her for Asmodeus getting in. I wanted someone else to be at fault. But the truth was it was *our* fault. We let the shadow demon have Henley. We let her stay possessed when we could have pulled her out. We left Frankie in that hospital instead of bringing her to Eden.

How the hell did he summon two greater demons? Two Princes of Hell?

The truth was we'd made decisions that set Nadia up for failure.

I sighed and pushed my hair back. "No, Nadia. You're not in trouble. But you're also not to leave our sides. Your ignorance, although understandable, is a risk factor. Make sure your family is safe. If you'd like, Tegan can call and give them a good cover story for why you won't be back for a few days."

"A few days?"

"We have to handle Asmodeus and Leviathan, and we're going to need every Card member we have—" Tegan frowned and glanced around the group. "Where are my parents?"

Emersyn groaned. "Mom hasn't woken from when you knocked her out."

"Dad broke his leg before we got to the archway." Cooper shook his head. "Dad is healing fine, but he won't leave Mom's side."

Tegan cursed and flicked her wrist. A white portal box opened up and then we all flew through it at her command. When the light faded, we were in the foyer of the Los Angeles Headquarters—which I only recognized because I'd visited with my father and Cooper a few times. Koth, Silas, and Maddox were still in their dragon forms, so their heads slammed into the ceiling. Their tails swept across the room and knocked people off their feet. Several people grunted and grumbled. I managed to jump over Koth's tail, but I was one of the few left standing. Only Jackson and my father were upright.

"*Whoaa,*" Braison grumbled.

Well, that was unexpected.

"OW, TEGAN!" Cooper growled from somewhere under Silas's tail.

"My bad." Tegan coughed and pushed Koth's tail off her chest, then pulled her own *still white* hair out of her mouth. "My bad."

"Your bad?" Maddox shrieked as he shifted back. "You could have killed us."

"I didn't succeed? Shit." Tegan pulled Koth's tail off Chutney. She was *grinning* like this was some inside joke. "My plan was flawless."

There were lots of unfriendly comments after that. Apparently, the novelty of my soulmate rejoining us had worn off quickly. I tried not to laugh and failed.

And then I heard Emersyn snorting.

Cooper sat up and turned wide incredulous eyes to his sister. "*Why are you laughing?*"

There was a creak from the stairs beside me and then someone shouted, "*Who's down there?*"

"I don't know—" Tegan snorted. "But I think I broke some of them."

"*Some of us?*" Braison snapped.

Emersyn rolled onto her side and laughed so hard she was tearing up.

Tegan bent over and laughed. "I think they're mad, dude."

Just then Hope's head popped up from under Silas's tail and she had tears running down her face from laughing—but there was no noise coming out.

Jackson scowled. "What's happening here, lads?"

Footsteps thundered down the stairs and then the Los Angeles Major, Hilary, came into view. Her brown eyes widened. She turned to me. "Emperor?"

I waved and shook my head. "Hi."

"*Hilary, how many are down there?*" The other Major, Brooke, shouted down the stairs.

"*Why, you wanna tally your score?*" Emersyn wheezed.

"Oh, feisty. I like it." Tegan cackled and helped pull Hope to her feet.

Hilary's face paled. She held two daggers up but looked to me in confusion.

Tegan, Emersyn, and Hope were lost in giggles that we clearly missed the memo on.

I shrugged. "It's been a weird few months."

"Sorry, sorry!" Tegan chuckled and wiped her gold and white eyes. She gestured to her twin and best friend. "That's almost literally how we met, and what was said."

I shook my head. "We've all officially lost it, Hilary. *Brooke,* you can come down. It's just us."

Brooke, wife to Hilary, came flying down the steps, then slid to a stop. "Hils?"

"I'm not sure. But The Coven and some dragons are here." Hilary frowned. "Which one of you is Cassandra? The one who called and ordered us to lockdown headquarters and stay inside?"

"And Bentley, the Hierophant who warned us this morning to lockdown Hollywood Boulevard as much as possible?"

Jackson spun on Bentley with wide eyes. "*C'mon, mate. What?*"

Bentley shrugged. "I saw it needed to be done, but I didn't know why."

"Such a wanker," Jackson whispered under his breath.

My pulse skipped. "*Cassandra* called you? When?"

Hilary pursed her lips. "Minutes before the attack started."

Tegan snorted. "I like her style."

"Tegan." I shook my head. "What do you know?"

My father sighed and turned to our two Majors. "Ladies, two greater demons attacked your city just now. They're gone, but there's major cleanup to be done. Do you need our assistance or are you prepared?"

"We've got it." Hilary nodded and tied up her curly brown hair. "We're ready to move."

Brooke, who was a petite and pretty little blonde thing who barely stood over five feet tall, pointed a neon-colored fingernail behind me. "And *what* is that? Is that the Moon Card in a cage?"

I glanced over my shoulder. Henley was still unconscious, which was probably a good thing. "Long story. Tegan? What do you know about Cassandra?"

Just then her phone rang from inside of her pocket. She pulled it out and hit the speakerphone button.

"Tegan." Cassandra's voice rang through the room. "*Get to Nashville.*"

THE KING's glowing blue river carried us right over the edge of the terrace before we could grab onto something to stop. Like barrels on a waterfall, we plummeted to the bottom, sinking beneath the water. Waves crashed and rolled, pulling us under before spitting us back out. I kicked and tried to get to the surface, but my body was not participating right. Riah's arm dropped down to my waist and squeezed—and then I was shooting straight up.

My head burst through the surface and warm air slammed into my face. I gasped for air, then choked on a cough. I spent far too long out of the water. It was like my body always needed a minute to remember what to do.

"*Saraphina?*" Riah's voice cracked.

I wiped my eyes and then opened them to find his face right in front of mine. His golden eyes were latched on me, but when I smiled and nodded they fell shut, like it took all of his strength to propel me out. I kicked myself. He was weak, I needed to stop needing saving.

My father coughed from the other side of Riah, with my soulmate's arm still hooked over his shoulder. He nodded to me and then squinted up to the palace looming over us. I glanced over my shoulder and sighed as I spotted Savannah, Willow, Amelia, and Landy all hanging on to each other and breathing. Ziva was riding Squishy's back, and he looked thrilled to be in the water.

Ziva's hazel eyes widened. She glanced around in a panic—

The water dropped again.

I gasped—

A loud screech ripped through the silence in the distance. *The beast.* Then it hit me. We were over the tunnels. I cursed and pushed up higher out of the water. The current was still gunning strong, but it was getting lower from water dropping into the tunnels.

The beast screeched again, this time almost beneath us.

The tunnels trembled.

There was a flash of light, then a person with blue hair appeared out of the corner of my eye. *THE KING!* I gasped and spun toward him—and froze. It was Princess Sage. She held her hands up and water gushed from her palms just like they had from her father's. I hadn't known either one of them had water power. She pushed the rushing tide over the edge of the holes and down into the tunnels. With each splash, the beast shrieked and the walls shook.

Yet we weren't sinking with the water. She was keeping us above ground.

Hope flared in my chest. Maybe Riah was right.

She looked to Riah with those violet eyes and scowled. There was a flash of light and cold air—and my knees hit the green vine floor of the Seelie tunnel. Riah crashed down beside me, his huge, heavy arm pushing my chest into the floor. But I held him up. My father helped me get him upright, but his head rolled. The bruises and wounds on his body seemed *worse*.

Sage cursed. She slammed her hand into the tunnel wall

and a hole opened up instantly. "Ziva, take Squishy and go. This will drop you at the village."

"What?" Savannah hissed. "She's not coming with us? Squishy?"

Squishy wined and licked Savannah's face, then hopped over to lick mine before hurrying to the opening in the tunnel wall next to Ziva.

Ziva turned to us with the cold expression of a warrior. "One day I will go home to Earth with you. For now, they need my help here until you can return. I'll see if I can save Paulina, but don't trust a hope."

I didn't want to accept it. I wanted to argue and demand they come with us. But I knew she was right. Ziva and Squishy were fierce warriors with skills The Circle needed to maintain their revolution. I nodded. "Be careful. I'll be back soon."

Sage caught Ziva by the arm and narrowed her eyes. "Fight smart."

Ziva nodded. She waved to us, then both her and Squishy leapt out of the tunnel opening and out of sight. Sage lifted her hand and the tunnel vines sealed shut instantly. Riah coughed and slumped in our hold.

"He'll get stronger on Earth. My father's magic is killing him here." Sage walked around us to the other side of the tunnel.

I glanced to my friends. "We okay? All here?"

Savannah cursed and held Willow up. Amelia and Landy were clinging to each other. They were alive. That was all that mattered. Lily's face flashed through my thoughts. My heart broke all over again.

"You better hurry," Sage said with a growl. When I looked up, I found she'd opened a new hole. She held her other hand out and my clothes instantly dried. Then she nodded to the hole. "Your Coven is in a war they can't yet win. GO."

My stomach dropped. My father and I lifted Riah up. I waved my other hand. "Girls, go first."

Sage smirked and arched one eyebrow. She waited until all four of them were gone to look at me and say, "If you don't trust me by now, we're all doomed."

A gust of wind slammed into my back, then my father, Riah, and I were flying through the tunnel opening. I glanced back in time to watch it close and vanish completely. *If you don't trust me by now.* Her words echoed.

"OH MY GOD!" Savannah screamed. "GET DOWN!"

I spun around just as a massive demon swooped over our heads. Amelia and Landy dove for the ground, but Willow was too slow. The wing of the demon knicked her in the head and she collapsed.

Amelia scrambled to her. "She's alive!"

Rainbow magic flashed left and right. I gasped. *TEGAN.* But then I looked up and my heart dropped right out of my ass.

Sage had dropped us right in the middle of a war.

Memories flashed in my mind from a long time ago. For a moment, I was back in Salem watching The Coven battle the twins *and* the surge demons coming through the open Gap. The sky was red and the air was cold. Demons swarmed the sky like stars. There was a river on my right and a small grassy hill on my left that led straight up to tall brick buildings. Demons with glowing red eyes emerged from the water one after another. Everywhere I looked were big black monstrosities.

"Where are we? What year is it?" I heard myself yell in a panic.

"This is not Salem," Riah said in a little bit stronger of a voice. "Look, Saraphina."

I looked up and my vision cleared. The memories vanished, leaving only awful truth in front of me. This was a new war. I didn't recognize the setting, but I knew that rainbow magic and it made me cry. Streams of fire streaked across the field. Red lightning flashed.

"Poison Roycy, you bitch!"

A horde of demons rushed toward us—then turned to ice and dropped to the ground. I saw two blond heads and red hair pounce on them. There was a roar and then a demon flew up *ripped in pieces*. My heart skipped. *The Coven. My Coven. They're here. We're back.*

A dark object with gold wings shot like a comet across the sky with a glowing six-foot-long sword in his hand. Demons burst to dust in his wake. *TENN!*

"*Oh my Goddess,*" Amelia whispered. "What...what..."

"*What do we do?*" Landy hissed.

Savannah turned wide blue eyes on her. "Stay the fuck down, ma'am. Stay alive!"

"SAFFIE!" Tegan screamed.

I couldn't see her in the chaos, but rainbow magic covered the sky.

STAY DOWN! She shouted in my mind.

The ground shook under my knees, knocking all of us off balance. We all crashed face-first to the grass. A roar like a dinosaur pierced through the chaos. I pushed up on all fours and froze. *What the hell is THAT?*

A creature I'd never seen stood up and towered over the fight. It was blood red—some kind of horrific mutant demon. It was like a giant worm with arms and legs like tree branches. Horns stood tall from its head above glowing red eyes.

My father cursed.

Riah gasped. "*Leviathan.*"

Savannah crawled over to me, then pointed down by the river where a man in a black tunic with a glowing green necklace stood still. He grinned and his eyes glowed a brighter green than his necklace. He held his arms out to the sides and demons seemed to pour *out of him*.

"RIAH!" Savannah hissed and waved her arm. "WHO THE HELL IS THAT?"

Riah's face fell. His eyes seemed to glaze over with a

haunted expression. He took a deep breath, then whispered, "*Asmodeus.*"

My jaw dropped.

Asmodeus?! The greater demon?

Two black horns stood on his head. Pointed ears poked out from dark hair that had two white stripes in the front by his face. He threw his head back and laughed.

"*The keeper of demons,*" Riah whispered, then pushed up on his knees higher. He growled and his gold eyes flashed. "He's a general for Lilith."

In the distance, coming from behind us, I heard humans screaming and crying hysterically. A massive black dragon shot into the sky and spit fire onto a dozen demons, then he ducked his head and sped toward the human screams. Silas and Maddox raced after him.

Landy gasped. "*Maddox.*"

Amelia's eyes widened. "He's here. They're all here?"

"Ma'am, those three have been worried sick," Savannah said in a rush.

Three spider demons jumped up out of nowhere right in front of us. Silver magic shot over my shoulder and slammed into their chests, killing them in an instant. *Riah!*

The giant worm thing's head snapped toward us. Glowing red eyes scanned the ground in a panic until they landed on Riah. It froze, then in an almost-human voice, it growled. "My fight does not dwell with a Prince of Hell."

He vanished out of sight.

Asmodeus scowled. He looked toward us and scoffed, then pointed to Riah. "Who *him*? He's nothing!"

And then an angel landed ten feet in front of us with massive white wings.

Asmodeus's eyes widened. "Ohhh. *HIM.*"

Then he was gone.

The angel pulled his wings in and fired black colored magic

out of his hands in a wave. Every other demon died instantly when it touched them, bursting to dust and ash. A black dog covered with black smoke billowing around its body leapt over our heads and landed at the angel's feet. It whined and stomped its foot. The angel sighed and pulled his magic back just in time to leave a handful of demons up ahead.

The dog bolted, moving faster than smoke and pouncing on the demons. Black blood splashed in the air and on the grass.

A blonde woman with white angel wings landed next to the male angel. She shook her head and laughed. "*Spot.*"

The male angel turned, and my heart stopped.

I knew that face.

I'd seen it in the past.

He had short dirty blond hair cut in the same style as Deacon and Royce and pushed back off his face. Gold eyes shined bright.

MALACHI!

Riah choked on a gasp in my ear.

Dark blue light flashed under my face, and I knew my soul-mate glyph had changed colors.

Malachi grinned and then pointed to Riah. "I'll be right back. Don't move."

Then, just as fast as the demons had, Malachi, the blonde angel, and the smoky dog vanished.

CHAPTER FORTY-TWO

SAFFIE

ONCE THEY WERE GONE, I looked up to see all of The Coven staring at us with wide, tear-filled eyes and smiles on their face.

My breath left me in a rush. I sagged into Riah. I couldn't believe it. We did it. We made it back. My heart was still breaking over Lily, but I knew she'd want us to rejoice in our return.

For a moment, we just stared at each other.

And then The Coven was running for us.

Willow groaned and sat up.

White light flashed and then The Coven was right in front of us. Chutney dove for Willow, tackling her back to the ground with a loud shriek. Deacon and Emersyn rushed over to where Amelia and Landy had somehow wound up a few feet away. The power couple had the young girls wrapped in a tight bear hug.

"Thanks for those nightmares," Savannah said with a giggle.

I looked over just as Cooper pulled her into his chest. He sighed. "Thanks for not dying. If you did and are already back, don't tell me."

Behind them, I saw Bettina, Jackson, Kessler, and Timothy smiling at us. Royce tackled Deacon and the girls. Bentley went right to *my father* and crouched down to give him a hug.

Tennessee and Tegan knelt in front of me. They reached out and put their hands on mine and Riah's shoulders. Tegan's hair was still snow white and her eyes that eerie combo of white and gold. I wanted to know why she was still like that, why it had not worn off yet. Words were coming out of their mouths, but it was mush to my ears. All I heard was my own heart pounding. My emotions were going haywire, or maybe it was *all* of our emotions. Or maybe it was just Riah's. His supposedly dead brother had just shown up as an angel like it was no big deal and then vanished again. Our soulmate glyph had turned dark purple—the color for heartbreak. I didn't think anyone else had noticed yet. They were too excited about our return, but I felt his pain like it were my own.

"Wait..." Braison's voice sliced through my emotional whirlwind. "Where's Paulina?"

I looked up and met his green gaze. My heart stopped. Words dried on my tongue.

Braison glanced left and right, then spun around. "Where is she? Where's Paulina?"

Easton pushed up between the group with wildness in his eyes and black demon blood covering his cast. "Where. Is. Lily?"

My chest tightened.

Deacon, Emersyn, and Royce rushed over to us with wide eyes and paled faces. Tennessee's face fell. Tegan closed her eyes and hung her head. Willow collapsed in Chutney's arms, sobbing. Amelia and Landy looked to the ground, cringing with tears running down their faces. Savannah was crying, but her cheeks were red and her brow furrowed like she was furious.

A broken sob escaped my mouth before I could stop it.

Braison and Easton flinched. They blanched and swayed into each other.

"No," Braison whispered, and his eyes watered. He sagged but Kessler caught him.

Silver body armor flashed on and off of Easton's body. He balled his fist and his lip trembled. "NO. No, don't say—"

A cold, broken silence fell over us.

"Did they...fall?" Jackson whispered.

I couldn't get the words out. They just wouldn't come. Fresh tears spilled.

My father cleared his throat, then in a soft voice said, "Paulina was alive when we left but...stuck. Ziva went to help her. And when we go back, we'll get her."

Bentley nodded. "Ziva will get to her. We can count on her."

Savannah nodded and put her hands on her hips, but she stared at the ground. Braison exhaled so hard he practically fainted. Timothy grabbed ahold of him and eased him down to the ground so he wouldn't fall.

Easton stared at me with red eyes. His energy pulsed in wild, raw waves. "And Lily?"

"I'm..." My father cursed and shook his head. "I cannot say for certain. The Queen...it was not conventional—"

"Easton—"

"*NO, DEACON!*" Easton screamed. "I don't believe it!"

Deacon cringed. "Easton, a new Sun Card was Marked—"

"*Maybe she sacrificed it!*"

"She did not," my father whispered. He hadn't known Lily, but he had tried to save her. His voice was hollow. "I tried to stop it. I could not. We could not. She's—"

"*You said, for certain! Like there's a chance!*" Easton's whole face was red now. Tears pooled in his eyes. He was fighting it and I didn't blame him, but that wouldn't make it easier.

"What the Queen did, I have never seen happen, therefore I

have no idea if it is reversible...if she is...savable. I fear to give you hope you cannot trust. I fear she is gone."

Easton collapsed and a strangled, awful cry burst out of him. Everyone else rushed to him. Kessler had him in a bear hug, rocking him back and forth as he broke. The others all put their hands on him, holding him in any little way possible.

A shadow passed overhead and then three huge dragons landed behind the Easton-huddle.

Koth shifted into human form instantly, his eyes wide and glistening. "LANDY?"

Maddox, the navy-blue dragon, shot like a rocket and landed right in front of Landy. He shifted into human form and started *yelling* at her. It wasn't in English, but it was obviously a scolding. Landy flinched and stepped back from him.

Maddox leapt forward—

Amelia jumped in front of her and shoved Maddox right in the chest. "BACK THE FUCK OFF!"

"*YOU!*" Maddox growled and shoved his finger into her chest. "This is all *your* fault."

"Bite me," Amelia snapped back. She pulled her arm back and let that fist fly straight into his nose. Silvery magic burst out of her and into his face, sending him flying backwards.

Maddox shifted in the air and dove for her, teeth bared.

Amelia screamed—silver magic exploded out of her entire body and then she shifted into a white-winged lion as tall as Maddox. White fur stood up straight. Amelia-lion stood on all four legs and growled so loud the ground rumbled.

"*Oh shit,*" Royce breathed.

Amelia-lion and Maddox-dragon were face-to-face, snarling and spitting at each other.

"*It's about to go down,*" Savannah whispered.

Landy's eyes were so wide I saw the whites all the way around them.

Koth marched over in his human form and grabbed Maddox

by the tail and yanked him back, throwing him up in the air. Silas jumped up and blocked him from coming back. Amelia-lion was still growling and preparing to charge at him.

Koth walked up to Amelia-lion in his human form and stopped right in front of her. She may have been taller than him in her lion-form, but when he growled she cowered and sank down low to the ground. Her whole lion-body trembled. She looked around with panicked violet eyes. A low cry rumbled out of her which only made her shake worse. She was now face-to-face with Koth.

"It's okay, Amelia." Koth reached up and pressed his palms to the sides of her face. His voice was calm and smooth, like this was no big deal. "Just breathe. The more worked up you get, the harder to shift back."

Amelia-lion cried and trembled.

"I know. Trust me, I know," Koth whispered. "Just close your eyes and breathe."

Deacon started toward her, but Tenn yanked him back and shook his head.

"Concentrate on your breathing. Feel your magic calm inside of you. Maddox isn't getting anywhere near you. You're safe. I promise." Koth shot a glare at Maddox over his shoulder, then turned back to Amelia. He kept his hands on her fur. "We're going to count out of order, do it with me....ten...four... two...seven..."

Each number he said she repeated. They kept going until her silvery magic swirled around her and she shifted back into human form, back in that same outfit the King had put her in. She looked down at her hands, then broke down into tears. Koth sighed and pulled her into his chest, rubbing calming circles on her back.

A few moments later, he pulled back. I noticed he was careful only to touch her on her biceps, like he *knew* something had gone down in Seelie. He ducked his head to meet her gaze. "Was that your first shift?"

Amelia nodded.

"I thought so." He glanced over his shoulder and waved for Deacon. He turned back to her. "You're okay now."

Amelia said something, but I couldn't hear. And then Deacon was pulling her into his arms. She sank into him but kept her eyes on Koth.

Koth sighed and shook his head. "I knew you were one of us the moment I first met you. I just wasn't sure when it would manifest."

Amelia's jaw dropped.

Koth smiled and shrugged. "I can smell my own people."

"But..." Amelia frowned and looked up at Deacon. "But I'm arcana."

"Yeah, so you're both?" Tegan shrugged. "It's a long story, which I'm sure Elan would explain much better than we can, but...there are a small amount of arcana who inherited the shifter gene, allowing them to be both witch and shifter."

Deacon whistled. "I did not know this."

Tenn grimaced. "It's a bit of a secret among our race. They used to be dangerously hunted. There aren't many of them left."

"We keep them safe now," Timothy added.

"We keep them secret for sure." Kessler nodded.

Deacon shook his head. "Did you know she was?"

"Yes," Tenn and Tegan said at the exact same time.

Deacon's face fell. "Why didn't you tell?"

Tenn threw his hands up. "She was a kid. The gene usually comes out as older teens for these witches. Besides, she was in the right place, surrounded by shifters *with* dragons there. I knew she'd be okay if she shifted at SOMA."

Koth nodded. "I've been keeping an eye on both of them."

Landy's face fell. "I'm full shifter and yet I cannot shift."

Koth reached out and tugged on her long hair. "You will. I have zero doubts about it. Just be patient."

Koth turned to Tenn and Tegan, then glanced to Deacon. "I would like very much to take Landy *and Amelia* back to Issale with me. Not permanently, but just for a time. Landy needs to see Elan and to be on homeland for a while. And Amelia, I would very much like to teach her about her new gifts myself. What do you say, Deacon?"

Deacon shook his head. "It's not my call, but I can't think of a better place for Amelia for right now. What do you think Amelia?"

Amelia nodded immediately.

Koth walked closer to Tenn and Tegan, then whispered. "She is afraid."

Tegan chuckled. "I bet."

Koth frowned and scratched his jaw. "Most of the time when an arcana is blessed with our gift, it is a significantly smaller animal, not a predatory one. And definitely a human-known one."

Tenn pushed his hair back off his face. "She'll also have her magic to go along with it. Are you prepared for that?"

"Elan is, yes. I want her to learn control in a safe place without witnesses." Koth's expression turned dark and cold. "She is still a child, and children can be ruthless."

"*A CHILD?*" Royce shrieked and pointed. "Is no one going to address the literal teenagers in front of us?"

Bentley sighed. "I thought I would've served as good enough warning for this."

Tegan appeared in front of the girls. She took both their hands. "Close your eyes. Picture the outfit you'd like to have on right now—whatever would make you happiest."

They closed their eyes.

Rainbow magic swirled around them in miniature torna-does. When her magic vanished, both girls were in baggy sweatpants and oversized hoodies. They looked at each other's outfits and giggled, then high-fived.

Deacon hugged them both to his chest and then pulled back. "I didn't say anything because I can sense you're not ready to talk about it. You both know where to find me, *us,* when you are. Okay? No worries. No pressure. Hakuna matata."

Landy snorted and nodded.

Amelia teared up and hugged him again. She came up to his shoulders almost.

"I'll call Heather and Sebastien and tell them she's safe and going to Issale to be with Landy," Tenn yelled out to them. "I do not want to alarm them about her sudden gifts until she can return home with control."

Koth nodded. "Agreed."

Tenn arched one eyebrow. "Amelia?"

She paled but rushed over to him.

Tenn ducked his head to meet her eyes. "You are not in any kind of trouble, okay? We're very happy you're home safely. I'm sure this is scary for you, but you do not need to fear this ability. Koth will teach you how to use it and then I imagine you will find it quite fun."

"Once things settle a bit, we can introduce you to the others like you." Bentley nodded.

Amelia smiled. "Thanks, Bentley. *Old man.*"

Bentley grinned and winked. "*Infant.*"

They were already joking with each other about shared trauma. That had to be a good sign. Had to be. *Right? Right. Goddess, I hope so. These three children lost so much time.*

Koth growled. "I'll also be taking Maddox with me for some disciplinary action."

Maddox grumbled and hung his head.

"Silas, please take Landy. Maddox, if you so much as look at either one of these girls, I will redecorate the spines on your back. Got it?"

Maddox nodded.

Koth sighed and rolled his eyes like an exasperated parent. "Amelia, you'll be with me. Don't worry. Even if you shifted mid-air, I'd catch you."

And then she smiled. "Does this mean I can fly now?"

He chuckled and waved for her to follow him over toward where Landy was expertly climbing onto Silas's back. In the matter of seconds, Amelia was loaded up on Koth's back and waving to us. I sighed with relief. Those girls needed a little down time to recover.

Deacon frowned and turned to Tenn and Tegan. "Does she get that from her other side of the family?"

Tegan chuckled. "Yes."

"Damn," Deacon and Royce both said.

"Right. So that's done. Um..." Bettina frowned and eyed us strangely. "Okay, but has anyone else noticed the newbie or nah?"

My father chuckled and held his free hand up. "Sorry, was caught up in the moment. Hello, I am Saffie's father."

"Hetron," I added.

They gasped. Their eyes bounced back and forth between us like they were looking for the similarities. They wouldn't find much. His hair was reddish-brown whereas mine was bright, *red* red. My eyes were lavender, his were a pale gray. We actually didn't share a single feature, even our wings were different.

Jackson strolled up between Tennessee and Bettina and nodded. "He's telling the truth."

"*Y'ALL*," Emersyn yelled with a thicker accent than her usual. "We need to get Riah to Katherine. Can we focus?"

I gasped and turned to him. I'd been so captivated and shocked by what happened to Amelia that I hadn't been watching Riah. He'd spoken and was holding himself upright. Hell, he'd used his magic to kill those demons.

But I tipped his chin up and forced his eyes to meet mine.

His face was still darkly bruised and bleeding, but he was somehow looking a smidge better. "Riah? Can you hear me?"

He closed his eyes and whispered, "I think hallucinations have caught me."

"Well, that wouldn't be the first time for you. Would it, brother?"

CHAPTER FORTY-THREE

SAFFIE

RIAH GASPED and his eyes flew wide open. His face paled. His breath left him in shaky puffs. He swallowed roughly, then looked down to me. He didn't speak, but I heard the question in his eyes.

I smiled and purposely looked to where Malachi stood patiently behind him. Then I turned back to Riah and nodded.

His golden eyes glistened. His chest rose and fell as he breathed. He pulled his arms off mine and my father's shoulders.

I couldn't imagine how he felt right now, even as I was literally feeling it with him. For six hundred years, he mourned his brother's death like it'd just happened. I remembered in Salem while my memory was gone how he'd spoke of Malachi's death and how much it tortured him still—only to find out now that he was alive and standing right behind him.

There had to be a story, a reason for the lying. If I'd learned anything in my three centuries of life, it was that. To Malachi's credit, he didn't rush Riah. He didn't speak or groan or even move around to the other side to get in front of him. He was an *angel*. He could have easily. But he knew his brother needed a moment, so he was giving that to him.

My eyes filled with tears.

Slowly, Riah turned on his knees. He was only halfway around when his gaze landed on Malachi. He choked on a gasp and fell backwards. My father and I reached out and caught him, but he didn't seem to notice. Riah's jaw hung open. He blinked several times like he was sure this wasn't real. I squeezed his shoulder.

"*Malachi?*"

Malachi smiled and his cheeks flushed. I felt his emotions raging as hard as Riah's. They were both torn up over losing each other. I knew that knowing Riah was alive hadn't made the time apart any easier on Malachi. I could feel it in his soul.

"Hello, Brother. I hear you only go by Riah now," Malachi said in a rough voice, like there was something caught in his throat. "Mother must hate it."

A broken kind of sob came out of Riah's mouth. I felt his desire to get up, yet he wasn't moving. So I subtly glanced behind me to Tegan with her white hair and nodded, then turned back around. Suddenly, Riah climbed to his feet gracefully and then stood there on his own. I smiled. Tegan had a way of moving people that made it look natural, like they'd done it themselves. Whether or not anyone else realized she'd done that didn't matter.

The brothers were now face-to-face, separated by only a few feet.

And they looked so similar it was unnerving. They stood at the same height with the same body frame and size. They had the same golden eyes and hair, even though Malachi's was cut short. Their cheekbones and jawlines were identical—well, perhaps not while Riah was injured, but I had his face memorized in my mind. They looked the same. I couldn't even put my finger on what the differences were. Hell, they even wore the same dark gray jeans.

Riah just stared with tears in his eyes. "*Malachi...*"

"I've waited for this moment for six hundred years, my brother," Malachi said softly. His jaw flexed and he shook his head. "Though I admit I had pictured it with a lot less blood."

Riah laughed in a strangled, tortured kind of way and then he was moving toward him. Malachi crossed the distance and the two brothers all but tackled each other. This was no macho-man embrace. No *let's not show our emotions* embrace. This was a full-on, arms wrapped tight around each other and squeezing as hard as they could embrace. Riah sagged into his brother's arms as his strength weakened. I jumped to my feet and rushed over to stand beside them. But when I got there and saw just how tight his fingers dug into Malachi's back, a river of tears burst from my eyes.

Malachi squeezed his eyes shut and tightened his grip. He was going to be covered in blood after, but he didn't care. Behind him, the blonde angel girl moved closer. Her lips trembled as she fell apart watching them. She lifted her hand to wipe her eyes and I saw a soulmate crystal glowing a color somewhere between dark purple and dark blue—between heartbreak and sadness. I glanced to Malachi's right hand and saw the same one. My eyes widened. *Oh, she's his soulmate!*

Rainbow magic swirled around them and then they vanished.

The angel girl and I both gasped and reached forward—

"They're fine," Tegan said in a rush. "I just thought they deserved a moment alone."

I sighed and nodded. She was right. I knew that. But I wasn't moving until I could see him again.

The angel girl did a double take on our High Priestess, then narrowed her eyes. "*Tegan Bishop?*"

Tegan wagged her eyebrows and it made her eyes look super creepy. "Wasn't sure you'd remember me."

She arched one eyebrow. "You tricked me into summoning the demon I thought was trying to kill me...just so you could see a hellhound."

Tegan grinned and shrugged. "He's a good boy."

The dog—*hellhound*—barked from beside the girl. He had one red eye and one yellow eye, both glowing. He was bigger than any dog I'd ever seen, even Squishy.

Tenn sighed and shook his head. "*Kitten.*"

"*What?* You tellin' me you wouldn't seize the opportunity to meet a hellhound named Spot?" Tegan giggled and held her arms out. "Come here, good boy."

Spot dashed for her, jumping up into her arms. His black, smoky tail whipped back and forth as he squirmed and licked her face.

Chutney giggled and rushed toward him, instantly burying her hands and face in his fur. He went nuts for her, too. She laughed. "Oh, yes, Spot. Very, very good doggy."

"*SPOT,*" Malachi yelled under his breath. "Pull yourself together, man."

I turned and found the brothers standing side-by-side. Riah looked to me with a look so full of emotion it made my heart swell. Malachi was holding him upright so nonchalantly I doubted anyone noticed.

Spot nestled into the crook of Tegan's neck and let out a purr-like noise.

"We've talked about this, Spot." Malachi shook his head. "You're supposed to remain in scary hellhound mode until I say otherwise *and then* floofy doggo mode. We've practiced."

Spot picked his head up and looked to Malachi with his mismatching eyes and ears that flopped. He whined and howled.

"Yes, I know you like her—*yes,* I know she's scarier than you.

More reason to maintain—screw it. Fine. Cuddle." Malachi threw his free arm up. "But no one feed him. He's still working through those ribs Chloe gave him—"

"*Hey!* You're the one who didn't save him a demon to eat." The angel girl, *Chloe*, said with a shrug. "I gave him a—

"*OI, lads.* Are we really skipping right over this? Are you tossers blind or have I gone bloody mad here?" Jackson yelled and gestured wildly around him. "*CHLOE*, did you not just have fucking angel wings?"

Chloe snorted and her white angel wings popped out behind her. "How mad do you think you could've gotten that quick, you daft plonker?"

Jackson made a choked groan kind of noise that was far too uncivil for his posh accent. "How do you bloody just roll up here like that and not a thing? Why am I being told by a fae Knight that you're over six hundred years old?"

Chloe's eyes widened.

The rest of us stared.

And then to all of our surprise, *Riah* chuckled.

"He sounds *just* like Henry, doesn't he?" Malachi shook his head and laughed. "All right, Lancaster, down boy. I know we have some explaining to do—"

"*EMPEROR?*" A woman screamed from behind me.

Tennessee cursed and spun around. "Sorry, Sarah. You guys good?"

I glanced back to find a young woman with blonde hair in a white sundress splattered with black demon blood and wearing cowboy boots.

Sarah waved. "Yeah, we're good. Y'all good? Need us for anything?" Her accent was almost as thick as Savannah's.

"No, we're good. Thanks, Sarah."

"Thanks, y'all!" She waved and then turned and bounced off.

Tennessee sighed. "Nashville Major. I may have forgotten we'd been fighting demons here."

"*Oh, THAT'S* why I recognized this place!" Savannah chuckled and shook her head. "It's been a minute, y'all."

Riah let out a long, hard sigh and his body swayed. "I don't understand."

Tegan snapped her fingers and a black loveseat appeared right in front of him. Malachi carefully helped his brother down to the sofa. Rainbow magic flashed again and a wooden chair appeared behind Malachi.

He grinned and shook his head as he sat down on it across from Riah. "She is *rather* convenient, isn't she? How do you handle when she's not around?"

"I don't," Tennessee grumbled. Then he shrugged. "If experience tells us anything."

Tegan leaned into him and kissed his shoulder.

I looked back to Riah and found him staring at his brother in amazement. The tenseness had been broken a few times, but he was still reeling. I hurried over and sat on the loveseat beside him, then hooked my arms around his body. Chloe stood just behind Malachi with her hands resting on his shoulders.

Riah shook his head. I didn't like the way his skin was looking more blue by the second. "Malachi...I don't understand. *You died.*"

"Yes, I did."

"I saw it. I *watched* him do it," Riah's voice broke a little.

"And I regret that you had to, but dying was always part of the plan for me." Spot sat down beside him, so Malachi ran his fingers through his fur. "I had hoped it wouldn't happen so soon, but I was prepared for it. My death was part of the plan. As yours will be one day."

I frowned. "Excuse me?"

Malachi sighed. "I was born mortal—a Seelie with a longer

life span, but mortal nonetheless. When I died, I became the angel you see me as now."

"*HOW? WHY?*" Riah groaned and leaned into me. Our soulmate glyph turned emerald-green, so I rubbed his back to soothe him. "What don't I know? I knew the plan with Edward and Henry. With Lilith and Chloe...but you dying was not something I was told."

Malachi's face fell. He wrung his hands in front of himself. "Riah, you understand better than most how some secrets must remain secrets in order for the plan to work. Our mother went to great efforts to ensure we'd be a part of Lilith's demise. Of the King's demise. I had planned on telling you if I survived the war, but then...I didn't. So I couldn't."

"Your mother, the Seer," I asked softly. "Girlfriend of Thorne?"

Malachi smirked. "Pretty sure she would not care for that second title being so highly ranked, but yes."

My father chuckled. Malachi and him seemed to exchange some secret joke between them.

"She saved us," Riah said just loud enough for us to hear. "In the palace. The King was going to kill us, and she saved us, using herself in the worst possible way."

I gasped. "*That exotic creature was your mother?*"

Royce snorted.

Riah nodded.

"Jaanda is her name. We do not resemble her but for the eyes." Malachi shrugged. "We look like our father, ridiculously so."

Chloe's eyes widened. "*Really?*"

Riah scowled but his energy was weakening by the second. All that activity had really worn him out. "No, we don't? Our father was—"

"That was not our father." Malachi glanced around The Coven that was all huddled by the loveseat. "I am unsure of the extent of your knowledge on this matter, but when an angel of Heaven creates a child with a mortal, that child can then become an angel upon their death."

Riah gasped. His skin turned gray. His mouth opened but nothing came out.

"*What?*" Bettina hissed. "Literally child of an angel or any of their bloodline?"

Malachi shook his head. "Direct child only. You, Hope Proctor, and your brother, Haven, are grandchildren of Michael and therefore cannot be reborn as angels. When you die, hopefully a long time from now, you will pass on to the afterlife."

Bettina sighed with relief and nodded.

"Our mother?" Tennessee's voice was barely more than a growl. "She died and is not an angel."

Malachi smiled sadly. "Ruth would have made a fierce angel. We all had hoped she would. But then her soulmate was a mortal man and soulmates cannot be parted for an eternity. She didn't want it either, even before she met Micah. But you see, it's not just that simple. A special ritual must be performed prior to said person's death in order for them to be reborn as an angel. We must fully die and then we are reborn."

Silence.

We all just stared.

"Yeah. Bloody heavy, right?" Chloe chuckled. "I got the crash course the other day."

Malachi smirked. "*Love,* your way was not the normal way."

"What's the normal way?" I asked. "What's the ritual? Does Riah need to do it?"

"He already has," Malachi said softly.

Riah scowled. "*No...*"

"Yes, when you were a child. Mother wanted it ready just in case. The war with Lilith was a bloodbath."

My body went cold. "Are you telling me when Riah dies he'll be reborn an angel?"

"He *can* be if he wants to. Angels of Heaven are rather strict about the free will of Earthborns." He sighed and I felt the building tension inside of him, like he was leading up to something he was worried to say. "Although, with our father being who he is...the rules are a little different."

Riah sat up straight and glared at his brother. "*Who...is... our...father?*"

Malachi took a deep breath. "Our father is Lucifer."

The world spun around me. I heard gasped from all my Coven-mates.

Riah fell forward and caught himself with his elbows on his knees. His eyes practically popped out of his head. His skin was so pale it was almost gray. "*WHAT?*"

"Lucifer is our father," Malachi repeated slowly.

My father cleared his throat.

"Hold up. Hold up." Savannah waved her arms in front of her face. "Lucifer as in *the* Lucifer. King Lucy of Hell."

"*King Lucy of Hell?*" Malachi shook his head and chuckled. "I cannot wait to call him that to his face."

Savannah's face paled. "Okay, but like maybe don't tell him I said it first?"

"Lucifer is well aware of who you are, miss black magic." Malachi winked at her.

"Malachi?" Tegan pursed her lips and waited for him to look to her. "What is Lucifer's role in this war?"

"Yeah, because I thought he was like...the bad guy?" Chutney said while cringing, like Malachi would attack her on the spot. "Ya know, fallen angels and fall of Eden and all that?"

Malachi sighed and scrubbed his face with his hands. "Lucifer is and has always been God's right hand, his strongest hand—his brightest light and most trusted angel. Lucifer was the first angel, the first seraphim—the highest order among Heavenly angels. He was, is, and will always be on the side of Heaven. Nor has he ever fallen."

I shuddered.

Riah's body turned cold. He sat rigid, just staring.

"God is the King of kings. He had to remain in Heaven. So, when he needed someone to run Hell, there was only one person he trusted with the honor—and believe me, it is an *honor*. My father, Lucifer, became the Chief Prince of Hell. And he took his best team of angels with him. There's a whole heavy story that is literally about the dawn of time, but now is not the time to dive into that. What you need to know is that Lilith framed Lucifer in the eyes of man. She destroyed the Garden of Eden. She tricked angels to fall."

Riah shuddered. "*Asmodeus, Leviathan, Azazel, Abaddon—*"

"Yes. *Them.*" Malachi pinched the bridge of his nose. "Lucifer has been working with Heaven since the fall to try and destroy Lilith, but Heaven had strict rules back then. It was only about seven hundred years ago that they realized mortals would never defeat Lilith without Heaven's hand. Until then, the only angel that had birthed a child by a mortal was Jophiel with the Lancasters. They were intended to be the keepers of the light—the angelic presence among the darkness of mortality. The One Hundred Years' War with Lilith changed everything."

Bettina scowled. "So, Uriel was the second angel to have a mortal kid? With Edward Proctor?"

Malachi smirked and shook his head. "No, Lucifer was second. God wanted his favorite son to send a hand to help the Earthborns."

"*You,*" Riah breathed.

"Me. But in order for Lilith to not know of my existence, he chose a Seelie Seer outside of Earth to mother his child." He looked up to Bettina. "Edward Proctor was third. At that point, Heaven set the one bloodline rule. But Lucifer does not believe rules apply to him, and he did not see a specification on how many within that same bloodline he could make. He said that technically having two children by the same mother was the same bloodline."

Tegan snorted. "Goddess, I love a loophole."

"In the middle of the war, I told my father we needed help. Edward was being stretched too thin when he needed to focus on slaying Lilith with Michael's sword. He said he would give me help...next thing I knew, my mother gave birth to a miniature version of myself." He smiled lovingly at my soulmate. "Riah was born just in time. We aged him quickly in Seelie to get him into the war, and without him we may never have succeeded that day with Edward."

Riah exhaled and slumped forward, resting his face in his hands.

"At this point, Riah knew the plan. Our *secret* plan that only the five of us knew, aside from the angels. The plan was for Riah to make sure Edward hit Lilith with that sword—the very one Haven calls his now—while my job was to get her necklace *first.*"

"Lilith's necklace. Riah told us about that when he first joined us." Tegan tapped on her chin like she was deep in thought. "He said you got it and then you placed it on Henry's daughter, Princess Chloe. And then once Lilith was gone, you shipped them all to a safe place only for them to get stuck in the Old Lands for centuries."

"I'm still not used to that fact, by the way," Chloe grumbled.

"And I saw Lilith's necklace under your gown at the Lancaster ball." Tegan cocked her head to the side. "But it does not look the same now."

"Timing is everything." Malachi frowned. "King Atzaran discovered my betrayal earlier than ideal and my mortal life had to end. Riah was forced to watch to prove his loyalty to the King. I did die. That was real. Rebirth is normally quick. However, I was the first to do it, and my father wanted to make sure I was okay before sending me back. And he wanted to conceal me from Lilith's snooping spy eyes. By the time I came out, Chloe and her mother were already lost to the Old Lands."

"*Why didn't you tell me?*" He cried in a broken voice. "Why wait—"

"Because I had to. For many reasons. The most important one, in my opinion, was to keep you safe. Atzaran and Lilith, and all their forces, would have had your head on a stick if they knew my fate. So I hung in the shadows, being a shadow myself. I spent a lot of time in the Old Lands, searching for Chloe and her mother to try and guide them out. I lost a lot of time in there, not as much as them, but a good amount—especially in the beginning. And then you were guarding Saraphina, for reasons which are now obvious."

Riah squeezed his eyes shut.

"I wanted to tell you, just as you probably wanted to tell Saraphina. But you and I understood the dire circumstances of our missions and why we had to obey the rules set to us. My job was to remain close to Chloe until the time to remove the necklace—"

"What is this necklace?" Tenn frowned and shifted his weight around. "That is what I want to know."

"*The soul reaper,*" Riah whispered and then coughed.

We all gasped.

Malachi nodded. "She used it to literally pull a soul from its body and trap it inside of her locket, and then she would live off it. Thrive on it. Do whatever she wanted to do with it. Which is why we had to steal it."

"And you did," I heard myself say. "I saw it—in the past when I went through the tunnels. You stole it and put it on Chloe."

"I did. We all thought it the safest way to protect and conceal it. Lilith despises children, she would never look to her." He sighed and glanced back at his soulmate. "What we didn't know until I tried to remove it in December, was that it was stuck to her—*on* her. It had become part of her."

Royce scowled. "Why did you wait six centuries to try?"

"The Lancaster curse," Tegan said with a firm voice. "As a human, touching the locket could've activated it and killed her on the spot. You had to wait until her magic came back, which meant you had to wait for Jackson to retrieve Michael's sword."

"*Again, so convenient.*" Malachi smirked but then sobered. "Yes. Exactly. I hid in the shadows while Jackson was on his quest. I was there the very moment Chloe's magic returned. I'll admit, hiding away with just my hellhound and not being around people did not aide me in my attempts to get the locket off."

Chloe snorted. Spot barked.

Malachi shrugged. "In the end, we discovered there were only two paths to take. *Option A*, we removed the necklace by force and Chloe died. Or *Option B*, we turned her into an angel and let the power of Heaven break the lock—which could've easily killed her too."

"Yeah, don't bloody recommend that," Chloe mumbled. She pulled the neck of her white t-shirt down to show us the glowing blue crescent over her soulmate glyph. "When it broke, it merely broke the physical object. The power was absorbed by *me*. I became the soul reaper."

"The angel of light, my love," Malachi whispered. "Chloe has a very specific role to play in this war, just like the rest of us."

For a moment, we were all silent.

Riah stared at the ground, unmoving.

Deacon whistled under his breath. "Shit, that's heavy."

"What you all need to understand is that none of you are here by chance. Each and every one of you was hand selected by the Goddess and *us* to be on this super Coven. Because we need the best of the best in order to defeat her once and for all. Some of you may not be here to see that job through, whether by death or replacement."

Tennessee cleared his throat. "The angel of tides?"

"Not quite rung yet. But soon. Sooner than any of you realize." He rolled his shoulders and cursed. "Look, I know this was a lot, and I know you'll have questions—*Tegan*. But what you need to know is that the angels are on your side, both in Heaven and on your couch. As angels, we have rules to obey, so we are limited in what we're allowed to do. For example, I was not allowed to interfere until I saw Asmodeus or Leviathan attack The Coven myself. I will help in every way I am permitted, and I'll bend the rules when I know it's safe to do so, but we are here to help you. And we are not leaving until Lilith is dead."

Riah hung his head and let his hair sway between his legs. He groaned, then looked up quickly. His face looked green and sickly. "Because I am a Prince of Hell."

"You are. As am I." He held his palms out. "We are gifted by our angel parents. Hope in her spells. Haven in his wings and overall non-humanness—*I can say that. I'm not human.*"

Tennessee chuckled.

"I can kill by a single touch, you know this. I got that from our father, Lucifer. But you, my brother, you got his greatest strength. You can heal by touch, like you did for Savannah. It is why you can heal so quickly and easily. That is Lucifer's power."

Riah nodded and scrubbed his face. His hands trembled. His skin was cold to the touch. Suddenly he jumped to his feet. "I...I need...a minute."

He stormed off without another word, but he moved in a zig-zag instead of a straight line. His legs wobbled. Something was wrong. Very wrong.

In front of him, my father's eyes widened. He threw his arms out and yelled, "RIAH!"

His body crumbled from under him. In slow motion we all

jumped up and dove for him. I moved as fast as I could. Tennessee and Malachi got there at the same exact time, catching him just before his face slammed into the grass.

Malachi cursed and flipped him over.

I choked on a scream.

Thick black lines streaked across every inch of his body. Around them, his skin was blue and purple. His lips turned black. His eyes were wide and entirely a milky white.

"*Atzaran,*" Malachi roared. "He cursed him!"

"What's happening?" I screamed.

Malachi growled and it wasn't even a little bit human. "He's dying."

CHAPTER FORTY-FOUR

SAFFIE

WHAT? "NOOOOO!"

White light flashed and then we were suddenly back in Kessler's house in Tampa.

Malachi lifted Riah up and threw him on the tan leather couch like he weighed no more than a feather. I dove for him, sinking to my knees beside the couch. Our soulmate glyph was flashing red faster than it had before.

"RIAH! *RIAH!*"

Malachi tipped his head back and forced his mouth open. Riah's tongue, his entire mouth, was black. That milky white film had completely covered his eyes, blocking out the gold. The black lines on his body raised up off his skin like mountain ranges.

Everyone was shouting, but I didn't hear a single word.

Because that faint, pale blue glow shimmered around his body. His soul was preparing to leave, to die. I screamed and slammed my hands onto his chest. *NOT AGAIN.* Flashbacks from that damn dinosaur bite filled my mind. I cried and pushed my magic into his soul. "*STAY!*"

White light flashed behind me. A woman shouted in alarm,

then I heard Katherine's voice, *"Tegan? What happened —RIAH!"*

Suddenly, she was right by my side. I had no idea what she was doing. This wasn't my area of expertise. I wasn't a healer. She didn't have any tools or potions or books. She just waved her hands over him rapidly.

She gasped and her eyes flew wide open. She jerked back and then shook herself like she'd been electrocuted. "That's a Seelie curse."

"Yes," Malachi and my father growled at the same time.

Katherine shook her head and turned to me with horrified, sad eyes. "I can't fix this. It was done with pure Seelie magic from inside Seelie. We-we-we just don't have it here, so I can't fix it."

The world caved in around me. Dark tunnels crept into the corners of my vision. My body trembled. "No. No, no, no. You have to save him. We have to do something. *There HAS to be SOMETHING!"*

"What if we take him back to Seelie?" Willow whispered from the back somewhere.

"NO." Bentley held his hands up in front of his face. His eyes were dark. "That'll kill him faster."

"That can't be true?" Chutney cried.

Malachi growled and the walls vibrated. "Yes, it is."

"We have to do something! We have to try!" I cried and ignored the tingle of death on my fingers.

Malachi looked up and his golden eyes met mine. "We let him die. He'll turn into an angel like he's supposed to be —like me."

I shook my head. Words poured out of my mouth in a panic, but I had no idea what I was even saying. *No, no, no, no. RIAH.*

"Saffie." Tegan dropped down beside me. "We can't heal him, Saffie. It's become an angel or die."

"No, he can't die yet." My father paced by Riah's feet. "He can't be an angel yet. That's not part of the plan."

Malachi scowled. "Yes, it is. What are you—"

"No! Not yet," my father practically yelled. His cheeks flushed. "It's too early, Malachi. Earthborn Angels cannot step foot in Seelie, or any other realm."

"We're not Earthborn," Malachi hissed.

My father pushed his hair back. I felt his panic and desperation. I felt him flipping through a million ideas but none of them being a solution. "Yes, you are. Your mother gave birth to both of you on Earth because this realm is the one that needs you, the one where you belong."

Malachi frowned. "Why didn't I know that?"

Riah gasped for air. His body shook like he was seizing and convulsing. His blue, glowy soul grew brighter and more solid.

"HE'S DYING!" I screamed. "DO SOMETHING!"

"Malachi," my father growled. "If he becomes an angel, then he can't help us kill the King, and we're going to need him."

Katherine covered her face with her hands. "But we can't heal him."

My father stopped pacing and faced Riah, standing just a few feet away from the couch. I felt something inside of him shift, some sacrifice he was ready to make. Magic poured out of his palms in a steady stream of golden glitter *just like mine.* It wrapped around his body for a moment, then began to fade away inch-by-inch, starting from his head.

His long, braided, reddish-brown hair that hung straight down turned a bright vivid red the same exact shade as mine. It fanned out around his shoulders in voluminous waves *just like mine.* Those pale gray-ish eyes darkened and flickered orange like burning embers under a bonfire. His skin paled and held a shimmery tone to it. His face grew longer, more narrow. The lines of his face turned sharp. A sharper pointed ear poked out from his red hair.

My breath left me in a rush. My jaw dropped.

All of my thoughts...vanished.

Because my father, *Hetron*, was gone.

In his place stood the one person I never thought I'd see on Earth.

Prince Thorne.

He held his hands out to his sides and magic filled his palms. "I can. *Move.*"

CHAPTER FORTY-FIVE

SAFFIE

"*WHAT?*" The entire living room shouted in unison.

I froze. My body felt like it'd turned to ice. The air was knocked out of my lungs as I stared up at the very man who had cursed me for three centuries. *THORNE?! H-HOW? This can't be happening?* I thought I'd met my father, finally, yet now he stood there as Prince Thorne. *Is he my father at all or was that a lie? Can we trust him? OR was this whole thing an elaborate trick to get him back into Earth?*

Panic flooded my veins. Riah was dying. Thorne said he could fix him. I had to let him try. I had to. For Riah's life. I was confused and conflicted. *Hetron* I'd felt I could trust almost immediately yet he was really Prince Thorne the whole time. *WAIT. Did Prince Thorne really take a near-fatal hit for me?* My mind and heart were a mess.

Prince Thorne's fiery ember eyes met mine and held my gaze.

My heart stopped.

Everyone was shouting.

"*Thorne!*" Malachi yelled and slammed his hand onto Riah's chest. "NOW, OR HE DIES."

RIAH! There were too many things happening at once. But Riah's life blocked the rest out. I had to focus on him.

Prince Thorne shook himself then shot across the room, clearing the space between him and Riah in the blink of an eye. Without speaking or even looking at me, he rested his knee on the couch cushion beside Riah's hip and then leaned over and slammed his palms into Riah's chest. Riah gasped and trembled.

"LET GO OF HIM," Thorne shouted as golden glitter burst from under his palms.

Tegan gripped my wrists and yanked my arms into my own chest. She kept her arms around me, holding me tight to her. *"Breathe. Let him fix it."*

Breathe.

BREATHE.

Prince Thorne is here.

Let him fix it, she said. I just need to breathe.

I wanted to go to him but Tegan had a firm grip on me. I was screaming inside.

Malachi was leaning over the backside of the couch. Chloe hugged close behind him. I felt each of my Coven-mates and friends, but I was numb—on the verge of breaking in a way I'd never recover from.

Thorne closed his eyes and leaned forward, his red hair falling onto Riah's chest. He chanted under his breath in a language I'd never heard. Lightning bolts of magic flashed from under his hands. Lush green and purple vines stretched around Riah's body like snakes slithering across his skin. In seconds, the colorful vines had shot across—*the black lines.* The vines had traced the raised edges of those black lines. Thorne pushed hard against Riah's sternum. Riah's back arched and his head tipped back. He gasped and sucked in fresh air.

That milky sheen on his eyes cleared.

The black on his mouth and face faded away.

His glowing blue soul was nowhere in sight.

I choked on my own spit as a broken sob ripped up my throat. Tears rushed over my eyelashes like a broken dam. Thorne lifted his hands—I dove for Riah. I knew he was hurt, sick, and had just been on the edge of death, but I basically tackled him. My arms coiled around his neck. I showered him with kisses and love.

Riah, Riah, Riah.

Thorne sighed over me. "He is healed now, but he may be weakened for a short while."

"That wasn't part of the plan," Malachi growled.

"We expected him to interfere with our plan once it was enacted," Thorne's voice was calm and steady. "We can expect more, though I haven't the slightest idea what that might be."

Malachi and Thorne launched into this whole new conversation *not* in English. They weren't arguing. They were planning. There were so many things to say and ask but in that moment all I cared about was Riah.

"Maybe he'll just let us pretend to be dead for six centuries," Riah whispered softly.

I gasped and pushed up off him, then cupped his face. "My love? Riah, can you hear me?"

The rest of The Coven moved in closer.

Malachi smiled and shook his head. "I had to, Riah. It was the only way to keep you safe."

"I've heard that before," Tegan and Emersyn said at the same time.

Riah licked his lips and his mouth quirked up to one side slightly. He looked up at his brother with matching golden eyes. "You will have to suffer through comments such as this for at least the next six centuries."

Malachi chuckled. He disappeared and then emerged right beside me. "Fair. Come on. Let's sit you up."

Thorne and Malachi grabbed ahold of Riah's hands, then

pulled him into a seated position with his back resting against the sofa. He reached out for me, so I took his hand and squeezed. My mouth was not yet working. There were too many warring emotions. But he was alive. Those black lines were gone. His skin was back to its normal tan complexion. His face looked like it'd never been in disarray.

Malachi sat beside him and squeezed his shoulder. "Just take it easy and breathe. You'll heal quick now that the curse is gone, but don't rush it."

I hopped up to sit on the other side of him. I took his hand in mine and the warmth in his skin made my pulse skip beats.

He lifted his hand and tipped my chin up. *"I'm sorry."*

I sobbed and shook my head. It wasn't his fault, but it hurt all the same. I buried my face in his chest, ignoring the scent of blood. "Are you okay now? Is the danger gone?"

"Yes. Yes, I am okay now." He tapped just under my face to where our soulmate glyph was back to our pretty aquamarine. Then he narrowed eyes. *"Thorne.* What the hell was that?"

Thorne cursed and pushed his long red hair back, running his fingers through the strands. "My father is a real piece of shit. That curse sleeps while in Seelie, but the moment you pass into another realm it activates. Real slow at first, then all at once. He most likely put it on you while in the dungeon just in case you escaped. Death is usually swift and awful. Fortunately, he did not anticipate me being here or *you* being the son of Lucifer."

Riah's eyes softened. "Thank you for saving me. Healing me."

Thorne smiled and held his hand out to him. "That's what friends are for. Is that not the saying here on Earth?"

Riah chuckled and instantly shook his hand. "But I blame you for me having to watch my mother make out with your father."

Thorne gagged and shuddered. "She's *my* girlfriend. Trust

me, I blame myself plenty for that nightmare. It is sure to haunt me. But she saved us."

"Wait, Riah, you knew he was *Hetron?*"

He frowned and shook his head, then he leaned into me and whispered, "If I had known he was your father I never would have kissed you."

I scoffed but my cheeks burned. "*I* kissed *you.*"

"I could have stopped you." Riah winked at me but then pursed his lips. "Or maybe avoided the hot tub."

Malachi chuckled. "Thorne, do you even know what a hot tub is?"

"Did you know about the hot tub?" Chloe gestured between me and Riah. "Or that they were together?"

Thorne sighed. "I cannot decide if it sounds enticing or horrific, but yes, I knew they were soulmates. That is why I sent Riah to watch over her."

Riah looked to his brother. "Later, when my strength returns, I'm going to break your face."

Malachi grinned. "I deserve that."

Tennessee cleared his throat. "So...Prince Thorne, eh?"

Thorne turned and I wondered what he thought in finding the entire Coven behind him aiming lasers with their eyeballs. He took a deep breath and then raised his hands up in surrender. "I owe you all a multitude of apologies. I cannot fathom what it has been like for you, to be seemingly tossed around. To think Sage and I were against you, when everything we've done for seven centuries was to help you. I'm sorry that our secret could not come to light until just now. The thing is, I've been playing this game of chess for seven hundred years and I assure you secrecy was the only way to win—to get where we are right now."

"Which is where, exactly?" Tenn crossed his arms over his chest.

"With the upper hand," Thorne said without pause. "I

promise I will answer *everything*. All your questions, all your concerns. I am an open book, as the saying goes. From this point on, Sage and I are transparently with you."

"Okay. Here's a question." I pushed to my feet and glared. "You said you were my father. Was that part of the lie?"

CHAPTER FORTY-SIX

SAFFIE

"I *AM* YOUR FATHER. I just didn't look like myself when your mother met me. In all fairness, meeting you as *Hetron* was as honest as I could have been – since I was him when I met your mother."

My father was Prince Thorne. *MY father was PRINCE Thorne.* It was going to take some getting used to. Right now, it felt like someone had hit me over the head too hard. I didn't understand. I had so many questions. I wanted to hug him. I wanted to strangle him. Most of all I wanted to cry for days and days and then burn all of Seelie to the ground.

"The dungeon. That's what you told us," Savannah snarled. "That she was born in that fairyfly tunnel."

He nodded. "That was true, all of it. *Well,* okay, maybe one teeny tiny bit wasn't entirely accurate—"

"Which. Part?" Savannah growled.

"The fairyflies," he said softly, then looked to me and smiled. His fiery eyes were warm and soft like candle flames. "They are drawn to you, in part, because you were born among them, but mostly because you are my daughter. A Royal."

Malachi smiled. "Princess Saraphina."

494

Riah's eyes lit up and sparkled. He looked down at me in wonder. "You're a Royal. That means you're immortal."

I gasped. "You did say that once, didn't you? Father?"

"It is true. You are immortal, as all Royals are."

Tegan sighed. "I just love how fate just weaves things together."

Riah and I turned to her.

She arched one eyebrow. "You're immortal. Once Riah becomes an angel, *he'll* be immortal. Is that not beautiful? It would be cruel to bind two souls that are destined to be parted for eternity."

Eternity. The idea of being immortal and living forever was overwhelming and scary but if Riah was going to be there with me...it did feel beautiful. I looked up into Riah's eyes and soaked in the warmth radiating off him. He was healing already.

"It was a nice disguise, by the way, Thorne. If not for being an angel with a particular penchant for souls, I would not have guessed it." Malachi wagged his eyebrows. "How long have you been—"

"*Hetron!*" Tegan grumbled. "Hetron! Thorne! The letters are scrambled!"

He chuckled. "Very good, Tegan. And to answer your question, I assumed the identity of Hetron after the war. I have been aiding The Circle since then."

Tegan clapped her hands and shook her head. "You sneaky little shit. You couldn't get to Earth unless Saffie brought you here."

My father grinned. "And you'll be glad she did. Trust me. This fight is only just getting started. If we want to win, we're going to have to trust each other real fast."

Chutney raised her hand. "I thought fae couldn't lie."

"Pure-bred Seelie civilians cannot lie. I am neither." My father grimaced and shrugged one shoulder. "My father simply never corrected anyone, and you aren't surprised to hear that."

Royce raised *his* hand. "Why can only those not lie?"

"My father cursed them a long, long time ago. Not that they ever knew." My father—which still felt weird to think when it was attached to Prince Thorne—held his hands up to ward off all the questions flying at him at once. "Listen, listen. I said I would answer you and I will. But I believe we, *you*, have some more pressing concerns that need handling before we have this chat."

Tennessee scowled. "Like what?"

"Well, for starters where is Easton? The boyfriend to Lily?" He squinted and eyed each person in the room. "Now that I revealed my identity, I wanted to give him some more information, more understanding. Is he hiding?"

Everyone glanced left and right, then back again.

My pulse quickened. I didn't feel them. I'd been so caught up with Riah I hadn't noticed.

"Where are Easton and Braison?" Cooper spun in a circle. "EASTON! BRAISON!"

Bentley cleared his throat. "They left."

WHAT?! Everyone was shouting their names and checking for them in the group.

Bentley held his hand up and fire danced along his skin. "While the panic erupted, they slipped away and headed for the Land of the Lore...for Seelie."

My father cursed. "That is not good. I knew you four were coming—I'll have to try and get a message to Sage."

Malachi stared at the ground. "We just have to hope they don't wind up in Unseelie—"

The door to one of the bedrooms flew open and Spot charged out with his red and yellow eyes glowing and his black, smoky fur standing on edge. Spot lowered his head and snarled viciously.

"Uh oh," Chutney grumbled.

Malachi stood. He cocked his head to the side and then his

gold eyes narrowed into slits. "*Do you have a shadow demon in this house?*"

Everyone gasped and turned to Tegan.

She rolled her eyes. "Well, I couldn't exactly send her to Eden since it's holy ground now. So, yeah, when we went to Nashville, I portaled her here to Cooper's room."

Malachi marched up to Tegan and narrowed his eyes. "You used angel magic to bind it?"

She grimaced. "Well, I used whatever magic comes with this White Witch ordeal."

"Angel magic. That's angel magic. *RIAH.*" He spun and darted for Cooper's room.

Riah flashed by me in a blur.

We all followed them into the room. By the time I got there, it was wall-to-wall packed but that didn't rob me of the sight before me. Laying in the middle of a cage made entirely of magic was Henley.

Riah crouched down and scanned her face. "He's been in there with her too long."

Malachi gripped the bars and cursed. Then he spun and marched right up to Tegan. His gaze travelled over her white hair, then he tipped her head back to inspect those gold and white eyes. "Later, you and I have to have a conversation about *this*."

Tegan nodded.

"Do you understand that when you're like this you're as close to an angel a mortal can get? Do you realize that you used so much Heavenly magic that *I*—the son of Lucifer, Prince of Hell—did not register it because I thought it was Michael's sword? *That's* how much you're using right now."

Tennessee cursed and ran his hand through his hair.

She grimaced. "I suspected as much."

"What triggered the onset this time?"

"The Strait of the Dead," I said and shuddered at the memory. "In the Land of the Lore, The spirits dragged her in."

Tegan nodded. "I was down for a while afterwards, then I woke still like this. I went right for where Asmodeus was fighting them. I didn't have much choice in the moment. I *had* to trap the shadow demon so that we can kill him."

"I believe you." He nodded and tugged on her white hair. "Once we eliminate the problem here, we will have to break you of this white."

"*Eliminate?!*" Royce screamed. "You mean save Henley, right? RIGHT?"

CHAPTER FORTY-SEVEN

SAFFIE

"I THOUGHT you got the demon out of her back in October?"

We all turned to Malachi with wide eyes.

He shrugged. "I am the eldest Prince of Hell. It is my job to know the happenings of demons and black magic."

Savannah's face paled.

Without even looking at her, he said, "We'll talk later, Savannah."

"I did get it out of her before Samhain...but..." Tegan grimaced. "He's back."

Royce pointed to where Riah was still crouched and watching Henley. "It was *HIS* idea."

"Brother? You suggested Henley be possessed a second time?"

Riah glanced up and shrugged. "In my defense, I had suggested one of the civilian children who summoned him in the first place be the one possessed."

"*In your defense?* You suggested possessing children?" Malachi blinked and shook himself. "Is that what you just said?"

My father, who was leaning against the doorframe, giggled.

Malachi pointed to him. "You've been with Thorne too long."

Thorne. My father. My father is Prince Thorne. My mind was still reeling over it.

Riah smirked and stood up straight. I could tell he was still a bit weak and worn out, but he was looking almost back to himself. He prowled the side of the cage. "These are almost impossible to kill."

Tennessee cursed. "Malachi?"

"He is correct." Malachi crossed his arms over his chest. "But it is possible. You'll just have to be creative."

Tegan cocked her head to the side and played with the crystal on her necklace. "Creative how?"

Royce snapped his fingers and then half skipped over to Riah. "Didn't Henley say this guy was terrified of Riah?"

I heard her words in my mind again, but it was still vague. "She did, but he and Malachi look so much alike..."

Riah scratched his jaw. "As much as I'd love to invoke such fear in said abomination, I have not had specific contact with this one before the night the kids summoned him here."

"I have." Malachi grinned and there was a wicked story in that smile. "But all demons know the children of Lucifer, even when you don't know it yourself."

Royce turned on him with glassy, puppy-dog eyes. "So, can you kill him?"

"He's not allowed—*no, Malachi*." Chloe slid up beside her soulmate and held his arm. "You need to not push the limits until they at least try. We both know you'll be breaking rules once the war officially starts."

"Chloe is right, Malachi." Tennessee towered over everyone else aside from Kessler. His black hair was a wild, tangled mess. "Let us exhaust all our options before we accept your rule breaking?"

Spot whined. Chutney chuckled.

Riah narrowed his eyes and tapped on the glowing magical bars. "Brother, do you remember that demon we killed with Henry and Edward, that first one?"

Malachi grinned. "Your memory is flawless. That is exactly what we're dealing with."

"WHAT?" Several of us yelled.

My pulse skipped beats. I had a sinking, horrible feeling about this.

Tegan snapped her fingers. "Okay, angel bros. Can you share with the class before I get on my bullshit?"

Riah nodded. He kept his eyes on Henley. "These demons can be stuck in a mortal body if the host has perished."

Royce whimpered and flinched.

Riah reached out and squeezed Royce's shoulder. "The idea I'm about to suggest you are going to hate in every single possible way. No one would think lesser of you if you left the room for this."

Royce paled and stumbled back.

Deacon jumped out and caught him, then dragged him to the door. "Neither of us want to see this, so let's go wait in the other room."

Once they were out the door, Tegan spun on Riah. "What's the idea?"

Riah sighed. "Chloe is now the soul reaper. So, I say we have Chloe suck Henley's soul right out of her body and into her necklace, because when the soul of the person they possessed is gone, they become that body permanently."

"Are you suggesting we kill Henley?"

"Yes." Malachi rolled his shoulders. "Chloe removes her soul safely and secures it in her locket. One of *you* have to kill her body. Once its dead, Chloe puts Henley's soul back into her own body and—"

"I heal her," Riah said in a deep voice.

Tennessee cursed a long string of violent obscenities. "I hate this. I *hate* this plan. But it's the only way to do it, isn't it?"

Riah and Malachi both nodded.

Tegan squirmed. "Full steam ahead, babe. If we could ask Henley right now, she would say yes and to stop wasting time. So, your call."

Tennessee groaned and scrubbed his face with his hands. "FINE. Goddess, I hate it. But fine. Let's just do it and get her out. What do you need us to do?"

"If there's anyone who does not want to watch this, now's your chance to flee." When no one budged, Malachi nodded. "Just stay back and watch our backs."

"Saraphina."

I smiled and turned toward the sound of my name coming from his voice. "Yes?"

He waved for me. "Stay with me, Saraphina. We need you to watch Henley's soul. Let us know if anything looks off."

With a nod, I hurried over and clung to his side. The Coven had all huddled against the far wall by the door. Their facial expressions matched the panic and worry racing through me.

"Tennessee, get Michael's sword out. You're going to kill the body with that. The Heavenly power will cleanse whatever it touched of evil and darkness."

He tapped the gold bands on his arm and Michael's glowing, six-foot-tall sword appeared in his grip. "Just give me the cue."

"I will." Malachi pointed toward our friend inside the cage. "Tegan, wake her up."

Rainbow magic slammed into Henley's spine. She arched her back and then rolled and jumped onto all fours—and then bright red eyes landed on her cage walls. She screeched and hissed. She dove for the walls and the power of Heaven threw her back to the floor.

"*Now, Chloe!*"

Chloe thrust her arms forward and white light shot out of her palms. It flew straight and strong right through the bars of the cage and into Henley's chest. White angel wings fluttered behind Chloe's back. Her soulmate glyph lines were dark red and were suddenly covering her entire body from the neck down. In the center of her chest, cutting right into the lavender crystal glyph, was a crescent moon that glowed a hypnotic-neon blue.

Henley screamed and flopped down on her back. She thrashed and kicked her legs like a small child having a tantrum. Her veins bulged. Loud, vicious growls that were *not* human bubbled up her throat.

"*Don't stop, Chloe,*" Malachi whispered.

I cleared my thoughts and focused on Henley. It took me a second to block out her screams and agonized wailing. But then I felt it. Henley's soul. It was clean, pure energy and full of light...and it was rising.

"*Almost,*" I whispered.

There was a *POP* and then a glowing neon-blue version of Henley lifted straight up out of her own body and into the air. I gasped and held my hands up, ready to catch her if I needed to.

"*Tegan, bars,*" Riah hissed.

Tegan flicked her wrists and her magic cage vanished.

Bright blue light the same color as Henley's soul shined from Chloe's chest. Chloe rolled her wrists and then curled her fingers like she was pulling on an invisible rope. The first few tugs fought her hard, but then the resistance snapped and Henley's soul shot like a rocket straight into Chloe's glowing crescent blue mark on her chest.

And then she was gone.

"I can't feel her soul anymore," I said in a rush.

Riah nodded. "It's being held."

A loud growl rumbled from where Henley's body was sprawled on the ground. We waited. We had to be sure. Tegan flicked her wrist and the demon was standing upright. Big red glowing eyes stared right at me. It tried to get out of her body. It tried to vanish into thin air, yet it couldn't. Instead, she flopped like a fish out of water. This was no longer Henley.

"She's gone," I whispered.

"*Now, Tenn.*"

Tennessee strolled forward with Michael's sword gripped in his palm. He walked straight up to Henley's body. "*LOOK AT ME.*"

The Henley-body looked up and those glowing red eyes latched onto him. He held her gaze as he raised Michael's sword —and slammed it right into her gut. Henley's body jerked. Her knees gave out and she crashed to the ground. White streaks of light seemed to shine *through* her skin. And then black dust crumbled all around her body and she collapsed.

Black blood poured from the wound and the scent of maple syrup filled the air. He yanked his sword back out and fresh blood bubbled out of her mouth and down her throat. Red eyes rolled.

Malachi and Riah walked over to where Henley lay lifelessly and crouched down. They pressed their palms to Henley's soulless body and closed their eyes.

Then Riah looked up to me and nodded once. "The shadow demon is dead."

CHAPTER FORTY-EIGHT

SAFFIE

Malachi, Chloe, Riah, and I all raced toward Henley's lifeless body.

Riah pressed both of his hands to the bloody wound on her stomach. *"Now, Chloe."*

I held Henley's head so that if this worked she wouldn't hurt herself.

"Get close for the return," Malachi said in a rush.

Over my shoulder, I felt the entire Coven, but mostly Tegan and Tennessee. They were watching every second of this.

Chloe held her palms on Henley's body's chest to make a diamond-shape between her fingers, like a frame right where the blue crescent moon would be on herself. Chloe took a deep breath and then pushed. I felt her magic rush out like a wave. That blue crescent pulsed like it was counting down.

The center of her chest ignited in bright white light that cast a crescent cutout shadow on the wall. There was a *POP* and then a high-pitched whistle. A split second later, a glowing blue orb popped right out of the crescent on Chloe's chest. Chloe held her hand out flat and the orb stretched until it was as long and wide as Henley's body.

Because it *was* Henley.

Chloe slowly and carefully guided Henley's soul back down to her body. That blue glow lit up all of her pale frame. The soul wiggled into place—her skin flushed. The blood in the wound ran red instead of black.

Riah pushed his magic without waiting. Bright light filled his palms and covered over the wound in her stomach. I watched in amazement as the severed pieces of skin reattached and reformed. Blood rushed *into* her body like a river flowing backwards. With every second, her face got less hollowed and her skin flushed a bit more pink.

And then Henley threw her head back and gasped.

Her eyes were a gorgeous *sapphire blue.*

White light flashed in my peripheral and then Deacon and Royce dropped to their knees beside me.

"*Henley?*" Royce cried and squeezed her hand.

Deacon leaned over at the same time and grinned. "Hey, Hen."

She blinked, then looked him straight in the eye and smiled. "*Royce. D.*"

Riah and Chloe were still finishing things up.

Henley's gaze moved over my shoulder ."*Tegan...*"

"I'm here, Henley," Tegan whispered.

Henley grinned and nodded. "*Ballsy move.*"

And then she passed out.

"She needs to rest," Malachi bit out. "Chloe, are you okay?"

"I'm fine, my love."

Riah stood but his body swayed.

Tennessee jumped up and hooked Riah's arm over his shoulder. "I've got you. Don't fight it. Let yourself rest."

What a day for Riah. I couldn't fathom how his body was still going.

"Malachi," Tegan said and bent down. "Can she portal like this?"

He nodded. "Get us to holy ground, where she'll be safe. Deacon and Royce, would you like to carry her?"

They leapt into action. Royce hooked his arms under her shoulders while Deacon lifted her legs. Tegan snapped her fingers and a white portal box opened a few feet away. The rest of The Coven descended like wolves. They each grabbed ahold of Henley and helped carry her to the portal. Tennessee and I carried Riah, which was mostly me just there for moral support while Tenn did all the work. Chloe and Malachi kept close watch on Henley the whole time.

Together, as one big team, we stepped through Tegan's portal...and right into the front field of Coven Headquarters in Eden.

I looked up and gasped. My feet stopped. There was a man I'd never seen before standing on the front steps to Headquarters. He had long, wild brown hair and seemed to be growing into his body as well as his scruffy beard.

Tegan gasped. "*Ellis.*"

Who is Ellis?

Tennessee cursed. "Is something wrong?"

"Was there another attack?" Tegan asked at the same time.

Ellis held his hands up and shook his head. His eyes shot right to unconscious Henley. "I made a blood oath to her once. Tonight, I felt...something. It was wrong and unsettling. So, I came here to help her in any way I possibly can."

Everyone froze.

Tennessee nodded. "Nice to have you back, Ellis. Yes, you can help her."

"Right, inside *now.*" Katherine rushed by them, waving for them to follow her.

Deacon, Royce, and Ellis shared the weight of Henley's body to bring her inside.

I sighed and leaned into Riah. "What a damn day."

He chuckled and wrapped his arm around my shoulders.

Tegan walked backwards in front of us. "Nadia, Malachi, Chloe, *Prince Thorne*. Welcome to Eden and Coven Headquarters. You're going to cause a stir when the others see you—*one of you more than the others*."

My father grinned and shrugged. *My father is Prince Thorne.* I was in denial. It'd happened too fast. I needed a minute to process everything that just happened and then I knew this revelation was going to rock me hard.

Emersyn groaned and hurried by us. "I'm going inside to make every type of comfort food I can find."

"Does that include hot *and* cold items?" Willow asked with a chuckle. She skipped ahead to catch up with Emersyn. "Can I help?"

We were almost to the house. Everyone was stumbling over their own feet, including our new Sun Card, Nadia, who was so quiet I kept forgetting she was there. I wanted to know her story, who she was. She had to be feeling awful, replacing a Card that has just died is always rough. I opened my mouth to call out to her when I felt a tingle on my spine.

My father froze in place.

He felt that, too. I stopped, which forced Tennessee, Tegan, Malachi, and Chloe to stop.

"What was that?" I heard myself ask.

"Thorne, are you doing that?" Riah asked over my shoulder.

But my father just shook his head.

Willow's face paled. "What is that?"

Blue light flashed in the air—and then the Seelie tunnel opened up right in the middle of Eden courtyard.

My Coven-mates freaked out, yelling that Riah and I had done a spell to keep uninvited Seelie out. They were right. We had. Magic flashed.

"Sage opened that just now," my father held his hands out. "Hold your fire one second. Let's see what this is."

We all turned toward the Seelie tunnel opening. Long blue

hair swung out of the hole, so I knew Sage was *there*. But I had no idea what she was doing. I glanced up to my father and found him frowning.

And then from inside the dark, dimly lit tunnel...Willow stepped out.

Wait, WHAT?

We all gasped and looked to our left. Willow was already standing there. I glanced back and forth. There were two Willows. That wasn't possible. Yet my eyes did not betray me. There they were.

The new Willow pulled out a nasty-looking sword and pointed it at the other Willow.

And then they charged for each other.

EPILOGUE

FRANKIE

I STOOD on a beach with crystal clear, turquoise water. My toes wiggled in the powder white sand and waves rolled over my feet. The clouds in the sky were so perfectly shaped it was like they'd been hand painted. I'd never seen a sky as blue as this one.

This was paradise.

I didn't know how long I'd been standing there—felt like forever while feeling like just a minute. The air was warm with a refreshing cool breeze that smelled of salt and coconut. There was a lounge chair behind me I could have been sitting in, but I preferred to feel the crunch of sand between my toes. I liked to watch the crabs and minnows scurry as the tide pulled the waves back into the ocean.

This was peace.

There was something I was supposed to be doing. Something that lingered in the far corners of my mind, like a song stuck in my head. Yet every time I focused on it to see what it was...it vanished.

The crystal ring on my finger, the one I had matching with my best friend, sparkled like a diamond in the rays of sunshine. I smiled and held my hand up. "Elizabeth, look. Have you ever seen so many colors?"

Silence.

"Elizabeth?" I frowned and spun around—and gasped.

A man stood behind me with long dark hair and black horns. His eyes glowed an inhuman green. He cocked his head to the side and pointed ears poked out between the dark strands of his hair. He smirked and it sent a chill down my spine. "I've been called worse."

I took a step back. "Who are you?"

Big black clouds rolled in from behind him, drenching everything in darkness. Thunder roared over our heads. The white sand under my feet turned black like soot. The waves burned like lava against my skin. I hissed and leapt forward to get out of the water and our bodies almost collided.

Lightning bolts the same green color of his eyes shot through the sky. He cocked his head to the side and smirked again. Black smoke billowed out from under his black boots and between the sand. It rose like fog, clinging to my body. I tried to move but my legs locked in place. Black, smoky tendrils reached out of the darkness and coiled around my wrists and neck.

My body raked and trembled. Fear like I'd never felt filled my veins.

The man closed the small distance between us, and I rose off the sand until our eyes were level. "You're strong."

I clenched my teeth and growled. "Who...are...you?"

"A *fighter*." He chuckled and it sent my pulse flying. Goosebumps spread across my skin. "I know you fear me, child. I can smell it."

"Who...are you?" There was no way in hell I was admitting out loud how scared I was.

He licked his lips and shoved his hands into his pockets. "This is going to be fun."

"*I said*, who are you?"

"Oh, I think you know exactly who I am..." He chuckled and winked. "Don't you, *Miss Proctor?*"

I gasped and my eyes flew open.

"FRANKIE!" Elizabeth leaned over me with wide, dark eyes and flushed cheeks. Tears pooled in her eyes. Her faded light pink hair fell over her shoulder and into her face. She blinked and then spun around and screamed, "NURSE! SHE'S AWAKE!"

I KNOW what you're thinking...*what the hell kind of middle earth bullshit is this?*

YOU'RE NOT WRONG. That was one hell of a ride, *amiright?* Not sure where to start? So much just happened at the end there. Riah. Malachi. Chloe. Spot. Asmodeus. Leviathan. Thorne. WILLOW...if you're dying to find out more then check out Book 4, the last book in The Coven: Fae Magic Series - **THE DEATH WITCH!** CLICK HERE to preorder now!

CLICK HERE TO preorder **THE DEATH WITCH!**

NEED TO TALK ABOUT MY BOOKS?

Become a Chandwitch and connect with me and other fans of The Coven! We're totally weird and crazy in there, but it's a whole lot of fun! Just CLICK HERE to join my Facebook group!

BUT FIRST, I've got a stand-alone story about two characters who will be important later in The Coven Saga. Read below to find out about Chloe Lancaster and Malachi in *The Rose Witch.*

HIS MAGIC LURKS in the shadows...

I feel his eyes on my back with every step I take. He's following me. Chasing me. There's nowhere for me to go, nowhere to hide that he won't find me. He moves in smoke and shadows. He *is* the darkness. He tracks my every move like a predator with gold glowing eyes in the night. I know he's going to catch me, the only question is...why do I want him to?

I have no idea who he is or what he wants. I know I should be terrified...but I'm not.

There are things happening to me...things I can't control or explain...things that only I can see. Magic pours from me like a scarlet river and this locket around my neck pulses with dark, electric energy. I think it's what *he* wants...but he isn't the only thing on the hunt for it. Demons hide around every corner, they attack mercilessly and relentlessly - the only thing they seem to be afraid of is *him*.

That should be a warning, except there's something inside me that begs to be near him. I feel it like a magnet, drawing me closer and I'm running out of reasons to fight it.

He is the Prince of Hell...and he's either my savior or my damnation...

The Rose Witch is a novel set in *The Coven* saga but is designed to be read as a stand-alone.

CLICK HERE to read **The Rose Witch** now!

FAE MAGIC is Season Three in The Coven Saga, if you haven't read Season One (*Elemental Magic*) and Season Two (*Academy Magic*) then check out the links and descriptions below and get caught up!

I THOUGHT magic was make believe...but I was *way* wrong.

I was nobody. No matter how hard I tried, I never fit in with anyone at my high school. Now I know why.

Turns out I'm a witch. A scary powerful one, too. Except The Coven that claimed me won't teach me how to use my magic.

Suddenly, I'm selected by the Goddess to hunt down a mythical locket needed to save the world from destruction. The only person who actually tries to help me is the alarmingly attractive Tennessee. He has immeasurable power and breathtaking mismatched eyes. I'm drawn to him on a level I can't explain...and he's forbidden from getting too close to me.

When the quest takes an unexpected dangerous turn, I have to improvise. This supernatural world is unraveling at my fingertips and I need to master my magic fast. If I don't, I could get everyone I care about killed...

CLICK HERE to read Season One: **Elemental Magic Series** now!

MAGIC. Isn't. Real.

At least that's what I thought. But now, my story is changing...

You know you're invisible when even your bullies forget to pick on you. That's me, Bettina Blair, hidden in plain sight. No matter how hard I try I just never fit in with my classmates.

Now I know why. I'm a witch...*apparently.*

One little demon attack and my parents confess their ugly secret...and ship me off to an elite academy of magic- for witches only.

I can't summon magic. I can't fight with my hands *or* my fists. I just don't belong here, and Jackson Lancaster keeps reminding me every single chance he gets. This boy is the most insufferable, intolerable, unbearable, judgmental person to ever have the right to be that gorgeous. I don't care how sexy his British accent is, or that literally everyone else on campus adores him. He hates me, and the feeling is mutual.

Suddenly, I'm sent on a quest into the Old Lands to find the only thing that can save Eden from a demon invasion. I'm in way over my head, and my best chance of coming back alive lies in the hands of the guy who wants me gone...

CLICK HERE to read Season Two: **Academy Magic Series** now!

For Moose, Houdini, and Bouwmeester.

You drew memories in my mind,
I could never erase,
You painted colors in my heart,
I could never replace.

THE COVEN READING ORDER

The Lost Witch

The Brave Witch

The Rebel Witch

The Broken Witch

The Eternal Witch

The Aether Witch

The Fire Witch

The Hidden Witch

The Fallen Witch

The City Witch

The Wild Witch

The Frozen Witch

The Secret Witch

The Uptown Witch

The Empire Witch

The Rose Witch

The Cursed Witch

The Rogue Witch

The Rotten Witch**

0 : The Fool : Chutney Burroughs – Cups Suit – Communicates with animals.

I : The Magician : Willow Walcot – Wands Suit – Illusion magic

II : The High Priestess : Tegan Bishop – *Aether Witch* – All Suits – All elemental Magic

III : The Empress : Emersyn Bishop – Wands Suit – Fire, smoke, & metal magic

IV : The Emperor : Tennessee Wildes – Swords Suit – Wind, water, & earth magic

V : The Hierophant : Bentley Bishop – Cups Suit – Divination

VI : The Lovers : Easton Corey – Swords Suit – Magical armor

VII : The Chariot : Devon Howe Bishop – Swords Suit – Astral projection

VIII : Strength : Kessler Bishop – Swords Suit – Super strength

IX : The Hermit : Timothy Roth– Swords Suit –
Speaks & reads all languages

X : Wheel of Fortune : Royce Redd – Wands Suit –
Nature magic

XI : Justice : Constance Bell – Wands Suit – Crystal
magic

XII : The Hanged Man : Braison Parker – Pentacles
Suit – Light & shadow magic

XIII : Death : Saraphina "Saffie" Proctor – Suit
Unknown – Communicates with the dead

XIV : Temperance : Hunter Bishop – Cups Suit –
Emotions magic

XV : The Devil : Deacon English – Pentacles Suit –
Persuasion magic

XVI : The Tower : "Frankie" – Suit Unknown –
Potion magic

XVII : The Star : Cooper Bishop – Swords Suit –
Dream magic

XVIII : The Moon : Henley Redd – Wands Suit –
Moon magic

XIX : The Sun : Lily Warren – Pentacles Suit – Sun
magic

XX : Judgement : Bettina Blair – Swords Suit – Ice magic

XXI : The World : Jackson Lancaster – Swords Suit – Truth magic

MMXVII

THE COVEN

ABOUT THE AUTHOR

Chandelle was born and raised in South Florida. She is the ultimate fangirl. Her love of Twilight, Harry Potter, and The Mortal Instruments inspired her to write her own books. When she's not writing she's on the beach soaking up the sun with a book in her hand. Her favorite things in life are dogs, pizza, slurpees, and anything that sparkles. She suffers from wanderlust and hopes to travel to every country in the world one day.

The Rotten Witch

Published by Wanderlost Publishing

Copyright © 2021 by Chandelle LaVaun

"Savannah Grace" Poetry & spells inside book written by Savvy Grace

Cover designed by Lori Grundy @ Cover Reveal Designs

Pentacle art by Samaiya Beaumont

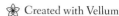 Created with Vellum

CHANDELLE LaVAUN

THE ROTTEN WITCH

THE COVEN: FAE MAGIC BOOK THREE

Made in the USA
Monee, IL
17 June 2022

98186591R00312